DARK SPECTRE

Michael Dibdin was born in 1947 and attended schools in Scotland and Ireland and universities in England and Canada. He spent four years in Italy, where he taught at the University of Perugia, and currently lives in Seattle. He reviews regularly for the *Independent on Sunday*.

Dark Spectre

MICHAEL DIBDIN

faber and faber
LONDON · BOSTON

First published in Great Britain in 1995
by Faber and Faber Limited
3 Queen Square London WC1N 3AU
This open market paperback edition first published in 1996

Printed in England by Clays Ltd, St Ives plc

© Michael Dibdin, 1995

A CIP record for this book
is available from the British Library

ISBN 0–571–17716–6

2 4 6 8 10 9 7 5 3 1

For Kathrine, who helped

And Tharmas calld to the Dark Spectre who upon the shores
With dislocated limbs had falln. The Spectre rose in pain
A Shadow blue obscure & dismal.

William Blake: *Vala, or the Four Zoas*

One

Jamie shot Ronnie Ho four times. Once in the head, twice in the chest, and once in the gut, where he'd heard it hurt real bad. Two shots went wide.

'Jamie!' yelled his mom from the porch. She'd been talking to Marsha Dawson for about an hour, and had gone outside, still talking, to pick up the mail.

'What?' he yelled back.

His mother appeared in the doorway, portable in one hand, her blue bathrobe billowing around her, sorting through the mail.

'What'd I tell you about using that thing in here?'

'But Mom … '

'Junk, junk, bill, junk. How come no one ever sends me a real letter?'

Jamie sulkily unpopped the suction caps of the darts from the mirror. Two misses wasn't bad, and if it'd really been Ronnie Ho he'd have got in closer before he squeezed the trigger.

'I bet Wayne gave you that darn thing, just to bug me.'

'I bought it with my allowance.'

'Get him to pay a dime in child support, no way. But any crap guaranteed to drive me crazy, no problem.'

'I'm *bored*, Mom!'

His mother sashayed through to the kitchen, pushing buttons on the phone.

'Do your homework.'

'I've done it.'

'Yeah, right!'

'I have *too*!'

He knew she knew he was lying, but if she called him on it

he'd ask her to help him out, and she didn't know diddly about math. They'd changed it all since she was at school. Plus he was getting OK grades, she'd back off.

'Did you get new batteries for my Game Boy?' he said, following her down the hall into the kitchen.

'Hi, Kelly!' his mom said in the chirpy voice she used for leaving a message. 'Friday's our girls' night out? I was wondering if I could catch a ride with you. Call me, OK?'

'Mom? Did you get those new … '

'I forgot.'

'Oh, *Mom*!'

'Why don't you go downstairs and play with Kevin and Ronnie?'

'They won't let me. They keep saying I'm too little.'

'Well, they'll just have to … '

The phone rang. His mother drifted around the corner, through the dining area and back into the living room.

'Hello? Oh hi, honey. You are? Is it OK with her mom and dad? Uh huh. Sure, as long as they don't mind. What time'll you be home? OK. See you.'

'Who was that?' demanded Jamie.

'Megan. She's spending the day with Nicole.'

'Not fair!'

Just then the Accident started up in the next room. Dawn sighed loudly and went to stick a pacifier in its face. Jamie threw himself down on the sofa, feeling sulkier than ever. Megan was fourteen and got to go to sleep-overs and goof off for the whole day with her friends, but what was *he* supposed to do? Once he and Kevin had taken care of themselves, tearing around the basement, staging fights, gradually stepping up the noise level until Mom had to come and tell them to shut up. But since Ronnie Ho came along, his brother had no time for him. Ronnie Ho was five-and-half months older than Kevin and smart and his parents were Chinese and took their shoes off at the door and ate wonton soup the whole time and neat stuff like that. Kevin thought he was the best thing since microwaveable popcorn. As for Jamie, he was just a kid. No one was interested in him.

2

His mom reappeared, the baby in one arm, its bottle and the portable in the other.

'What am *I* supposed to do?' Jamie exploded.

His mom heaved another sigh. She set the Accident down on the sofa, where it started to howl again, and jabbed at the phone. She'd got Kevin and Megan their own private line, so they could firm up their social lives without bothering her.

'Kevin? Listen, I've got to take care of the baby and I want you and Ronnie to do something with Jamie. He's driving me nuts with that dart-gun his dad bought him.'

Jamie lifted the pistol and took aim at the Accident, blew its head apart with a single shot.

'Well, you better, you want your allowance this week,' his mom snapped.

She switched off the phone, picked up the baby and the remote control and channel-surfed until she stuck on some cheesy old black-and-white movie. Typical, thought Jamie. He loved his mom, but she had no class.

Nothing stirred downstairs in the basement. Kevin and Ronnie were staying put, hoping Mom would forget about the whole deal. Jamie'd have done the same thing. Ever since Dad walked out, Mom had been like a hard-pressed pitcher facing a line-up full of gritty hitters. At the moment she was one-and-o on Kevin, but she still had a long way to go if she wanted to strike him out. Jamie reloaded his gun and took careful aim.

'Jamie!'

He snuck over to the TV, giggling, and pulled the dart off the screen.

'Sorry, Mom.'

It worked. She hit redial on the portable.

'What'd I just tell you, Kevin? I don't care if you're … Well, how long is … ? Just finish and get your butt up here is all.'

She looked at the gun in Jamie's hand.

'Get that thing *outta* here!'

'It's only a toy, Mom!'

'Go clean your room.'

'What did Kevin say?'

'He'll be up as soon as he's died.'

Jamie let his body slump in an expression of despair. If Kevin and Ronnie were playing Mortal Kombat, they'd be at it all afternoon. Mom thought that when you died it was like the power went off or something, like it was something *real*, but on the video you could die over and over again, as many times as you wanted. It was so frustrating! There was so much parents didn't understand! They should make them take a test or something. It wasn't fair, putting people like that in charge of kids. It meant that nerds like Ronnie Ho ended up getting away with murder.

He rolled up off the sofa, leapt over the coffee table and froze up against the window. Mr Valdez across the road was flat on his back on the drive under his Pontiac, 'giving head to her front-end' as Kevin had said to Ronnie. Jamie wasn't sure exactly what that meant, but he could tell by the way they laughed that it had something to do with sex. That was a whole world he wasn't looking forward to. It sounded like going to high school. You had to leave all your old friends and routines and get bussed across town to some new place where they were all bigger than you and everything was for real.

Some guy on a bike cruised past, turning to look at the house, holding Jamie's eyes for a moment. Cool ATB, Cannondale or Bridgestone, he couldn't be certain, but eighteen gears for sure, the seat high and the bars wide, like bucking a bronco. Jamie had seen stuff like that in the catalogues, and downtown you saw guys riding them, but he couldn't imagine who'd have one around here. People had that kind of money, they'd trade in their car. Still, Jamie made an effort to keep up product availability, even though all he had was the hand-me-down BMX Kevin had stopped using when Dad gave him a nearly new Giant for his birthday.

A muffled, whumping beat started up downstairs, making the floorboards shake. Jamie turned around, eyeballing his mom. She sat holding the baby like a sack of groceries, gazing moodily at the TV, where some guy in a suit and hat and moustache was talking to a woman having a weird hair day. For a moment, Jamie thought his mom wasn't going to get it. It wasn't like the

4

music was loud enough to drown out the TV or anything. Then she looked up, caught his intent stare. He didn't need to say anything. She reached for the phone.

'If you're not up here in fifteen seconds, Kevin, I'm phoning Viacom and cancelling cable.'

She tossed the portable down on the sofa dismissively. Snoop Doggy Dogg's punchy rap immediately faded to a murmur. Jamie turned back to the window to hide his smile. Kevin would sooner have his wiener cut off than TV. He'd won. It wasn't so much that he wanted to play with Kevin and Ronnie, but they sure didn't want to play with him, and now they were going to have to.

Another bicyclist passed the house, going the other way this time. A different bike, nothing fancy, one of those old-fashioned drop-handlebar numbers. The guy was different too, older-looking, with a beard and kind of long greasy hair, like that boyfriend of Mom's who hadn't worked out. The only thing the same was that as he passed, he turned to look at Jamie, as though he'd known all along he was standing there. It was kind of weird.

Footsteps clomped heavily up the narrow stairs from the basement. Jamie's smile grew, then disappeared as he turned around to watch the payoff. Kevin slank moodily into the living room, shoulders hunched, scowling at his mom, ignoring his younger brother. Three paces behind came Ronnie Ho, looking polite and concerned as always. What a jerk!

'I'm so sorry we didn't come right away,' Ronnie said in his smarmy voice. 'We were kind of locked into the game.'

Jamie's mom smiled. She thought Ronnie Ho was 'so polite'.

'That's fine, Ronald. But listen, I need some quality time with the baby and Jamie is driving me up the wall. Can't you guys do something with him?'

'Like what?' snarled Kevin.

After Ronnie's smarm, Kevin sounded even more in-your-face than usual.

'Oh gee, I don't know!' his mother exclaimed girlishly. 'Whatever you guys do.'

5

'He's just a *kid*!'

'So are you,' snapped his mom. Her voice had hardened right up. No more buddy-buddy stuff if he wasn't going to buy into it. Kevin stared back at her angrily. Ronnie Ho stood looking on with an embarrassed smile, pretending that nothing was going on, or if it was then he hadn't noticed. Jamie bet Chinese people would rather commit hara-kiri or whatever it was than throw a scene like this in front of guests. Well, screw 'em, bunch of FOBs! This is America. Deal with it.

'Come on, guys!' their mother exclaimed wearily. 'Go chase each other around in back or something.'

'It's too cold.'

'Watch TV.'

She stood up, cradling the Accident.

'There's nothing on but a bunch of dumb shows and crappy movies,' said Kevin, looking pointedly at the glowing screen in the corner.

'Well, let Jamie play your video game,' Mom suggested.

'He's no good.'

'That's because you never let me play,' Jamie protested loudly.

'Listen, I don't care *what* you do, just get outta here, all right?' snapped their mom. 'What's the matter with you kids? Play hide-and-seek or something.'

She disappeared into the bedroom with the baby. Kevin looked at Ronnie Ho, rolling his eyes and shaking his head. Hide-and-seek! What planet did this woman live on? Kevin had long since moved on to sardines, where one person hid and everyone had to find them and then hide in the same place, which gave you a chance to kind of rub up against some of the good-looking babes. Hide-and-seek was for little kids.

'Or maybe you'd rather clean that room of yours?' his mother yelled threateningly from the next room.

Kevin leant over and whispered something to Ronnie, who nodded.

'OK, we'll play hide-and-seek,' he called back.

'You won't play fair!' retorted Jamie. 'You'll make me be it and then goof off somewhere I can't find you!'

6

'OK, you hide,' Kevin replied.

He beamed innocently at Jamie. Too innocently.

'You won't come looking for me!' Jamie protested loudly.

He knew there had to be a catch, and he was determined not to be suckered by the older boys.

'Yes, we will,' replied Kevin. 'And I bet we find you right away.'

'Oh yeah? How much?'

'A dollar.'

'A *dollar*?'

Jamie thought furiously. He was still sure it was a scam, the way they'd whispered to each other, but he couldn't figure it out. And a dollar was a dollar.

'How long have you got to find me?' he demanded suspiciously.

'Twenty minutes.'

'Ten.'

'OK, fifteen.'

'Shoot, you can search the whole house in fifteen.'

'That's the deal,' his brother said. 'Take it or leave it.'

Jamie reflected for a moment. Then he nodded.

'OK.'

Kevin smiled swaggeringly at Ronnie Ho.

'We'll be downstairs in my room,' he told Jamie. 'We'll give you a couple of minutes to get hid. C'mon, Ronnie.'

They disappeared. A few moments later the rap was up to strength again, making the floorboards quiver underfoot. Jamie set a fifteen-minute timer on the el-cheapo digital watch his dad had got free at some gas station and passed on to him. Then he headed for the stairs. Through the open bedroom door, he could hear his mom cooing and murmuring to the baby. The way she carried on, you'd have thought she'd *wanted* the damn thing.

Jamie started down the cramped, twisting stairs leading to the basement. He was careful to avoid the second and fifth steps, which creaked. When he was far enough down he checked the door to Kevin's room. It was closed. He carried on down to the bare concrete floor of the basement. To his right, a door lay open into a utility room housing the washing machine, drier and freezer. Straight ahead was the rec room containing the half-finished bar his dad had been building as part of a project to turn it into a den, even though he'd never even got around to carpeting the basement. Empty liquor bottles gathered dust on flimsy glass shelving. To the left was Jamie's room, and next to it Kevin's. They had the music on again in there, a strident twangy thumping beat that would cover any noises Jamie might make.

The centre of the floor was occupied by the furnace, screened off with plywood panelling. Jamie walked slowly around it, inspecting the housing intently with eyes and fingers. A couple of months earlier the furnace had failed to light and they'd had to call the repair man. Jamie had been home from school with a sore throat the day he'd come. He'd watched from his bed as the guy removed a section of panelling and fiddled around with a vast array of cool-looking gadgets from his toolbox. Jamie had known about the hatch which gave access to the controls at the front of the furnace, but he had never suspected the existence of a removable panel at the side, used for servicing the jets. The joint ran right along one of the bevelled black lines cut into the plywood to make it look like real planking. You'd never guess it was there, unless you knew. After the guy had gone, Jamie had taken it off himself and looked inside. The space was pretty small, but so was Jamie. Kevin would never find him there, not in a million years.

Upstairs, the doorbell rang. Jamie heard his mom's footsteps on the boards overhead as she went to answer it. Then he saw the thin black crack in the plywood and the grubby marks of the repair guy's fingers. He worked the panel loose and started to crawl inside.

It was more difficult than he'd thought. The surface of the furnace inside the hatch was covered in valves and pipes and stuff sticking out at crazy angles. It was tough to wriggle in between them, feet first, unable to see where he was going. The real problem, though, was replacing the panel from the inside. There was nothing to hold on to, and in the darkness it was tough to line up the metal tabs and slots which held it in place, particularly with your body twisted like a stick of liquorice. He'd only managed to get one fastener in place when he heard the creak on the stairs.

He crouched there in the darkness, pressed up against the pipes and ducts of the furnace, waiting for his mom's call. Probably it was some friend of Kevin's, either that or Ronnie Ho's dad was here to take him home. But instead of a voice he heard the shriller squeal of the other loose step. His mom must have realized they wouldn't hear her calling over the music. It was kind of weird, though. Normally she would have phoned down. Mom didn't set foot in the basement that much any more. It was their territory, now that Dad had gone. As long as they stayed out of her hair, she left them to their own devices.

Jamie worked his left hand down to the wrist of his right, which was holding the free catch of the plywood panel, and pressed the light button on his watch: 11.36. Almost four minutes since he made the bet with Kevin. Why hadn't they come looking for him? They must have lost track of time, boxed in with the music, curtains pulled and the light on. Well, that was fine with him. A deal was a deal. Another ten minutes and the dollar was his. He started to think about what he would get with it. Candy was out. He'd put it towards the collection of baseball cards he was amassing. A dollar would buy another six, including hopefully that one of Barry Bonds he'd been after for months, and which no one wanted to trade.

Then he felt a familiar sick feeling, the humiliating sense of having been outwitted yet again. Maybe they'd never *meant* to find him. Maybe a dollar was the price Kevin was prepared to pay to get his little squirt of a brother out of the loop for fifteen minutes without screwing things up with Mom. He'd split it with Ronnie, who got a big allowance from his parents. That's what they'd been whispering about together upstairs. Fifty cents each for a quarter of an hour's peace, they'd pay that. It got them off the hook, and put Jamie in his place, someone who could be bought for a buck.

But just then there was a sudden surge in the music as the door to Kevin's room opened. He and Ronnie must have decided to get up off their butts and start looking for him, finally. Jamie gripped the metal tab on the hatch as hard as he could. If they noticed any gap or irregularity, they would be on to him immediately. He listened intently for their voices, trying to pick up some clue about where they thought he might be hiding, where they were going to look for him first. All he could hear was the metallic synthesized crashes and explosions of the funk rap, and then even that was drowned by a dull whump and a loud roaring as the furnace started up.

Jamie started to panic. It had never occurred to him that the thing might light while he was in there. Would the pipes he was lying on start to heat up? He was already wedged tight between them. If they expanded and turned red-hot, he would be trapped and scalded to death! No one would hear his screams. The darkness grew dense and choking, an unbreathable mass in which he lay suffocating like that guy they'd buried alive in the video he and Kevin had rented from Blockbuster while their mom was out with that creep from work.

He had to get out, *had* to. The time must be almost up anyway. He was afraid to check his watch again because his fingers were sweaty and ached from keeping hold of that little sliver of metal. If only he could hear them going upstairs, he could crawl out and go hide in Kevin's room, under the bed or something. They'd never come looking for him there, not when they'd been in the room the whole time.

A widening glimmer of light appeared as he began to lose his grip on the metal fastener. The panel dropped down about half an inch on one side. Jamie desperately clenched his fingers tight again, ignoring the pain, and managed to stop the hatch slipping any further. He couldn't get it back in position, though. He didn't have enough of a grip on the thing to lift it up *and* pull it in. If he tried, he'd lose it altogether. He just hoped that the triangular crack at the top of the hatch didn't show too much from the outside. But was there anyone there? Surely Kevin and Ronnie must have searched the basement by now and gone upstairs. That's if they were looking for him at all. Maybe they'd just gone to grab a snack or something.

All he could see through the gap between the hatch and the panelling was a patch of bare concrete floor and a strip of unpainted baseboard. He felt as though he'd been trapped in there for hours, not minutes, and although the pipes beneath him weren't getting any hotter, the air was. Jamie remembered something he'd seen on TV about some guy who'd died from working on his car in the garage with the engine running. There was this poisonous stuff, silent and invisible and deadly. You never even knew what was happening until it was too late. Creepy.

He tensed up. There was a flicker of movement in the triangular sliver of light above the hatch. Even when it came to rest, it took Jamie a moment to figure out that he was looking at the leg of a pair of faded blue jeans, a patch of white sport sock and a shoe.

And what a shoe! A Nike Air Jordan! Jamie recognized it right away, black all over with the silhouette of the basketball star Michael Jordan picked out in bright red on the side of a sole as thick as a Big Mac. A shoe to *kill* for! $125 a pair! No one he knew had stuff like that, not even Jamal Davis, who'd once told Mr Olson not to dis him, right there in front of the whole class.

Jamie shut his eyes tight and counted to ten. When he opened them again, all he could see through the crack was the patch of floor, the strip of baseboard. The shoe was gone. He must have imagined it. No one in the house had shoes like that, and none of Kevin's friends either. Maybe the fumes were getting to him, warping his brain, making him see things and act strange, like Dad when he'd been drinking.

Something close by started beeping, a high-pitched electronic sound. Jamie cursed as he remembered setting the alarm on his watch. Even if the time was up, he didn't want to reveal his hiding place. He might want to use it again. He stabbed frantically at the button with one free finger of his right hand. As he did so, the metal fastener slipped from his tired fingers and the hatch clattered to the concrete flooring.

With a sigh, the furnace turned off. Jamie lay there without moving, as though his cramped, painful stillness could somehow cancel the noise of the falling cover, erase it so that no one would hear. But he knew it was pointless. If Kevin and Ronnie came to investigate, they'd see the hatch lying on the ground and find him right away. But maybe they were upstairs, out of hearing. The music seemed to have stopped, and he couldn't hear anyone around.

There was a creak on the stairs, then another. Someone was coming down. Footsteps scuffed on the concrete floor.

'Just a piece of wood fell off the … '

It was a voice Jamie had never heard before. A man. He was just inches away, on the other side of the plywood panelling.

'What?'

Another strange voice, this time upstairs. There was no reply, only the scuffle of footsteps close by.

'Russ?' the second man called again.

There was a pause, then the creak of the stairs. Going up this time, the fifth step and then the second.

'C'mon, let's go.'

The first voice. There was no reply, no further sound of any kind. Jamie huddled up between the pipes. The dark, confined space which had oppressed him just a moment earlier had become a haven, a refuge. It was the open hatchway which scared him now. He expected a face to appear there at any moment, a strange face, smiling a strange smile. He wished he could reach out and replace the panel, but he was afraid to move a muscle. Play dead, he told himself. Play dead.

When he dared move a hand to check his watch again, he found that time had speeded up. Five-and-a-half minutes had gone by. The house was completely still, but Jamie made no move. Even the dull pain of the pipes digging into his back and shoulder seemed a kind of comfort. But in the end the throbbing of his cramped muscles became unendurable. Taking as much care as he could not to make any noise, Jamie started to struggle out of his hiding place. It was even harder getting out than getting in. His ankle had got wedged between two pipes, and there seemed no way to wrench it loose. He remembered the kid in seventh grade who'd gone into the wrecking yard over on 33rd and got trapped when a parted-out car collapsed on him. A surge of panic almost made him cry out for help, but he bit his lip and forced himself to calm down.

Eventually he found the trick to free himself, by pushing his foot *into* the cleft and twisting it. After that, it was just a matter of squeezing through the narrow opening and lowering himself on his hands, carefully avoiding the loose hatch cover. He crouched on the concrete floor, taking up no more space than he had inside the panelling, listening intently. Silence lay on the house like a fall of snow. The only sound was the whine of the freezer in the corner and a car engine revving up outside in the street. Jamie recognized the deep, throaty roar of Mr Valdez's Pontiac.

The thought that normal life was going on close at hand gave him the courage to stand up and look around. Everything looked the same as it had when he came down to hide. Jamie stepped cautiously, on tiptoe, to the door of Kevin's room. He turned the handle and opened the door a crack. His brother lay stretched out on the bed as though asleep. Jamie opened the door wider, and sniffed. There was a funny smell, kind of nice, like fireworks or something. Then he saw Ronnie Ho lying face down on the floor. Jamie's fear abruptly left him.

'C'mon guys!' he said in the edgy tone he knew Kevin hated. 'Pay-up time.'

Neither of them moved. Jamie began to feel irritated. They were playing one of their stupid games, ignoring what he said, acting like he wasn't there.

'You owe me a dollar, Kevin!' he said, taking a step into the room.

Still there was no response. The stress and strain of the past twenty minutes had left Jamie's nerves ragged. Being treated like a dumb younger brother was the last straw. He picked up a social studies textbook lying on the chest of drawers and spun it across the room like a frisbee. It was a heavy book, and the corner struck Kevin just below the ear. Realizing that he'd gone too far, Jamie sprinted quickly across the basement and upstairs before Kevin could catch up and give him hell.

In the hall at the top of the stairs, he paused. There was no sound of pursuit. In fact there was no sound at all. Even the Accident had stopped whining for attention. Jamie was still standing there uncertainly when the phone began to ring, doubled by the electronic warble of the portable. He waited for his mom to answer, but the phone kept right on ringing. Jamie walked through to the living room. The portable was still lying on the sofa where his mom had thrown it. He picked it up and pushed the button.

'Hello?'

'Hi! Is that Jamie? This is Kelly Shelden. Your mom left a message on my voicemail. Can I speak to her?'

'Hold on.'

He lowered the phone.

'Mom!'

There was no reply. Jamie wandered down the room towards the dining area.

'Mom!'

He stumbled on something and grabbed the back of the sofa to stop himself falling. The portable went flying. Jamie looked at the thing he had tripped over. It was wrapped in shiny blue fabric, with pieces of crinkly white appearing here and there.

Mrs Shelden was hollering something in a squeaky voice. Stepping carefully over the obstacle on the floor, Jamie reached down and picked up the portable.

'Hello?' he said.

'Jamie? Are you there?'

'I'm here.'

'What's going on?'

'I dropped the phone.'

'Oh, OK. Did you find your mom?'

'Yeah.'

'OK.'

Jamie turned and looked down again.

'Hello?' said Kelly Shelden.

'I'm here,' said Jamie.

'Well, are you going to put your mom on or what?'

'I can't.'

'How come? Is she in the bathroom or something?'

He did not answer.

'Jamie? What the heck are you playing at?'

'Could you get over here, Mrs Shelden? Like now?'

'Oh boy, you must be kidding! I've got a zillion things to do. Listen, I'll call back in ten minutes. Will she be able to talk then?'

'I think she's dead.'

'Well, have her call me when she's free. I'll be home till four, then I have to bring Ryan to baseball practice, but I should be back by … '

'You've gotta come!' Jamie shouted. 'I'm only a kid!'

Kelly Shelden's voice softened into concern.

'Why, Jamie! What's the matter, honey?'

Jamie broke into sobs.

'I'm feeling weirded out. Like totally.'

Two

The time I remember best is the night we ended up down at the Commercial, and all that happened afterwards. It would be nice and neat to be able to say that that's where the whole thing started, but there must have been a lot more behind it, a slow shifting of psychological fault lines under the pressure of life events about which I know nothing, about which maybe no one ever knew anything, and never will now.

Minneapolis is not exactly notorious for its seedy low life, but there is – or was, back in the seventies – a part of downtown, a couple of blocks either side of the railroad tracks, which got reasonably lively after dark. The Commercial Hotel was right in the middle of it. They knocked it down later and built a mall with fountains and escalators and shops selling things which no reasonable person could need, but I don't recall anyone circulating a petition to save the place.

The Commercial was one of those oppressively huge hotels which went up all over the country around the turn of the century near major railroad depots. Its fortunes exactly mirrored those of the transportation system it was built to serve, and during its last decade the rooms were used only by prostitutes, winos and other down-and-outers. What kept the place in business was its liquor licence. The bar was the biggest and rowdiest in town and they had pretty tight bands at the weekends, but for us the main attraction was the atmosphere of sleaze and failure. It appealed to our sense of living on the edge.

Maybe that was what held the group together. It's hard, in retrospect, to see what else we had in common. Even calling it a group is misleading. We were just a bunch of guys who liked to hang out together. The membership was never clearly defined.

The basic core – Greg, Sam, Larry, Vince and me – was more or less stable, but it also included a temporary assortment of girl-friends, buddies, hangers-on and anyone who happened to be crashing at our pad at the time.

We were all young, of course, but so was everyone else back then. Greg, Sam and I were all connected in one way or another with the university, but the links were so tenuous and diverse that this too is a false trail. Greg had been an athlete, a college football star, but had been dropped from the team in his second year following a much-publicized drug bust. Sam had studied English for two years – we'd taken some classes together, which is where we met – before dropping out to complete his studies at the University of Life, while I was in my third year of Comparative Literature.

As for Larry and Vince, they came from other worlds altogether. Larry worked for a painting contractor, and got home every night covered in specks and streaks of various hues, stoned out of his mind on paint thinner. Vince's means of support remained a mystery. We suspected that he was subsidized by his parents, but that was not something you could either admit or enquire about in those days. He spent most of the day fiddling with a bank of stereo equipment he had put together from kits and spare parts, which provided a mind-numbing volume of sound that was the envy of our friends and the despair of our neighbours.

What brought us together originally was the house. It was a pleasantly decrepit wood-framed place with an overgrown yard and a huge maple out front, in a run-down blue-collar neighbourhood south of the river. Many lots had been demolished and rebuilt as condos or walk-ups, and the surviving older houses had a provisional, doomed look accentuated by lack of care and upkeep. Respectable renters steered clear of such properties, but the combination of low rent and no hassle was just what we were looking for. The landlord, an old Swede, was waiting for some redevelopment company to make him an offer he couldn't refuse, and he didn't much care what we did with, to, or in the house just as long as the rent was there on time every month.

It's all part of the general pattern that the guy who originally found the place didn't go on to become a member of the group at all. He was a dour jock who'd been a wide receiver on the same team as Greg, but had now graduated and was working as a salesman at a Dodge dealership. He and a co-worker took the house and invited Greg to share it with them. Greg brought in Sam, who in turn mentioned the place to me. I was living with a girlfriend that year, but I was looking for an excuse to break up so I said I'd give it a try.

The arrangement was doomed from the start, of course. The two car salesmen may have looked and sounded very much the same as us when we met them over a beer one Saturday night, wearing their weekend tie-dyes and faded Levis, but they had in fact crossed the shadow line which separated our floating world from the uncompromising grid of straight society, and were none too happy about this transition. Monday through Friday they had to be up at seven, showered and shaved, suited and wide-tied, and get out there and move stock. Their servitude was thrown into sharp relief by our anarchistic lifestyle, and they tended to react particularly badly when we staggered back in from an all-night party just as they were leaving for work, or decided to play *The Who Live at Leeds* at the appropriate volume around three in the morning.

But what brought things to a crisis was the question of drugs. We had a fairly large stash of these on hand at any given time, mostly pot and hash, but also more exotic treats. This gave the car salesmen the jitters. If the house got busted, their careers would be over before they'd started. At first they came on heavy and tried to enforce a ban, but there were three of us and only two of them, plus we had the advantage of being able to drop some uppers to improve our attitude, or toke up and mellow out if the vibes got too heavy. It must have been a bitch. They finally gave up and moved out to a squeaky-clean highrise near the dealership, leaving us to find replacements quickly to make up the next month's rent. Larry turned up on the first trawl – he'd been to school with Sam and they used to shoot pool together once in a while – along with another guy who didn't last, and the following month Vince materialized from somewhere, I still don't know how or why, and stuck.

Such a casual, disparate grouping seems pretty unlikely now, yet at the time none of us thought twice about it. Later, looking back nostalgically from the far side of my own shadow line at that lost world of ease and excitement, I spent a lot of time trying to figure out just what it was that made the whole thing work. I can't speak for the others, but I think I know what drew me to them: a passion for the tawdry and the transient, a weakness for the power not just of cheap music but of cheap emotion, cheap ideas and cheap thrills of every kind.

To Greg and Larry, all this came naturally. It was where they had grown up, a language they had spoken all their lives. With Vince it was a little more forced. He never talked about his parents, but one or two comments he let drop in unguarded moments suggested that he'd been raised in the kind of small-town home where they subscribed to the *New Yorker* and listened to the live broadcast from the Met every Saturday morning. He had to work his catechism of popular culture, but did so with all the zeal of a recent convert. For Sam, the journey had been even longer. His parents had permitted only one book in the house, the family Bible, and regarded television and popular music as works of the Devil. Even the radio was only turned on for farm bulletins and religious broadcasts on Sunday.

But despite their differences, the other four were merely expressing or reappropriating a culture native to them. They were Americans. So was I, on paper. I had been born in Maine and carried an American passport, but none of this made me an American, in my own eyes at least. My father had been European marketing director for a Boston-based company, and from the age of six to eighteen I lived and went to school in Holland, Switzerland and France. Despite summer vacations back in the States, when I enrolled at the University of Minnesota I felt a foreigner in my own country.

So my association with Sam, Vince, Greg and Larry meant more than just a good time. At the risk of sounding pompous, it was a rediscovery of my roots, an affirmation of my identity. I was discovering for the first time the unique experience of

American *low* taste, the authentic, unexportable cultural product. I revelled in its shameless excess, its triumphant vulgarity, and looked to the others as my guides through a heritage I possessed in name only. They were naturally flattered by this, and the fact that I embodied various qualities which they aspired to – a classy veneer of sophistication and cosmopolitanism – helped soothe any tensions which might have arisen from our differences in other respects.

That Saturday night at the Commercial was a good example of the way the relationship functioned. As I said, the bar at that hotel was notoriously the roughest and scuzziest in town. The bouncers at the door checked the ID of anyone who looked remotely under age, but that and money were all you needed to get in. You ordered a tableful of beers from one of the hard-faced waitresses, and as long as you drank up and didn't get too rowdy, no one would bother you. The noise level was pretty high, particularly when the band started up, but the bouncers ensured that there was very little real trouble. Occasionally a pack of frat boys running the trap-line would start making assholes of themselves, but that was just local colour, like the hookers who trolled the bar between glasses of Seven-and-Seven.

So there we were, that Saturday night, sitting around a table of half-drunk brewskis and discussing what theologians term the Problem of Evil. There was nothing unusual about this. When it came to conversation, we went straight from the trivial to the cosmic without batting an eyelid. We could spend hours discussing what kind of pizza to order, or rehashing the plot lines of old movies, and then move right on to such topics as the meaning of life or the theory of reincarnation. We were equally at home with the sublime or the ridiculous. It was the stuff in between we didn't have any time for, the earnest middle ground of the straight world with its rules, regulations and responsibilities.

Drugs had a lot to do with this, of course. People who weren't part of that scene often don't realize that it was governed by a code of etiquette every bit as rigid as a Long Island dinner party. If a fellow-tripper decided that some object in the room – an ashtray, say – was of intense beauty and significance, it was simply not done to point out that it was just a fucking ashtray, for Christ's sake. On the other hand, if someone brought up the fact that the toilet kept overflowing, or that the electricity would be turned off if we didn't pay the bill, he would immediately be told to stop heavying everyone out. It was considered gauche in the extreme to mention practical problems or future arrangements, but absolutely OK to raise the question of the origins of the universe, or to argue for hours about whether the physical world has an existence independent of our perceptions of it.

So there was nothing out of the ordinary about our discussion that evening at the Commercial. It was a television news item which sparked the whole thing off. At home we almost never watched the news, considering it to be a propaganda tool of the military-industrial complex designed no less than its Soviet equivalent to manipulate and suppress the truth. But there was a TV set in the bar to entertain patrons while the band took a break, and this particular report had gotten to us. Sure, it was another repressive pre-emptive strike at the drug culture of which the power-trippers in Washington were rightly terrified, but it also related to issues which directly concerned us, and we had to talk it out.

Here's what happened. A single mother living in some tenement in New York set out to bathe her baby. Since there was no running hot water, this involved heating a pan of water on the stove. The mother in question was a junkie, which gave us an out to some extent. We didn't approve of hard drugs, although if anyone had managed to score some cocaine we would have given that a try because word was it wasn't physically addictive. But heroin, no way. We were drug *users* – radical, innovative individuals for whom illegal substances were just one more tool in the unending search for personal growth and enlightenment. People who took heroin were mindless addicts. The distinction in our minds was absolute.

Anyway, while the mother is waiting for the water to heat, she decides to fix up. When the water is nice and warm she pops her six-month-old in the pan, only unfortunately she forgets to turn off the burner. I think it was this simple domestic detail which got to us. It was the kind of thing we were doing all the time. None of us would forget the night Larry set the kitchen on fire when he got the munchies and started to fry up some food, then switched trips and wandered off leaving the pan on the stove. But there were five of us, and at least one usually had his head straight enough to keep track of what was going on. The woman in Chicago wasn't so lucky. She was alone, and she'd miscalculated the dose when she fixed up. Result, she passed out and the baby was boiled alive.

OK, it was a real bummer, whichever way you looked at it, but any other time we'd have had a moment of silence and moved on. These things happen, life's a bitch, gotta keep on truckin'. But that evening, for some reason, we all got hung up on this thing. Maybe the grotesque nature of the tragedy had something to do with it. People getting boiled alive sounded like something from the Middle Ages, or some wacko late movie scenario. Plus the details were hard to work out. How big was the pan? Couldn't the kid climb out? How much water was there? Why didn't it drown? *How long did it take to die?*

The only way to exorcize all this was to find someone or something to blame. For the TV people there was no problem, of course. They blamed the mother, and the dealers who had supplied her habit. But even though we disapproved of heroin, and despised anyone who let themselves become enslaved to it, we couldn't get off the hook that easily. We'd all been equally out of it at one time or another, and although dropping when alone was against our code, who was to say what we might have done if we'd had kids to raise and poverty to contend with and nothing else to ease the pain? There was no way we were buying into the newscasters' smug, judgemental line.

But if the mother wasn't to blame, who was? For a while it looked like society was going to take the rap. If the woman had been brought up in a caring, supportive, communal environment, like the indigenous peoples before the white man fucked everything up, this would never have happened. There would have been plenty of old people with time on their hands who were only too glad to look after chores like bathing babies, leaving the mother free to go out and get royally laid by a selection of super-studs like us. Plus she'd be living in harmony with nature, so she wouldn't need drugs or other artificial stimuli to combat the colonialization of her mind by the propaganda machine of late-capitalist consumerism, right?

We had all more or less agreed on this solution when Sam put a new spin on the whole thing by bringing up the religious angle. This was a personal thing with him. He'd never talked much about his fundamentalist background until a couple of months earlier, when his mother was killed by an intruder at her home in Milwaukee. They caught the guy right away, a local loser who'd already done time for break-ins. Another conviction would send him to the pen for ten to fifteen, so he'd taken a gun along and, as guns will, it had gone off.

Sam had never given the impression of having much time for his parents. When he talked about them at all it was as a big joke, a couple of hicks given to quoting the 'good book' and dwelling at great length on the moral failings of others, so we were surprised to see how hard he was hit by his mother's death. His father had succumbed to cancer five years earlier, and his mother had begged Sam to attend the University of Wisconsin so as to be near her. He had been equally determined to keep his distance, but when the old woman died in such a shockingly gratuitous way he naturally felt guilty for having left her all alone in the house. Rather than admit this, however, he deflected his feelings into an all-out assault on God. His parents had given up everything for Him, laying waste to their lives, pursuing a scorched-earth policy lest Satan find a crumb of comfort, and what was their reward? His father was consumed by a slow and agonizing illness, his mother gunned down in a robbery gone wrong. Thanks a lot, God.

So Sam's line on the boiled baby story was fairly predictable: it was just one more proof that the idea of a wise, loving, all-powerful God was a crock of the ripest bullshit, and that anyone who believed in Him was mentally deficient and in dire need of counselling. We'd heard all this before, and duly nodded, murmured 'Right on!' and reached for another beer. Then Larry, who hadn't said anything much up to then, suddenly broke out, 'I believe in God anyway.'

For a moment no one said anything. We were too stunned. If Larry had remarked that personally he enjoyed eating boiled baby, maybe with a little relish on the side, that would have been fine. But this abrupt declaration of a faith whose existence none of us had imagined left us deeply shocked. It was uncool.

'Anyway, it's all like a matter of faith,' Larry went on a little sheepishly. 'I'm only saying there's no way you can prove God doesn't exist just 'cos bad stuff happens.'

We belatedly realized that Larry must have been suppressing this statement for a long time, not wanting to challenge Sam on the sore point of his mother's death. But this was neutral ground, and the time had come to take a stand.

'Sure, you're right,' Sam replied in a slightly patronizing tone, as though he was managing Larry the way you did someone who was having a bad trip. 'All it proves is that if God *does* exist, then He's an evil fucker.'

'God is love,' Larry retorted heatedly. 'Evil is the work of Satan.'

Years of Bible study had left Sam well prepared for an argument such as this.

'That's the Manichean heresy, Larry,' he replied cheerfully. 'Couple of hundred years ago you'd have got burned at the stake for dividing up good and evil like that. Listen, according to the Scriptures, God is all-powerful, right? "I am the Almighty God", Genesis seventeen, verse one. "The Lord God omnipotent reigneth", Revelations nineteen, verse six. But we are also expected to believe that "God is love", First Epistle of John, chapter four, while Psalm Thirty-Four tells us that "the Lord is good: blessed is the man that trusteth in him". All I'm saying is that you can't have it both ways. If God is all-powerful, he could have saved that baby. If he is good and loving, he would have.'

This broadside understandably left Larry reeling. Apart from a theological expertise which none of us had suspected Sam possessed, we'd each had about fifteen beers by this time, to say nothing of the joint we'd passed around in the car on the way there.

'Religion isn't about that, it's about eternal salvation,' Larry protested. 'It's about the soul, not the body.'

Sam rolled his eyes and nodded earnestly. His lean, angular face and sharp, close-set eyes made him look like a ferret going in for the kill.

'I see! So our pain doesn't matter to God, that's what you're saying. Have you ever stuck your hand in boiling water? Can you begin to imagine what that child must have suffered? But of course that's as nothing in the eye of eternity. Probably the kid hadn't been baptized. That would explain everything. Original sin. It's going to burn in hell anyway, so why not boil it up a little first, get it used to the idea. Right?'

'It's not for us to judge the Almighty!' Larry broke out.

'Why the fuck not?' Sam shouted. 'What would you have thought of Phil here, or me, or Vince, or Greg, if we'd been in that apartment and just stood there and watched the kid stew? Would you have got down on your knees and worshipped us? No fucking way! You'd have called us sadistic perverts who should be locked up for ever. So where does that leave your just and loving God?'

An embarrassed silence fell. We knew Sam as a good-time guy, laid-back, mellow and very funny, someone for whom nothing was worth hassling about. This was a Sam none of us had glimpsed before: engaged, angry, articulate, dominating. He seemed to pick up on the vibes himself.

'What do the rest of you think?' he asked with a visible effort to lighten up.

Greg scowled into his beer.

'I think this whole thing's a downer,' he said.

'I think we should get stoned,' added Vince.

'We could go home and smoke some more,' I suggested.

Vince stood up.

'I mean *really* stoned. I'll go see what I can score.'

Just then the band came back for another set, we all sunk a few more beers and Greg launched into a story about a cheerleader who'd reportedly been slamdunked by the entire U of M basketball team after their recent triumph over a rival institution out in the sticks known around campus as Moo U. By the time Vince returned, the earlier incident seemed to have been forgotten. We had blow-ups like that all the time, and they didn't faze us too much. Worse things happen when you're stoned. Straight people might get hung up on disagreements and dissent, but we knew it was all in your head.

Vince had bought six tabs of what was billed as 'organic mescaline'. This evoked a round of sceptical groans. Ever since Huxley and Castaneda, mescaline was the buzz word in drugs, but the chances of being sold the real stuff was just about zip. This almost certainly wasn't mescaline at all, and sure as hell not organic. What we'd scored was most likely some cocktail such as acid cut with downers. Vince said he knew the dealer, though, and it was bound to be good shit whatever it was. That silenced any complaints. Another aspect of drug etiquette was that it was a point of honour never to refuse anything supplied by a friend of a friend. If Vince's buddy said it was OK, that was good enough for us.

Riding home in the car, we passed another joint around and fiddled with the radio. Larry sat up front beside Greg, who was driving. Sam, Vince and I swayed from side to side in the back, singing along to the Allman Brothers' 'Whipping Post' with Vince playing a mean air guitar. Suddenly a flashing blue light flooded the car.

'Holy fuck!' said Greg, glancing in the mirror. 'It's the pigs.'

We totally lost it. Some friends of ours had got busted a couple of weeks earlier. They were only holding a couple of grams of hash, but they'd been charged with possession and were in jail awaiting trial. We had six tabs of some unknown psychedelic plus a whole bag of weed. To make matters worse, the thought flashing through each of our drug-and-booze-hazed brains was that Vince's 'friend' had done a deal with the narcs. How else could they have got on to us? It all made sense. The dealer had copped a plea in return for fingering his clients so that the cops could bust them on the way home. Now they would strip-search us, do a rectal frisk and pack us off to the state pen where we'd be buggered and beaten up by redneck cons who thought hippies were faggot commie scum.

'Open the windows,' said Sam. 'Vince, pass me the shit.'

Vince handed Sam the stapled plastic pouch containing the tablets. As the car slowed to a halt, we wound down the windows in an attempt to flush out the sweet, herby smell of marijuana. The police cruiser came to a stop right behind us, lights still flashing. Greg turned off the radio and took a deep breath.

'Jesus Christ,' said Larry quietly.

The patrolman sidled up to the driver's door and asked for Greg's licence. We all sat very still while he scrutinized it.

'Get out of the car,' said the cop.

We obediently opened the doors and struggled out. The policeman stared at us irritably.

'Not *all* of you!' he snapped. 'Just the driver.'

We climbed back into the car again. The patrolman led Greg away. I thought about another night, when I'd been driving from one party to another with some people I didn't even know. We'd done some speed before leaving, so we drove *very* carefully, chanting 'Take it easy!' like a mantra. We thought we were maintaining really well until the State Patrol pulled us over on the highway. 'You know how fast you were going?' the cop asked. 'Gee, officer,' said our driver, 'I was just keeping up with traffic.' 'You were doing ten miles an hour,' the guy replied. That time, fortunately, we were clean.

After a few minutes, Greg reappeared and the police cruiser pulled out and roared away. We all stared at him as though he'd come back from the dead.

'What happened?'

'What did he say to you, man?'

Greg got back behind the wheel.

'The rear passenger light's out,' he announced laconically. 'He gave me a ticket.'

'That's all?'

'That's all.'

'*Far out!*'

We laughed like maniacs all the way back to the house. We'd beaten the system yet again, put one over on the whole Establishment crock of shit. The episode just confirmed our conviction that we were cooler, smarter and better adapted for survival than our enemies. They got so obsessed with their uptight rules and regulations they didn't even notice what was going on right under their very noses! There we were committing a major drug offence, and the dumb patrolman cites us for a traffic violation!

It wasn't till we got inside the house that someone sobered up enough to ask, 'So where's the mescaline?'

'I ate it,' said Sam.

There was a stunned silence.

'I thought the guy was going to bust us,' Sam went on calmly. 'A few ounces of weed we might talk our way out of, but not the tabs.'

'You ate them *all*?' asked Greg incredulously.

Sam nodded.

'What strength were they?' I asked Vince.

He shrugged.

'Who knows? Couple of hundred migs, the guy said.'

'We've got to get him to the hospital fast, get his stomach pumped.'

'No way!' said Sam forcefully.

'Sam, you've just dropped over a gram of whatever that shit is. You could *die*.'

He shrugged and smiled.

'We're all going to die, man.'

'For Christ's sake, Sam! This is serious. Even if it doesn't kill you, it's going to screw your head up completely!'

Sam stared at me.

'You figure I can't *handle* it?'

There was nothing I could say to that. Our cardinal rule was that drugs don't fuck you up, hang-ups do. An oft-repeated story described how when the Beatles made their first pilgrimage to India to see the Maharishi, he noticed that they were stoned and asked to see the stuff they'd been taking. They hand over their stash and the guy swallows it like candy right in front of their eyes. Fifty tabs of acid, man! Grade A, unadulterated, full-strength sunshine, nothing but the best for the Fab Four! And the Maharishi gobbles the lot and then sits there all night, calmly discoursing on the Path of True Knowledge until the sun comes up! Even a dose big enough to turn on a small town couldn't disturb his Inner Peace and Purity, dig?

So while in a similar situation nowadays someone would have dragged Sam off to the hospital, by force if necessary, back then it was out of the question. If I'd attempted to press the issue any further I would have risked being branded a power-tripper, projecting my own insecurities and anxieties on to Sam. Certainly none of the others would have backed me up. Their attitude was pretty well summed up by Larry's response when Sam assured us grandly that he would be all right.

'Sure *you*'ll be all right, man, but what about the rest of us? How are we supposed to get fucked up now you've cleaned out the stash?'

'Don't heavy me out, man,' replied Sam, closing his eyes.

Vince suggested dosing him with orange juice to bring him down, but we didn't have any in the house and Greg wasn't too crazy about driving after what had just happened. Anyway, Sam said he didn't want to come down.

'I'm kind of looking forward to it. I'm tired of low-level tripping. I've always wanted to go to the limit, and this is my chance.'

'Maybe you'll have an out-of-body experience,' said Greg, a trifle enviously. Everyone had read about out-of-body experiences, but no one we knew had actually had one.

'Maybe you'll see God,' added Vince.

'If I do, I'll ask him why he let that kid boil.'

The fact that he could joke about it made us feel more relaxed about the whole thing. Sam was an experienced tripper, and the dealer had probably been lying about the strength of the tablets. We smoked another joint and listened to some music, and then one by one people drifted off to their rooms. Sam lay stretched out on the sofa, his foot tapping in time to the music. I was the last to leave. I asked Sam if he was OK. He didn't reply.

'You want someone to stay up with you?' I asked.

His eyes opened, big and blank, but there was still no reply. I didn't insist. I had an early class I couldn't afford to cut, and I knew from experience that even good trips are bad trips when someone else is having them.

By the time I got up the next morning, Sam had crashed. He didn't surface again until late that night. I was sitting in an attempted lotus position on a beanbag, making notes for a paper I had to write. The others were out somewhere.

'Hey, man!' I said. 'How did it go?'

He looked at me in a strange, expressionless way.

'Phil,' he said flatly, as though recognizing someone from the distant past.

'What happened?'

He frowned.

'Nothing.'

'Last night, I mean. You dropped all that shit.'

A ghostly smile appeared and disappeared on his lips.

'Oh, that. The usual stuff, man.'

I shrugged and got back to my paper. Everyone's trips were their own responsibility, but also their own business. If they wanted to share them with you, fine – unless of course they carried on about them at excessive length, as though they were somehow better and more interesting than yours. But if they chose not to talk about them, you had to respect that too. A fundamental tenet of our shared philosophy was that language was a highly suspect medium of communication, clumsy and imprecise, a tool used by the straight world to impose its rigid, normalizing concepts on the infinite, threatening freedom of the human spirit. We weren't any more consistent about this than about anything else. Whereof one cannot speak, thereof one frequently went on and on about at ball-breaking length. But Sam had chosen to exercise his right to remain silent, and anyone who questioned him further would stand revealed as an undercover agent for the thought police.

Within a few days, the whole episode had turned into the stuff of myth, one of the heroic exploits to be celebrated whenever members of the tribe gathered late at night and the communal joint passed from hand to hand. Its connection with real events became increasingly tenuous. Before long we were telling people how we would have been busted by a crack narcotics squad that night if it hadn't been for the quick thinking of Greg, or maybe Larry, who'd dropped the whole stash of twelve – count 'em! – *twelve* tabs of high-grade acid, and how we'd worked all night to keep him together while he went on about the wall-to-wall shag being a heaving mass of maggots.

Sam never contested this version of events, or talked about what had really happened. In fact he rarely said anything much any more. He had changed, becoming quieter, more serious and withdrawn, less accessible to our noise and nonsense. The reason seemed obvious. A month or so earlier, Sam had received his 'Greetings from the President' letter from the draft board. He had been shocked at the time, because he had drawn a pretty high number in the lottery and had thought he was safe.

Now that the date when he had to report for induction was looming closer, however, he seemed strangely resigned to his fate. Again, we thought we knew why. With his level of education, Sam would almost certainly be able to land a clerical job and put in his year's tour of duty filing reports and typing letters. Nevertheless, the situation inevitably created tension in our midst. Larry's turn was also coming up soon, and he had a number in the low teens, making it almost inevitable that he would be drafted. From time to time he talked of taking a bus up to Canada, or maybe applying to join the National Guard, but he never did anything about it, and we all knew he never would.

The rest of us were safe. Vince had already been turned down because of his bad eyes and generally poor health, while Greg and I were protected for the moment by the student deferment. We never openly discussed the matter, but this manifest inequality slowly drove a wedge into the heart of our intimacy, splintering it apart. One night just before he left, Sam freaked out for the first time in our company, raving on about the world being divided into two kinds of people, the ones with real souls and feelings, and a bunch of phonies who were just pretending to be alive.

Nothing came of it, however, and a couple of days later Sam

packed up his belongings and set off to start his two months' basic training at Fort Lewis, in Washington State. Our farewells were awkward and subdued. A month later a woman I'd been seeing on and off for the past year invited me to move in with her. I was glad to leave. Larry had also been drafted by then, and Vince and Greg were spending more and more time with people I didn't know. That stage of my life was over. It was time to move on.

I never expected to see any of them again.

Three

Pearce and Robinson were sitting in the parking lot at Taco Time when they got the call.

'I wouldn't've went if I would've known,' Pearce said through a mouthful of chicken tostada.

Kimo Robinson sipped his banana shake tentatively. He'd felt like grazing on something, but his stomach couldn't hack spicy food any more. He felt queasy just watching Pearce feed, lettuce shreds hanging off his bristles, hot sauce dribbling down his chin.

'But you're there, what you going to do?' the rookie demanded, spraying a gobbet of refried beans at the windshield. 'Can't walk out on the wife's best friend's dinner. Mandatory detail.'

'It's my way or the highway.'

'Pardon me?'

Pearce was regarding him quizzically. Robinson shrugged.

'I saw this programme on TV. Some guy who's written a book, you know? He says men are from Mars and women from Venus.'

'Jean's from Omaha,' said Pearce, frowning.

Two weeks ago Robinson showed up for work, sarge tells him, 'Congratulations, Kimo, you're an FTO for the next three months.' No one liked field training assignments, stuck every shift with some guy fresh from the eleven-week course watching your every move, time to time saying, 'Gee, that's not what they taught us at the Academy.' Plus Robinson didn't want to hear about Pearce's marital problems. He wanted to tune into KING-FM and relax with Haydn, Handel, those old guys who knew how to kick back and have fun.

'Not only is Chari a bitch on wheels,' Pearce continued, 'she's cranked up on medication the whole time. Obsesses over every goddamn thing, never shuts her mouth … I spent the whole evening processing anger. You know?'

Robinson set his shake down on the dash. He could feel the burn starting up already. Maybe he should see a doctor. 'Your core is good,' the guy down at the garage had told him. Guy was talking about the transmission, but somehow the words had stuck. 'Your core is good.' Kept coming back to him like the slogan from some cheesy commercial you can't shake. Maybe because he knew it wasn't true for him any more than for the goddamn car. Fact was, their cores were both fucked.

We should never have moved here, he thought for the thousandth time. It had seemed like a great idea at the time. For the price of a studio apartment in Honolulu, they could get a family home with a yard and a garage in Seattle. True, he'd had to start at the bottom of the ladder again, going from sergeant in Hawaii back to plain officer with the King County Police, but that had seemed a price worth paying. Marti was delighted with her new home, the kids were happy at school, he had his RV to go hunting and fishing. Everything was just great, except that his core was fucked. I wasn't meant to live in this cold, wet, timber-haunted landscape, he thought. I was meant to live and die on the islands, and my gods are punishing me for my desertion.

The call was the one cops dreaded most: domestic disturbance. Then Robinson heard the address, and eased up a little. Pearce rolled up the remains of his tostada in the 100 per cent recycled paper bag and tossed it in back.

'Don't break the limit getting over there,' Robinson told him. 'We let him work on her a little, maybe this time she'll press charges.'

'These guys regulars?' asked Pearce, putting the Chevy in drive and hanging a U across the oncoming traffic. 'Kinda strange timing.'

Robinson grunted. Pearce still wasn't up to speed on the precinct. In town, most domestic violence occurred in the evening, when folks were tense from a day's work and a long commute and had had a couple of belts to unwind. But Renfrew

Avenue South East was in the slurbs, the swathe of suburban slums in the unincorporated areas of the county stretching inland from the southern tip of Lake Washington. You were talking high unemployment, mothers on shift work, the kids at the childcare centre, the men spending all day down at the stuccoed, mirror-windowed licensed restaurant where no one had ordered a meal in twenty years. Domestic tensions could flare up any time of the day or night, particularly at 14218 Renfrew Ave.

Robinson had lost count of the times he'd been called to the Sullivan house, maybe because it always seemed like the same call. Guy beats up on his wife, someone calls 911, soon as you show up they both turn on you and tell you it's none of your fucking business, wife denies he ever laid a hand on her, guy says she hurt herself falling, not a goddamn thing you can do. Robinson had hoped things might improve when they finally split up. Some chance. Wayne still hung around there half the time, the only difference was he had another woman down in Renton he was beating up too.

They drove up a hill dominated by a huge water-tower and a sprinkling of conifers, degenerate offspring of the giants which had preceded them, past a bowling alley and a bingo hall, the Thrift Store and the Splash 'n' Dash car wash, the Silk Plant Center and the Hallmark outlet, by signs reading 'Rent-2-Own' and 'No Hassel Loans'. It had started to rain again. Overhead, a suffocating mass of clouds miles high pressed down on the land-scape. Robinson thought of the candid azure skies of his home state, and shivered.

Pearce took a left at the lights, passing a strip mall and the 'Faith in Focus Worship Center' whose reader board said 'If life hands you lemons, make lemonade'. Then they were into the grid of residential streets, GI starter homes originally, small squat boxes with gravel lots surrounded by chain-link fencing, 25 mph limits, lots of all-way stops, no sidewalks. You had to be rich to walk these days, like the yuppies down by the lake. These people were too poor.

Except for a few decorative details, the house was identical to its neighbours. Woodgrain-effect vinyl siding, skimpy windows, a worn afghan draped over the sofa on the front porch, three pick-ups in various stages of cannibalization in the yard. There was no one around. Pearce parked by a telephone pole, blocking Robinson's door. A yellow sign peeling off the pitted surface of the pole read 'Neighborhood Crime Watch: We report all suspicious persons and activity to our local police'. Robinson logged in their arrival and squeezed painfully through the half-open door. Pearce was already striding up the path in a take-charge manner.

By the time Robinson caught up, the rookie had knocked several times at the door. There was no reply. Pearce rapped again, even more insistently.

'Police!'

A soft tintinnation of wind chimes from a neighbouring house, the busy hum of a light aircraft overhead. Looking down at the rain-glistened porch steps, Robinson caught the reflection of a float-plane heading east towards the mountains, Lake Chelan maybe. He thought of the camping trip he and the boys had taken last summer up by Snoqualmie. That week his core had been good.

'Police!' Pearce yelled again. 'Open up!'

He glanced at his partner.

'What do we do? Is this an exigent situation? That'd give us the right to go in.'

Kimo Robinson could have told him it didn't make a damn bit of difference, this thing was never going to come to court. Instead he tried the handle. It turned. Robinson pushed the door open and stood on the threshold, scanning the room. Nothing seemed to have changed. Plastic leprechaun, three foot high, weighted for use as a doorstop. Doormat reading WELCOME TO THE SULLIVANS. White plastic cross on the back of the door with BLESS OUR HOME in gold. Thing played the 'Hallelujah Chorus' in electronic chimes when you walked in, except the batteries were always out. The air was hot and thick and full of smells, food mostly, but also something else, something with an acrid edge. Robinson stiffened, his eyes searching the room.

An entertainment centre dominated the end wall, the big

wood-effect TV flanked by dusty gaps where Wayne had moved out his stereo and speakers. His plush velour recliner rocker was still there, though, lined up with the TV, Dad's throne. A chunky sofa too big for the room, upholstered in bright mustard and tomato soup brocade, faced an octagonal coffee table with a smoked glass top standing on a stained, simulated sheepskin rug. Beneath that lay brown deep-shag carpeting with plastic strips to protect the heavy traffic areas.

It was Pearce who spotted the bare leg thrust out from behind the sofa. The foot was clad in a pink fluffy slipper. Motioning the rookie to stay put, Robinson walked along the ridged plastic runner until he could see the rest of the body. It was a woman. She was wearing a faded blue bathrobe over a white synthetic nightgown. Her henna-tinted hair was arranged in a tightly interlocking mass of whorls, her face pressed into the carpet.

'What is it? What's the matter?'

Pearce sounded panicky. Robinson knelt down and turned the woman over. It was Dawn Sullivan. There was blood in her hair. She didn't seem to be breathing, and her skin felt cold and clammy.

'Go take a look in the other rooms,' he told Pearce, just to get him out of there.

As the rookie headed off towards the master bedroom, Robinson unclipped the portable radio from his belt.

'Frank Three, Frank Three. Woman down, unresponsive. Get me an aid car.'

He was responding to a follow-up question from the call receiver when he heard Pearce's scream. Running to the doorway, he collided heavily with the rookie on his way back out.

'What the hell?' he demanded.

Pearce shook his head. He looked as though he was about to cry. Grabbing his mouth with one hand, he plunged past his partner and out of the front door. Robinson started after him, then turned back. He drew his pistol and stepped warily into the room. The bed unmade, female clothing strewn around, no sign of any serious disturbance. The light was dimmed by layers of grimy net curtains and a dust-laden valance of folds and flounces that resembled bad meringue. A flicker of movement caught his attention. A mobile suspended over a crib. Plastic figures of animals and birds in bright primary colours revolved slowly in the draught from the heating vent.

Then he heard a noise, somewhere between a groan and a gurgle. It seemed to be coming from the crib. Robinson remembered that the Sullivans had had another child just before they broke up. The 'Accident', Dawn called it. Kimo Robinson thought that was kind of gross, even though the little thing couldn't understand. The noise was repeated, more urgently. He walked over to the crib, feeling awkward and incompetent. Hopefully the EMTs would know how to calm a baby.

But this baby did not need calming. Even before he reached the crib, Robinson realized that the noise he had heard was coming from beyond the window, out in the front yard, where Bill Pearce was hurling up a curdled mess of half-digested Tex-Mex. The baby, by contrast, lay quiet and still, its tiny fingers clutching at nothing, its pale blue eyes wide open, a neat, blackened hole punched in the centre of its forehead. The mass of blood and brain fragments which had haemorrhaged from its nose and mouth lay congealing on the pillow and quilt.

*

By the time Patrol Sergeant Alex Mitchell arrived at the house, the body count had risen to four. The Fire Department's paramedics had been and gone. Those guys would do CPR on anything with a heart left to pump, but once they looked the scene over they knew they were wasting their time there.

Mitchell had driven fast – siren and lights, touching a hundred – down Highway 169 from the headquarters of Third Precinct at Maple Ridge. 'Get me a sergeant,' Robinson had blurted hoarsely over the radio. Everyone knew what that meant. To make matters worse, the field trainee had flipped completely, and it was only after another patrolman showed up to hold his hand that it had been possible to complete the search of the property. That was when they'd found the other victims downstairs in the basement, two boys about ten years old.

Next thing some woman name of Kelly Shelden turned up at

the door, saying she was the person who'd called 911 in the first place.

'When I saw what'd happened I just freaked. I mean, I know Wayne's crazy, but I never thought he'd do nothing like this. So I called Chuck, that's my husband, and then I took Jamie across the street to the neighbours. Mr Valdez was real nice, even though I hardly know them. He wanted to come over and take a look, but I told him, "You keep out of there till the police get here." I knew there was nothing we could do for Dawn, not that I'm a doctor or anything, but you can tell, right?'

Alex Mitchell listened with half an ear as the woman blathered on. He didn't have time to follow the ins and outs of her story. What he had to do was call downtown. All the local TV and radio stations had scanners tuned to the police frequency, and one word about a case like this over the air would have them all banging at the door before the homicide dicks had even got their coats on. He needed a land line. The phone in the house could be evidence, so he couldn't use that. Mitchell had never gotten over being bawled out for mishandling a scene-of-crime following a drug shoot-out in Cascade Vistas. 'Procedural irregularities impacting the investigative assignment,' the report had said. That would stick with him the rest of his career, filed away in a computer somewhere.

'Let's go back across the street,' he suggested to the woman. 'You can tell me all about it there.'

The neighbour, Valdez, was an intense Hispanic with pockmarked skin and pure black eyes. His wife was talking softly in broken English to a boy of about seven or eight who sat on the sofa, staring down at his knees. Mitchell asked to use the phone. It was in the bedroom. The air was filled with musky, intimate smells.

Down at Precinct One, they went ape-shit. A quadruple slaying meant pictures in the paper, prime-time TV, you name it. When Mitchell put the phone down he found the Shelden woman at his elbow. She started in again right away, but Mitchell cut her off, telling her the detectives were on their way and would want to hear it all from her own lips. Back in the living room, the kid was in tears, weeping and sniffling. Kelly Shelden walked right by him, still trying to interest Mitchell in her story. He found it kind of weird, her showing more interest in bugging him than comforting her own son, but life was full of things he didn't get, and some he didn't want to.

The homicide dicks were there in twenty minutes flat. There were four of them – 'One per stiff,' thought Mitchell cynically – plus all the personnel who travelled with the Van. Thanks to the grisly and still unsolved Green River murders, King County had one of the best Mobile Crime Scene Units in the business. While the detectives nosed around getting a feel for the scene, the technicians donned their protective suiting and got busy photographing and fingerprinting and vacuuming, looking for all the world like some maid brigade.

In charge of the case was Kristine Kjarstad, who ran homicide and assault investigations in the south-east district of the county, where 14218 Renfrew was located. Mitchell knew her slightly from the time they'd both spent working out of Second Precinct, and they kidded around some, the way everyone does when they're nervous. Kjarstad was wearing a well-tailored suit and carrying one of those metal executive cases with combination locks. Like many tall women, she stooped slightly, giving her a round-shouldered slouch which undercut the power look she projected in other ways. There was almost nothing about her to suggest that she was a detective. Most people would have spotted her for a realtor or maybe an executive secretary, some wannabee high-flyer gradually discovering that she was trapped between sticky floor and glass ceiling. Only Mitchell noted the little clues: the sensible shoes, the cheap clip-on earrings, the absence of rings or other jewellery. Fashion shoes slow you down, pierced earlobes can get torn off, rings can snag on fences just long enough to get you shot.

Kjarstad's partner was a guy named Steve Warren. Mitchell marked him down as one of those nerds with a taste for cop toys, the kind who drops a couple hundred of his own dough every month at Blumenthals on a high-tech baton or some snappy gizmo to hold your Mace canister. He wore a cheap clone Brooks Brothers outfit with a snazzy tie and carried his automatic in a soft rawhide holder clipped to the inside of his pants.

The other two dicks had just come along for the ride, but Kristine Kjarstad didn't seem to mind. Mitchell could understand that. There may be no such thing as a good homicide, but by the looks of it this was one of the worst. It helped having colleagues around to talk you through it, to make it all seem just another detail, part of the job. The detectives weren't even too bothered when Davidoff, the patrol lieutenant, showed up and started giving them the benefit of his wisdom and experience. Davidoff had put in time working out of the courthouse before being promoted. Now that the biggest thing in years had landed on his territory, he wasn't about to miss out.

All this activity had drawn a small crowd of spectators, so Mitchell went to tell Kimo Robinson and one of the other patrolmen to secure the street in front of the house. The roll of official POLICE LINE DO NOT CROSS tape ran out half-way through, and they had to use a length of orange tow-rope instead. While he was rooting around in the trunk looking for more tape, Mitchell noticed one of the plastic-bagged soft toys which every patrol car carried. These were donated by members of the public, dry-cleaned and bagged so that they could be given to distressed children following automobile accidents, domestic shootings and so on. 'Yo, kid, your mom and pop are road kill but here's a stuffed animal.' It sounded sucky, but sometimes it helped, if anything could.

That gave him an idea. Picking up the bagged teddy bear, Mitchell walked back across the street to the Valdez house. The moment he got inside, he regretted his impulse. Kelly Shelden started in on him again without even pausing for breath.

'One of the detectives will be along to take your statement real soon,' Mitchell told her. 'You just wait here till they get here. Don't want to have to tell it all twice, right?'

He pushed the plastic-wrapped package into her arms. Kelly Shelden broke off in mid-sentence, staring with amazement at the floppy-eared teddy bear.

'For your little boy,' Mitchell explained. 'Help him get over the shock.'

'*My* boy?' queried the woman. 'How do you mean? Chuck and I don't have any kids.'

She sounded indignant, as though Mitchell should have known this. He looked at the boy, who was sitting absolutely still on the sofa, legs clenched together, arms crossed. His eyes, dry now, stared blankly out over a comic book Mrs Valdez had given him to read.

'I thought … ' Mitchell began.

'Jamie?' Kelly Shelden cut in. 'I *told* you. He lived there! He was there when it happened! He saw everything!'

*

An hour later, Kristine Kjarstad had the familiar feeling that she'd exhausted the immediate possibilities of the situation. When Alex Mitchell returned to tell her there was a material witness across the street, she'd dropped everything and gone to interview him, leaving Steve Warren to handle the scene-of-crime notes. This involved marking, measuring and recording every conceivable physical detail, relevant or not, just in case some smart-ass defence lawyer tried to throw doubt on the prosecution case by pointing out to the jury that the police didn't appear to have noticed whether or not the windows had been washed recently, so how could their testimony in other respects be credible? It was the kind of thing that Steve Warren could be trusted to handle well, and she was happy to leave it in his hands.

Before Kristine Kjarstad could speak to the boy, she had to listen to the Shelden woman's version of events. This was of no particular interest to her, but Kjarstad had no desire to antagonize anyone at this stage, particularly a witness who was clearly in shock. It took her the best part of thirty minutes – it felt more like ninety – to sift the facts of the story out of a mass of confused and repetitive responses. The root of the problem was that instead of calling 911 herself, Kelly Shelden had called her husband.

This is after she gets to the house and finds Dawn Sullivan

lying face down on the floor. She has no idea what's happened or what to do about it, and Jamie just sits there howling, so she calls Chuck at work, who calls Emergency. He knows all about the Sullivans, of course, so he naturally assumes that Wayne and Dawn have been duking it out again, which is why the call went out as a domestic.

Once she'd got that straightened out, Kristine Kjarstad spent another five minutes getting Mrs Shelden out of her hair so that she could talk to the boy. She tried everything she knew, not just from training but from her own experience with her son Thomas, who was about the same age. She talked about Mr and Mrs Valdez, about Jamie's clothes, about his new toy, about anything except the horrors he had allegedly witnessed. She tried to get him to look at her, to address a single word to her – any word.

And she failed. Jamie just sat there, hugging the bear listlessly and gazing into space. She might as well have been speaking a foreign language. She might as well not have been there. To all intents and purposes she wasn't. Jamie was alone at the epicentre of a psychic blast which had wiped out all life in the vicinity. It would take rescue workers days if not weeks to get through to him. The question was what to do with him until then.

A confusing session with the attention-seeking Kelly Shelden and the idiomatically-challenged Valdez couple elicited the information that there were two more members of the Sullivan family unaccounted for, a teenage girl and the estranged husband. As far as they knew there were no other family members living locally. Mrs Shelden insisted stridently that Jamie should come and stay with her and Chuck, but Kristine Kjarstad did not feel that this would be in anyone's best interests. In the end she called in to DSHS and arranged for a social worker to get out there and place the boy in temporary foster care.

It wasn't the ideal solution, she reflected as she made her way back across the street, but it was the best one available. The only responsible adult relative was the boy's father, Wayne, and at this stage he was also the principal suspect.

The crime scene technicians were still at work in the basement, but in other respects the preliminary investigation was almost complete. The medical examiner had come by and certified that the victims were dead, and the corpses of the mother and baby had been removed to the morgue. Steve Warren had compiled notes and sketches of every room in the house, and the other two dicks, Harrison and Borg, had interviewed the neighbours.

Mr Valdez had been out in the front yard the whole time, working on a car, but neither he nor anyone else had seen or heard anything unusual, despite the fact that at least four shots had been fired. A magnum or a shottie might have attracted attention, but not the small-bores which inflicted these injuries. Even in the next room, a .22 or .25 sounds no louder or more alarming than a book falling to the floor. In the next house, or outside in the street, you wouldn't even notice it.

As for Wayne Sullivan, none of the neighbours knew where he'd been living since the couple split up, or if they did they weren't saying. Where the police were concerned, most of these people had been on the receiving end most of their lives. Talking to the cops didn't come easy.

'But it's got to be him,' Steve Warren asserted confidently. 'He has a record of domestic violence. Only this time he went all the way, took out the whole family.'

He and Kristine Kjarstad had drifted instinctively into the kitchen, the only part of the house untouched by death. In the corner, the fridge hummed sturdily away as though nothing had happened, and at any moment the family would appear and start rooting around for something to eat.

'Except he didn't,' said Kristine. 'The boy survived somehow, the daughter wasn't around. And what about the other kid?'

She'd just been downstairs. The basement was another world, raw, inconclusive, a place of botched projects and provisional arrangements become permanent by default. There were various utility rooms and a half-finished bar-cum-den. In the centre of the floor, the furnace roared hollowly. Two rooms opened off the other wall. The bedrooms looked identical at first sight, full of boy's stuff: maps and posters on the wall, a globe, an empty fish tank, wooden dinosaurs, a shelf of tattered books and comics, a football, a catcher's mitt, unwashed clothes strewn on the floor, Lego pieces, a marble, coins, a shell collection. But the two cadavers which lay stiffening on the bed and the floor didn't conveniently fit the matching décor, because the fourth victim was clearly Asian.

'Then there's the MO,' Kristine Kjarstad continued. 'This guy sounds like a violent slob, a wife-beater. You'd expect him to use a shotgun, something messy like that, not a neat shot to the back of the head. This looks more like an execution.'

Warren shrugged uneasily.

'Maybe there's a drug angle. They could have gotten involved with the gangs … '

His voice trailed away. He looked around at the line of stoneware jars marked 'Dawn's Kitchen', the dirty dishes stacked at all angles in the sink, the stove cover set with pictures of birds, a pizza delivery box with one limp slice inside, an open box of Cheerios, the unicorn spice rack, an empty plastic gallon milk container, the mock-crochet sign reading 'Bless This Mess' …

His face sagged suddenly. He looked old and lost.

'Jesus Christ,' he said quietly. 'What *is* this?'

*

A week later, there was still no answer to this question.

By now the identity of all the victims had been established. Three were members of the Sullivan family: Dawn, thirty-three, a checker at the local K-mart, and two children, Kevin, eleven, and Samantha, fifteen months. The fourth was Ronald Ho, twelve, resident at 2337 Fourth Avenue, a classmate of Kevin Sullivan at Renton Heights School.

All had been killed with a single CCI Stinger .22 round fired at very close range. Such bullets break up on entry, splitting up to six times inside the body, and it was thus impossible to recover any further ballistics information. The mother and the two boys had been shot in the back of the head, the baby in the forehead. There was no sign that anything had been stolen from the house, and none of the victims had been sexually molested before or after death.

Three members of the family had survived. Megan, fourteen, had been spending the day with a friend, Nicole Pearson. Her brother Jamie, eight, had apparently been in the house at the time of the shootings. It was not clear why he had been spared, or whether he could identify the perpetrator. At present he was in foster care under the nominal supervision of social workers. Kristine Kjarstad had interviewed him on three occasions, without result. The boy now seemed to hear and understand her questions, but responded only by shrugging his shoulders and shaking his head. On each occasion the social worker had brought the interview to an end, indicating that further pressure could compromise the child's eventual recovery.

The remaining survivor and primary suspect was the estranged husband, Wayne Sullivan, thirty-seven. The fact that the door had not been forced suggested that the perpetrator was either known to Mrs Sullivan or possessed a key. The couple had a history of domestic violence, and the crime seemed to fit a pattern of cases in which depressive or vengeful spouses killed their entire families shortly after a separation or divorce.

Two factors weighed against this hypothesis. The first was that the spouses in question usually killed themselves at the same time, or gave themselves up to the police immediately afterwards. The second emerged from the autopsy report on Mrs Sullivan and the two boys, which revealed mild contusions and abrasions around the wrists and traces of adhesive on the lips and surrounding skin, suggesting that the victims had been bound and gagged before being shot. That, like the choice of weapon, seemed to indicate the work of a cold-blooded professional killer, not an emotionally wrought spouse, but no one had been able to come up with a convincing reason why such a killer should choose to execute a housewife, two schoolboys and a baby – unless of course it was a case of mistaken identity.

Police work is a percentage game, and at the moment the smart money was on the estranged husband.

If he hadn't given himself up, Wayne Sullivan would have been a hard man to find. His driver's licence was still registered to the Renfrew Avenue address. He didn't have a bank account or hold a regular job, and was staying at a semi-derelict house he shared with two other men in a forgotten patch of Renton blighted by the Burlington Northern tracks on one side and Highway 405 on the other. Fortunately he made life easy for everyone by turning himself in just a few hours after the all-points bulletin went out.

Sullivan's story was that he had spent the day painting an empty apartment in Bellevue, a subcontract he'd picked up from a friend in the construction business. It wasn't much of an alibi, but Kristine Kjarstad didn't get too excited about that. One look at Wayne, you knew this guy didn't have a *life*, so why should he have an alibi? And while he did admit to having a gun, it turned out to be a .30-calibre Remington hunting rifle. He claimed that he had spent the day painting the Bellevue apartment and had heard of the killings on the radio as he was driving home. He was offered and accepted a polygraph test, which he passed. Tests for nitrates on his hands and face proved negative. His fingerprints had been found at the scene, but not on the bodies or clothing, and since he regularly visited the house, and had lived there until recently, this proved nothing.

There wasn't enough evidence to hold Wayne Sullivan for the killings, but Kristine Kjarstad ran a computer scan which showed that there was a warrant out in his name for unpaid traffic fines amounting to $145. Sullivan couldn't pony up, so he was taken across the street to spend the night in the King County jail. Meanwhile Kjarstad obtained a warrant and ordered a search of the house in Renton. This turned up a .22 automatic pistol belonging to one of the other residents, but it was loaded with a different type of ammunition from that used in the killings and showed no sign of having been recently fired. Moreover, the absence of spent cartridges at the scene meant that the perpetrator had either carefully collected them after shooting – in itself inconsistent with the domestic scenario – or had used a revolver instead of an automatic.

Then two things happened which changed the whole tenor of the case. The first was that the social worker looking after Jamie Sullivan contacted the police with the news that the boy had started to talk about what had happened. Kristine Kjarstad tried without success to get him to respond directly to her questions, but the foster mother reported that Jamie had told her that he had been concealed behind a service hatch in the furnace housing as part of a game of hide-and-seek with the other two boys. While there, he had heard strange voices in the house. One had said something about 'a piece of wood', presumably referring to the panel covering Jamie's hiding place, which had fallen off. The other man had used the name 'Russ'.

If this was true, it explained why Jamie had survived the slaughter. However, its real significance lay in the fact that it suggested that there had been at least two killers, neither of them known to Jamie. Unfortunately its value was diminished by the source. Jamie Sullivan had had plenty of time to think the situation through and decide what story to tell. The part about hiding in the furnace hatch might well be true, but suppose the person he had seen from his refuge had *not* been a stranger. That would explain his shock, his initial refusal to speak, and the elaborate and unlikely tale he had finally come up with, as well as his continuing reluctance to expose himself to cross-examination by the police. The cover story must be as different from the truth as possible: two men, not one, and safely anonymous strangers, not the all-too-familiar figure of his own father.

But even as Kristine Kjarstad was digesting the implications of Jamie's reported statement, a second development promptly superseded it. One of the two men Sullivan had been sharing the house in Renton with appeared at the courthouse and paid the fines outstanding in Wayne's name. Since they still lacked sufficient evidence to press murder charges, the police had no choice but to release Sullivan. When he was informed of this, however, the prisoner refused to be released and demanded to speak to Kristine Kjarstad.

Fearing some kind of protest against his unjust detention, Kristine asked Steve Warren to sit in on the interview. Sullivan was tall and rangy, with a sad, defeated face framed by a bushy brown beard. His piercing green eyes looked restlessly around the room as though on the alert for insult or aggression. He sat down opposite the two detectives and asked for a cigarette.

'This is a no-smoking facility,' Warren told him sternly.

'But you can smoke all you want outside,' added Kristine Kjarstad.

Wayne Sullivan looked at her, shaking his head slowly. Tears trickled from his eyes and fell, getting tangled up in the mesh of his beard like dew in a spiderweb.

'Can't do that,' he mumbled.

'That buddy of yours paid your fine,' said Kjarstad. 'You're free to go.'

The movements of Sullivan's head became ever faster and convulsive.

'I don't care about the fine!' he said. 'It's the babies I care about.'

His tone was so pathetic that Kristine Kjarstad had to look away. Dead bodies didn't bother her, precisely because they were dead. The grief and suffering of the living was much more difficult to deal with.

'We're doing everything we can,' she said in a kindly tone, forgetting for a moment that Sullivan himself was the principal suspect, in fact the only one. 'I'm sure we'll find out pretty soon who did it.'

Wayne Sullivan looked up at her in astonishment.

'Find out?' he exclaimed. 'What the hell's to find out? *I* did it! That's what I came to tell you. I didn't want to do it, but there was no other way to save them from that bitch.'

Four

I never expected to see any of them again, and when I did it was pure coincidence. I was passing through O'Hare on the way back from Boston, having visited my parents on the occasion of my father's sixtieth birthday. He had recently retired, and they had moved to a house on Cape Cod. Because of my mother's poor health they had been forced to cancel a planned trip to come to see us, and since Rachael hadn't wanted to travel so far with David, I ended up going there alone. On the way back my connection in Chicago was delayed, and I was killing time in the bar when someone walked up to me and said, 'Phil?'

The face looked vaguely familiar, but it was only when the man noticed my blank expression and said his own name that I realized who it was. Recognition came tainted with a sense of unease. Of the whole group, Vince was the one I had been least close to. His interests – sex, drugs and rock-and-roll – were also ours, but the single-mindedness with which he pursued them set him apart. To Vince, time not spent balling, tripping or bopping, preferably all at once, was time wasted. We admired his purity, but even then it seemed a little extreme. I had never forgotten the time I'd unguardedly mentioned some novel I was currently enthusiastic about, and Vince had remarked crushingly, 'You still read books? I'm too busy living.' After that I'd never quite known what to say to him. What on earth would we have to say now?

It immediately became clear was that Vince was no longer Vince. The former acid-head, sack artist and lead guitar manqué was now a highly paid sound technician for a TV station in Chicago with a profitable sideline in freelance assignments. He looked fit, tanned and relaxed, and sipped a Perrier while I slurped my scotch. The duds he had on looked like they cost more than my car, and instead of a commuter plane to St Paul he was catching a direct flight to Tokyo, club class, to film a documentary on sumo wrestling.

Worst of all, he was *nice* about it. He made no attempt to cold-cock me with a blow-by-blow account of his glamorous lifestyle, and even showed some polite interest when I filled him in on the banal data of my own. I told him that I was teaching English at a community college, that I was married, that we had a child. What more could I say? That I liked my work? That I loved my son to distraction? That I was happier than I had ever been in my life? It would have sounded false and forced. I let the lame facts speak for themselves with no attempt to explain or excuse. Vince was very kind and correct.

'Boy or girl?' he asked.

'A boy. David.'

'How old is he?'

'Going on seven.'

'Great. I'd love to have kids one day. Right now, though, a family life's kind of impossible.'

He even managed to sound slightly envious! I started to warm to him.

Having exhausted every other topic we had in common, we began to talk about the others. Vince had lost touch with Greg, who had last been heard of working on the Alaska pipeline, but he had news of Sam and Larry. It was bizarre and a little disturbing.

'When they got drafted, we all figured Sam would get some cushy desk job while Larry ended up as a grunt, right? Wrong! The army found out that Larry had worked as a painter, and he got to stay right here fixing up the mess and recreational facilities at the base. Never even went to Vietnam.'

I laughed.

'Good for him.'

Vince shook his head.

'Two days before he was due to go home, he got hit by a truck. Some guy had been drinking, came around the corner with no lights on, didn't even see him. Larry didn't stand a chance.'

I was shocked. I'd read about the war, of course, and seen the familiar, horrific pictures on TV, but it had all seemed as remote from my own existence as gang-land killings in Miami or race riots in Los Angeles. But Larry was someone I'd known. He'd painted our house in his spare time, using up leftovers from whatever job he happened to be working on. The results were quite spectacular: strips and patches of every hue, shade and finish, some matt, others shimmering satin, a few in high gloss. I'd joked and smoked with Larry, eaten and drunk with him. Once in a while we even talked. I suddenly remembered that last time, down at the Commercial Hotel, when he'd clashed with Sam over the existence of God.

As so often in the past, when the joint had passed and the vibes were good, Vince must have been having the same thought.

'Well, I guess Larry knows the answer to all the big questions now,' he said. 'Shame he can't come back and have the last word.'

'Sam made it OK, then?' I asked, glad to change the subject.

'Uh huh. Which is almost as weird as Larry getting killed.'

'How do you mean?'

Vince looked at me.

'You remember how the system worked? After induction you did two months basic training, and then you got to find out what classification they'd assigned you. The one no one wanted was Eleven Bravo. That meant you did two more months training as a rifleman, then got shipped to 'Nam to replace the guys who were coming home in body bags. But there were eight support personnel for every man at the front, so if you had any kind of qualifications or education your chances of avoiding combat were pretty good.'

'Like Sam,' I prompted.

'Yeah. Except Sam volunteered.'

'*Volunteered*?'

Vince nodded.

'Doesn't make sense, right? Anyone that crazy to see action

had already joined up, and they'd mostly all been in ROTC at college and were into all that military bullshit. But for someone to wait to get drafted and then deliberately lay his life on the line when he could walk away with a job as a filing clerk! And a guy like Sam!'

I shook my head.

'I don't get it.'

'Me neither. But that's what he did, and he spent his whole tour of duty under fire. The company he was in took 80 per cent casualties in one fire-fight. He was out there the full year, and he came back without a scratch on him.'

'You met him, then?'

'He wrote me. We talked about getting together, but nothing ever came of it.'

We chatted some more about this and that, and then my flight was called. Vince and I hurriedly exchanged addresses, phone numbers and formulaic promises to keep in touch. By the time my plane was airborne, the whole encounter seemed unreal. I didn't bother to mention it to Rachael when I got home.

It must have been almost a year after that when Sam called me at home one evening. It was not a good moment. David had recently developed chronic asthma, and although the medication normally kept the symptoms in check, he was still liable to have periodic crises. This was one. He had caught a heavy cold the week before, and this had precipitated an asthma attack which kept him – and us – awake for hours every night while he coughed and cried and struggled for breath.

As a result, Rachael and I were both ragged from lack of sleep, and oppressed not just with a rational anxiety for our son's health but with something neither of us could mention, even to each other – a sense of failure, of inadequacy, of what I might once have called 'bad karma'. However much you reject the idea rationally, a child becomes a symbol of the relationship which brought it into being. Any congenital weakness in the former inevitably reflects on the latter.

As well as nursing David, Rachael and I had our jobs to deal with. Her work for the Children's Protective Service continually brought her into contact with stressful situations involving, as she once said, people who shouldn't be allowed to keep a cat, never mind a child. There was no solution to the problems she dealt with, only damage control and the least harmful option. Sometimes, as that evening, this knowledge left her feeling depressed and vulnerable.

When the phone rang, she was telling me about the case she was currently working on, a ghastly affair involving systematic physical abuse over a period of years. Just hearing about it brought me down – I was exhausted myself, and had my own, less dramatic problems at work – but I knew that sharing these horrors with me was therapeutic for her, and forced myself to listen. David was running around screaming his head off in a desperate attempt to attract our attention. Before us loomed another sleepless night.

So I may have sounded slightly abrupt when I answered the phone. I thought it might be someone trying to sell me a home improvement scam or a carpet-cleaning service. This was the time they usually called. Instead, I heard a hazily familiar voice.

'Phil? How you doing, man? This is Sam. Remember me?'

It took me a moment to work it out.

'Oh, hi,' I replied flatly. 'How are you?'

'Good! Vince wrote me with your number. So what are you doing?'

'I'm a teacher.'

Sam's laugh made him real for me again. How often I had heard it ring out as we cracked up helplessly over some nonsense which tickled our drug-fused synapses!

'No, man! Like what are you doing *now*? Tonight?'

'Tonight?'

I frowned.

'Where are you calling from, Sam?'

'I'm right here in town.'

'In St Paul?'

'Other side of the river. Where are you at? Vince gave me the street address. Maplewood, right? Can I get a cab out there?'

There was no way I wanted Sam to come to our modest tract-

54

house, identical to all the others in our neat, convenient suburb. The distance between my present lifestyle and the one I had shared with Sam and the others could not be measured in years. I had become the kind of person we all despised then, myself included. I was faithful to my wife, my strongest drug was whisky, and although some of my rock albums were still lined up beneath the stereo, I never played them any more. But part of my new persona was a concern for the feelings of others, and although I had no desire to see Sam again, neither did I want to seem rude. So after conferring with Rachael, I eventually agreed to meet him for a drink.

My choice of venue was Shaunessey's, a self-styled 'Irish pub' located in a new shopping precinct in downtown Minneapolis. It was snowing lightly, and I drove with care. The Mississippi was frozen over, as bleak and bare as the concrete freeway. I left our sensible Chevy Nova in a multi-level parking garage and walked the three blocks to the bar, trying to figure out how to fill a decent amount of time with someone I would never have chosen to see again. Still, it was no big deal. A couple of hours, a couple of drinks, and Sam would be history.

The first thing that struck me was how relaxed he seemed, how serene. Unlike Vince, or for that matter me, he didn't seem to have changed one iota from the person I remembered. He had aged, of course, but his lean, bony frame and ferrety features had taken it well, merely tautening up a little, shrinking to a sinewy, leathery essence. His straight mousy hair was as long as ever, tied back in a pony-tail, and his clothes – jeans, denim jacket, check shirt and boots – epitomized the no-bullshit, low-maintenance look we all used to strive for. By comparison, I felt staid and conventional in my V-neck sweater, tweed slacks and moccasin-style loafers bought at sale prices from a department store in our local mall.

Sam didn't seem to notice, though, or maybe didn't care. In fact he showed almost no interest in me at all. He didn't ask any questions about my life, and when I mentioned a few details he didn't bother to conceal his indifference. References to my work, my marriage and my child elicited only a nod, a grunt and a slightly contemptuous smile. It was as if all that was irrelevant, and he was faintly amused that I hadn't realized this.

Nor was he any more forthcoming about his own life. He didn't volunteer any information, and when I asked what he'd been doing the smug smile stayed right in place.

'I've been through a lot of changes, man.'

There was no hint of irony in his voice. I nodded warily.

'We all have.'

Sam's smile grew broader than ever.

'Some more than others.'

I was beginning to get annoyed. This kind of supercilious, cooler-than-thou posturing had been standard operating procedure in our former life, but it had not worn well.

'So where are you living?' I asked shortly.

He hesitated before answering, as though this was a difficult question. At the time I dismissed this as just another mannerism, an attempt to make himself look deep and mysterious.

'Out on the coast,' he said eventually.

'Any particular coast?'

I was no longer bothering to hide my irritation. But he wouldn't be drawn.

'There's a bunch of us,' he said. 'We've got a place out there.'

He looked me in the eye suddenly.

'Why don't you come out and visit us some time, Phil? See for yourself.'

For the first time, it sounded like what he was saying mattered to him. This made his complete lack of interest in my actual circumstances all the more maddening.

'I've got a job, Sam. I've got a wife and child. We go to see my parents once in a while and go camping in the summer. Vacationwise, that's about it.'

He didn't seem to hear.

'Do you remember that night we went down to the Commercial Hotel and Larry and I got into that argument about God?'

He was speaking in a quiet, intense tone, leaning across the table as though he didn't want to be overheard. I was afraid he was going to lay the whole story on me with some pseudo-philosophical spin about Fate and Chance.

'Sure I do,' I replied. 'It happened right here.'

Sam looked around at the Guinness posters, the Irish flags, the leprechaun figurines and all the other laboriously inauthentic décor, contrasting with the bustling team of attractive young waitpersons and the well-heeled, well-groomed clientele.

'Here?' he echoed.

I had the advantage for the first time, thanks to local knowledge, and I seized it.

'The Commercial's long gone, of course, but this is what they put up on the same spot. That's why I suggested we meet here.'

Sam nodded intently, as though I'd said something profound.

'That's good, Phil. I'm real glad. Because this is where it all started.'

'Where what started?'

He looked down at his beer, which he'd hardly touched, and then back at me.

'You remember we scored all that shit, and then the cops stopped us on the way home and I ate the whole stash?'

'How could I ever forget?'

'Something happened to me that night. Something I've never told anyone.'

I groaned inwardly. Surely to God he wasn't about to lay some wacko acid insight on me after all these years? Sam was still staring at me unblinkingly.

'You're someone I could tell.'

Not if I can help it, I thought. Some hint of my feelings must have showed in my expression, because he suddenly backed off, drank some beer and went on in a normal tone of voice.

'I always really respected you, Phil. You were different than the others. You'd been in Europe and all. Plus there was that class we took together. That makes a big difference, the fact that you've read Blake.'

'What's Blake got to do with it?'

It occurred to me for the first time that Sam might be slightly crazy. Maybe that year in Vietnam had taken its toll after all.

His next words seemed to confirm my suspicions.

'Blake is very important,' he whispered, as though confiding a great truth.

I shrugged.

'Try telling that to my students. Most of them don't read anything except the funnies.'

Sam nodded.

'Do you ever get the feeling that some of them aren't exactly real?'

I frowned. Once again he'd thrown me for a loop.

'What?'

'Don't you ever feel that there are some of them who just don't get it? Who never will get it? I'm sure you're a great teacher, Phil. An inspirational teacher. But I'll bet that when you look around the class, you see maybe five or ten people out there who just aren't picking up the signals you're sending. You know? They don't get it, because they don't *have* it.'

'Don't have what?'

Sam gave me his meaningful look again.

'Soul,' he said.

It was the first time for years I had heard the word except in a religious context. 'Soul' was one of those loose, capacious words we used so much, into which we could pour our feelings without having to analyse them at all. If you liked something, it had soul. If you didn't, it hadn't. A neat way of not thinking, but one which had also worn badly with the passing years. I felt slightly sickened by Sam's hippie one-upmanship, with its unearned suggestions of superior insight and more radical consciousness.

'Some of my students are more gifted than others, of course,' I replied stiffly. 'Some are going to get the credits they need to get into a four-year college, others will wind up delivering mail or driving a bus. My job is to educate them up to the level of their abilities, not pick out the brightest and best and stroke their egos.'

Sam smiled and shook his head.

'That's not what I meant.'

'Then what did you mean?' I shot back.

He tossed his head slightly. The smile disappeared.

'It's not something you can discuss over a beer. Words are such little things, Phil. You should know that.'

'Words happen to be my business,' I replied huffily.

Again he didn't seem to hear me.

'All those nights we sat up tripping together,' he said, gazing dreamily at the table-top. 'What happened then was real, wasn't it? Realler than anything you'd ever felt before. But you could never talk about it after, never describe what you'd seen and heard. You had to have been there. You had to have lived through it.'

I eyed him coldly.

'I don't do drugs any more, Sam.'

'Neither do I,' he said. 'I haven't touched them since that night we were just talking about.'

Given what I'd heard about the dope intake of our boys in Vietnam, I found this hard to believe. But it was none of my business.

'OK,' I said, 'so what was it that happened that night? You didn't make a big deal of it at the time. In fact you hardly said anything about it.'

Sam smiled and nodded.

'Sure, I know. It took me months to come to terms with it at all. I couldn't believe it, couldn't accept it. It was all too new, too overwhelming. It wasn't till I got back from the war that I really mastered it.'

Our eyes met.

'Is that why you volunteered to become a rifleman?' I asked.

Sam grinned delightedly.

'That's right, man! You understand!'

He spoke with such feeling that I was almost reluctant to disappoint him.

'I just figured that since you'd done two oddball things, they might be linked.'

He nodded, still grinning.

'I had to put it to the test.'

I stared at him.

'By risking your life?'

He nodded.

'If what I learned that night was true, you see, then I possessed a secret which would give me the power of life and death over every single person on the planet.'

So he was crazy after all. I felt slightly disappointed, but also relieved.

'That's why it was important to make sure,' he went on in the same conversational tone, 'and the only way to do that was to lay my own life on the line. If I survived, against all the odds, that would prove I was right.'

My only wish was to get the hell out of there, but I controlled myself. If I walked out now, leaving him with a sense of unfinished business, I might never hear the end of this. Better to let him get it off his chest now.

'So what's this all about, Sam?'

He didn't reply for a moment.

'Remember that argument I had with Larry?' he murmured. 'I said that God either wasn't omnipotent or He wasn't loving, but you couldn't have it both ways? Well, I was wrong. You can have it both ways. And that night I was shown how.'

'Uh huh,' I murmured.

He sat looking at me.

'Well, are you going to tell me?' I asked.

He laughed.

'It's not something that can be *told*, man.'

'But you said I was someone you could tell,' I retorted, childishly pleased to have caught him out.

Sam turned over the bar tab and wrote a phone number on the back. He pushed it across the table towards me.

'Come out and see us some time,' he said. 'It's very quiet, very peaceful. A good place to kick back and get your head together.'

I tried to keep a straight face.

'So what's the deal on this place? Is it some kind of commune?'

'Kind of. We've got some land, all the basic stuff you need for survival. There's about twenty of us hanging out there. They're nice folks. You'd like them. Some great-looking chicks, too.'

I imagined a ragtaggle group of ageing hippies camping out in some clearing in the woods, their hand-knit clothes reeking of woodsmoke, a pack of grimy children crawling around their feet while they strummed out-of-tune guitars and cultivated a cosy sense of moral superiority.

'I'd really like for you to join us, Phil,' Sam continued seriously. 'That would complete the circle. And for you it would mean a whole new life, something you can't even begin to imagine now. But first you have to change. That's the key to the whole thing. The old must pass away before the new can be born. First you change, then you are changed.'

I had had enough.

'I *have* changed,' I replied calmly. 'I've changed a lot. Not in the twinkling of an eye, after ODing on acid, but day in, day out. That's the kind of change I believe in, the kind that lasts.'

'My kind of change outlasts everything,' Sam said softly. 'Even death.'

This was intended as a challenge, but I wasn't going to rise to the bait. I had made my point. Now it was time to throw in the sweetener and get this guy out of my life for ever.

'I really admire you, Sam,' I said. 'I like it that you're still tackling the big questions, the big issues. We were all like that once, but most of us have lost it somewhere along the way. I think it's great that you're still out there on the edge, but personally I can't live like that. It turns out I work best with my feet on the ground. I'm neither proud nor ashamed of that. Maybe you're more flexible. All I know is the kind of change you're talking about would break me.'

Sam looked at me solemnly a long moment. Then he smiled, as if dismissing the whole matter.

'Well, it's been good to talk to you, Phil.'

'Sure has,' I agreed heartily. 'If you're ever in town again, give me a call.'

The idea was to reduce everything that had been said to the level of a banal social encounter. I knew he wasn't likely to pass through the Twin Cities again.

Sam shook his head decisively.

'Next time, you'll call me.'

I edged out of the booth, gathering my things around me, asserting my separate existence.

'What are you doing here anyway?' I asked.

'I came to see you, Phil.'

This time I couldn't ignore him.

'You came all this way just to have a beer with me in a bar?'

He said nothing. Never underestimate the power of silence. It made me lose it completely.

'You should have told me you were coming! We could have had dinner, gone out somewhere … You should have let me know.'

His supercilious smile reappeared.

'That's not the way I operate.'

And with that he walked away, across the bar, out the door. I left some money on the table and went after him, feeling resentful that he had somehow managed to gain the upper hand, despite all my efforts. But when I got outside, the street was empty. Downtown Minneapolis had changed since the old days. The street life which had flourished then had been exterminated, but nothing had replaced it. Consumers drove in from the suburbs, like me, had their fun and went home. The sidewalks were empty, the concrete slabs decorated with a faint flurry of snow.

I got my car from the parking lot, jammed a tape of the Brandenburg Concertos in the stereo and drove home, seething internally. I felt intolerably nauseous, as though I might throw up not just the beer I had drunk and the pretzels I had nibbled but my very brains and being. The whole weight of my hippie youth rose in my throat like a greasy, undigested feast. The evening had been a disaster from start to finish, a farcical misalignment of intentions and personalities. It was futile to try to revive old friendships.

I had tried to be polite and positive to Sam, praising his refusal to compromise and apologizing for having settled for less. This was hypocrisy, a strategy for sending him away happy, for getting him off my back. The fact was that I had come to

62

terms with life. I had accepted its conditions, signed the contract and was now enjoying the modest but solid rewards. Nothing else was real, and anyone who went on trying to pretend that it was would end up like Sam, marginalized and crazy, someone people shied away from in bars.

The whole episode seemed an irrelevance, a freak occurrence of no relevance to my present circumstances. If it hadn't been for that chance meeting with Vince, it would never have happened. As I drove up to our modest tract-house, identical to all the others in our neat, convenient suburb, I made a vow never to let chance interfere in my arrangements again.

Five

Bonnie Kowalski drew up by the kerb and yawned loudly. It was OK, she was on time, in spite of the traffic. The guy would most likely be late, anyway. He'd phoned in the day before to check the time of their appointment, even though she'd sent him a confirmation in writing. Your typical academic ditz, thought Bonnie. She'd had lots of dealings with them, the campus being so close, and she'd yet to meet one who didn't seem to be a few dishes short of a combination platter.

She pried the plastic lid off a mug of coffee which read 'The beverage you're about to enjoy is extremely hot'. Bonnie remembered reading something where some woman had scalded herself and sued the company for half a million bucks. She sipped the coffee cautiously and stared out through the windshield at the big trees in the parking strip, gaunt and bare in the morning sunlight.

When she'd started up the car that morning, to take Nathan to the orthodontist and then on to school, the windshield wipers had started too. Their painful scraping across the dry glass had brought it all back to her: the evening which had started so promisingly and ended so brutally, the suddenness with which everything had gone wrong, their inability to turn it around again, Ed's cold words and unyielding silences, the fit of anger and despair which had forced her out into the rain-sluiced streets, the fact that he hadn't come after her. The fact that he hadn't come after her.

And she hadn't even gotten laid. That's what it had all been about originally, and even now, after all these months, Ed had only to give her a certain look, and put one hand on her breast and another on her leg, and everything else fell away. That's what had always held them together. She'd never known a lover so masterful, so greedy, so sure of what he wanted and how to get it. His occasional moods and sulks had seemed a small price to pay for such ecstasy, plus he'd always been at his best in that way after being at his worst in others.

If anyone had told her, six months before, that she'd fall for a man like that, Bonnie would have dismissed the idea with contempt. She'd always thought she liked being in charge in bed, setting the agenda, controlling the pace and the progress. Now she wondered what had made her waste so much time dating men who bought into that kind of micro-management. With Ed she'd known from the get-go that she was in safe hands. Sex with him wasn't a matter of consultation and compromise. He took what he wanted, turning her body this way and that, having his way with her. And she *loved* it. For a couple of days she'd worried about betraying her principles, then she thought, fuck it. No one need ever know, anyway.

She glanced at her watch. Still five minutes to the appointment. She'd give him fifteen after that, just to be safe, then head back to the office. A wave of depression hit her like a blow, forcing a sigh from her. She suddenly felt that men were standing her up, ignoring her feelings and needs. Even Jerry had been cool and distant when she got back the night before. Maybe he'd guessed. Maybe her pain had showed in her face. It was easier to conceal a happy affair than an unhappy one.

As usual, her alibi had been that she'd had to show a home. Her work was useful that way. Many people could only view a property at night. Bonnie had gone into great detail about the listing, a young contemporary colonial on Indian Ridge, five beds, four-and-half baths, boasting a gourmet kitchen, a butler's pantry and a cathedral ceiling. She'd even described the clients, a gay couple from out of state. Maybe she'd said too much. She wouldn't have bothered if the story had been true, or even if things had gone better with Ed. She would have felt confident and relaxed, and Jerry would never have suspected a thing. He never had before, she was sure of that.

She took a gulp of the coffee, which had cooled considerably by now. Sherman *was* late, God damn him. She'd tried to get him to meet at the office, but he'd claimed his time was too valuable. The same apparently didn't apply to hers. At the office she could have buried herself in her work and joked around with the others instead of sitting moping all alone in her car. Plus, although she tried not to think about this too much, it was safer. There'd been a couple of horror stories involving female realtors recently, rapes, even a murder. But that was some place else. There were neighbourhoods where she wouldn't have shown up alone, but Evanston wasn't one. Anyway, it was broad daylight, and the guy was a professor. He'd probably be so scared of ending up in a harassment case he wouldn't make eye-contact with her without a witness.

A couple of joggers passing by glanced at the house with its immaculately tended lawn. A metal sign embedded in the turf displayed the logo of the firm along with Bonnie's name and the Hot Line number in red. This one was hot, all right. $600,000 was the asking price, although Bonnie was pretty sure they'd go down to the low fives for a quick sale. The seller had been transferred back east and needed cash fast. As for Samuel Baines Sherman, recently appointed MacSomebody Distinguished Professor of Something at Northwestern, he'd already sold.

The joggers passed by again. Bonnie looked them over as they padded along the sidewalk. In their twenties, one a little taller than the other, clean-cut student types. That's the kind of place Evanston was – college kids, professors, yuppies and rich businessmen, espressos and French bakeries and fresh pasta. Far enough from the city to be safe, near enough to be convenient.

Then there were the properties themselves. This one was a classy Victorian, maybe a little rambling – or 'spacious', as the ads said – but definitely toney. Ten rooms in all, five bedrooms, two fireplaces, hardwood floors, leaded glass, you name it, this baby was loaded. It didn't have a lake view, but Maple was a very nice street tucked in between Ridge Boulevard and the CTA tracks, quiet and leafy but still only half an hour from the Loop and a five-minute commute to the Northwestern campus. Sherman could bike it, even walk there, or run if he was the type. It was a perfect home for him. Everything looked good, and Bonnie stood to clean up on the deal. These North Shore places sold themselves. It had been dumb to let herself get thrown by what had happened. It was only a lover's tiff, every couple had them. As soon as she got back to the office she'd give Ed a call and fix up a time to see him again. Then they would talk everything over, get it all worked out.

A car came up the wide, tree-lined street and pulled in right in front of Bonnie. It was a bright red Impala, but the man who got out of it didn't look like the Impala type. He was of average height and build, but gave the impression of occupying more space than he actually did, and being entitled to it. His hair was dark and curly, his beard grizzly grey and neatly trimmed. He wore a double-breasted astrakhan coat over what looked like a tweed suit, with well-polished oxfords and those Italian-framed glasses that don't make you look like a nerd. The Impala had to be a rental. The family Volvo or Audi, or whatever distinguished import the Distinguished Professor drove, would be in storage with the rest of his stuff back in New Hampshire. Lifting her purse from the passenger seat, Bonnie Kowalski switched on a smile and got out to greet him.

Ten minutes later, she knew that it had all been a waste of time. Less than ten, in fact, but she'd tried to kid herself for a while there. However the sale went, Bonnie normally got along really well with her clients. That was one reason why she was such a successful realtor. Maybe that was also one reason why Jerry didn't ask too many questions about her being out so much in the evening, seeing as she had been paying the bills ever since his job with a marine brokerage turned out not be recession-proof. Real estate is a people business, and Bonnie liked to think of herself as a people person. Plus there was always a little buzz in the air when the client was a man. Men had always gravitated towards her, drawn by her looks and a sense that they could relax around her. She enjoyed this for its own sake, and knew how to turn it to her practical advantage. And if the guy happened to be gay, she could work that room too, with her sassy sister act.

So it kind of shocked her to discover there was no way she could relate to Professor Samuel Baines Sherman. Not only did Bonnie's social firepower fail to make the slightest impression on the Sherman Tank, as she privately dubbed him, but it turned out that he had no intention whatever of buying. For a while she thought he might be trying to work some leverage on the price, but when she hinted that there could well be some flexibility in that area, he just carried right on enumerating all the defects of the property. After a while she gave up. It was like the guy was giving a lecture on whatever the heck he was Distinguished for. There was no way to stop him short of walking out, and she couldn't afford to do that. Losing the sale was bad enough, but if the client complained to Jack Capoccioni she could be in deep shit. Marine brokerage wasn't the only job description where there were more applicants than positions these days.

Sherman's basic bitch was that the property had been wilfully misrepresented in the description he had been sent, describing it as a 'gracious and immaculate rehab in move-in condition combining sophisticated family living and oodles of charm'. OK, so it was a bunch of bull, but Bonnie didn't write the copy. Plus everyone knew that was just a come-on, feel-good stuff. All that really counted was the location and the price. After that you had to go look. But Professor Sherman evidently felt he'd been deliberately conned out of an hour of his valuable time, and wasn't going to leave until he'd made damn sure that Bonnie never tried to pull a fast one on him again. As a result he led her through every room in the goddamn house, pointing out at great length why it was totally and utterly inappropriate for a man of his status.

'These rooms have been insensitively remodelled at some stage, probably the late forties or early fifties to judge from the mouldings. The whole rationale of the original groundplan has been destroyed thereby, creating an architecturally psychotic ambience. Just look at the shape and dimensions relative to the height of the ceilings! It's like a rat maze designed by Piranesi. No claptrap about graciousness and sophistication can change that.'

They had reached the bedrooms by now. Bonnie Kowalski figured she had to eat shit for about another ten minutes, then he'd be through. Give him satisfaction, she told herself. Keep him sweet for the future. Nevertheless, she felt a huge surge of relief when she heard footsteps on the stairs. Jack Capoccioni had told her he would drop by if he got through with the Schlumberger deal in time, see how she was doing, maybe work a squeeze play if the client was hard to close. This way he'd get to see for himself what an asshole the guy was, and she'd be off the hook.

'I must confess myself stupefied by your inability to grasp the nature of my requirements, Ms Kowalski,' Sherman was saying. 'I think it would be fair to say that I boast a certain renown as an effective communicator in academic, civic and political circles throughout the country. I am therefore mortified and dismayed to discover that in this instance I have evidently been unsuccessful in enabling you to grasp something as straightforward as the type of house I am looking for. Whether the responsibility for this failure is mine or yours is unclear, but at all events it is something we must rectify momentarily if we are to continue to do business.'

Behind them, the door creaked on its hinges.

'Hi, Jack!' said Bonnie, turning.

But the man who stood there wasn't Jack. He was younger and fitter, wearing some kind of sports outfit and holding something in one hand, a personal stereo maybe. There was another guy behind him, standing in the shadows. Then they came into the room, and she recognized the two joggers who'd passed by while she was sitting outside waiting for Sherman.

'Don't do anything stupid, you won't get hurt,' the first man said.

It was an uneducated voice, sullen and constrained. He was about twenty, twenty-five, with a face that tapered to a protuberant jaw. He had meaty lips, slightly buck teeth and evasive, widely spaced blue eyes. He raised his hand, and Bonnie realized that the thing he was holding wasn't a Walkman.

'Yeah,' said the other man, moving forward into the room. 'That's right.'

This was the shorter one. He had bleached blond hair and a little slit of a mouth, and he was also carrying a pistol. He reminded Bonnie of one of the other realtors called Randy who'd been pink-slipped a couple of months back, and for a moment she thought of those news stories you see where some guy who's been fired comes back to work and starts shooting at random. But she knew it wasn't Randy.

'Kneel down on the floor,' the tall one said.

Both men were wearing transparent plastic gloves, Bonnie noticed, the kind her gynaecologist used for pelvics.

'I've got two hundred dollars in my wallet, and a gold Rolex,' Samuel Baines Sherman announced calmly. 'You're welcome to both.'

'Kneel the fuck down!' the squat guy shouted tensely.

Sherman gave out a long sigh, as though this were just one more of the tedious and unnecessary inconveniences he had to face every day of his life, due to the incompetence of others.

'Kneel?' he repeated with a peeved frown. 'What on earth for?'

'Do what they say!' Bonnie Kowalski told him, all the fury and frustration she'd suppressed now gushing out. 'I don't want to get shot just because you're an asshole!'

Sherman looked more shocked by this than by the gunmen's appearance. Well, screw him. She didn't care about losing the sale any more. She didn't even care about Jack Capoccioni getting mad. Setting her purse down carefully, she knelt beside it, facing the two gunmen. After a moment's hesitation, Sherman gave a little weary shrug and got to his knees. The tall guy unzipped the pocket of his backpack, watching them all the while.

'Hands behind your back,' he said.

'It's not even our house,' Bonnie replied. 'The owners have moved out. There's nothing here to steal.'

'Shut up! Shut up!' screamed the squat one agitatedly.

'Hey, lighten up,' his partner murmured.

He crouched down behind Sherman. There was a sharp click. Sherman gave a grunt of surprise, or pain. The man straightened up and moved in front of Sherman, blocking Bonnie's view.

'This is completely un … ' Sherman began.

The gunman bent down, and Sherman's voice ceased abruptly. The shorter man gave a jagged laugh which broke off as his partner swung around to face him.

'Well, don't just stand there!' he snapped.

The other gunman started rooting around in the backpack. All his movements were jerky and urgent. He ran around behind Bonnie, who flinched.

'Please!' she pleaded. 'I have a family!'

She could feel his breath on her hair and at the nape of her neck. Something hard and sharp gripped her left wrist, then the right, locking them together. The man seized her jaw from behind and pressed something over her mouth in a sticky kiss. Smelling the heady reek of raw plastic, she realized it was a patch of adhesive tape. There was one on Sherman's mouth too.

The taller man surveyed the scene for a moment.

'OK,' he said.

His companion looked at Bonnie, then at Sherman. His expression was one of panic. The other man had set down his pistol and was taking something else out of the backpack. Bonnie noted dully that it was a video camera, a Sony, the new lightweight model she had been meaning to get Jerry for Christmas, but the store had had a JVC on sale for a hundred bucks less so she'd gone for that instead. The salesman had assured her it was just as good, maybe a tad heavier was all.

The squat man stood looking at the two trussed and gagged figures kneeling on the floor. He took a step towards Bonnie, then paused and stepped quickly over to stand behind Sherman. The other man raised the viewfinder of the video camera to his face, targeting his partner, whose pistol was pointing at the back of Sherman's neck. Bonnie fought to control her bladder. If she peed now it would form a puddle on the floor, everyone would see. She would just die of shame.

'I can't!' the short man said in a tone of desperation.

'C'mon, Dale!' said the tall man, switching on the camera. 'Hit the mitt! Straight down the pipe, baby! You can do it.'

The gunman took an audible intake of breath and pressed the muzzle of his revolver to Sherman's neck. At the contact Sherman's head jerked back instinctively, knocking the barrel aside. There was a dull crack and the gunman jumped back with a horrified expression.

'Christ!' he gasped.

Sherman was thrashing around on the floor. His muffled roars reverberated in the empty room.

'Jesus Christ!' the gunman cried in obvious distress. 'Jesus Christ!'

The victim's overcoat had ridden up, revealing a patch of dense red blood spreading across the seat of his tweed pants.

'Fire it in there!' the tall man shouted.

'I can't! I can't do it!'

'Hustle up, Dale! Finish the job!'

Bonnie could feel the waffle and bacon she'd eaten for breakfast rising in her throat, and the thought of choking on the vomit, unable to get rid of it because of the gag, made her panic.

The gunman bent over Sherman, who was twisting around and around on the bare floorboards, his feet kicking convulsively. There was another shot. Splinters of the oak planking went flying. Then a sudden spasm of Sherman's leg knocked the gunman off balance. The revolver went off again as he fell heavily on his side. The window broke, and for a moment Bonnie thought that someone outside had thrown a rock or a ball at the glass, like the time Nathan was pitching to a friend in the back yard and a fly-ball went through the kitchen window.

'Fuck! Fuck! Fuck! Fuck!' the gunman howled desperately.

He had scrambled to his knees, his clothes and hands streaked with blood.

'Help me, Andy! I can't handle it! You've got to help me!'

A series of warbling sounds filled the room. Bonnie glanced down at the purse where she kept her cellular phone. It must be Jack, calling her to see how it was going. The phone rang eight times, breaking off with a truncated beep.

The gunman called Andy switched off the video camera and

set it down on the floor. He looked at Sherman, then at the kneeling gunman.

'Lemme have it,' he said.

The other guy didn't react until the command was repeated. Then he raised the plastic-sheathed hand which held the pistol. Andy took the weapon by the barrel, turned it around and shot his partner between the eyes. The man's mouth popped open as though in amazement. He toppled forward slowly, crashing to the floor without uttering a sound.

Sherman was moving more slowly now, feebly pedalling his legs and jerking his spine. Carefully avoiding the patch of blood-stained flooring, the gunman crouched down and aimed his pistol at the side of the wounded man's head, just above the ear. He fired once. Sherman stiffened, then relaxed and was still.

The killer observed him for a moment. Then he straightened up and turned towards Bonnie Kowalski.

*

Coverage was big in Metropolitan Chicago, fair in Illinois and surrounding states, patchy to non-existent elsewhere. NU PROF, REALTOR SLAIN IN SHOWHOME SHOOTING was the *Chicago Sun-Times* headline. The article began:

Urban-style random violence struck at the quiet, leafy college town of Evanston Thursday when three bodies were found in a house in the exclusive Grey Park area of the Lakeside suburb. Two of the victims were named as Samuel Baines Sherman, fifty-one, and Bonnie Kowalski, thirty-seven. The other, a man who police suspect may have been the killer, has not yet been identified.

The crime was discovered by John Capoccioni, president of the Evanston real estate agency where Mrs Kowalski worked. He had grown concerned when she failed to return to the office or to answer her cellular phone, and drove to the property on Maple Street. He found Kowalski's car parked outside, and on searching the Victorian mansion discovered the bodies in one of the upstairs bedrooms.

Samuel Sherman had recently been appointed as MacDowell Distinguished Professor of Corporate Law at Northwestern University. He had made an appointment to view the Maple Street house with Mrs Kowalski at 9.30 that morning.

According to Detective Eileen McCann of Evanston City Police, all three victims were shot at close range with a .22 calibre Smith & Wesson Model 34 revolver which was recovered at the scene. Marks on the bodies suggest that Sherman and Kowalski were bound and gagged before being shot. Police are working on the theory that the gunman then turned the weapon on himself.

The motive for the crimes remains a mystery. Neither of the victims had been robbed, and there is no evidence that either was known to the presumed killer. The property itself, which had been on the market for several weeks, contained nothing of value. A sexual attack has also been ruled out.

The article continued with an appeal by Evanston Police to any members of the public with information about the shootings. They were particularly concerned to identify the gunman, who was described as a white juvenile aged twenty to twenty-five, of medium height, heavy build, with light brown hair and brown eyes. Efforts were also being made to trace the murder weapon. Home security specialists, hardware stores and gun shops in the Evanston area were reported to be doing record business.

It was a slow news day in the Northwest, and the early edition of the *Seattle Times* featured a heavily condensed version of the story in its 'Across the Nation' column, squeezed up against an advertisement for a shoe sale at Nordstrom's department store. In the night final which Kristine Kjarstad read that evening at home, this had been dropped in favour of a piece about the drugs charge which had been brought against one of the pitchers for a leading American League team. Kjarstad skimmed the column briefly before turning to the Arts section to read about a movie she was thinking of seeing.

Almost two months had gone by since the shootings at Renfrew Avenue. The news that Wayne Sullivan had confessed had created a sense of euphoria and relief that was as intense as it was short-lived. Seattlites liked to think of their city as a civilized haven, as temperate as its mild, cloudy climate, immune by its very nature to the epidemic of crime which had turned so many other urban centres into virtual war zones. At the same time, everyone knew that out-of-staters were moving there, partly because of the area's reputation as peaceful and liveable, and there was growing concern that they would bring their problems with them.

So when something like the Renton killing occurred, a houseful of people shot dead in broad daylight without any evident motive, everyone's worst fears appeared to have been realized. *Any* outcome would have been a relief from the swirling, formless terrors of the community's collective imagination, but Wayne Sullivan's confession was the very best news anyone could have hoped for. People might be shocked by what Sullivan had done, but at least they could understand it. Hell, we've all been there at some moment or other, if we're honest.

Above all, they were relieved to find that it posed no threat to them. Far from being the random slaughter it had at first appeared, this was a situation-specific killing. What had taken place was a private affair between Wayne Sullivan and his family. As for that poor Chinese kid, he'd just been in the wrong place at the wrong time. Could've happened to anyone.

There was thus intense pressure on the police in general, and on Kristine Kjarstad in particular, to come up with evidence to corroborate Sullivan's statement so that charges could be brought. This they had failed to do.

Kristine had known the attempt was doomed from the moment she and Steve Warren had interviewed Sullivan at the courthouse following his unexpected admission of guilt. Things had begun promisingly enough, with Wayne giving vent to obviously genuine feelings of hostility regarding his ex-wife.

'She tried to take the little ones away from me,' he explained in a voice filled with hurt. 'She shouldn't ought to've done that. I don't care about her, but those were my children, the only thing I have in this world. She tried to take them away and form them in her image. No one has the right to do that. I told her. "My boys'd be better off dead than brung up by a slut like you," I said.'

Kristine waited for him to go on, but he seemed to have lost the thread.

'What happened then?' she prompted.

Sullivan's eyes darted around the room, as if searching for inspiration.

'She started in at me, calling me a no-good, worthless loser who wasn't fit to father a dog. I just lost it. I took out this pistol I'd brought with me and I blew her away. Then I got to thinking 'bout the kids, all alone in the world with no one to look after them. And them knowing their dad killed their mom and all. So I knew I had to kill them too. It was for the best. I didn't know what else to do.'

Kristine Kjarstad nodded sympathetically. So far, so good, she thought. Everything Sullivan had said rang true. Now they just had to sort out the details and type up a statement for him to sign.

'Where did you get the gun?' she asked.

Wayne Sullivan hesitated.

'Guy in Seattle sold it to me. You can get anything you want there, you got the cash.'

'And where did you get the cash?'

Another hesitation.

'I'd saved it up. I was going to take the kids to Disneyworld, but she wouldn't let them go, the bitch. Said I was a bad influence.'

Kristine frowned slightly. She had the feeling she was listening to something which *almost* made sense, but didn't quite. It was easy to imagine Wayne making extravagant promises to his children, particularly after a few drinks, and equally easy to imagine Dawn putting him down contemptuously. What wasn't

76

so easy to believe was the idea of him actually getting the money together. She'd seen how Sullivan had been living. He didn't strike her as someone who was into delayed gratification for himself, never mind others.

'What kind of gun was it?' she asked.

Sullivan glanced at the uniformed man who had brought him over from the jail, and who was now chewing his nails at an adjoining desk. He shrugged.

'I don't know. I just know it worked. Guy I bought it from took me down the alley, loosed off a few rounds. I knew it would do the job.'

'But it was an automatic?' Steve Warren put in.

Kristine glanced at her partner in surprise. Luckily Sullivan didn't catch her expression. He nodded.

'Sure.'

'So how come there weren't any ejected cartridges at the scene?' Warren demanded.

Sullivan looked around nervously.

'The, uh ... ? Oh, I guess I picked them up.'

'Why did you do that?'

There was no reply.

'And where is the weapon now?' asked Kristine Kjarstad.

This time, Wayne Sullivan had his answer ready.

'Bottom of Puget Sound. I rode the ferry over to Bremerton, dropped it over the side half-way across.'

'Let's go back to the killing,' said Warren. 'You said your old lady started badmouthing you so you shot her.'

Sullivan nodded.

'So you two were just sitting there ... '

He broke off.

'Sitting? Standing?'

Sullivan shook his head.

'I don't know. Standing, I guess.'

'You were standing there chatting, and she said something you didn't like. It was an impulse thing, right?'

'Right.'

'You didn't tie her up first, anything like that?'

'Why would I do that?' said Sullivan with a puzzled look.

'And the kids?' demanded Kristine, keeping up the pressure. 'How did you kill them?'

Wayne Sullivan flinched visibly. He didn't mind discussing his wife's death, but his children were another matter.

'Same way,' he replied shortly.

'What about the Chinese boy? You said your own children would have had no one to look after them, but Ronnie Ho had a family. Why did he have to die too?'

Sullivan shrugged.

'I guess I kind of got carried away.'

'What time did all this happen?'

'Some time in the afternoon.'

'When we first questioned you, you said you'd been painting an apartment in Bellevue all day.'

'That's right!' Sullivan exclaimed indignantly.

Kristine Kjarstad nodded.

'We checked into that, and we found a witness who saw you at the apartment block shortly after two that afternoon, just after the bodies were discovered. That's a twenty-minute drive from Renton. There's no way you could have got back in time.'

She glanced quickly at Steve Warren, who seemed to be about to protest. Leading questions about the type of gun used were one thing, inventing non-existent witnesses another. She gave her partner a hard look.

'I did it earlier,' Sullivan said at last.

Kristine Kjarstad nodded helpfully.

'How much earlier?'

'On my lunch break. I didn't want the boss coming by and finding I wasn't at work. It's tough to get jobs these days.'

He looked up at Kristine, as though to confirm the clinching effect of this down-to-earth detail.

'So what time would that have been?' she asked.

Sullivan considered.

'Between twelve and one, maybe.'

'And you were back at work by one?'

Sullivan nodded.

'How do you know?'

'I was listening to the radio while I got the paint ready. Thought there might be something about it on the news.'

Kristine Kjarstad was silent.

'What's the deal here, anyway?' Sullivan demanded with a touch of anger. 'I told you I did it! That's all that matters.'

He was clearly aggrieved at the way he was being treated. He had voluntarily confessed to the murders, thereby saving the police a whole lot of trouble, and what happened? They started fussing over details and looking for discrepancies, just as though it was his innocence he was trying to establish, not his guilt! Why didn't they just book him and be done with it?

Kristine Kjarstad would have been only too happy to oblige, if she'd thought she could take the case to the DA's office with the slightest chance of success. Unfortunately that was out of the question. Wayne Sullivan's spirit might be willing, but his story was weak. The chronology he'd come up with to accommodate the imaginary witness who'd seen him at Bellevue shortly after two o'clock was the final blow. Before she was shot, Mrs Sullivan had left a message on her friend Kelly Shelden's voice-mail. Like all such messages, it had been dated and timed, proving beyond doubt that Dawn Sullivan had been alive at seventeen minutes past one that afternoon. If Wayne was at work by one o'clock, there was no way he could have killed her.

Over the next two days, Kjarstad and Warren, working in relays with Harrison and Borg, took Wayne Sullivan's story to pieces like kids disassembling a junked appliance. It was hard work. Sullivan had clearly hated his wife's guts and resented her influence over the children, particularly the two boys. He was also grieving in a mute, inarticulate way for their deaths, and feeling guilty for having left them alone and defenceless. The scenario he had invented satisfied and explained all these emotions, as well as casting him as a star player instead of a weak, ineffectual onlooker in his own tragedy. It took a long time – much longer than it would have done if he *had* been guilty – to break him down and force him to admit that his confession was false.

With Wayne Sullivan's release, the investigation had to start all over again from scratch. But in the absence of any other leads, the case was in practice relegated to inactive status. In most homicides the perpetrator is arrested within hours of the crime, often at the scene. At the very least his identity is established, and it is just a matter of waiting until he is picked up. Intensive, time-consuming investigations of cases where there is no known suspect are simply not cost-effective.

Kristine Kjarstad had gleaned only one additional piece of information since then. A month after the shootings, Jamie Sullivan and his sister Megan moved to Nebraska to live with their maternal aunt. Before they left, Kristine spoke with the boy. By now he had recovered, as much as he ever would, from the shock of what had happened. It had become a story, and Jamie no longer had any problems talking about it. He confirmed to Kristine Kjarstad the account which had been passed on earlier by the social worker, and added one further detail: the man who had come down to the basement of the house that day had been wearing a pair of expensive athletic shoes. He had even been able to identify the model, the Nike Air Jordan.

Six

I made a vow never to let chance interfere in my arrangements again. My presumption was punished, as it seemed, in the most terrible way.

One day in early spring, three or four months after my meeting with Sam, our son David came back from school with an invitation to a birthday party in his lunchbox. A bunch of the kids in his class were going, he told us, displaying the card decorated with red and blue balloons and a clown's exaggerated rictus.

Like many only children, David found socializing problematic, alternating between bouts of bossy domination and moody withdrawal. Rachael and I were the more disturbed by this because we knew that he was not going to have any siblings. Her second pregnancy had been terminated as a result of complications which precluded the possibility of her having any more children. Birthday parties, with their structured activities and reassuring rituals, were one of the few occasions for peer interaction which David didn't have to be talked into. Neither of us knew the child whose party it was, a girl who had only just moved to the school, so we called another couple whose son was the nearest thing David had to a friend. They said that he was going too, and offered to collect both boys from school and drop them off at the party. I would then pick up David on my way back from work.

The afternoon the party was held was not an easy one for me. A group of students had lodged a formal complaint against the low grades I had given them, on the grounds that they were the result of 'white male Eurocentrist bias'. My initial reaction was to laugh this off, but in the course of an hour-long meeting with the Associate Dean I quickly learned that it was no laughing matter. I had told one of my better classes a few anecdotes about my experiences at schools in Europe, naïvely thinking that this would help overcome the teacher-student barrier and foster a sense of shared purpose. This story had apparently gone the rounds of the college, and when I penalized a different group of students who had persistently under-performed, it was raised as a way of bringing my judgement into disrepute. I had expected the Associate Dean to back me up, but by the end of the interview I had been made to feel that it was I who had flunked some basic test, not the students.

Having ditched out of the Dean's office at the earliest possible opportunity, I was the first parent to arrive at the house. I parked at the kerb and walked up the path to the front door. Inside I could hear kids screaming and shouting. It sounded a little out of control, but we'd given similar parties ourselves and I knew that they always tended to come apart towards the end.

I rang the doorbell. There was no response. Close up, it was apparent that not all the screams inside were of excitement or overtiredness. Some of the children sounded seriously panicked. I rapped on the door. I was expecting a rapid response, an adult face corroded with stress, relief and a sense of failure. 'Hi, I'm David's father,' I'd say with a big smile. 'Looks like you've got your hands full here. Just remember, next time *you* get to go shopping.'

No one came. I rapped again, then tried the handle. I thought at first the door was locked, but it was just jammed against the frame, and gave when I pushed hard with my shoulder. Something nudged up against me, about the same height as David. Then I saw that it was a balloon, one of those shiny metallic pillow-shaped ones filled with helium. It moved past me on a current of air and drifted away, rising rapidly until it was just a dark shape against the eggshell-blue sky.

There were more balloons inside, taped in bunches to the walls, streamers and paper chains looping down from the ceiling and lengths of crêpe paper winding all over the floor. But despite these festive touches, the scene which met my eyes was the stuff of every parent's nightmare. Some children were fighting, others were crying. One boy was busily smearing chocolate cake on the wall, another was throwing everything he could get his hands on at a sofa where two others lay cowering in terror. In the corner, a girl with glasses and curly blond hair sat with a blank expression, clutching a teddy bear.

Hearing footsteps behind me, I turned. A woman I didn't recognize was coming up the path, looking at me apprehensively. I immediately assumed that this was the party-giver, who had sneaked out to the corner store, leaving the children unsupervised.

'Are you supposed to be in charge here?' I demanded aggressively.

'I'm here to pick up Tara,' the woman said, coming up the steps and looking in. 'Jesus! What the hell's going on?'

With a cry of 'Mommy!', the girl with the teddy bear scrambled to her feet and rushed across the room to embrace her mother.

'I was scared!' she sobbed.

I looked around for David. He didn't seem to be there. I called his name. No one answered.

A door opened off the living room to the left. I opened it and looked inside. It was empty, the walls bare, the air musty. I rushed to the only other door, leading to the back of the house. It was locked.

I ran back to the front door. By now, the other parents had started arriving. I pushed through them and dashed around in back. A flight of steps led to a door lying open. Inside was the kitchen, a bedroom and a staircase down to the basement. I searched them all. There was no one there.

The key to the connecting door was in the lock. I turned it and went through to the living room. David *had* to be there. But he wasn't.

I stood paralysed, hyperventilating, unable to think or act. Eventually one of the mothers asked if I was all right. I told her I couldn't seem to find my son, apologetically, as if it was my fault. It was she who called the police.

The process which followed was as long and thorough as the

one which follows an airplane crash, and as futile. The investigators painstakingly collect all the scattered fragments of the wreckage and patch them together again, they draw detailed maps and plans showing exactly where and when the accident took place, they interview witnesses and analyse every scrap of evidence. It is a retrospective victory of order over disorder, a triumphant demonstration of human ingenuity and control, a reassuring ceremony around the open grave.

Above all, perhaps, it provides a pretext for speech in the face of the unspeakable. There are no words for the experience Rachael and I had to endure, moment by moment, over the following days and weeks. I should say *experiences*. She had hers and I had mine, and they were as impossible to share as two acid trips whose only point in common is that they started from the same external stimulus. I was locked into my grief and she into hers, but they were configured differently. Any attempt to discuss these differences invariably ended in mutual recrimination and pointless self-validating conflicts in which we worked off our urge to give and receive the punishment we both longed for.

For my part, I focused on just one aspect of the situation: David's asthma. I told myself that everything would be bearable if only he had had his medicines with him, his various inhalers and the pink hydrocortisone pills to be used as a last resort. I imagined him coughing endlessly, with that patient, bewildered look he always had at such moments, struggling for breath in the middle of the night. All other possible horrors I excluded by dwelling on that one problem, as though the whole thing was just a question of bad management. *If only he had his medicine. If only he had his medicine.*

Rachael's demons were less tractable. Her work with the Children's Protective Service had exposed her to endless examples of the ways in which careless or ill-intentioned adults can abuse the children in their care, and she now replayed all these scenarios with David as the victim. Unlike me, she had met the woman who had sent the invitation to the party, known to her as Carol. It was a casual meeting, just a few words exchanged after they dropped the children off at school, but now Rachael recalled that she hadn't liked the woman. 'Affectless' was the word she had used to describe her. And so she had to live with the knowledge that she had let our son, her only child, go unescorted to the house of a person she hardly knew and didn't care for. As a professional in the field, part of whose job was to assess the suitability of those responsible for children, this was almost unbearable.

Penned in these separate hells, we were visited from time to time by envoys from the outside world: policemen, psychiatrists, media ghouls. The story of David's disappearance gradually took shape. After interviewing the fourteen children who had attended the party several times, as well as the parents who had delivered them to the house, the police pieced together a picture of what had happened.

The party had apparently begun normally. As the children arrived, they were given paper hats and party favours. There was a table laid with snacks, drinks and a birthday cake. One mother had asked to stay, claiming that her daughter was too timid to enjoy the occasion otherwise, but 'Carol' had refused on the grounds that it would be unfair to the other children. To start with, there was a round of games. They played pin-the-tail-on-the-donkey, musical chairs, statues, and then, as a grand finale before the food, treasure-hunt. This involved each child following a length of crêpe paper which wound all around the house before leading to a present of some kind. Each paper ribbon was a different colour, and the children selected their colour – and hence the present – by dipping their hand into a bag and picking out a short strand of the same paper.

After that it was a free-for-all as the children milled around, falling over each other, getting their paper trails confused, before finally finding and unwrapping the present. When they eventually calmed down, they discovered that the woman in charge was no longer there. But children are used to adults drifting in and out on mysterious errands, and for a while none of them thought much of it. They played with their toys, then, left to their own devices, some of the more aggressive ones started to attack the food. After that the situation gradually deteriorated. No one noticed that the woman's daughter and David were also missing.

All attempts to trace 'Carol' proved fruitless. She had rented the house six weeks earlier, paying the deposit and two months rent in advance with a cheque drawn on a local bank. The account had been opened with a cash deposit of three thousand dollars, the balance of which had been withdrawn the day before the party. The Social Security number and other details the woman had given all proved false, as was her name. She had of course been seen coming and going at the school and at her home, but no one seemed able to give a precise description of her. Even estimates of her height varied wildly.

The teachers at the school told police that her daughter had been withdrawn and uncommunicative, and the same seemed to apply to her mother, if she *was* her mother. The FBI was already working on the possibility that the girl was the victim of an earlier kidnap – there were some similarities with an unsolved case on their files – and that the woman had wanted to add a son to her 'family'. I found this marginally comforting, just as I did the knowledge that the aggressor was a woman. What I most dreaded, of course, the unspoken horror that surfaced at four in the morning, was the idea that David had fallen into the hands of someone for whom evil, the deliberate infliction of pain, was an end in itself.

The police did their best to reassure us, and to make themselves look good, but it was obvious that there was little they could do except hope that the massive searches, roadblocks and appeals to the public produced some result. It didn't seem likely that we would receive a ransom demand. If that had been the object of the kidnapping, there were several children attending the party whose parents were in a much better position to pay than Rachael and I.

Besides, all the evidence suggested that the victim had been chosen at random. Only one of the lengths of crêpe paper led out into the kitchen. The woman had presumably waited until the child following this trail passed through the connecting door, then locked it and decamped. But since the process of selection was done by the children themselves, and done blind, there was no way of determining in advance who that would be. All the woman knew was that *one* of the children would fall into her trap. It just happened to be David.

This sense of arbitrariness was almost the hardest thing for Rachael and me to face. Our son had been taken from us by someone whose identity was unknown and whose motives did not bear thinking about, and all by chance. Our suffering and appalling sense of helplessness, to say nothing of whatever David might be going through, were all mocked by the knowledge that they were the product of nothing more than a mere lottery, a casino sideshow whose odds were precisely calculable: fourteen to one.

It was three weeks to the day after David's abduction that a maintenance worker at Elm Creek Park, a nature preserve northwest of Minneapolis, came upon a pile of bloodsoaked clothing and alerted the police. The description of the clothes David had been wearing when he disappeared had been widely circulated, and the garments were quickly identified as his. They were all there, every last one. I had to go to police headquarters to make the formal identification, and I wept when I saw his tiny shorts and socks. The denim shirt had been slashed in several places, and was heavily stained with blood. There were other stains on the jeans.

About a year earlier, David had exhibited symptoms which led our doctor to believe that he might be suffering from anaemia, and a series of blood tests had been done. The results of these were still on file, and a comparison with the stains on his clothing produced a virtual certainty that the blood was his.

I was the one to tell Rachael. Maybe I did so badly; maybe there is no good way to break such news. I felt absurdly resentful at having been miscast as a character in some trashy made-for-TV weepy. My revenge was to read my lines as flatly as possible. The police had found David's clothing in a state which suggested that he had been the victim of a violent attack. They were now searching the scene for his body, but Elm Creek Park was very large and the remains might not be discovered for some time, if at all.

'That's impossible,' Rachael replied, shaking her head.

I was stunned at her calm, confident tone. For two weeks now, Rachael had been in a state of continuous agitation which even the powerful barbiturates the doctor had prescribed seemed unable to reach. Terrible panic attacks ripped her brutally out of her brief spells of broken sleep, and her mood swung from frantic bursts of pointless activity, in which she would go around the house moving furniture and other objects until each was positioned just so, to periods of almost catatonic inertia when she would not respond to the simplest remark. Yet now she had just heard the worst news of all, and it had seemingly been powerless to touch her. The reason soon became obvious: she *hadn't* heard it.

'I've seen him several times,' she went on casually. 'He's alive.'

I sat staring at her across our walnut-grain coffee table. In one of her manic phases, Rachael had arranged copies of the *New York Review of Books* and *Atlantic Monthly* and other detritus of our former life into neatly aligned quadrilaterals, like the base layers of a pyramid.

'You never told me,' I said weakly.

'You wouldn't have believed me,' she shot back.

Well, that was true enough.

'I saw him just today,' she continued in the same creepily conversational tone, 'on my way back from seeing Mom. He was with that woman. They were driving the other way. I saw him clearly. But there was a central divider, so I couldn't do a U. I turned around the first chance I got, but I never caught up with them. But it was definitely David.'

She went on to describe the other sightings, always brief glimpses in some situation which, conveniently enough, made it impossible for her to make contact. My response to this was no doubt unhelpful. I should have passed the whole thing over to the professionals we were consulting and let them handle it. But I was under considerable strain myself that day, having seen what I'd seen and heard what I'd heard. I needed sympathy and support in facing what had to be faced, not a course of self-serving delusional fantasies.

'Rachael, he's dead. He must be. It's just a matter of time before they find the body. I'm sorry, but there's no point in either of us trying to pretend otherwise. It merely delays the process of healing.'

I suppose I sounded sanctimonious and insincere. She gave me a withering look.

'He's always been dead to you,' she said. 'You never wanted a child in the first place.'

This was true enough, although the moment David was born and I held him in my arms, what I had or had not wanted became irrelevant. But Rachael had never forgiven me for not responding the way she had hoped when she announced that she was pregnant. Now she was taking her revenge.

'It doesn't matter what you or the police think,' she went on with an icy calm. 'I *know* David is alive. That woman is just trying to throw me off the trail. She knows I've seen her, and that sooner or later I'll catch up with her. She's trying to make me despair and give up. Well, it won't work. She may have fooled everyone else, but she can't fool me. I'll never abandon David whatever happens. Never.'

Nor did she. When her fanatical faith finally deserted her, she joined him.

Two days later Rachael went to visit with her mother. When she didn't return, I called and discovered that she had left the house at six. It was now almost nine. When another hour passed with no sign of her, I alerted the police, but there was little they could do at that time of night. Even when a full search began, it was two days before they found her body in the car, parked in a clearing off a back road in a state forest thirty miles out of town.

Maybe it was that final conversation with her mother which finally broke the self-induced spell which had been protecting Rachael. By now the story of David's bloodstained garments had appeared in the papers and on TV, and Rachael's mom – a matter-of-fact Mid-Westerner from a German farming family – must have drawn the same conclusions as everyone else, and would not have hesitated to tell her so. Rachael's comforting illusions could survive my scepticism, but she was defenceless against her own mother. Having postponed the reckoning with the truth for so long, she was swept away when it finally occurred. On the way back from her mother's she stopped at a pharmacy and filled the repeat prescription for sedatives which the doctor had given her a few days earlier. Then she went to a liquor store and bought a bottle of vodka, and drove to the lonely glade in those woods and consumed them both.

I had already been through so much that Rachael's death merely confirmed me in my state of total numbness. I seemed to have been exiled to a zone beyond feeling, and I never expected to return. In the end I did, but gradually, and with frequent relapses. It was two months before I started to feel even fitfully normal, or rather to realize how abnormal I had been feeling for so long. It was another month after that – much of which time I spent with my parents back East – before I could even think about picking up the threads of my life. As soon as I did, I realized that they were like the threads of David's shirt: slashed and drenched in blood.

Take the Chevy Nova, for instance. It was no longer a car but Rachael's death chamber. How could I use it to drive to work or to stock up and save at Safeway? I soon realized that the house would have to go too. Every square inch was mined with memories, any one of which was enough to blow my fragile sanity to shreds. I put it on the market and moved into a rented apartment downtown. The idea was to put what had happened behind me and start again in a new place, with new friends and a new life. The college had given me the rest of the semester off, as much to avoid unwelcome publicity as anything else, I suspected. With the summer vacation coming up, I had several months in which to pull myself together and – the phrase seemed appropriate for some reason – 'get my head together'.

Instead I fell apart more completely than ever before. For days at a time I didn't even get out of bed. I unplugged the phone, which brought a succession of calls from over-solicitous people wanting to know how I was 'getting along'. I didn't open my mail or read the papers. I turned the television to face the wall and left the drapes drawn all day long. Dishes and clothes went unwashed. I hardly ate.

At the time I thought I was just having another relapse into the shock and grief which had overwhelmed me for so long. I realize now that it was more than that. What had happened was hard enough to deal with in itself, but it also called into question everything I had been doing in the years before, and what I was going to do now. Ever since awakening from the acid dream, I had dedicated myself to coming to terms with the realities of life. I had traded in the cheap thrills of my youth for a package which, so I believed, would make up in security and substance for what it might lack in other respects.

Despite the high tone I had taken with Sam, the truth was that this had not always been easy. I had married Rachael because she seemed to epitomize the solidity I was searching for, but there were times when this very fact made her seem an unappealing mate. Our sex life had never been better than perfunctory, and fell apart completely after her abortive second pregnancy, but I had been faithful to her out of principle. My job often seemed little more than an obstacle course designed to test my endurance to the limit, but I'd stuck at that too.

And the result? A woman had staged a fake birthday party in order to abduct a child, any child, and that child was mine. Both David and Rachael had been taken from me, and the whole way of life I had given up so much to preserve had been destroyed. I felt as if I was being mocked for ever having tried to do the decent thing.

There was no way I could simply start again. I had lost my faith, and had nothing to replace it with. After what had happened, I could no longer believe that responsibility, self-sacrifice and hard work were their own modest reward. But I had invested so much time and energy in that illusion that I no longer believed in anything else either. The result was a paralysis of the will which was reflected in the weeks I spent in that apartment, staring at a wall as blank as my own mind.

I was roused briefly from my lethargy by the news that our house had been sold. I made arrangements for a moving company to strip the place of our possessions and put them in storage until I felt able to deal with the task of going through them and deciding what to do with everything. The day before the movers came, I drove over to Maplewood to remove a few more clothes and sort through my papers and documents for anything I might need. While doing so, I happened to come across the bar receipt on which Sam had written his name and phone number. The area code was 206. I looked it up in the phone book. It covered the western half of Washington State.

That chance discovery sparked an idea which firmed up into a project over the course of the next few weeks.

Seven

One Saturday evening in May Kristine Kjarstad got back from dinner at Ray's Boathouse with a couple of gay friends and a woman called Betty whose sister had just had an operation for cancer, and who needed cheering up, to find a message on her voicemail.

'Hi, Kirsty, it's Steve. Listen, if you're around, tune in to Channel 13 right away. *America's Most Wanted* is doing a scene that's just like that Sullivan case, and I figure if the Kansas City cops can get air time then why not us? Give me a call when you get in, I want to see the rest of it.'

Kristine gave a sigh of relief. Steve Warren's burning ambition to get on television was one of the many features of her partner which failed to endear him to her, but her first thought had been that the message was from her ex-husband. Thomas was spending the night at his house, which gave Kristine a chance to go out. The price she paid in return was giving Eric the chance to nag her about some detail of the way she was bringing up their son.

It was now four years since she'd thrown Eric out, having belatedly realized that he was never going to change his ways. He'd appeared genuinely astonished by her decision, and maybe even more by the fact that she'd finally got around to making one. That had always been *his* role in the relationship. He'd picked Kristine out at college, where he was majoring in dentistry and she in social science, and dated her assiduously for two years. Once they both graduated, he had proposed and she'd said why not, even though the idea of her marrying a Swede hadn't gone down too well with her Norwegian family. Looking back at it now, Kristine could see that she had passively bought into his programme all along. What she didn't understand, even now, was why.

Once they were married, Eric had been the one to decide where they should live, who their friends should be, which restaurant or movie to go to, even the most appropriate moment for having a child. Kristine had followed the path of least resistance, standing idly by while he organized every aspect of their life with the same obsession for detail that he lavished on his patients' dental problems. In a weak, Pollyanna-ish way that now made her shudder, she had kept telling herself that things would soon get better. He would mellow out once they were engaged, once they were married, once they'd settled down, once they started a family. It had taken her eight years to realize that she was living with a control freak. Underneath the masterful exterior which had charmed her at first lay a deeply disturbed individual, weak and anxious, with a compulsion to organize every single aspect of his own life, and that of everyone around him. By the time they finally separated, they were like the impacted branches of trees which have grown too close together, both distorted, both rubbed raw.

But even though Kristine had got him out of the house, she couldn't get him out of her life. When you have a child, you not only give a hostage to fortune but also to a person you may eventually come to wish you'd never met. With Thomas as a pretext and go-between, Eric could continue to exercise a measure of creepy control over Kristine for the foreseeable future, and there wasn't a damn thing she could do about it.

Sometimes Thomas relayed the messages himself. 'Dad says you shouldn't cook hamburger so often, it's full of cholesterol.' Sometimes they came by phone. 'I see Thomas is only in the ninety-fifth percentile in English. How rigorously do you supervise his homework? He seems to be spending a lot of his time watching TV.' So although Kristine had no particular wish to feed Steve Warren's fantasies of fame and fortune, she felt a measure of warmth towards him simply for not being Eric, and called him back to explain that she had been out all evening. Steve Warren cut her off.

'As soon as I started watching it I thought, hey, this sounds familiar. The MO was pretty well identical. Two guys and a woman get blown away in a walk-up. Twenty-two to the back of the head, victims bound and gagged, nothing taken, no sex angle, no prints, no clues, no manifest perp. Jesus, you should have seen the homicide dick hamming it up for the cameras. You could tell he was just *loving* it. Like, "Hi, Mom, it's me!"'

'When did this happen?'

'Couple of months ago. Takes them a while to set it up and do the filming, I guess.'

'Too bad I missed it.'

'No prob, I taped it. Got a library of every episode dating back to March of 1989, all except one where my VCR went ape and chewed up the tape. I'll bring it over tomorrow and we can talk about putting together a package to send them. Someone told me one of the segment directors lives right here, on Mercer Island. We could go over there, pitch it to him direct. Hey, we could be stars! The camera's gonna love you, babe.'

Kristine Kjarstad viewed the video the following evening. The next morning, she put in a call to the Kansas City Police and after some delay got to speak to Fred Polson, the detective who had handled the case. He insisted on calling her back at the office, just to check that she was who she claimed to be. Once this had been established, Polson was ready enough to talk, but it soon emerged that he was sceptical of the alleged parallels between the two cases and suspicious of his caller's motives in trying to establish one.

'You're talking what sounds like a straightforward domestic, Ms Kjarstad, except you can't come up with the goods on the guy. This one here's something completely different. You see the show? Did a great job, huh? Course they had my complete input the whole time, not just the parts where I was on camera. Anyway, what we've got is an old man, his daughter who was visiting, and the guy they had in to paint the kitchen. Right? These guys arrive at the door, tie them up, blow them away and then just disappear. I mean it's like in a different class, you know? Which is why the TV people decided to go for us instead of you guys.'

Kristine frowned.

'Mr Polson, did you already receive a call from someone in this department?'

'Guy name of Warren? And I told him just the same as I'm ... '

'Can I just clarify something? Whatever my co-worker may have said or implied, this is my case and I'm not interested in TV exposure. OK? I couldn't compete anyway. You're a natural, Mr Polson, and just let me say that your necktie looked *great*. We don't see many bolo ties here in Seattle, not the real classy ones.'

'Hell, that old thing! My wife Gertrude gave me that for my birthday, way back in ... '

'Here's what I'm up for,' Kristine continued in her most hokey tone of voice. 'You send me the notes on your case and I'll send you the notes on mine. That way we both get a chance to compare and contrast. You're probably right, there's no there there. But just supposing there *is* some link, or we can make it look that way, you get to go right back on *AMW* and update the story. I guarantee to stay out of it. And you can have that in writing if you want.'

'Hell, Ms Kjarstad, you should get a piece of the action too.'

Kristine turned on a mildly flirtatious voice.

'Well, in that case let's get together and work something out.'

Polson laughed richly.

'Be more than my life's worth, Ms Kjarstad. Gertrude is one jealous woman. You got fax machines out there on the coast?'

The report on the Kansas City killings arrived on Kristine Kjarstad's desk while she was typing up her case notes on an alleged sexual assault at a school in a town called Selleck. The first page was signed by the patrolman who had been called to the scene.

Kansas City Police Department

Case Number: 47-94-0076 *Offense*: Homicide

Victim #1: Howard Selby W/M DOB: 03-16-27
Victim #2: Sandra Selby W/F 09-07-49
Victim #3: Unknown B/M unknown
Suspect #1: Unknown W/M
Suspect #2: Unknown W/M
Location: 2930 East 64th Street, # 33

Details: Reporting officer arrived at scene at 14.35 hrs, in response
to a reported disturbance. Complainant Wanda Neuberger, fifty-
seven, resident at 2930 East 64th Street, #35, stated that she had
heard cries for help from the neighboring apartment, inhabited by
Howard Selby, who was confined to a wheelchair. She went to
Selby's apartment and knocked on the door, which was opened by
two young men. One of them was drenched from head to foot in
rose pink paint. The men pulled a gun and forced complainant to
return with them to her apartment, where they confined her in a
windowless bathroom off the kitchen and blocked the door by
moving the refrigerator against it. Complainant struggled with the
door for some fifteen minutes before succeeding in opening it
enough to escape and telephone 911. Having conducted a search
for the suspects, R/O proceeded to apt. 33, where he discovered
the body of victs. 1 & 2 in the living room, and vict. 3 in the
kitchen. He called in for assistance and remained at door to secure
scene from intruders until arrival of detectives. Case was then
turned over to Detective Fred Polson.

The following pages contained Polson's report:

Kansas City Police Department

Case Number: 47-94-0076

In response to Officer Kimball's request for detectives to work a
reported multiple homicide, I went to 2930 East 64th Street,
Apartment 33. Victim #1, identified to me by neighbour Wanda
Neuberger as Howard Selby, was in living room sitting in a wheelchair. The chair was facing the north wall, the head slumped forward and the wrists taped to the arms of the chair. Gunshot entry
wound visible at back of head. Victim #2, identified to me by same

witness as Sandra Selby, daughter of vict. #1, was also in the living room, lying on floor under window in east wall. The body was lying on its right side, facing east, in a foetal crouch. Gunshot entry wound at back of head. Victim #3 was found in kitchen, which was being repainted, lying on back in middle of floor, right arm outstretched above head. Victim was wearing housepainter's overalls. Three gunshot entry wounds were visible, in the mid-chest, right shoulder and forehead. A large irregular splash of pink paint lay on the floor to the north-east of the body. A series of clear shoeprints in the same paint were visible on the vinyl flooring, and more faintly on the living-room carpet leading to the front door of the apartment. I directed Crime Scene Technician Traci Moore to make a full investigation. I then took a full statement from Wanda Neuberger (see document attached) and put out an urgent call for the two individuals she described to me, including a description of the winter coat and scarf she reported missing from her wardrobe. At that point John Boychuk, the janitor of the apartment block, appeared at the scene and identified victim #3 as Winston Jones, of 4711 East 53rd Street, who did light maintenance work for many tenants in the building.

Kristine Kjarstad read through the neighbour's statement, which added nothing of any substance to what she had told the patrolman. She then skimmed the lengthy supplemental reports by the CST, the pathologist and the forensic laboratory. Selby and his daughter had been shot at close range, Jones twice from a distance of several feet and once, to the forehead, at close range. The ammunition used was CCI Stinger .22 calibre. Traces of adhesive on the mouths of Howard and Sandra Selby matched that used on the duct tape used to secure Howard's wrists to the arms of his wheelchair, indicating that they had been gagged. Marks on Sandra Selby's wrists suggested that she had also been handcuffed.

But the piece of evidence which interested Kristine Kjarstad the most was hidden away in the dry catalogue of the CST report. The shoeprints created by the paint on the vinyl flooring of the kitchen were so clear that there had been no problem in matching the make, model and year against the sample books which are supplied to police authorities by leading shoe manu-

facturers. In this case identification had been simplified still further by the fact that the sole of the Nike model in question featured the silhouetted figure of the basketball star Michael
Jordan.

*

Detective Eileen McCann of the Evanston City Police did not see
that particular episode of *America's Most Wanted*. For one thing,
she had gone into Chicago that evening to watch the Black-
hawks fight a losing battle for a playoff spot in the Stanley Cup.
For another, she didn't own a television.

By this time, there had been a number of developments in the
Maple Street case. One related to the murder weapon, which
had been traced to a gun shop in Portland, Oregon. It had been
sold eight years previously to a certain Willard Sumner, resident
in the Errol Heights neighbourhood of that city. Two years later,
Sumner had returned home from work to find that his house
had been burgled. Amongst the inventory of missing items he
gave the police – two VCRs, a brand-new fax machine and a
'priceless' collection of country and western CDs – was the .22
calibre Smith & Wesson Model 34 revolver which Sumner had
bought over the counter at Joe's Guns following a previous
break-in at his house.

After that, there was no further trace of the weapon. Evanston
Police circulated its ballistic characteristics to law enforcement
agencies in the North-west, hoping that they might match a set
held on record in relation to other crimes, but without result.
The burglar who stripped Sumner's house might have kept the
revolver for his own use, or sold it privately to one of the many
people whose professional activities require the use of firearms
but who prefer to avoid the formalities associated with the
mandatory five-day waiting period. That purchaser might then
have experienced a temporary cash-flow problem and sold the
gun on to someone else. There was no way of knowing how
many hands the gun had passed through before it turned up in
Evanston.

But the major breakthrough concerned the identity of the
third victim and presumed perpetrator of the killings. By the

time it happened, Eileen McCann had almost given up hope of ever being able to tie a name-tag to the anonymous cadaver which was stored, like some art work of dubious provenance, in the basement of the city morgue. An extensive poster and media blitz immediately following the shootings had induced a flurry of claims to recognize the unknown man, but these had always failed to hold up to sustained scrutiny. Then, when all the furore had died down, along came one that stuck.

The informant was a private investigator named Lou Gelen, with an office in Decatur, Illinois. He had been hired three years earlier by a local couple named Watson to find their son. Gelen had managed to trace Dale Watson as far as Boise, Idaho, where the boy had worked briefly in a lumber yard. There the trail ended, until Gelen visited a police station in South Chicago to look up a friend and happened to see one of the posters featuring a tastefully retouched photograph of the unknown individual in the Evanston killings.

Lou Gelen immediately contacted the Watsons, then the Evanston Police. The next day, Eileen McCann drove down to Decatur, bringing with her a portfolio of photographs of the dead man. Joseph Watson returned with McCann to Evanston, where he viewed the body in the morgue and positively identified it as that of his son.

Hopes of a swift breakthrough in the case rapidly faded, however. Bank, medical, telephone, utility, DMV, voter's registration, IRS, consumer credit and Social Security agency records were all checked, without effect. Dale Watson's name did not feature on the National Crime Investigation Computer, and there was no record that he had ever been charged with a crime.

By interviewing the parents and following up leads provided by them, the police gradually built up a profile of Dale Watson's life. He had been born in Shelby County and raised in Decatur, where the family moved in the mid-seventies. He had achieved average grades at school. People remembered him, if at all, as a pleasant, unexceptional young man. The caption to his High School Yearbook photograph read: 'Noted for his ready smile, Dale participated in Frosh football and Varsity baseball … he belonged to the Baptist Youth group outside of school … he will remember shop class because of Mr Booker's inspirational teaching … his secret ambition is to travel throughout the world … Dale plans to attend college next year.'

But he hadn't. Instead he'd gone to Chicago, where he'd worked at a variety of low-paid jobs from pumping gas to delivering pizzas. If his parents were worried by his lack of ambition, they didn't make a big deal of it. Joseph and Olive Watson were plain folks – he ran a garage, she took care of the house – and made a clear distinction between 'doing well for yourself' and 'getting above yourself'. Going to college wasn't needful for the former, the way they saw it, and could all too easily lead to the latter, if not to worse things. As long as Dale continued to fear the Lord, it wouldn't do him any harm to have a taste of big city life, get it out of his system. Then he could come home to Decatur, find some nice girl and settle down to a steady job.

The first sign that this modest scenario might not work out was when the Watsons received a letter postmarked Omaha, Nebraska:

> Dear Mom and Dad,
>
> Well, as you see I've moved out West for a while, I guess I just got the travel bug. I got work at a garage, nothing fancy, but I can do lube jobs and replace shocks like you showed me, Dad. Once I get a few bucks together I might head on a little farther, try and see something of this great country of ours. Hope you're well. Say hi to Trish and Howie. Did Ronda have her baby yet? I guess she must.
>
> Love,
>
> Dale

For the next eighteen months, similar letters arrived irregularly from towns and cities all over the Western states. On special occasions – Christmas, his parents' birthdays – Dale would telephone, but his calls were as brief and vague as his letters. He never left a forwarding address or phone number where his parents could contact him, explaining that he would soon be moving on.

One of the letters had been sent from Portland, Oregon, and for a moment Eileen McCann thought she might be on to something. But it was dated six months before the burglary at Willard Sumner's house, by which time Dale Watson had once again 'moved on', and she reluctantly conceded that this was a mere coincidence.

Mr and Mrs Watson had not been too happy about Dale's continuing and indefinite absence, and still less with his nomadic way of life, but they had other problems to contend with, notably Olive's health – a kidney infection – and the marriage of Dale's sister Patricia, which was well on its way to becoming Topic A in the community.

Just over a year earlier, they had received yet another of Dale's letters, this one from Los Angeles. It mentioned that he intended to 'head south for a while, maybe go to Mexico'. There was nothing else remarkable about it, certainly nothing to suggest that this was the last contact they would ever have with their son. But there the series ended. When two months went by without any more letters or phone calls, the Watsons – alarmed more than anything else by that word 'Mexico' – notified the police.

About a million Americans are reported missing each year, and the numerous city, county, state and federal agencies whose job it is to locate them are understaffed and underfunded. As the months went by without any news, the Watsons reluctantly decided to employ a private investigator. Lou Gelen did not find their son, but he discovered a tragic and possibly significant secret which Dale Watson had been keeping from his parents.

As one of his routine search procedures, Gelen contacted the Illinois Drivers Services Section in Springfield, hoping that Dale might have registered a change of address which would give him a starting point to work from. He drew a blank there, but Dale's accident history showed that he had been involved in a traffic-related fatality in Idaho the previous year. Gelen applied to the Motor Vehicle Division of the Idaho Department of Law Enforcement, enclosing the search fee of five dollars, and ten days later received a copy of the accident report.

One summer night, just before two in the morning, Dale Watson had been driving a car which was struck by an eighteen-wheeler tractor-trailer rig which had crossed the median on Interstate 84 near Nampa. Watson was taken to the hospital suffering from shock and minor injuries. His passenger – Starr Costello, seventeen, of Boise, whose parents were the registered owners of the car – was killed. The trucker was charged with reckless driving. No charges were brought against Dale Watson.

Using the Haines Tele-A-Key locator service, Lou Gelen obtained the phone number corresponding to the street address in Boise where Dale Watson had told police he was living at the time. The person who answered his call said he'd only been there a couple of months and had never heard of any Dale Watson. The Watsons weren't prepared to pay Gelen's expenses to go out there in person, so there the matter rested until the police got involved.

After a flurry of faxes and phone calls from Eileen McCann and the Idaho State Patrol, the Boise Police dug out their files on the accident. According to Dale Watson's statement, he had been at a party given by some people he'd met in a bar. He'd got a ride to the party, which was in a town called Caldwell, but the people he'd come with had left early and he'd had no way of getting back to Boise. Then a girl called Starr Costello offered him and another couple a ride in her parents' car, which she'd borrowed. At the last moment the couple had got a ride with someone else, and Dale and Starr had set off together. She'd asked him to drive because she was feeling 'unwell'. Watson had agreed to take a breath test, which showed a level of alcohol slightly over the legal limit, but since the accident was clearly not his fault, and he was 'severely traumatized' by what had happened, the police decided not to press charges.

At Eileen McCann's request, the Boise Police interviewed a number of people who had attended the party in Caldwell, and eventually traced three who had known Dale Watson. One of them had since moved out of the area, but she was able to contact the other two by phone.

The first, Kathy Lawson, twenty-two, sounded like a female equivalent of Dale himself, a rootless migrant moving from state to state according to whim or weather. She was from South Dakota originally, but had moved around quite a lot since then, and had a record of convictions for drug possession. Despite this, she was perfectly prepared to talk to Detective McCann all day – or even longer, Eileen suspected, given half a chance.

'Dale was like, a nice guy, you know? Someone you could trust? Like I know he kinda had a thing for me, but he never hit on me or anything. You get guys hitting on you the whole time, but Dale was different. He was like, *gentle*. I mean you could talk to him. He was real intelligent too, read books and everything. But like he never came on like heavy. It was like he was really interested in you, what you were thinking, your personality.

'That thing that happened, with the truck? It just … I don't know what to tell you. It was like it destroyed him. Like he didn't even know the person who died. I was there that night, and we kinda had a little thing going for a while there. He kinda started to come on to me, you know, and then this other guy, a real asshole name of Arnold, he came over and got me to dance and Dale kinda drifted away. He wasn't like real flexible, you know?

'It's like with the accident. I mean it wasn't even his fault, the other guy was going too fast and just lost control. And the girl who died wasn't even a friend. It was just some mall rat who offered him a ride home, for Christ's sake. It wasn't like it was someone he really knew and cared about. But he took it really hard. I went to see him in the hospital, they thought he had maybe a cracked rib or something? And he was going on about how it was all like just a total chance, what happened. And I thought, right, so what's your problem? This is life in the big city. But Dale, well, you know he had a kinda strict religious upbringing, that Bible Belt stuff, and I guess that makes it tougher to go with the flow. Like if you grow up thinking there's like a reason for everything, and then something like that happens, and there's no reason …

'Last I heard of, he was talking about moving to Seattle. He said he wanted to go all the way to the edge and then fall off. That's what he told me, or it might have been someone else he said that to. I was kind of out of circulation just then, with this … Well, I won't bore you with the details. A medical thing. And when I felt like seeing people again, Dale wasn't around any more. It's too bad. If the kid had been his, I would've maybe thought about having it. I'd like to have told him that. Maybe it would have like made him feel better, you know?'

The other witness, Eugene Vandestraat, twenty-eight, worked as a bouncer at a club described by police as 'frequented mainly by younger individuals'. Eileen McCann asked him if he'd ever had any professional encounters with Dale Watson.

'You mean like trouble? Hell, no. Dale … Listen, I called him the Philosopher. That was something I got called at school, on account of I was so dumb. Some jerk in the honours programme started it off and the thing stuck. But Dale, well, he wasn't no philosopher, I guess, but he was a guy who lived in his mind, you know? Like you'd look at him, and you could almost hear his brain working, kinda like a dishwasher.

'Dale never gave anyone any trouble, far as I know. It was just the opposite. You were in trouble, he'd come and fix it. Not like the way I would, but there's kinds of trouble you can't just walk in and say "OK folks, you're outta here", right? Like I recall one time there was this guy, his woman'd left him, he was a big drunk, we all kinda felt she'd done the right thing there, but he just couldn't take it. Used to come in and sink a few, next thing you know he'd be going up to the other tables, people he'd never even met before, and telling them how this bitch'd dumped him after all he'd done for her.

'What you going to do? You can't throw the guy out, he ain't getting violent or abusive, plus he's one of our best customers. But guys didn't want to know. Maybe they had problems too. They'd gone out to forget that shit, and here was Clark – that was his name – wouldn't shut up about it. But Dale, Dale was a genius. He went over to the guy and sat down at his table, said "Tell me about it." Clark didn't know what the fuck to do. He'd made a career outta breaking people's balls about his problems and here was some guy *asking* him to talk about it.

'So anyway he starts into the whole story, same as usual. After a minute or two Dale looks at him – I heard all about this from a guy at the next table – Dale looks at him and says, "You supporting this woman?" Clark kinda frowns, what the hell's this? "Hell, no," he says, "we weren't even married." "Yes, you are," says Dale, real quick. "You're carrying her around on your shoulders like a monkey." And you know? After that, we didn't hear one goddamn word from Clark about it ever again.'

Vandestraat hadn't seen Dale Watson after the accident on the highway, but he said he'd been talking about going home. 'Said he was tired of drifting around from place to place, wanted somewhere to lay down his head.'

Eileen McCann reviewed the progress she had made with mixed feelings. On the one hand, the breakthrough she had initially hoped for had not happened. She had learned nothing which would enable her to close the file on the Evanston killings. On the other hand, she now had a clear image of who Dale Watson had been, a small-town 'philosopher' who had never had a chance to test his ideas against a coherent system of thought. He probably wouldn't have got very far if he had, but at least some formal education might have helped him deal better with the demons which menaced him, with his sense of being different from everyone and everything around him, and his need to grapple first-hand with the big questions which his parents had conveniently packed up and shelved away in a box marked Religion.

Those demons had always been there, she guessed, nagging away at his peace of mind, continually pushing him to 'move on'. When the truck had smashed through the traffic barrier and killed Starr Costello, they had emerged in force, precipitating the crisis which he had managed to stave off for so long. As soon as he got out of the hospital, he had no doubt headed out to the coast, as Kathy Lawson had said, all the way to the edge of the continent, hoping to 'fall off'.

She contacted the Seattle Police, but they had no record of a Dale Watson. But somewhere out there, Eileen McCann was sure, he had crossed paths with Willard Sumner's stolen revolver. After that, the other idea in Dale's shocked, guilt-ridden mind had taken over, the one he had mentioned to Eugene Vandestraat about going home. 'He was tired of drifting around from place to place, wanted somewhere to lay down his head.'

But where was home? Not Decatur, where parents and relatives and friends who had never understood the way he saw things, even in the good times, would expect explanations and a 'normal', easy-going, brain-dead mentality which Dale knew he couldn't fake any more. No, he would go to Chicago, where he had first tasted the joys of independence, a city he knew and where he no doubt still had friends (but who were they, and why hadn't they come forward when he died?).

That much McCann was fairly sure of. The rest, which was everything she needed to close the case, remained obscure. She could understand that Dale Watson might have come to believe that the only place he could finally 'lay down his head' was in death. But if suicide was his aim, why kill two total strangers too? And why choose a deserted house in Evanston to do it?

Maybe the question was the answer. Maybe Watson had deliberately set out to create an insoluble mystery which would enlighten others as he had been enlightened, an action as random and meaningless as the passion he had suffered, and which had made his life unliveable.

Maybe. Maybe not. As Eileen McCann tidied her papers away and prepared to turn her attention to other matters, the one thing she felt reasonably certain of was that no one would ever know.

Eight

The chance discovery of Sam's phone number sparked an idea which firmed up into a project over the course of the next few weeks. The more I thought about it, the more excited I became. I had always wanted to visit the Pacific coast, but had never been farther west than St Cloud. Now was the ideal opportunity to indulge in a prolonged bout of white-line fever. I had plenty of leisure and no other plans or commitments. And if I needed further justification, I could always claim that it marked another essential stage in my quest for full citizenship, a kind of personal manifest destiny. What have Americans always done, given half a chance, but head west?

I bought maps and guide books, then a car. This was also a Chevy, but a very different animal from the Nova, one of those elephantine gas-guzzlers which Greg had been driving that night we were pulled over by the traffic cop on the way back from the Commercial. I found it both comforting and exciting, but couldn't be bothered to figure out why. That was another sign of the way I had changed. Analysis once again seemed as irrelevant and misguided as it had back in the seventies, a futile attempt to understand what can only be seized and lived. Understanding hadn't saved my wife or my son. Why should it save me?

The day I left was mild and sunny. I drove through the commuter traffic like a whale through minnows, heading for deep water. I found a country and western station on the radio and cranked up the volume. My classical records and tapes were in storage, along with the whole way of life they represented. I was heading north to Grand Rapids, then west on to Highway 2, the old route to the coast which I had chosen in preference to the sterile efficiency of the interstate.

I felt deliciously light of head and heart, like a teenager again. I had no idea where I was going, still less what would happen when I got there. That *was* the idea. For years I'd done nothing which had not been scheduled, priced and planned down to the last detail. Even a trip to the movies had become a major logistic exercise involving extensive coordination and consultation. And yet we might just as well have thrown a dice for all the good it had done us. Now I was prepared to take my chances. What had I got to lose, after all? I had already lost everything.

Calling in on Sam was a minor aspect of the trip. I didn't think about him once during the drive across the agricultural grid of North Dakota and the badlands of northern Montana, past innumerable isolated farmsteads, each with its pick-up and barn and satellite dish and gaunt tree from which a tire swing dangled like a noose, through innumerable small towns whose most memorable feature was their names: Niagara, Petersburg, Devils Lake, Palermo, White Earth, Wolf Point, Wagner, Harlem, Kremlin, Galata, Cut Bank. The road had led me on across the mountains and out on to the plains of Eastern Washington, then through another chain of mountains to the ocean and a town called Everett.

Everett is not a pretty place. In fact it was one of the uglier towns I'd seen on my trip. The chatty motel clerk gave me the whole story. Originally built to serve the pulpmill industry, it was now a big naval base, a status for which the local citizens had lobbied long and hard. If that hadn't worked out they'd probably have tried to get a nuclear power station, or have the state pen moved there. It was that kind of place. It was also the end of the road, where Highway 2 meets the Pacific.

I stopped at Dairy Queen on the outskirts of town and ordered a cheeseburger and rings to keep my indigestion up to speed. At the table across from mine, a couple of economy-size women in muumuus and elaborate perms were loudly discussing a friend's colostomy in graphic detail. On the other side of the divider, next to me, a trio of teen tarts were rehashing their Saturday night live.

'So he goes, "No fucking way!", and I say, "Way!" And it's

like I'm getting weirded out, OK? And I'm going, *uh*-oh! You know? So I tell him, "I'm *out*ta here," 'cos I'm getting like major-ly, *majorly* stressed. So I'm home later, and I'm like, wow, this is totally *out there.*'

It was there that I remembered Sam. For the first time since leaving home, I had to make a decision. I could go north, or south, or I could turn back, but I had to decide. My week on the road had been interesting, but it had also been enough, at least for now. I couldn't face the prospect of any more meals in truck-stops where everyone was either on the move or wished they were, or any more nights in motels where I woke at three in the morning with images of David and Rachael swarming in the darkness all around me, and got up and sat on the tweed-uphol-stered sofa and watched CNN until it grew light outside.

Now darkness had fallen again, and Dairy Queen was filled with happy families who thought of themselves as unhappy, who squabbled and whined and bitched and left in tears, little knowing their luck, their incredible, unearned good fortune at simply being able to go home together. It was not their happi-ness that I envied so much as their unhappiness. I too wanted the luxury of carping and complaint, the safe thrill of sniping at sitting targets, of taking your distance from the place where 'they have to take you in'. But I had no home to go to. The only person I knew for a thousand miles in any direction was Sam. In retrospect, it was inevitable that I would call him.

A man I didn't know answered. Sam wasn't there, he said. He'd try to contact him and have him call me back. I was at a payphone outside Dairy Queen. It had started to rain, a fine per-sistent enveloping drizzle which furred my clothes and skin. I gave the guy the number, went back inside and had another cup of coffee. It was another forty minutes before the phone outside started to ring. It was Sam. He sounded preoccupied, and not particularly pleased to hear from me, as if I represented a prob-lem of some kind.

'So where are you at?' he demanded.

'Everett. You know it?'

'Yeah. You're pretty close.'

There was a pause.

'Want to come tonight?' he said.

'Well, is that OK? I mean I don't have any other plans, but I don't want to put you to any trouble.'

'It's OK,' Sam said flatly. 'I just got to think.'

Another pause.

'You got wheels?' he asked.

'Sure.'

'What are you driving?'

'An old Chevy. Kind of a blue-green colour. It's got Minnesota plates and a big antenna on the back.'

'OK. Here's what you do. Take I-5 north to Highway 20, then turn off for Anacortes. Go into town and park on Main Street, across from the clock. Aim to be there in about an hour and a half. It's less than fifty miles, so you can take it easy. I'll send someone to meet you.'

'Hey, are you sure this is not a problem?' I said, slightly disconcerted by his abrupt tone. 'I mean I didn't let you know I was coming or anything, and ... '

'I knew you were coming, Phil.'

I smiled at this hint of the old familiar bullshit.

'You did? That's interesting. I didn't know myself until a week ago.'

'I don't mean I knew you were coming today,' Sam replied a little sharply. 'It could have been any time, next month, even a year from now. But I knew you'd come in the end.'

I smiled secretly to myself.

'You'll really like it here,' he went on, seemingly making an effort to sound a little more enthusiastic. 'You've got your own room and everything. I've been looking forward to this for a long time, Phil. Believe me, it'll be just great.'

'Sounds good,' I replied unconvincingly.

Traffic was heavy on the concrete ribbon of the interstate. Headlights slashed through the curtain of rain, passing trucks plucked and tugged at my old Chevy. I was glad to reach the exit.

Anacortes turned out to be a sprawl of modern homes and

shopping malls surrounding the original town centre. It was right on the water, and must have been a fishing port at one time, but its Main Street looked almost identical to many of those I had passed through on my way to the coast: a core of sturdy two-storey brick business buildings with a scattering of big wooden houses. I had no problem finding the clock that Sam had mentioned, one of those models with Roman numerals and a double face standing on a wrought-iron pillar which small-town jewellers used to put up outside their stores as an advertisement.

I sat there for over half an hour, getting colder and colder and wondering how reliable Sam and his friends were. There was hardly anyone around. By now it was after nine o'clock, and the citizens of Anacortes were presumably hunkered down in front of the TV or tucked in with a cup of cocoa. So when the headlights appeared behind me, I noticed them at once. The only vehicle which had passed me so far was a cruiser with a cop in a Smokey the Bear hat who had given me the beady eye, as if I were casing the jeweller's premises across the street.

A VW van pulled up alongside me. I could just make out the silhouette of a man sitting in the driver's seat. He seemed to be looking in my direction. The van was covered in garish magic-bus artwork, amateurish swirls of colour depicting naked bodies in various poses surrounded by stars and flames. There was a brief peep from the VW's reedy horn, then it revved up and proceeded down the Main Street. I restarted my motor and followed.

We drove in tandem out of town along the highway I had come in on, then turned off down a narrow road winding through dense woods. The rain had ceased by now, and the clouds were breaking up, allowing glimpses of the almost full moon. After several miles, the VW slowed down and signalled left. A battered mailbox with a number crudely painted in white was nailed to a post at the entrance.

We turned on to a dirt road which zigzagged steeply downhill. It was deeply pitted with potholes filled with water and ruts formed by the run-off. The Chevy scraped painfully several times, and I had visions of losing my muffler. After about five minutes the ground levelled out, the woods dropped back, and we emerged on to a patch of level grassland. Up ahead was an isolated house. As we approached, an external light high on the eaves came on, the door opened and a figure appeared in silhouette. I assumed at first that it was Sam, but as my headlights passed the doorway I saw that it was a man I didn't know.

The VW drew up beside one of the barns. I parked behind it and got out, savouring the odours of pine sap and salt water. I could hear the ocean somewhere close by. Seagulls circled invisibly overhead, screeching intermittently. A light breeze stirred the tall, seemingly impenetrable barrier of conifers all around.

The man who had emerged from the house walked over to the VW and spoke briefly to the driver, then they both came over to where I was standing. The driver was in his late thirties, short and chunky, with a soft beer gut. His face was chubby and battered, and he had a droopy moustache and long hair pulled back in a ponytail. The other man was taller and sparer, with the kind of leanness which looks like the result of malnutrition or bad genes, not diet and exercise.

'I'm Rick,' the driver said. 'This is Lenny.'

'Phil,' I replied. 'Good to meet you.'

'We've got some stuff to unload,' Rick remarked, jerking his thumb at the VW. 'You want to give us a hand, it'll go quicker.'

'Sure thing.'

When I looked more closely at the kitschy designs painted on the VW van, they reminded me of something I had seen before, although I couldn't place it – an album cover, maybe. Rick opened the side door, lifted out a large package and walked off with it. Lenny did the same, and then it was my turn. The inside of the van was filled with shrink-wrapped multipacks and rows of institutional-size drums and jars. There were packs of canned spaghetti and wieners and nukeable chicken noodle soup and industrial desserts and containers of peanut butter and ketchup and Coke like characters from a child's nightmare, the familiar form and features swollen to monstrous proportions.

I chose the lightest-looking item, a plastic bag containing sixty packs of cheese-flavoured corn snacks, and set off the way the other two had gone, following a barely visible path in the rough grass. The sound and scent of the ocean grew stronger. Then the moon glowed from behind the clouds and I saw it, a seething dark surface stretching away on all sides. The house, I realized, was built on a promontory. The next moment the ground beneath my feet turned hollow and I stumbled on something, almost falling.

'Take it easy,' said Lenny. 'We don't want to lose any of that stuff.'

I discovered that I was standing on a narrow pier of wooden slats built out into the water. There was a boat alongside, and what I had stumbled on was the heavy metal ring to which it was moored.

'Just set it down here,' Lenny told me. 'Rick'll load her.'

He brushed past, heading back the way we had come, his lanky figure outlined against the yard light on the house.

It took us another twenty minutes or so to lug all the groceries down to the water, while Rick manhandled it aboard the boat and stowed it away.

'You got any baggage?' he asked when we were done.

'Just an overnight case.'

'Better get it.'

I finally understood.

'You mean we're going in the boat?'

Lenny chortled.

'You'd have one heck of a hard time driving there!' he said.

He walked back with me to the house, where I got my case out of the trunk of the car.

'Leave the keys with me,' Lenny told me. 'I'll put her in the garage later.'

I wasn't particularly happy about giving my car keys to a total stranger, but presumably Sam's friends weren't going to rip me off. With a weak shrug, I handed them over. A diesel motor gurgled into life down by the water.

'Better get going, you don't want to be left behind,' said Lenny, turning back into the house. A moment later the light

114

went out. The moon was obscured again. I made my way slowly back to the pier, trying to dilate my eyes to the point where I could distinguish grass from rocks and land from water. The lights inside the boat were on, and once I found the pier I got aboard without difficulty. It was a surprisingly roomy old motor cruiser, with an enclosed wheelhouse.

While I stowed my overnight bag below, Rick untied the ropes and pushed us off from the pier. He put the engine in reverse until we were clear of the shore, then revved up and spun the wheel to turn the boat around. I peered out through the windshield. I could see nothing whatever. We appeared to be heading out into an expanse of total darkness.

'Where are we going?' I asked.

Rick stood grasping the wheel and staring straight ahead.

'Heading due west right now,' he said. 'Once we get out into the strait we'll turn north until we clear Orcas, then head on in.'

None of this meant anything much to me, but that's usually the way I feel when I talk to boat people.

'So how do you know where you are?' I asked. 'I can't see anything out there.'

Rick tapped a circular glass inset in the dashboard. I leaned over and saw a white line revolving slowly around a screen. In its wake, a ghostly outline faded slowly until the line passed once again, refreshing its vigour.

'Didn't use to be able to do this run at night,' Rick remarked with satisfaction. 'Not till we got this baby. Cost plenty, but it's doubled our mobility.'

The gadget was some kind of radar, I supposed. The ghostly outline was an image of the shoreline apparently moving past the boat, which remained eternally stationary in the middle of the screen. For some reason I thought of David, the still centre of a world which seemed to move around him, safe and navigable, and something gave way inside me. 'It will only get better,' the psychiatrist had advised me. 'You will have bad patches for a long time to come, but they will be farther and farther apart.'

I was having one now. It was not just his death I was grieving for, I realized, but the brief life which had preceded it. Children are vectors aimed at the future. All the doubts and anxieties about how they will turn out are balanced by the knowledge that their course and final destination are ultimately out of your hands. Whatever happens to them will happen when you are different, or dead, and the world an unrecognizable place. But no such perspectives existed in David's case. The only things that would ever happen to him had already happened. His death seemed to make a mockery of his ever having existed at all, and of my continuing to do so. For the first time, I understood why Rachael had decided that she could not go on.

As we emerged into the open channel, the waves grew steeper. We passed a large unladen oil tanker coming the other way, its high sides towering over us. Later a car ferry crossed our bows, decked out in lights from stem to stern. It was almost eleven o'clock by my watch when Rick finally eased the throttle and the roar of the motor died away to a gentle gurgle. The boat wallowed lazily on the slight swell. A few moments later, I made out a light in the darkness up ahead.

'Are we there?' I asked.

Rick's head moved in what might have been a nod. He had hardly spoken a word to me the whole way. If the rest of Sam's friends were as much fun as Rick and Lenny, this was going to be a visit to remember.

The boat crept imperceptibly towards the beacon. It was impossible to tell how far off it was, and I thought we still had several hundred yards to run when the light suddenly loomed overhead and we bumped heavily against something. The boat tipped, the door of the wheelhouse opened and Sam was there, flinging his arms about me.

'Phil! It's so great you're finally here, man!'

His manner couldn't have been more different from his cool response on the phone. He stood there slapping me on the shoulders and grinning delightedly. I smiled at him with real pleasure. Sam's was the first familiar and friendly face I had seen in what seemed like a very long time. My earlier doubts about the wisdom of coming were swept away.

As we stepped off the boat, I saw that there were three other men standing on the pier beside some kind of hand-truck.

'Get the stuff unloaded, guys,' Sam told them casually. 'Bring Phil's bags too. I'm going to take him straight up to the hall. He must be wiped out.'

I was slightly surprised at this peremptory tone, but the men obediently climbed aboard the boat and set to work. I also thought it kind of strange that Sam made no attempt to introduce me. Still, this was his scene, not mine.

We walked along the pier to a trail winding up a wooded hillside. The only sound was our footsteps, the only light the faint glimmer of the moon behind a screen of high cloud. Superficially, Sam had hardly changed since we met in Minneapolis. His body was as spare as ever, his features as sharp, his hair as long. But something was different. He had a new poise, a gravitas, a centred, controlled energy. The very exuberance of his greeting revealed a confidence that had been lacking on that previous occasion, when he had been so stiff and guarded. Now he could permit himself what seemed like a genuine and spontaneous display of affection. In all our previous dealings, I had always felt older and more mature than Sam. Now the relationship seemed to have been mysteriously inverted.

'How come we had to take a boat to get here?' I asked.

'Because it's an island.'

I stopped and looked at him.

'An island? You never told me that.'

Sam's smile was visible even in the half-light.

'There's a lot of things I haven't told you, Phil. This way, you get to find out for yourself.'

This sounded more like the old Sam.

'So where the hell are we?' I demanded.

'We don't usually use the boat to go all the way to the mainland,' he said. 'But Rick was doing a Costco run anyway, so we figured we might as well do it this way instead of hassling around with the ferries.'

I couldn't decide whether he'd evaded my question deliberately, or was just continuing his earlier train of thought.

'So anyway, how've you been doing?' he asked suddenly.

The question startled me. Stupidly, I hadn't given any thought to how I was going to answer it. The last thing I wanted to do was to discuss what had happened and 'how it felt', but I couldn't very well avoid the subject. Or could I? Sam's question had sounded casual enough.

'Oh, not so bad,' I replied.

'Really?'

This time I thought I caught a little edge to Sam's tone, but I decided to bluff it out.

'And how about you?' I demanded.

He laughed.

'Just great. Everything's going according to plan.'

'And what plan's that?'

'God's plan,' he replied.

I decided this had to be a joke.

'You aiming to crack the televangelist market, Sam?'

'How do you mean?'

'Those smoothareno sleazebags with toops and bad dye-jobs you see on TV. They're always talking about God's plan for humanity and stuff like that.'

'We don't have TV here, man. That shit just fucks up your head.'

This was a great relief. It now made perfect sense that David's kidnapping hadn't penetrated this lost colony of born-again hippies. I could remain anonymous, instead of having to play the hackneyed role I'd been dealt by fate.

'But there's a plan all right,' Sam added softly. 'It's just that those suckers don't know what it is.'

'And you do?'

'That's the only thing I know,' he replied in the same quiet tone. 'And the only thing I need to know.'

'Keats,' I retorted pertly. '"Ode to Beauty".'

Sam stopped and turned to me. For a moment I thought he was angry. Then he smiled.

'Still the same old Phil. You were always so fucking *smart*, man! I was amazed at the stuff you knew. Like just then. I didn't even know that was a quote, but you spotted it right away. Awesome, man!'

I felt embarrassed by his effusiveness, embarrassed for him.

'Everything we say these days is a quotation,' I replied. 'Just like everything we think is a rerun of an idea someone's had before. These are the latter days, Sam, the end of history. The new's all mined out. All we can do is recycle post-consumer materials.'

'Right!' he cried. 'That's so right!'

He clapped his hands together in his enthusiasm.

'Jesus, I can't tell you how happy I am to have you here, Phil! You're someone I can talk to about this stuff. You really *get* it. The latter days, the end of history, that's it exactly!'

My embarrassment redoubled. I had meant the whole thing as a joke, but Sam had taken it literally. I shrugged.

'That wasn't original either. The idea that everything's been said before has been said before.'

Sam leaned towards me and touched my chest with his forefinger.

'But what if there was something that *hadn't* been said before? What if there was something which no one had ever even thought before? Imagine the power of something so fresh and original in a world where everything else is grubby and second-hand! It would be like a nuclear explosion!'

He gave a sharp laugh and started to walk again. To the right, a light had become visible through the trees.

'I care not whether a man is good or evil,' Sam remarked in a stilted voice. 'All that I care is whether he is a wise man or a fool.'

He looked at me expectantly.

'Another quote?' I murmured.

Sam smiled and nodded. I'd travelled a long way that day and was in no mood for party games.

'Beats me,' I said.

Sam didn't reply. We had emerged on to a gently sloping clearing. I could just make out what seemed to be a number of huts and other buildings. We made for the largest of these, a long structure made of roughly-hewn tree trunks with a steeply pitched roof. The light I had seen, a dull yellow glow, came from two small windows in the wall facing us. We walked around to the other side, where there was an imposing doorway with three steps leading up to it. Sam pushed the door open and ushered me inside.

The interior of the building seemed at first sight to consist of one huge room. The flooring was worn wooden planks and the walls made of the same tree trunks as outside, only painted white instead of dull red. The only light was provided by two naked bulbs which dangled on their cords from the ceiling some twenty feet apart. At the back of the room, opposite the door, a wood fire smouldered in a huge fireplace made of beach rock. The air was drenched with the pungent smell of cedar smoke.

I took in all this at a rapid glance, but the feature of the room which most struck me was a large television set standing against the right-hand wall. A group of about five men and three women were sitting and lying in front of it, watching a movie featuring Sylvester Stallone blasting away with a weapon the size of a rocket launcher. They mostly looked to be in their early thirties, and were wearing the sort of cheap and durable clothes you can see on any street in the country. I was relieved to see that there was no sign of homespun fabrics or hippie regalia.

Sam picked up a remote control unit from the arm of a chair and stilled the video. Instead of protesting, the people who had been watching it all greeted Sam loudly, breaking into wide grins. Sam waved like a star restraining excess adulation with a mixture of appreciation and hauteur.

'This is Philip,' he said, turning to me. 'He's an old friend of mine. An old, old friend.'

They all stood there, studying me with expressions I could not exactly gauge, envy perhaps, or awe.

'Phil's going to be staying with us,' Sam went on. 'I'm really happy he's here, and I want him to be happy too.'

The men and women all got to their feet and came towards me, smiling and holding out their hands.

'It's great!' one of them said.

'Fantastic!' echoed another.

'We're really happy you're here!'

'Cool having you around!'

'Good to meet you!'

It all sounded crude and forced. Why were they coming on so strong to someone they'd only just met? They reminded me of salesmen welcoming a newcomer to the 'team' under the beady eye of the manager.

'Way to play!' cried a tall man, gripping my hand forcefully. 'You're the man!'

Sam's smile broadened.

'Andy used to be a baseball coach,' he said. 'He treats everyone like they're in the Little League.'

The others laughed uproariously at this quip.

'Hey, some of us are playing in the Majors now!' the tall man remarked in mock protest.

One of the men had stayed behind, munching on a package of corn chips and drinking beer from the bottle. He was staring at the frozen frame from the video, which showed Rambo in midburst, trembling as though from the pent-up frustrations of this enforced *coitus interruptus*.

'Hey, Mark!' called Sam. 'Come and say hi.'

Mark got up with obvious reluctance and shambled over. He looked older than the others, more Sam's age. He was a big guy, six one or two, and built to match. He wore a long beard divided into nine tiny pigtails tied up with silver bands, while his head was shaved almost bare, leaving just a dark stubble showing on the scalp. He wore a silver ring in his right ear and another in his left nostril, and glowered at me in a way I found physically intimidating.

'Hi,' he said with deliberate flatness.

Sam slapped him on the shoulder.

'Hey, loosen up, man!'

He turned to me.

'Mark's kind of pissed because I kicked him out of his room so you'd have somewhere to sleep.'

'You didn't need to do that!' I protested. 'I could have slept anywhere. I don't want anyone to have to give up … '

'Hey, it's OK!' Sam replied. 'Not a big deal. Right, Mark?'

Mark shot him a look, shrugged and walked back to the TV. I wasn't the only person who was embarrassed by this, I realized. Several of the others shuffled about and looked at the floor as though they wished they were somewhere else. I found myself looking especially hard at one of the women.

I hadn't noticed her the first time around, but now something about her struck me. She seemed different from the others, in a way I couldn't quite pin down. She was dressed equally shabbily, in a pair of old khakis and a baggy grey sweater, but she managed to suggest that this was meant to conceal a great body, and had almost succeeded. Her face looked tired, but her brown eyes had an intelligent wariness which contrasted strongly with the flat, vapid expressions all around.

Our eyes met briefly. There was definitely a flicker of interest there, an intensity that made me realize that the facile smiles of the others had been directed at Sam, not at me. If I existed for them, it was simply as an extension of him.

'Come on, Phil,' Sam said, putting his arm around me. 'I'll show you where to bed down. We can talk in the morning.'

He led me around a massive rectangular dining table to a door at the end of the hall. The small room inside was furnished with a bed, a chair, a chest of drawers and an empty bookshelf. There was no window, and the air felt cold and damp.

'The Hilton it ain't,' said Sam wryly. 'This place was an old summer camp used to belong to some nutty sect. We've made a few improvements, but everything's still kind of basic.'

'It's great,' I murmured. 'I just wished you hadn't inconvenienced that guy for my sake.'

'It wasn't just for your sake,' Sam replied, lowering his voice. 'Truth is, Mark had it coming. He's been getting out of line lately. This'll be a good lesson.'

I wondered which line Mark had been getting out of, and why such a mean-looking dude would let someone like Sam push him around.

'Anyway, it's just for now,' Sam went on. 'Later on we can

make other arrangements.'

'Oh, I won't be able to stay long,' I said quickly. 'I've got to be getting back in a week or two, and there's a couple of other places I want to see first.'

I wanted this established right away. I planned to stay a few days, a week at most. It would be something to look back on later as an 'interesting experience'.

'If you need the can, there's one across the yard,' Sam continued, ignoring my comment. 'It's kind of primitive, but you'll get used to it.'

He stepped forward and grasped my hand.

'You're going to find happiness here, Phil. A happiness you never dared dream would come to pass. I know that may seem kind of strange now, but it's true. I'll prove it to you.'

I smiled weakly and nodded.

'Great. Thanks a lot for inviting me.'

Sam turned in the doorway. He shook his head solemnly.

'You invited yourself, Phil. Everyone who comes here invites themselves. They're the only invitations we accept.'

He turned and walked out, closing the door behind him. I undressed quickly, turned out the light and got into bed, pulling the covers over my head just as I had as a child in our badly heated house in Holland. Shivering with cold, I lay there sorting out stray sounds which seeped in through the cracks in the walls: a flurry of indistinct voices next door, rapid spasms of gunfire from the video, the dull thud of the Costco goodies being stashed away, and then the disturbingly familiar sound of a child crying somewhere in the distance. That was the last thing I was conscious of, and when I thought it over in the morning I wasn't sure if I had really heard it or if it was part of a dream.

Over the next few days, I explored my new home and fell in love.

Nine

Beyond the window streaked with grime, the flat, featureless landscape slipped past like a loop of film repeated interminably. Where the hell were they? After three days on the road, he'd even lost track of what state it was. The occasional towns they hit offered no clue, just the usual run-down main street, a few parked cars and pick-ups, a cluster of people waiting to board the Greyhound, a row of hard-scrabble businesses, a water-tower with some no-hope name painted on it.

Pat glanced at his watch. Still another three-and-half hours to go. He looked across the aisle at the girl in the leather jacket and tight jeans. She had sweet, mean, trailer-trash looks, and a body to match. He knew just how she'd fuck, but how would she die? He imagined pressing the pistol to her head, just behind the ear, the way he'd practised so many times. Ease the muzzle right in there, in the little hollow he'd have licked if he'd been going to fuck her.

She'd like that. After all the guys who'd just climbed on top of her and shot their wad, she'd appreciate a little gesture like that. She'd think he was classy. But not if it was a revolver he was sticking in there. That would make him just like all those other guys, plus she'd be dead. But then maybe she already was. You couldn't tell, that was the whole point. Not until you tried.

Sensing Pat's eyes on her, the girl turned and stared right back at him, sassy and challenging. He looked away, feigning a sudden interest in what was happening outside the window. Which was nothing. And if he'd had to shoot her? Would he have blown that, too? In that case, of course, everything would be different. He'd be psyched up and ready to go, and Russ would be there to help. Even so, nothing could guarantee that he'd be able to go through with it. Dale had proved that once and for all.

Pat still found it very difficult to accept what had happened to Dale. For a couple of days in there, he'd almost lost his faith. And he wasn't the only one. Even the real hard guys like Mark and Lenny had been shaken.

Andy had laid the whole thing out for them: how he and Dale had found the house empty, how he'd tricked the real-estate agency into revealing the time of the next viewing, how they'd dressed up as joggers and circled the block until the client and the agent showed, then followed them inside. Everything had gone without a hitch. The victims had been positioned, cuffed and taped. All that remained was the act itself, the ritual revelation of Life and Death which would raise Dale to the ranks of the initiates.

But then it had all gone wrong. Pat and the others had listened in stunned silence as Andy described how Dale had broken down and then turned the gun on himself, leaving his partner to execute the witnesses and withdraw as best he could.

It was a brutal reality check for all of them, but especially for Pat. He and Dale had been real close. They had arrived at almost the same time, and a bond had formed between them back in those early days when everything could seem kind of creepy at times. Plus they had similar tastes in music and movies, even food. They'd even shared the same woman for a while. And now Dale was gone. Even worse, he'd never really been there in the first place. That was the hardest thing to accept, but there was no other possible explanation. Facts were facts. Get over it.

Pat had tried, but the best he could do was to separate the two Dales in his mind: the dead one, and the person he'd talked and joked and bullshitted with for hours on end, day in, day out. He hadn't admitted this to any of the others, of course. He knew it was heresy. But there was no way he could convince himself that the Dale he'd known had been any less real than he was himself.

But how real *was* that? Pat shivered. That was the scariest thing about the whole business. Not only had none of them known the truth about Dale – Dale himself hadn't known. If he had, he would never have gone along in the first place, knowing what the outcome must be. Why take a test you're bound to fail? So he hadn't known. No one had known. Until the moment of truth, no one could ever know. The people at 322 Carson Street didn't know, Russ didn't know, Pat himself didn't know. That's why he was going, to find out. That's what the whole thing was about.

'You got the time?'

It was the girl across the aisle. Pat checked his watch.

'I've got a quarter of two.'

The girl made a face.

'I could really use a rest stop.'

She straightened up, turning away from him. For a moment Pat was tempted to try to keep the conversation going. It would help pass the time, and take his mind off what was going to happen when he arrived. But that was against the rules of engagement.

His palms were sweaty. He rubbed them against the smooth, faded denim over his thighs. If only he had the gun with him. Knowing that it was tucked up in his bag, up on the rack, would make him feel better. Just knowing it was there. The gun was solid enough, at least, while the rest of it sometimes seemed kind of flaky, even weird. It was one thing back home with the others, everyone buying into it and no distractions. Everything made perfect sense then, as Los expounded the scriptures, laying out their hidden meanings and making you see how it all related to your own life. But out here, bombarded by headlines and billboards and neon signs and reader boards and electronic counters telling you how much Americans had saved by switching to MCI, there were moments when Pat felt himself losing touch. Everything seemed brighter and louder and faster and more confusing than he remembered. Sometimes he found himself reeling under the onslaught of sensations, even though there was nothing really happening, just a bunch of people hanging out in some greasy spoon where the bus stopped. Above all, it was the people who bothered him. There were too many of them, and they were too different. He had to struggle to recall that this was all an illusion, repeating the lines of scripture he'd memorized as part of his self-reprogramming exercise.

That's why they hadn't let him take the gun, of course. They had it all figured out. As it was, there was nothing to tie him in to them. If he flipped out and went to the police, he would have nothing to give them but a story so crazy that no one would believe it for a moment. He didn't even know where Russ was staying. All he knew was the address of the house they were going to hit, and that wouldn't mean anything until afterwards. And afterwards he would be guilty of first-degree murder, videoed in the act by Russ, a permanent record of his initiation which would send him straight to the gas chamber or the electric chair or however they did it in Georgia.

When he thought about it now, that seemed kind of crazy too, having to come all this way, spending days and days on buses, and all because his dad had happened to be posted to Fort Benning the year Pat was born. In fact his childhood had resembled this cross-country journey more than it did his destination. The family had moved when he was two, and he'd never been back. He couldn't remember a damn thing about Georgia, but he had plenty of memories of other places all over the States, mostly unhappy. His sister had taken new homes and schools in her stride, settling down and making friends, the perfect military brat. For Pat it had been a struggle. By the time he was ten, his life already seemed like a school notebook full of botched attempts, unfinished assignments that never got beyond the first paragraph.

That's why he was so determined not to screw this one up. It wasn't so much the Secret itself that attracted him. If he was honest, he kind of felt the same about that as he did about Dale. Looked at in one way, it was a really neat idea which explained everything, and he was proud to be one of the chosen few to whom it had been revealed. But if he closed his eyes and looked again, it could seem no more part of him than a new set of clothes, a really zippy outfit that made him look and feel great, but which he could put on or take off depending on how he felt.

Maybe it would be different after his initiation. Anyway, what really mattered wasn't that but the sense of belonging. For the first time in his life, Pat had a real home and real friends, a stable centre and a shared sense of purpose. For that, he was ready to kill, even to die. If he had to go back to the life he was leading before they'd taken him in, he'd be as good as dead anyway.

He lay back and closed his eyes, trying to imagine what the house would look like. It was impossible, of course. It might be large or small, old or new, stucco or brick or wood or aluminium siding. At the moment it was just a number and a street name, but somewhere up ahead of him, getting closer every minute, was a real building on a real block, with real people living in it. Only they weren't real. Either that, or he wasn't. Soon he would find out.

A crinkling sound drew his attention. The girl across the aisle was opening a package of cookies. She saw him watching her.

'You want one?'

He hesitated just a second, then smiled.

'Sure.'

She moved over to the empty seat next to the aisle, her long legs dangling down, and handed him the bag.

'Going all the way?' she asked.

He nodded.

'You?'

'Uh huh.'

Beneath the open flaps of the leather jacket, Pat could see her breasts outlined against the T-shirt she had on. They were small and tight, with slightly raised nipples.

'Visiting your family?' he asked.

She shook her head, stirring her dank, bleached hair, the roots already growing out a mousy brown.

'Other way around,' she said.

Her accent was lightly spiced with the sweet sensuality of the South. Pat remembered her getting on in some small town they'd stopped at in the middle of the night.

'How do you mean?'

'I got sick and tired of running interceptions on all the passes my step-dad kept throwing at me.'

Pat frowned.

'You mean he tried to … '

'He sure did. He tried *real* hard.'

'Did you tell your mom?'

'Uh huh. She said it was all God's will. Meaning, this guy is my meal ticket, so just play along and keep him sweet so I can sit around here all day without having to do jack shit. So I figured I could do better on my own. This way, if I end up having to peddle my ass, at least I get to keep the cash. You want another cookie?'

Pat took one.

'So you've run away from home?' he said. 'Jesus.'

All his own fears of rootless dispossession rose up like a waking nightmare. But the girl merely shrugged.

'It's not that big a deal. I took about fifty bucks and my mother's charge card. I can forge her signature real easy and it'll be a couple of weeks before she even notices it's gone. Till then, I aim to go spastic with the plastic. How 'bout you?'

Pat opened his mouth and closed it again.

'I'm … Well, I … I guess I'm kind of in the same position myself. I lost my job, see. And I heard Atlanta was a good place to find work, so I thought I'd head on down there and see if maybe something will go right for a change.'

The girl nodded.

'You got a place to stay?'

Pat shook his head.

'You?'

'Nope.'

They were silent for a while.

'Listen,' she said at last. 'You want to do me a favour? When the bus gets in, you want to make it look like we're together? Thing is, all these pimps hang around the bus station looking for fresh meat. A friend from school came down last year, real nice person but the worst buckteeth you ever saw. I mean this little gal could eat corn through a picket fence, and they were still all over her like stink on shit. So I'd really appreciate it if you'd kind of stick around for a while.'

Pat hesitated. He knew he should refuse, but he also knew that he couldn't. This girl's situation reminded him too much of his own previous existence, after his dad and mom broke up and he'd faded into the blurred anonymity of the streets, sleeping outside and panhandling and searching trashcans for scraps of half-eaten hamburger.

'I'd be glad to,' he said.

She smiled, a sweet pucker of her thin red lips.

'We'd better meet. I'm Cindy Glasser.'

Pat thought furiously. He couldn't give his own name, of course.

'Dale,' he said.

The girl gave a heliated laugh.

'Really? My first boyfriend's name was Dale! What's your last name?'

Pat tried to make one up, but his mind had gone blank.

'Watson.'

The girl pouted charmingly.

'No, he was Krumdiack. Crummy Dick, everyone called him, poor guy. Still, isn't that amazing? I bet I know what sign you are, too. Gemini, right? I get along real good with Geminis, 'cos they're kind of indecisive. I'm just the opposite, being an Aries. Can I come sit here beside you? The edge of this seat is killing my butt.'

It had started to rain, the drops transformed into streaky lines of water by the speed of the bus. Pat snuggled down in his seat. For the first time since his long trip began, he actually felt good. He knew this was wrong. He wasn't supposed to be feeling good, not at this supreme moment of his life. But he couldn't help it. And what difference could it make, after all? If stuff was meant to happen, it happened. If it wasn't, it didn't. That was the basis of the whole thing, so why give himself a hard time about feeling good? No one need ever know, anyway. Just because they all shared the big Secret didn't mean he couldn't have his own little one. He relaxed, feeling the warmth of the girl's body beside him.

*

Kristine Kjarstad sat on the steps of her front porch, looking up at the sky, which was tinted an ethereal shade of peach. Although it was almost nine o'clock, the light was only just starting to fade. The mild, balmy air was perfumed with the odour of resin from branches cracked by Thomas, who had taken up residence in the tall cedar which grew next to the front fence. She could just see his head as he sat ensconced in his nest, reading about orca whales.

Summer was always a mixed blessing for a single mother. Once school was out, the whole business of organizing the day became an exhausting exercise in logistics and scheduling. This inevitably involved her ex-husband, whose meticulously organized agendas were just one of the many hurdles she was going to face in the coming months. To make matters even worse, Kristine had just learned that Clark and Donnie Wallis were going to Europe for four months.

The Wallises owned the house which backed on to Kristine's, and their son Brent was Thomas's best friend. Kristine thought Brent was kind of dorky, if the truth were told, but she recognized that he and Thomas together possessed the key to a magic kingdom she would never enter. They played happily for hours on end, massaging each other's fantasies and fears in ways that were incomprehensible to any adult, but which kept them occupied and only rarely ended in tears. Clark Wallis had confided to Kristine that the relationship with Thomas had been 'really helpful with Brent's anger management'.

So when Donnie called with the news that Clark, a systems analyst with Microsoft, was being sent to Frankfurt to oversee the installation of a new computer network for a German bank, and that she and the kids were going along, Kristine felt as if the long-threatened Seattle earthquake had arrived, demolishing some structures, rendering others unsafe, and opening up giant fissures in the texture of her life. Donnie's interest was in finding someone to rent their house, not an easy task given the short notice and limited period of availability.

Kristine had promised to do what she could, not out of a sense of loyalty to the Wallises but because that would enable her to add a condition which Donnie hadn't mentioned: that the prospective renters should have children, preferably boys, ideally of about Thomas's age. She loved the Wallingford neighbourhood where she lived, but its demographic mix tended to be split fairly evenly between older couples whose children had left home and younger ones whose offspring were still in diapers.

To the left of the cedar where Thomas was perched rose a gaunt telephone pole, a stripped tree trunk with metal climbing brackets imitating the vanished branches. The stave of cables running up the street was intersected by three wires strung at an angle, feeding her house and the one next door. Where they crossed, the wires appeared to thin out, as though melting into each other. One of the crows which had started infesting the neighbourhood sat on an insulator, emitting raucous cries. Kristine briefly fantasized about getting her pistol from the locked drawer where she kept it and blowing the evil thing away in a shower of blood and feathers.

She knew very well that far from being evil, the crows probably fulfilled some vital function in the internal economy of the biomass, but to her they were as much intruders as the non-native species of plants imported by nostalgic immigrants. Like holly or Scotch broom, the crows, arrogant and rapacious, seemed to symbolize other, more sinister forms of invasion which Kristine sensed at work behind the Renton massacre.

Her attempt to demonstrate that this was not an inexplicable anomaly but part of a campaign of organized killings had taken on the character of a crusade whose fervour, she knew, had made her something of a joke at work. It was true that she was over-motivated. As a native Seattleite, she felt affronted by the idea that something like this could happen here, and as a devout though lapsed Christian she was appalled that it could happen anywhere. But if she was obsessing, then her superiors, it seemed to her, were in denial.

'Close, but no cigar,' Dick Rice had replied when Kristine had given him her dog-and-pony show on the possibility of a link with the case in Kansas City.

Rice, a tough, taciturn man in his mid-forties whose first reaction to any topic was what could it do for or to his career, was head of the Criminal Investigation Division of King County Police. Kristine knew his wife, who was a pillar of the smells 'n' bells Episcopal church on Queen Anne Hill which she attended on the increasingly rare occasions when the urge took her, and she had taken advantage of this to go straight to the top.

'OK, so they both bought the same kind of shoes. BFD. You know how many pairs of those Nikes they sell every year?'

'The gun was the same too,' Kristine put in defensively, and immediately regretted it.

'The same *calibre*,' Rice shot back. 'We don't even know it was a six-shot or automatic, never mind the make or model.'

'And the shells, and the tape, and the handcuffs ... '

Rice stared at her for a moment with his wary, reptilian eyes. Then he shook his head.

'I took a course, Kristine, statistical theory? They got some numbers-butt from UW in to explain the whole thing. One of the things he did, he gave us these lists of random numbers and got us to see if any of them had any significance in terms of our lives. And it was just amazing! One guy found his complete date of birth, another got almost all his phone number, someone else found his car registration plus his daughter's age. But none of it means a damn thing. They're just strings of numbers churned out by a computer some place.'

Rice tapped the memo which Kristine had sent him.

'It's the same with this. Sure, you've found a few corresponding features in one other case among the hundreds of thousands reported all over the country every year. You know what? It would be amazing if you *hadn't*. If we asked HITS to run a search for homicide victims with green eyes, a birthday in March, fallen arches and a grandparent living in Spokane, I bet it would come up with a few matches. That's because computers are so smart they're dumb enough to answer any question you ask them. What I'm saying, even if you came up with half a dozen matches a lot tighter than this, you'd still be well within the statistical norm. And since you're pitching this KC job so hard, I take it you didn't.'

Kristine Kjarstad looked away, conceding the point. Initially, she had been optimistic about the outcome of computer searches, both at state and federal level. In fact it had been the routine chore of filling out the mandatory HITS form on the Renton killings which had originally forced her to confront her growing doubts about the way the case was being handled.

All police and sheriffs' departments in Washington State were required to submit information on murders, attempted murders and predatory sex offences to the computerized Homicide Investigation and Tracking System run by the State Attorney General's Office. The paperwork was supposed to take thirty minutes to complete, but in this particular case Kristine had spent over an hour puzzling out the most appropriate answers. The basic facts were easily transcribed from her full report: the date and time parameters, victim characteristics and background, method of operation, cause of death and forensic details. Things started to get tricky at the section headed INCI-DENT CLASSIFICATION.

There were thirty-two choices, ranging from 'Heat of anger' and 'Drug-related' to 'Psychopathic' and the chilling 'Fun/amusement'. Confronting this list, Kristine quickly realized that she could check five or six completely different categories, each of them as plausible as the others. Was it 'Domestic violence' or 'Serial/possible serial'? 'Hate' or 'Cult (ritualistic)'? 'Conspiracy' or 'Mental/insane'? She finally opted for 'Unable to determine'.

But when she came to the next question – 'Based on your experience and the results of the investigation of this case, do you believe this offender has killed before?' – she found herself, after a considerable struggle, marking 'Yes'. It took even longer to complete the sentence 'Evidence suggests the victim in this case is … ' Here she hesitated still longer, before choosing response three, 'a victim in a possible series'. And the pattern which had been lying dormant in her mind finally became clear when for 'Victim—offender relationship' she passed over 'Spouse', 'Family member (other)', 'Friend', 'Acquaintance (business, drugs, etc)' and checked 'Total stranger'.

Data submitted to HITS was not only entered into that system, but also automatically generated a parallel report which was transmitted to the FBI's Violent Criminal Apprehension Program, there to be matched against similar incidents reported from other states. Kristine Kjarstad had nourished high hopes that this process would provide her with evidence to support her tenuous and largely intuitive theory about the Renton case, but there had been no response, either from HITS or VICAP.

'The problem is, the system isn't complete,' she had protested to her Chief of Detectives. 'You know that, Dick! It isn't mandatory for LEAs to submit data, and a lot of them don't. New York, California, Texas – some of our biggest violence producers don't even participate. We do, so anyone who looked at the VICAP stats would end up thinking that the Northwest is the murder capital of America, which is absurd. Plus any cases which are 'solved', quote unquote, get wiped from the Feds' system! So if the original investigators in Peoria or wherever decide, rightly or wrongly, that it was just an attempted robbery gone ballistic or a family feud or a gang-related hit, whatever, it won't show on the computer. And that must happen all the time. After all, we almost wrote this one off as a domestic.'

'Which I still think it was,' Dick Rice replied calmly. 'OK, so we can't make a case against the guy … What's his name?'

'Wayne.'

'Right. That doesn't mean he didn't do it. He *confessed*, for Christ's sake! That makes sense to me. We buy into this idea of yours, what've we got? Some guys hit a house here in Renton, then hop on a plane to Kansas and start over. That's not the way multiple killers operate. They work their territory, wherever it may be. Look at our Green River guy. He killed at least forty-one women, maybe fifty, and all between here and Tacoma. He didn't waste his time racking up Frequent Flyer points.'

'Bundy moved around,' Kristine objected.

'Only because he was moving anyway. Utah, he went to law school. Florida, he was on the run after busting out of Aspen. As long as he was living here, this's where he hit 'em up. Didn't even bother to change his MO, just kept working the campus.

Whereas you want us to believe that there are these guys flitting around the country like sales reps, shooting up houses at random from sea to shining sea. I'm sorry, Kristine. I appreciate your enthusiasm and dedication, but this just doesn't fly.'

Coming from a man who had served on both the Bundy and Green River Task Forces, Rice's words had a certain authority, but Kristine Kjarstad still retained a blind, dogged faith in her idea. What really disturbed her was something which Fred Polson said when she called him to get his views on the file she had sent him in return for the one on the Kansas City murders. Polson hadn't been any more impressed than Rice by the alleged similarities between the two cases, but his parting words had stuck firmly in Kristine's mind.

'I'm pretty sure you're wrong about this, Ms Kjarstad. I certainly hope so. Because if someone *is* doing what you say, then it's theirs to screw up.'

A plane roared overhead, banking into the approach path to Sea-Tac airport. Off to the west, another was moving in towards the city, its landing lights glowing brightly against the bank of cobalt cloud which dwarfed the mountains of the Olympic peninsula. Above the clouds, another point of light, unmoving, pricked the gathering dusk: Venus.

Kristine thought of all the other planes which must be taking off and landing just then, all over the country. Someone had calculated that at any given moment one and a half million Americans were in the air. Add to that millions more in cars, buses and trains, and you had a continual flow and counterflow from city to city, state to state, coast to coast. It was as if the original impact of the *Mayflower* on Plymouth Rock had set up a shock wave across the whole continent, amplified by the later waves of immigrants.

For a time, all that energy had been channelled into the epic drive west. Now, thrown back on itself, it produced only this ceaseless turbulence, millions and millions of people perpetually on the move. And somewhere amongst them, perhaps, were two men equipped with .22 calibre revolvers, plastic handcuffs and rolls of duct tape. Sitting on her porch in the quiet evening,

Kristine felt a chill run through her. Fred Polson was right. As long as they didn't make a mistake themselves, such killers would be virtually immune to detection.

Because beneath the superficial restlessness which the European immigrants had brought lay the very different America of the native peoples: rooted, tribally based, rich in local traditions, fiercely independent. That culture had been destroyed, but its ghosts had come back to haunt the one which replaced it. Every town and city jealously defended its rights and privileges against the county authorities, which in turn resented any interference by the state, and all made common cause against the federal government. As a result, law enforcement was divided among thousands of different agencies, each operating independently of the others and responsible only to their own elected officials.

Most of the time this worked pretty well, since most crime is local too. But if someone took it into their head to exploit that gaping fissure between the two Americas, by committing random, motiveless crimes all over the country, they could just disappear right into it. They would be operating nationally, and there was no national police force.

People thought there was, of course. A diet of thrillers and movies had convinced them that whenever the local cops hit a case that was too big for them to handle they simply called in a glamorous FBI special agent played by Kyle McLachlan or Jodie Foster, who promptly sorted the whole thing out. In fact the Bureau had no power to investigate murder, for the simple reason that murder was not a federal offence. The Feds could only muscle in if they could demonstrate that the killings were linked to crimes which were, such as kidnapping or racketeering. Otherwise all they were empowered to do, and then only on request, was to send a representative from the Behavioural Science Unit at Quantico to liaise with local police on a consultative basis. Responsibility for the investigation itself remained with the law enforcement agency having jurisdiction in the area where the murder occurred.

In theory, of course, such agencies were supposed to co-operate fully with each other, sharing information and pooling resources. Sometimes it worked out that way, other times it didn't. But even discounting the usual rivalries, how could a pattern emerge if each part of the emerging puzzle was in the hands of a different player, each of them unaware that the others existed, and struggling to make sense of their own individual fragment?

A rustling in the branches above her brought Kristine's thoughts back to the present. There was Thomas, clambering nimbly down the tree to finish with an athletic leap into the yard, rushing up to hug her and bug her, demanding food and attention. As they stepped inside the warm, well-lit, wood-sprung house, Kristine promised herself that tomorrow she would lock the file away and devote herself to other work. Maybe she should phone Paul Merlowitz. He still seemed interested in her enough to want to take her out to lunch. It might even be worthwhile mentioning the Wallis house to him. Lawyers knew loads of people. It would make all the difference if Thomas had someone to play with over the summer vacation.

Ten

Over the next few days, I explored my new home and fell in love.

The first part did not take long. The island turned out to be much smaller than I had imagined. Despite the rough terrain, I was able to walk from one end to the other in less than an hour. The rain of the previous evening had stopped, the sky had cleared and the sun shone brightly in a pale blue sky.

'That's the way it is here in the islands,' Sam told me later. 'If you don't like the weather, just stick around for five minutes.'

'But I suppose the same thing applies if you *do*,' I replied.

He didn't seem to get it.

The island was roughly pear-shaped, rising from the coastline of smooth, sloping rock slabs and small stony beaches where we had landed to a single jagged peak sticking out into the open waters of the strait to the west. It was difficult to estimate distance, given the twists and turns in the overgrown trail which ran the length of the island, but the whole thing was probably not much more than a mile long and about five hundred yards across at the widest point, the relatively flat and low-lying plateau where the trees had been cleared for the buildings.

The rest was densely wooded with a mixture of evergreen and broadleaf trees: alders and sycamores, hemlocks and vine maples, cedar, fir, spruce, dogwood, and arbutus with its heavy, fleshy leaves and its trunk patched orange where the bark had stripped away. The undergrowth was lush with sword ferns and horsetails, every trunk and fallen branch verdant with moss, shafts of sunlight making distinctions between infinite subtly different shades of green.

I made my way along the overgrown trail which ran up the

spine of the island towards the westerly peak. The vestiges of other, narrower paths could be seen at intervals to either side. Like all reminders of how provisional any of our projects are – uprooted railways, old lengths of highway superseded by the interstate, cracking concrete runways among flourishing acres of wheat – they were both melancholy and fascinating. I wanted to know who had made them and where they led, to what enchanted cove or sunstruck glade where time stood still. Once or twice I set out to follow them, but soon gave up, defeated by outbursts of sharp brambles, barricades of fallen trees and eruptions of monstrous ferns.

The trail curled up to the top of the peak and stopped abruptly, overlooking a cliff which fell maybe fifty feet in a sheer drop to the water below. The view was stupendous. To the south, a long line of brooding mountains massed against the sky suffused with the tender Pacific light. To the west, a snow-covered volcanic cone rose high above a range of foothills. A thick layer of fog spilled out from the invisible coastline, funnelling down valleys and spreading out across the water in a shallow layer.

Nearer at hand, the surrounding islands were tucked one behind the other so that no open water was visible, their tone fading from clear green to hazy blue with distance. The shoreline consisted of a band of bare rock chewed by the waves, after which the vegetation began. Huge tree trunks bleached to a silver-grey lay piled like garbage at the tideline. Depending on its depth and exposure to the wind, the water itself varied in colour from a bright reflective glitter through a cloudy green to cold, steely blue. Where the turbulent currents met, huge circular patches, eerily smooth, basked on the surface like monstrous jellyfish. Above my head, seagulls hung like toys on a string in the stiff breeze scooping up and over the headland.

It felt wonderful to be all alone in the midst of such beauty. I was pleasantly rested after my sleep, and the doubts I'd had the previous night about coming had faded like a bad dream. This was exactly what I needed to help me forget what had happened and to give me the courage and the energy to start again. I sat there for a long time, beguiling myself with pebbles and twigs like a child, feeling the vast ambient peace of the place seeping into my pores, unkinking all my tension, stilling my jangled nerves.

Inevitably, the return to the compound was something of a downer. The peak experience I'd just had was an impossible act to follow, but the sight of the crudely logged clearing and its slum-like jumble of shacks and shanties, dominated by a rusted metal water-tank, was enough to destroy my mood of elation entirely.

The clearing itself consisted of two areas. There was an inner zone, about fifty feet square, where the trees and other vegetation had been dug out and the ground levelled, leaving a more or less flat table of packed dirt flecked here and there with patches of grass and clumps of horsetail. Around this stretched a desolate wasteland of rocks and scrub extending about a hundred feet up the hillside. Most of the trees here had been felled, presumably for firewood, but no attempt had been made to remove the roots or level the soil. As a result, all the buildings were crammed into the first area.

I had not paid much attention to them when I left that morning, but returning with my eyes attuned to the beauties of the landscape, I was appalled to see what an eyesore they were. The hall itself, clearly the oldest structure, was also the least offensive, its weathered timbers blending into the natural environment. There were two smaller outbuildings in the same style, one of which housed the equipment for generating the electricity supply, the other collapsing under the assault of a mound of brambles.

The rest were all more recent. Judging by the way they were jammed in at all angles, some just a few feet apart, they had been put up as needed, with no attempt at advance planning. It looked as if Sam's little commune must have expanded pretty rapidly, particularly in the last few years. The earliest ones were mere shacks, mostly of timber which looked as though it had been scavenged from previous structures dating back to the same era as the hall. They had corrugated iron roofs and incongruous modern doors, or in some cases just a length of gaudy plastic sheeting – one was clearly a shower curtain – nailed to the frame.

Finally there were six cabins of identical design and construction, probably built from kits. These were mounted on a poured concrete foundation and sported aluminium siding, double-glazed windows and felt roofs. Some of the men were at work on a half-built one. Among them was Andy, the ex-baseball coach I had met the previous night. He and another guy I didn't know were throwing up the sheetrock on an inside wall, and Andy waved in a friendly way as I passed.

I waved back with some relief. The blank stares and sullen faces which had greeted me when I appeared at breakfast had almost been enough to send me scurrying back to my room. I hadn't recognized any of the people seated around the long dining table. They were younger than the group Sam had introduced me to the night before, mostly in their twenties, and their taciturn, guarded manner couldn't have been more different from the exaggerated welcome I received then. Sam himself was nowhere to be seen, and I felt like an unwanted older intruder.

The food consisted of plastic-wrapped slices of spongy white bread, a huge jar of peanut butter and a selection of sugary cereals. There was also a percolator of industrial-strength coffee. Since Rick had forgotten to buy fresh milk the day before, the only kind available was a concoction resembling runny wallpaper paste which had been made up from powder.

I poured myself some coffee and a bowl of Cheerios, which I ate dry. There had been some desultory conversation in progress, but this ceased as soon as I sat down. My comments elicited only grunts or shrugs. After a while I gave up. We sat in silence, munching and crunching like animals at the trough. The fire was out and the air felt cold and dank.

An hour after breakfast, Sam still hadn't appeared. I asked several people where he was, but they either didn't know or wouldn't say. I thought at first that they were resentful that I wasn't pulling my weight, acting like the place was a hotel, but when I offered to lend a hand with the dishes or some other chore they just looked blank. I approached one man who was chopping wood beside a stack of timber at the edge of the clearing.

'Want me to take over for a while?' I asked.

He shook his head silently.

'I kind of enjoy outdoor chores,' I told him. 'I'd be happy to help.'

The guy just walked off, taking the axe with him. I was about to try my luck with someone else when Mark suddenly appeared.

'You got a problem?' he demanded.

'I was just offering to help.'

'We don't need help. Everything's under control. Just let these people get on with their work.'

'You know where Sam is?' I retorted, to remind him that I had some official standing there.

Mark looked me up and down with undisguised hostility, then spat thoughtfully between my legs.

'I don't know anyone by that name,' he said.

This was the point at which I decided to remove my unwelcome presence and explore the island. There was still no sign of Sam when I got back, so I went to hole up in my room until he appeared.

At one end of the hall, four men were gathered around the TV watching a fuzzy video featuring a woman who claimed, as far as I could make out, to be an alien who had been sent to earth to foster relationships between humans and other inhabitants of the universe and had taken over the body of a 'terrestrial' who had died in an accident. It seemed to me that in her position I'd have chosen a classier body than the pudgy, zit-ridden, bad-hair one she'd opted for, but maybe aliens see these things differently.

At the dining table, three children were watching a woman hold up flashcards with the names and pictures of animals. As I passed by, I recognized her as the one who had caught my eye the night before. I made a detour and went up to them.

'Hi there!' I said. 'You all look very busy.'

The children, two boys and a girl aged about six or seven, eyed me solemnly. I thought they looked scared.

'We're learning to read,' the woman said. 'Aren't we, guys?'

She was wearing a man's shirt, open at the neck, and jeans. I could see her breasts moving slightly as she breathed.

'Yes, Andrea,' the children chorused.

'That's great,' I said. 'I wish you'd teach me some time.'

The woman's brow creased in a small frown.

'You don't know how to read?'

She didn't seem terribly surprised.

'Yes, but I only read writing,' I explained.

'What else is there?'

I waved theatrically.

'Looks. Portents. The future.'

The ghost of a smile appeared on her lips. By daylight, she looked older than she had the night before. Her figure was attractive, her face pretty enough but unremarkable. I still couldn't understand why she fascinated me so much. Just as she appeared to be about to say something, a door opened at the far end of the room and Sam appeared. The children immediately rose to their feet.

'Good morning, Los,' they chanted in unison.

'Hi, kids!' he called out breezily.

He stopped for a moment to exchange a few words with one of the men watching TV. Then he caught sight of me, broke off his conversation and strode over.

'How you doing, man? Sleep all right?'

'Fine. I was just admiring the old school-house scene.'

He narrowed his eyes, as though realizing for the first time what was going on at the table.

'Oh yeah, we home-school here,' he said. 'Can't schlep them over to Friday every day.'

'What?'

'Friday Harbor. That's the nearest school. Nearest stores, everything. But Andrea here does an OK job. It's legal in this state, lots of people do it. You can buy kits and stuff.'

He waved towards the door.

'C'mon, let's take a walk. We've got lots to talk about.'

I shot Andrea a quick glance, but she was already bent over the textbook, her short brown hair concealing her face. I followed Sam out of the hall and across the compound, where he responded with nods and smiles to the greetings of the people we encountered. Like the night before, everyone seemed excessively pleased to see him, hanging with childish eagerness on his slightest word or gesture.

'You're sure popular around here,' I remarked.

He smiled smugly.

'I'm the landlord. They've got to keep me happy.'

'How do you mean?'

'I own the place, Phil. They don't get along with me, they're out of here.'

I stopped and looked at him.

'You own this whole island?'

Sam nodded casually. I stared at him in genuine amazement. If he was trying to impress me, he'd sure found the hot button.

'But it must have cost a fortune!' I gasped. 'Where did you get the money?'

He smiled.

'Didn't cost me a cent.'

This was the familiar old Sam, being mysterious in order to provoke further questions which would cast him as the source of wisdom and me as the humble seeker after truth. I decided to back off and let him make the first move. After all, he was the one who'd said that we had lots to talk about.

The shoreline was visible by now, a stony beach surrounded by smooth planes of inclined rock. Small waves surged in, teasing the pebbles, while tall grave firs looked on like parents watching their children at play. I felt again the sense of joyful tranquillity which had overwhelmed me on my walk.

'It's so beautiful!' I exclaimed.

Sam nodded like a teacher whose student has given the correct answer.

'I knew you'd get it, Phil,' he said. 'It took a leap of faith, but I knew. Some of the others were opposed to having you come here, but I overruled them. Everything is coming together.'

He looked me in the eye.

'Amazing things will happen to you here, Phil. Things you

wouldn't believe if I told you.'

This was too gushy for me. I decided to get back to solid ground.

'Those people who didn't want me to come, I take it they include Mark.'

I told him about our confrontation by the woodpile. Sam smiled and nodded.

'Don't let Mark get to you,' he said. 'He's basically an OK guy, although he's kind of in-your-face sometimes. But I can handle him.'

He turned off down a steep path cutting through the trees to the left. Eventually it came out on a rocky bluff, where we had to scramble down, using a series of knobs and ledges worn smooth by many hands and feet. At the bottom was a small cove where a slab of basalt protruded out over a natural pool formed by two curving lines of rock. On the other side of a stretch of open water, only a few hundred yards away, rose the precipitous, fir-covered flank of another island.

'You can swim here in the summer,' Sam said, pointing to the pool. 'The water comes in at high tide and then gets trapped and warmed by the sun. We go skinny-dipping here a lot.'

He sat down on the smooth rock, his long thin legs extended in front of him. In addition to his regulation work shirt and jeans, he was wearing a pair of fancy sports shoes with inch-thick soles and the logo of a basketball player.

'Wow, cool shoes!' I remarked in a teen-speak voice.

Sam glanced at them indifferently.

'Oh, yeah. Russ bought a pair, and I said I liked them, so he got me some.'

He said it casually, as though this was standard operating procedure.

'On account of you being the landlord and he has to keep you happy?' I queried with a touch of irony.

Sam shrugged.

'I was just kidding about that.'

'So who does own the place?'

'No, I was kidding about them having to suck up to me.

Everything they do is done out of love, man. No one lays any power trips around here. We're all in this thing together.'

He gazed out across the water at the island opposite for a moment, then began to talk in a slow, steady voice, as though reading a speech.

'The island used to belong to a group of Theosophists. This was back in the twenties. Then Theosophy went out of fashion. The place was deserted for years, then in the sixties it was bought by this woman from Seattle. She was working in the naval base at Bremerton, in the kitchens, and one day she put her hand through the meat grinder and lost two fingers. I happen to know she was stoned out of her skull at the time, but she sued the federal government and used the money to buy this place.'

'So where do you come in?'

'Well, what she did, she got all her hippie friends together and they all came over here to set up a commune. That was everyone's dream at the time, right? Get away from it all, live off the land, all that shit. Well, that lasted as long as those things usually did, and then people began drifting away. In the end Lisa, that was her name, was hanging on here pretty well alone.'

I looked out over the reach of open water glinting and shifting in the raw sunlight. Gulls swooped and plunged for fish, efficient feeding machines, aerial rodents.

'By then she wanted out too,' Sam went on, 'only it turned out this place wasn't so easy to sell. There are a couple of hundred islands round here, but only some of them have a good supply of water, and even then there are shortages all the time. This place had enough for the Theosophists and the hippies and guys like us, but not enough to support people who want showers and washing machines and dishwashers and jacuzzis. So Lisa found that having invested all her dough in this place, she was kind of stuck with it.'

'I still don't see where you come in,' I said.

Sam grinned broadly.

'I got in, that's how,'

He made a circle with the thumb and first finger of his left hand and inserted the forefinger of his right rapidly several times.

'We fell in love,' he added in a tone of contempt.

I thought of Andrea, of my inexplicable attraction to her. Was I too 'falling in love'? How lame the phrase sounds, how hackneyed and banal! We need more and better words to describe the experience, a vocabulary as rich as the one that some cultures have for different varieties of snow. Presumably the reason we don't is the same in both cases: an inability to distinguish, a feeling that neither snow nor love is important enough to our lives to warrant that degree of discrimination.

'Lisa and I had a friend in common,' Sam explained. 'That woman who was teaching the class? I got to know her while I was hanging out in Seattle. Andrea used to spend a few months out here in the summer, but she had a job teaching back on the mainland. She introduced me to Lisa, who used to come over every now and then. It started off as a straight mercy fuck, but Lisa thought I was the hottest thing to come down the pike in a long time, and I was kind of at loose ends myself then. Next thing I knew we were married.'

'Oh, so it's really your wife who owns the place,' I said. 'Which one is she?'

I was irrationally furious at the discovery that Sam had known Andrea, and presumably slept with her.

'She's dead.'

He pointed to the island on the other side of the strait.

'She tried to swim across to Orcas. Lisa was a good swimmer, but the currents around here are very treacherous.'

The sun had disappeared behind the firs massed on the heights behind us, and the air suddenly felt cold.

'I know things haven't been easy for you recently,' Sam said in an almost inaudible voice. 'But soon you will regain everything you have lost, and more besides.'

I stared at him, wondering again if he knew about David.

'Speaking of loss,' I said, 'why did those kids call you that?'

Sam's irritating little smile reappeared.

'Ah, you noticed that? Well, I guess you should know the

148

answer to that one, Phil.'

'I wouldn't ask if I knew,' I replied shortly.

'You *do* know. But you don't know you know.'

I laughed derisively.

'What the hell is that supposed to mean?'

Sam turned to me, looking me in the eyes.

'You're like all of us, Phil. You know more than you think, but you also know less.'

I sighed impatiently.

'That's gobbledygook, Sam.'

'No, Phil, it's a great truth. A sublime truth.'

He smiled suddenly and slapped me on the arm.

'But just stick around, kid, and pretty soon you'll know it all.'

I'd had enough.

'Sam, listen!'

I paused, trying to find the right words.

'Can we just get something straight? I get the feeling that you guys are into some kind of religious or philosophical thing here. Is that right?'

Sam's eyes left me, gazing out over the stretch of water where his wife had drowned.

'I guess you could put it that way,' he said at last.

'OK. Well, let me just say something. I appreciate you inviting me here, and it would be a great pleasure to spend three or four days in such a beautiful spot. *But* – and it's a big but – you've got to understand that I'm not in the market for any kind of new ideology. I'm not knocking your ideas, whatever they may be. I'm simply saying that I'm not interested in signing up for anything. If you can accept that, I'll be happy to stay. If not, it would probably be better for me to leave right now.'

Sam looked at me with a frown.

'Chill, man!' he said with a slightly forced laugh. 'No one's asking you to do a damn thing except veg out and enjoy yourself.'

'Great. And I'll have to leave on Wednesday or Thursday in any case. My car's at that house on the mainland. Lenny took the keys. Does he live there or what?'

There was a slight pause before Sam answered.

'He's staying there this week, while Russ and the other guy are away, case they need to call in.'

'But there must be a phone here,' I replied. 'You called me in Everett, remember?'

Sam looked uncomfortable for the first time. Then he shrugged.

'I've got a cellular, but we try not to use it too much. You never know who might be listening in.'

I laughed.

'Have you got secrets to hide, then?'

Sam jumped up.

'I better get going,' he said, turning away. 'I've got to choose a reading for this afternoon. You stay if you want.'

I got to my feet.

'No, I'll come.'

The truth was, I was already looking forward to seeing Andrea again.

I had been faithful to Rachael for the ten years we had been together, and since her death I had not thought of finding someone else. This was not a question of high-minded morality. I was simply out of practice. Without realizing it, I had sealed myself off from contact with the other sex. I had invested all I had in one relationship, and lost everything. The idea of starting all over again seemed more trouble than it was worth.

But Andrea had somehow penetrated the cocoon of indifference and sloth with which I'd surrounded myself, and had done so – this is what really disturbed me – without even trying. There was no evidence whatsoever to suggest that she was remotely interested in me. On the contrary, she was almost certainly fixed up with one of these guys who, for reasons beyond my comprehension, were kissing up to Sam. Nevertheless, for reasons equally beyond my comprehension, she had gotten to me, and before I left I wanted to know why.

I was also mildly curious to know exactly what kind of scam Sam was working. I had no doubt that it was one. If he'd bothered to get married to this Lisa, who must have been quite a lot older than him if she'd bought the place back in the sixties, it could only be because he knew that she was sitting on a nice chunk of real estate. This indicated a degree of financial planning I wouldn't have suspected in Sam, even if he couldn't have known that Lisa would be out of the picture so soon. But the way he'd parlayed this attractive but unsaleable asset into a permanent meal ticket was even more impressive. I didn't know who was grabbing the check for the cost of keeping the operation going, but it clearly wasn't Sam. Probably the followers he'd recruited had to go and work on the mainland every so often, and hand over their earnings to him. Maybe that was what this Russ was doing. That would explain why Sam had seemed reluctant to talk about it.

But what were they getting in return? It didn't have to be anything very much. Most of the people I'd seen so far struck me as classic high-school drop-outs. Nevertheless, Sam had to be offering them something they felt they couldn't get anywhere else, the way they were treating him. Even if it hadn't been for Andrea, I think I would have stayed just out of curiosity, to find out what it was.

At that point, of course, I still thought I had a choice.

Eleven

The moment Russell Crosby saw the venue, he knew it was going to be OK. This was Russ's third time. By now he had a feel for these things.

It was a one-storey frame house with a deep veranda located on a backstreet a couple of miles south of the city centre, in an area called Pittsburgh. The main drag was called McDaniel, which ran all the way up to Peachtree. The time he went to scope it out, Russ got off the bus at the next neighbourhood up, Mechanicsville. *That* was what he had been dreading: a mix of late-stage urban decay and scorched-earth redevelopment, housing projects ranked like prison blocks on a bare hillside. There was no place to hide, no reason for whitey to be there, and you didn't need to read the spray-paint to know who ran the streets after dark.

Russell had grown up in rural Washington, and had never actually seen a black person except on TV until he was fifteen and went into Seattle with some buddies. Even now, twenty years later, he had hardly had any dealings with them, good or bad. Nevertheless, the idea of going into a black neighbourhood terrified him. Blacks were tough and proud and mean and *different*. You could never be sure what they were thinking or what they were going to do. The only thing you knew was that a hell of a lot of them had learned the hard way how to look after themselves.

But above all what scared him was the question of visibility. Russell knew he shouldn't be thinking this way, as though something other than God's will might be done. That was heresy. But looking at it from a strictly practical point of view, the success of the operations they had undertaken so far depended to a large extent on a profile so low as to be invisible. They came and went virtually unseen by anyone other than their victims. No one else noticed them at the time, and there was no one left to remember them afterwards. But Russell knew that no white person could be invisible in a place like Mechanicsville. It didn't matter that people had never seen you before and would never see you again. They already knew you. You were the enemy. There was nowhere you could go without being watched, nothing you could do without it being an object of interest.

So Pittsburgh came as a big relief. It was predominantly black, but with a way different feel, an old-fashioned neighbourhood with a certain battered charm and a lush, green look which was almost rural. On McDaniel there were a couple of jerry-built food stores with heavy wire-mesh over the windows. There were no national franchises at this end of town, no big-name brands or fancy advertising. Hand-written posters spelt out the price of fatback and beer and beans. There were also two places of worship, the Freedom Holiness Church of God in Christ and the African Methodist Free Church of Full Gospel.

That was down in the valley, on the flat. On either side, the cross-streets ran steeply up, the blacktop pitted with cracks and potholes. The houses were all small, a few barely more than shacks. All were of wood, some of it unpainted. Most had big porches with beat-up chairs set out and screens to keep out the bugs. But the basic look was country: mature trees laden with an abundance of verdure, gauds of foliage spilling out and over every surface, explosions of crêpe myrtle, nature gone nuclear. A pall of kudzu vine had transformed some of the lower trees and shrubs into fantastic shapes, castles and monsters.

Kids of all ages were running loose in the street. A skinny old black guy with braces and a cane stopped to chat to a white-trash mother with three children in a stroller built for one. A real sharp dude in a powder-blue suit with a purple shirt and white slip-on shoes was having a loud argument with a spectacular woman with a peach-shaped ass sheathed in a tight white dress which showed the outline of her panties. Behind a picket fence, two toddlers played in the copper-red earth.

Russ moseyed around a little, just to get the general feel, then walked down Carson Street itself, just once, and caught the bus back into town. He'd seen enough to know that it was going to be OK as far as the location was concerned. But that was only one of his worries. The other was his partner.

It was a big honour, of course, being the one chosen to handle this difficult assignment. By rights, Andy should have come, but after what happened with Dale his nerves were understandably shot. In the end, Rick had proposed Russell. He'd accepted, but with a heavy heart, because he knew that the subject of the initiation was Pat. The problem wasn't just that Pat'd been born in the South, which meant blacks. The problem was Pat himself.

Any doubts he might have had about that were erased when he went down to the Greyhound station on International Boulevard to meet Pat off the bus from St Louis, and the jerk had walked down the steps practically arm-in-arm with some babe he'd picked up. Russell hadn't made the mistake of saying anything then, of course. He'd just strolled across as though heading for another bus himself, barged into Pat and slipped a business card into his hand. The card was from a motel on Ponce de León, a short walk from the hotel where he himself was staying. On the back of the card, Russell had drawn a map showing how to get there from the bus station.

The idea was that Pat should go straight to the motel, check in and wait for Russell to call him. Instead, the stupid ditz hung around the Greyhound station for about ten minutes while the girl worked the payphone, and then they both went inside and sat there for another half hour over a couple of shakes. Next thing, they started sucking face across the table with a fervour that got noticed by plenty of people besides Russ. 'Hey, get a room!' someone murmured. The young lovers were still swapping spit when the waitress came up and said something to them. Pat threw a bill on the table and they headed outside, climbed into a cab and drove off together.

Russell would have aborted the whole operation there and then, except that he was worried about the effect that two fuckups in a row might have on morale. If people got the idea that they were on a losing streak, it would get harder and harder to turn the thing around. His next thought was to bone Pat in the ear but good when he called the motel later, but he thought better of that too. Pat's breach of discipline had been so serious that it had to be dealt with face to face. He didn't say a word about it on the phone, just set up the meeting for that evening and then headed off to check out the target.

Russell had chosen the location for the meeting with care. It was right downtown, just east of Five Points, a big chain pizza house with seating for over a hundred on two levels. In the early evening, the place was pretty busy with a youngish crowd that they'd fit right into. Turnover was fast, service impersonal. He got to the place early, found a table in a corner and ordered a slice of pizza and a coffee. He'd finished both and accepted a refill before Pat showed, twenty minutes late.

'Kind of got lost,' he said by way of greeting. 'Went the wrong way on the subway, ended up in some suburb way to hell up north.'

Pat looked like a male hooker in his battered leather jacket, tight jeans and a huge Western-style belt. When the waitress came around, he ordered a whole pizza with pepperoni, double cheese and extra anchovies, plus a side of rings, a large Coke and a Caesar. Maxed-out as she was, that got her attention.

'That supper just for you, honey, or should I fix a plate for your friend?'

'I'm OK,' said Russell quickly.

'He could use a little meat on his bones at that,' said the waitress, glancing at Pat's skinny torso.

When she'd gone, Russell gave Pat a cold, hard look.

'You're something else, you know that? We can't even go to a fucking pizza house without you coming on like the most unforgettable person anyone's ever met!'

Russ expected Pat to be crushed by this. Instead, he looked offended.

'Hey, what's the problem? I'm hungry, OK?'

'I bet! You've been up all night slamming body with that 'ho you snared on the bus, right?'

Pat tried to speak, but Russell overrode him.

'You know the rules! No contact beyond what's absolutely necessary. I took Andy to Kansas, we spoke maybe ten words to anyone the whole time we were out! But you? You meet some fresh nugs on the road, next thing you're playing tonsil hockey in the middle of a crowded bus station! Then you take off in a cab together, and now she's shacked up with you, right? Even the geeks at that dirtball motel are going to remember that!'

'Maintain, Russ,' Pat warned as the waitress approached with his Coke.

His patronizing tone was just about the last straw. The way he was talking, you'd think Russ was the one in danger of flipping out.

'I guess that scene at the bus station was maybe notso-hotso,' Pat resumed in a more conciliatory tone. 'But you're making way too big a deal of all this. Cindy doesn't know a thing about me. My name, where I'm from, what I'm doing here – nothing.'

'Yeah, right! She only knows what you look like, when you arrived, where from, where you've been staying … '

Pat leaned across the table.

'Don't be such a worry wart, Russ! We're doing God's will here. What can go wrong?'

Russell squirmed and looked away. The little shit had endrun him. Although he knew that the outcome was in God's hands, Russell couldn't help seeing the thing in human terms. They had a job to do, and his partner was acting like a flake. And one thing he'd learned from his previous two experiences was that you had to be able to depend absolutely on your partner. Because if he screwed up, it was *your* ass that was going to be in a sling. But he couldn't admit that, and Pat knew he couldn't, which is why he was sitting there giving him that slimy grin.

'I've been to the house,' Russell said shortly. 'We go in tomorrow.'

That knocked some of the sass out of Pat.

'Tomorrow?'

He sounded shocked.

'No point in hanging around,' said Russell. 'The sooner it's done, the sooner we can get out of here.'

Pat nodded slowly two or three times.

'How many … How many are there?'

'No idea,' Russ replied brutally. 'I didn't see anyone home when I walked by. Maybe one, maybe a dozen. God will decide.'

He accompanied this final phrase with a telling glance.

'Sure,' said Pat. His voice was still unsteady. 'Only I was expecting a little more time. I only just got here.'

The waitress came with Pat's food. He sat there, picking at it idly. His appetite seemed to have deserted him.

'So where do we meet?' he asked.

Russell outlined times, routes and places. Then he went through it all again, and got Pat to repeat it back to him.

'There's a discount clothing store one block north of the bus station,' he continued. 'Go in there tomorrow morning and buy yourself a black suit, white shirt, dark necktie, pair of plain black shoes, nothing fancy. I'm handing you a hundred and fifty bucks under the table now.'

Pat reached down and took the roll of bills.

'What if it comes to more than that?' he asked.

'Then you bought the wrong outfit. We're talking Dacron, Ohio, here. The cheap nerd look.'

'But what's the deal?'

Russ gave him another of those looks. He was back in charge now.

'The deal is that you get to do what I say, when I say, and keep your mouth shut. OK?'

They went over the details once more, then Russell got up, leaving Pat to deal with his cooling pizza and soggy onion rings. He leant back over the table.

'Oh, and this Cindy … '

'She's history,' Pat said, a little too quickly. He had obviously been expecting the question for some time. But Russell knew better than to contest something he couldn't control.

'Let's hope she feels the same way about you,' he said.

Despite the implied threat, he had no serious doubts about this. The very fact that getting laid had acted like such a drug on

Pat's ego proved he was a wimp in the sack, Russ reckoned. Look at the way he dressed. The bigger the belt buckle, the smaller the dick.

Russell walked back up Peachtree, passing an old flatiron office block, the winos and addicts in the park, the chic strip with its convention hotels. The air was clammy and still. By this time tomorrow it would all be over. It'll be all right, he told himself, just like the other two times. Neither of them had been a smooth ride either. The baby had been the worst. Russ thought he'd prepared himself for anything that might come up, but the idea he might have to do it to a baby had never entered his head.

Rick had seen him through that one. After what he'd seen and done in the war, to say nothing of his own uniquely challenging initiation, Rick had been able to talk him through the whole experience. The gooks were so different, he explained, you could learn to kill them easy. With spectres it was a lot trickier, because they *looked* just like anyone else. You needed faith. That's what the whole thing was about, a test of faith.

But it wasn't until Dale Watson had failed that test that Russell realized just how lucky he'd been. In the end he'd done fine, put the gun to the kid's head and pulled the trigger as sweet as if they were back in practice. Even that noise from the basement later, as they were leaving, hadn't freaked him out. He'd been sure there was someone else in the house, but Rick kept real cool, told him to check downstairs, and sure enough it was just a piece of wood that had fallen off the furnace housing.

The next time out, he'd been in charge. That had been a whole lot tougher, but he'd still managed to justify Rick's commendation after his initiation in Renton: 'This guy is the real deal.' First of all they'd had to get there. Kansas City wasn't as far as Atlanta, but it still meant days on buses. It wasn't a question of the money. They could have taken a plane and stayed at the best hotel in town, but that would mean passing through the hands of endless service personnel, any of whom might remember them. It would mean presenting documents and credit cards, and ending up on a computer somewhere. It was safer to travel poor and anonymous, down in the uncharted, free-flowing depths where no one cared where you were coming from or what you were doing, or even whether the name you gave was your own.

The hotel Russell was staying at in Atlanta was far from being the best in town, and by midnight he began to wonder whether it might not have been better to take the slight risk involved, pay extra and get a good night's sleep. Nothing too fancy, maybe a HoJo, something like that. He'd had a lot of trouble adjusting to the climate ever since he arrived, but so far he'd been able to dismiss this as a matter of no importance, a trivial local particularity like the way Southerners spoke. Now it took its revenge.

The night was sticky, hot, damp and airless. In theory the hotel had air-conditioning, but all the unit in Russ's room produced was a flimsy draught only slightly cooler than the air in the room itself. Being from the Northwest, Russ automatically opened the window. That was a big mistake. The whole room started throbbing with the noise of traffic on the interstate right below the hotel, while a syrupy influx of moisture-laden air instantly pushed the conditions from the uncomfortable to the unbearable. The electric fan did nothing but stir the miasma around.

Calling the spook at the desk didn't help either. Russ hesitated before taking this step, not wanting to impress himself on the guy's mind. Some chance. The clerk's mind was tuned to a whole other wavelength.

'No outlet!' he told Russ when he phoned to ask if the AC could be turned up.

'A vent?' Russ replied, not getting it. 'Sure there's one. It's just it doesn't condition the air worth a damn, you know what I mean? I'm like suffocating up here is what I'm saying. And I've got a big day tomorrow, so I need my sleep.'

'Limited sight distance!' said the clerk, and hung up.

On top of everything else, Russ had a recurrence of the vicious migraine which had tormented him for so many years. When he was accepted into the Sons of Los, it had ceased, as though to prove the power of the Secret. Now it was back, and he was powerless to deal with it. He'd given up carrying painkillers since the migraines had left him, and even if he found a drug-store open this time of night, the stuff they sold without a pre-scription wasn't worth shit.

He tried everything: a cold shower, push-ups, light on, light off, lying down, sitting up. He even tried reading some verses from the scriptures he'd brought with him. Nothing made any difference to the particle of agony lodged in his skull. It wasn't just the pain that drove him wild but the prospect of the next day. He'd need to be at his very best, and the way things were going he'd be about his worst. Laid out on his bed, the raptor pecking at his brain, he thought about Andy's initiation in Kansas, replaying it like the video he'd made at the time.

Jesus, that had been tough! They'd done everything right. The woman had come to the door, Andy'd shown the gun and forced her back inside. Far as they knew, there was just the old guy in the wheelchair and her to deal with. They'd gagged him with a patch of duct tape and tied his wrists to the arms of the chair the same way, then trussed the woman. How were they to know there was a guy painting the kitchen? He'd opened the door, tak-en one look and dodged back inside. Luckily there was no lock on the door and no phone in there. But when they went in after him, the guy had thrown the contents of his paint tray at them before Andy could take him down, and the very next moment the old bitch next door starts hammering at the front door!

Realizing they couldn't kill her too had been the worst. It would have been so easy, a shot to the skull and another corpse to add to the pile on the floor. But she hadn't been in the desig-nated house, so they had to keep her alive, same as Lenny and his initiate in St Louis had been forced to do with the security guard they had to con to get into the high-rise in the first place. There wasn't a damn thing they could do except tie him up and gag him, even though he'd seen them both and could identify them later.

He and Andy had backed the woman into her own pad, then barricaded her in the bathroom by pushing a big fridge up against the door. They'd taken a coat and scarf to cover the stains on Andy, who'd caught most of the paint, then coolly walked out and waited for the bus while the cops swarmed around like wasps around a barbecue. It had taken a lot of nerve, knowing the woman might identify them at any moment. But everything had gone smoothly. The whole secret was not trying to hide. No one would believe that the men who'd just wiped out a household in cold blood would be standing at a bus stop just a few blocks away.

They would use the same scenario here. Where everyone thought cars, taking the buses was like putting on a cloak of invisibility. Sometimes, like Russ's initiation, they couldn't do that. That time they'd gone on bicycles, bought for cash from a shop with a high turnover and later abandoned to be stolen. But around Seattle was different. Anyone on a bike in this part of Atlanta would stick out a mile. They would take separate buses, so they wouldn't be seen together until they reached the scene. And afterwards they'd leave the same way, Pat direct north-bound, Russ heading south to the terminus at Hapeville, where he could pick up MARTA back to his hotel.

He lay on his bed of pain, clutching his head in the dense, sultry atmosphere, trying to hold the whole thing together. It was all there, he just had to contain it, to stop it from slipping away. Plus he must remember to make that call home. After what happened with Dale, they were going to be real anxious if they didn't hear. He'd do it right after he called Pat.

After a night of bloodless torture, the migraine suddenly abated just as the sky outside was starting to grow light. Utterly exhausted, Russell collapsed, hugging his pillow damp with sweat. When he awoke, it was full daylight and the room was vibrating with the noise of a demolition project in progress on a neighbouring block. Russ looked at his watch. It was twenty past ten. He reached for the phone, dialled the number of the motel. It rang and rang, then someone picked up.

'Uh huh?'

A woman.

'This 118?'

'Uh huh.'

There was a silence.

'Who *is* this?' the woman demanded.

Russ hung up. So his instinct last night had been right. Pat had lied about Cindy. There was no telling what she might have found out about him, and how much more she might have guessed. She would have asked questions, the way women always do, and Pat was a lousy liar.

He dressed and walked seven blocks down Peachtree to Macy's, where he bought an outfit identical to the one he had specified for Pat the night before. He also bought a plain black suitcase. Putting the other purchases in this, he returned to the hotel, picking up a Big Mac and fries to eat in his room.

That afternoon he slept some more, a fitful, oppressive drowse infested by dreams so real it was like watching clips from a movie. The last featured a ringing telephone, and the noise of the bell was so loud and peremptory that Russell woke up, convinced that someone was calling him. The phone by his bed was silent. He checked his watch and realized that it was time to go.

He showered and changed into the clothes he had bought, then checked his appearance in the mirror. The hair was maybe a little long, but he would pass. He took the Gideon Bible from the drawer by the bed and put it in the empty suitcase, along with a copy of *The Watchtower* and some leaflets with titles like 'Can the Dead Harm the Living?' A guy had been handing them out some place he'd changed buses. Russell had been about to tell him to go piss up a rope when he'd had an idea.

Religion was big down in the South. Everyone was into it, whites and blacks alike. So he'd got chatting with the guy and come away with a wad of literature which they would put to good use that evening. No one would think twice about a couple of guys in suits pitching their particular brand of redemption door to door. All they had to do was visit a couple of houses on the street first, then hit the target. 'Hi, how are you folks doing today? We're calling on people in this neighbourhood to tell them about God's plans for you.' Which was true enough, except they weren't planning to *tell* them.

At six forty-five, Russell checked his preparations for the last time, picked up the suitcase and rode the elevator down to the lobby. Russ gave the night clerk a curt nod. An extravagant smile split open the man's shining face.

'Wrong way!' he breathed.

Russ walked out on to the street, pocketing his key. The bus stop was three blocks away. He walked at a steady pace, occasionally shifting the suitcase from one hand to the other. It was pretty heavy. As well as the Jehovah's Witness material, there were the two revolvers, fully loaded, plus a box of spare ammunition, the handcuffs, a roll of duct tape pre-cut into four-inch lengths, and the camcorder to tape the ceremony.

The bus was almost empty. Once south of Alabama Street it drove fast, hardly stopping, through a wasteland of car lots and small industrial businesses. By the time they bumped over the railroad crossing on McDaniel, Russ was the only passenger. It was only then that he realized, too late, the meaning of the unconscious summons which had woken him. He had forgotten to call home. He had been so disturbed by missing Pat that morning, and still more by finding Cindy there in his place, that it had completely slipped his mind. Oh well, he'd call tomorrow with the news that the operation had been a success. They wouldn't freak out if they didn't hear from him for one day.

He got off at the stop he'd used that afternoon, crossed the road and walked up the street opposite. It was even hotter and stickier here than it had been downtown, and the air was laced with patches of exotic scent. Cicadas grated away in the undergrowth over a bass section of whinnying frogs. Russ felt as though he'd stumbled into one of those old jungle movies they had on TV about three in the morning.

He climbed the hill, gripping the suitcase in a palm already damp with sweat. Quite a few people seemed to be out on their porches. He hadn't noticed them at first, mere shadowy presences in the pervading darkness. It was only the soft murmur of voices, punctuated by the occasional throaty laugh, which gave them away. But once he started looking, he realized they were everywhere. No one said anything as he passed, but he knew they were watching him.

This was something he hadn't expected. Why the hell couldn't they have drawn a place like that suburb where Pat got lost the night before, an all-white neighbourhood where everyone homed in, clustering around the electronic hearth in their widely spaced, secluded properties? He'd much rather have gone in there, even if it had a security system and those little metal tags in the lawn marked 'Armed Response'. But you didn't get to choose. They'd performed the calculations the usual way, and this was the address that came up. It was meant to be, so it would be. He tried to comfort himself with this thought.

When he rounded the corner of the block, near the top of the hill, a figure detached itself from the still torrent of vines which had engulfed a retaining wall on the other side of the street. Russ found himself wishing that he'd taken his gun out of the case. Then something about those jerky, uncoordinated movements reassured him that this was one of his own kind. A moment later he recognized his partner.

'You got the piece?' Pat asked him.

'Piece?' Russell queried vaguely.

'The gun, man! C'mon, let's go!'

Pat was transformed, taut and wired like one of life's natural go-to guys. Despite his narbo outfit, the suit a size too small by the looks of it, you could sense the energy he was giving off. Just being around him made Russell feel woozy from lack of sleep, stale air and too much thinking. He opened the suitcase and handed Pat one of the revolvers, pocketing the other himself.

'We'll cruise by a couple of the other houses first,' he said. 'Set up our cover.'

Pat waved impatiently.

'Fuck that, man! Let's just do it! Get in, get out, don't screw around.'

His air of urgency was so strong that Russ hesitated, a moment too long to insist.

'OK,' he murmured.

It was all wrong, he knew, letting the initiate lead like this. On the other hand, Pat's mood might change again at any moment, leaving him with a cowering wimp on his hands. Better to ride the moment.

164

They set off along the side-street running parallel to McDaniel. Up here there didn't seem to be so many people out on the porches. In fact many of the houses looked abandoned. Maybe they were going to clear the area and put up more projects. Pat strode along, humming some staccato melody under his breath. Russell could hardly keep up. He glanced curiously at his partner.

'You been drinking?'

'I had a shot with a greeny back,' Pat replied carelessly. 'Man, that stuff sure works, you don't use it all the time.'

'That's way out of line!' Russell snapped. 'You know we're not supposed to do drink or drugs when we're … '

'Hey, what is this? The floggings will continue until morale improves? Don't treat me like a little kid.'

'Hold it right there!'

Russell gripped his partner's arm and pulled him around.

'You want me to call this whole thing off right now?'

Pat shook his head quickly.

'OK! Then remember I'm in charge here. I don't want to go down because you're too smockered to stick to the game-plan.'

They rounded the corner into Carson Street. 322 was the sixth house on the left. Russell opened the suitcase again. The copy of *The Watchtower* was lying right on top, but the pamphlets seemed to have wriggled down to the back somewheres.

'Hey!' said Pat.

The beam of light falling on the suitcase from the streetlamp behind was suddenly cut off.

'Hand it over, motherfucker!'

Russell straightened up, still holding the magazine. There were three of them, no more than fourteen or fifteen years old by the looks of it, all black. The one who had spoken had a body like a barrel. He was wearing a StarTrek T-shirt and a pair of jeans which looked two sizes too big even for him. He and one of the others had pistols, the third a knife.

'We're just children of God,' Russell found himself saying, holding up *The Watchtower* like a sign. 'We're spreading the word of the Lord in this neighbourhood.'

The squat guy waved his chunky snub-barrelled automatic.

'I don't give a fuck who you are, honky! Hand over your shit or your ass is history!'

That was all they'd needed to do, Russell realized a moment later, when it was too late to do anything. Just hand over their wallets and watches and the suitcase and let the three youths run off with them. Instead, Pat pulled his pistol and shot the guy in the chest and stomach.

'Christ Almighty!' cried the other gunman, a skinny kid in tight red pants and a basketball jersey.

Russell could have taken him there and then, but he hesitated a second too long, knowing he wasn't empowered to kill them. There was a flash of steel, then a grinding sound as the knife hit one of his ribs. Another shot, much louder, sent Pat spinning away, his face amazed. Then something huge hit Russell harder than he had ever been hit before. He tasted blood, mixed in with the dirt of the street. There were other sounds, other sensations, but he had no names for them. It didn't matter. Pretty soon they faded, like everything else.

Twelve

At that point, of course, I still thought I had a choice. Not just about staying or going, or even falling in love, but about things like how I spent my time. So I was disconcerted to find that, like all the others, I was expected to attend a lecture on the poetry of William Blake every afternoon.

The lectures were given by Sam. That first one lasted two and three-quarter hours, and seemed even longer at the time. I learned later that they often *were* longer, particularly when things threatened to fall apart. The one Sam had given on the day after the news about Dale Watson came through apparently lasted well over six hours, starting right after lunch and going on until well after dark. I didn't understand then, of course, that Sam was struggling to retain control, and that his laboured exposition of Blake's so-called 'prophetic books' was merely a means to this end. This was just one of many things I didn't understand.

My only previous contact with Blake's work had been in a class I took at college. Like a lot of people back then, I'd been seduced by the idea that Blake was an acid-head born ahead of his time. All that stuff about seeing the universe in a grain of sand, we'd been there, done that. Hell, we'd seen it in an empty Coke bottle, a crumpled cigarette packet, a capsized cockroach. We were old hands at relative reality, and although Blake had never actually dropped himself (but it was hard to score good shit back then) and tended to maunder on at times (but it could have been really neat if Pink Floyd had set it to music), we decided in a slightly patronizing way to add the old buffer to our gallery of proto-hippies like Huxley, Hesse and the rest. We knew where he was coming from. It also didn't hurt that the professor who taught the class was young and hip and, according to the student guide, graded generously.

As I said earlier, it was there that I had first run into Sam. We wrote our final papers together over a thirty-six-hour period, with the help of twelve tabs of high-grade amphetamine we had pooled our money to score, knowing we would never get the damn things finished any other way. Sam managed to scrape by with a passing grade, although only after I had gone through his paper and suggested numerous changes and additions. It was therefore all the more of a shock to see him stride into the hall after lunch that afternoon and launch into a lengthy exegesis on a passage from *Jerusalem* in front of the assembled company. There were nineteen of them in all, six men and thirteen women, ranging in age from the mid-forties to a girl who looked no more than sixteen, if that. So I was doubly chagrined to discover that the one person I wanted to see, and if possible sit next to, was not there.

For some reason, Andrea didn't appear. No one remarked on her absence, and I didn't know anyone well enough to ask where she was. This was a bitter blow. She hadn't been at lunch either, and I had been counting on seeing her at the lecture, given that attendance was apparently obligatory. That was certainly the impression I had got from Mark when he approached me while I was finishing up my bowl of Rice-a-Roni.

'Right after this we have the reading. Stick around. Maybe you'll learn something.'

'It's never too late, they say,' I replied lightly.

His hard, glazed gaze transfixed me.

'Some people, it's too late when they're *born*.'

Despite this heavy hint, the only reason I stayed was in hopes of seeing Andrea. Whatever Mark might say, Sam clearly had the last word, and he had told me that morning that I didn't have to do anything except 'veg out and enjoy myself'. But I stuck around, and of course Andrea didn't show. And once there, wedged in among all the others, I found it impossible to get up and walk out.

Not only did everybody else turn up, but they all stuck it out to the very end, listening attentively in reverential silence. When I was teaching, I'd had a hard enough time getting my students to concentrate for twenty minutes at a stretch on texts with far more to offer than Blake's homespun comic books, with their apocalyptic bombast and jejune mythologizing. Yet Sam had these waifs and strays and drop-outs, not to mention tough sons-of-bitches like Mark, hanging on his every word for almost three hours.

We were seated cross-legged on the floor throughout, as if to dispel any lingering doubts I might have had that Blake was a pain in the ass. Once we had taken our places, Sam strode in, carrying what turned out to be a facsimile edition of Blake's illuminated edition of *Jerusalem*. He was dressed the same way that he had been all morning, but his bearing and presence were very different. He moved in a springy, feline way, and he radiated confidence, knowledge and power.

The session began with a reading:

I see the Four-fold Man. The Humanity in deadly sleep
And its fallen Emanation. The Spectre and its cruel Shadow.
I see the Past, Present and Future, existing all at once
Before me; O Divine Spirit sustain me on thy wings!
That I may awake Albion from his long and cold repose.

Having declaimed these lines in a loud, stagy voice, Sam closed the book like a Bible and looked at us in silence, as though to gauge their effect on us. After a protracted pause, he went on in a deliberately contrasted tone, quiet and husky, as though talking to himself.

'You've listened to the word of God. But have you heard it? Do you understand it? Do you know what it means?'

I glanced at my neighbours. *The word of God*? I was thinking. But none of them appeared to share my consternation.

'DO YOU KNOW WHAT IT MEANS?' Sam screamed suddenly at the top of his voice.

No one answered. I had a terrible urge to say 'Beats my pair of jacks!', but in the circumstances I felt that such levity would be frowned on.

'Of course you don't,' snapped Sam, answering his rhetorical question. 'You don't have the first fucking idea! Even the blowhards out there who are always ready to give attitude about the decisions I make. *Especially* them.'

He fixed Mark with a glare.

'If it wasn't for me, you zit-brains would still be hanging out on some street corner trying to find the truth at the bottom of a quart of Mad Dog Twenty-Twenty. Think about that, next time you dare question the word of Los!'

I remembered the children addressing Sam that morning as 'Los'. When I had asked him why, he'd told me that I should know the answer. At the time, I'd thought he was just being his usual smart-ass self, but now I realized he was right. Los, of course, was one of Blake's allegorical characters. I couldn't remember much about him, except that he was called 'the Eternal Prophet'.

His introductory harangue over, Sam started in on his exposition of the text. This was unconventional, to say the least. 'The Humanity in deadly sleep' supposedly referred to the masses of people living in ignorance of the truth. Commingled with them were 'emanations' and 'spectres', which Sam apparently conceived of as zombie-like creatures of human appearance but lacking a soul. He, Los the Prophet, had an overview of all time, past, present and future, and was engaged on a programme to awaken 'Albion' – the 'Eternal Man' – from his ignorance and thus bring Time to an end.

This, I think, was the gist of Sam's speech. Just like a regular preacher, however, he kept throwing in other snippets of text in an attempt to buttress his position with a show of scriptural authority.

'Blake says of these spectres, "To be all evil, all reversed and for ever dead: knowing and seeing life, yet living not", chapter ten, lines fifty-seven and eight, and again in chapter eight, lines thirteen through eighteen, "My Emanation is dividing and thou my Spectre art divided against me. But mark I will compel thee to assist me in my terrible labours. To beat these hypocritic Selfhoods on the Anvils of bitter Death I am inspired. I act not for myself: for Albion's sake I now am what I am, a horror and an astonishment."

'And in line thirty-five he says, "For I am one of the living: dare not to mock my inspired fury!" Think about it, you guys! Anyone out there who figures just because he knows the truth means he doesn't need to respect discipline and absolute obedience needs to read chapter eleven, lines five through seven, "Striving with Systems to deliver Individuals from those Systems; that whenever any Spectre began to devour the Dead, he might feel the pain as if a man gnawed his own tender nerves." Now you might say, "Huh? Spectres can't feel pain, any more than the dead." Right?

'*Wrong!* These are no ordinary spectres! These are the "cruel Shadows" Blake talks about in our text for today. The truth has been revealed to them, but they have rebelled against Los's System and tried to go their own way. They have been received into the body of Albion and granted the gift of eternal life, but they prefer to "devour the Dead". And their punishment is to be cast out and hunted down, made to "feel the pain as if a man gnawed his own tender nerves".'

And so on. For all Sam's talk of disobedience and rebellion, every single person there crouched docilely on the floor for almost three hours while Sam ranted and raved and swaggered and strutted in front of us, cowing us into submission with his lunatic gloss on Blake's allegory. I tried not to listen, to think of other things, or of nothing, but Sam's voice kept breaking through my defences.

At one point he held up the book he was reading from to show us one of the engraved illustrations, and I suddenly realized why the painted designs on the VW van had seemed so familiar. They were all motifs from Blake's work, airbrushed on to the VW to form a collage. 'Blake is very important,' Sam had told me when we met back in Minneapolis. I was beginning to understand just how important he was to Sam, but the key to the whole charade continued to elude me.

Then, at last, it was over. Sam stormed through a final bout of bullying, exhortatory rhetoric, then abruptly turned and stalked off without another word, disappearing through the same door from which he had emerged that morning, and slamming it behind him. For a moment no one moved, as though they were awaiting permission to dismiss. Then Mark, followed closely by Rick and two other men, got up and everyone started to stir.

I got painfully to my feet and wandered outside. The weather had turned again. A cold wind seethed in the woods all around, and ridges of slowly moving grey cloud covered the sky. I went back inside, put another log on the fire and tried to make sense of what I had just witnessed.

In principle, the set-up seemed simple enough. Sam had created a religion using Blake's work as his bible and casting himself in the role of Los, the prophet. What I didn't understand, no matter which way I twisted it around, was how he had convinced his followers to buy into it. What were they getting out of it, except an obligatory series of lectures from someone whose only distinction was that his interpretation of the subject was even wackier than Blake's own?

Still, what did I care? None of this had anything to do with me, I reminded myself. Meanwhile I decided to solve the more specific mystery of Andrea's whereabouts. I went over to the door through which Sam had disappeared and knocked gently. There was no answer, so I turned the handle and peered in. What I saw was so amazing that I opened the door and went inside.

The dimensions and the construction of the room were all it had in common with the one I had been allocated, or the two next door where Rick and Andy slept. The floor was thickly carpeted, there was a window with curtains, the air was warm and dry, the lighting bright yet muted. But what stood out above all was the quantity and quality of consumer durables on view. There was a Bose home-theatre stereo system right next to a fifty-inch Mitsubishi slimline television. A desk to one side supported an Amerigo multimedia computer with CD-ROM and assorted peripherals, including what looked like a laser printer. A vintage Stratocaster guitar lay on the sofa. The cellular phone Sam had mentioned, an expensive Motorola flip-down model, was on the matching chair opposite. There were shelves and shelves of CDs and video cassettes, and the small amount of vacant wall space was covered in framed colour reproductions of illustrations from the Blake canon.

I stood staring at all this in amazement. I had figured that Sam must be doing all right from whatever scam he had going, but I'd had no idea just how sweet it was. How the hell did he manage to justify this kind of lifestyle when his followers were living in boot-camp conditions all around him?

Although the room was empty, I could hear noises from next door, the kind I associated with someone taking a shower. I wandered over to the shelves and perused Sam's CD collection. This provided another surprise. There was some jazz, and a few reissues of the rock albums we had used to listen to back in Minneapolis, but the bulk of the collection was classical. Wagner was largely represented – there were three complete *Ring* cycles alone – but also Bruckner, Mahler and Shostakovich. I moved on to the videos, but most of them were blank tapes whose labelling – *Andy (Russell): Kansas City* – made no sense to me. I was examining one of these more closely when I happened to glance to my right.

I had been so preoccupied by all the things that were in the room that I had totally overlooked the one thing that *wasn't*: a bed. I'd also forgotten that Sam couldn't be taking a shower, because the water shortage on the island meant that such an amenity was unavailable even to him. The solution to both these puzzles now became clear. While Mark, Rick and Andy had to make do with a single room each, Sam had commandeered an entire wing for his own quarters. The room I had entered was just the first of three in line. In the next I noticed yet more incongruous luxuries, including a pool table and what looked like a cue case mounted on the wall. But my attention was drawn by the third room, at the end of the suite, where Sam stood groaning before a woman on her knees who was enthusiastically blowing him.

Jostling somewhere at the back of my mind was the conviction that the woman was Andrea. *That* explained why she had not attended the reading. She was Sam's personal sex slave and had to remain in his quarters in order to service him as soon as his performance was concluded. I left quickly, closing the door quietly behind me. A group of about half a dozen people were sitting in front of the TV. They all stared at me as I emerged, and I realized that I was still holding the video cassette I had taken from the shelf.

'Hi, guys,' I said as casually as I could, and headed off across the hall to my room. The contrast with the sybaritic conditions I had just left made it seem even more squalid than before. Setting the cassette down on the chest of drawers, which was still full of Mark's clothing, I lay down on the bed and tried to rest. But it was impossible. The more I tried to relax, the more agitated I became. After a few minutes I gave up and returned to the hall.

It was another fifteen minutes before Sam finally emerged. The transformation from his previous appearance could not have been more marked. It was like glimpsing an actor leaving the stage door of a theatre. His charismatic aura had totally vanished. He was one of us again, a mere human, with human needs and frailties.

He saw me sitting by the fireplace and came over.

'How's it going?' he asked dully.

I couldn't make out if his subdued mood was the result of his thespian or sexual exertions.

'Good,' I said. 'Great talk you gave there. Kind of amazed me, though. I never expected to hear you lecturing on William Blake. Back when we took that class together, I recall you saying … '

Sam held a finger to his lips.

'Hey, don't scare the horses!'

I smiled back. For the first time, Sam had made a clear distinction between me and the suckers he was doing such a successful number on. Emboldened by this, I decided to relieve my hurt about the sex scene I had witnessed with a little gentle joshing.

'The only thing I don't get is why Andrea didn't show. How come she gets to play hooky?'

I paused significantly.

'Or is she on some special duty roster?'

I was prepared for Sam to look sheepish. Instead, he shot me a glance I found unnervingly penetrating.

'Andrea? You interested in her?'

'Oh, I'm sure she's already spoken for.'

Sam just shrugged.

'Help yourself. She's no one's squeeze, far as I know. I used to give her a turn once in a while, but now I've got Ellie to take care of that. You met Ellie? Cute little thing. Just turned sixteen, but she's got tits out to here, firm as avocados. Loves to fuck, too. They all do, but the young ones even more. Validates them, see? They're still unsure about this adult stuff, how they fit in, all that shit. They see that look on your face as you cream into them, they know they've just joined the club. Turns them on like crazy.'

He slapped my shoulder.

'Good thinking, Phil! Get yourself a woman. I'd go for Melissa if I were you. Tall blonde number? Used to be a junkie, but she's straight now. Kinda flat-chested, but man, that pussy! Hasn't seen much action, either, since Dale left. That's where I would head first, tell you the truth. But if you got the hots for Andrea, I can fix that up, no prob.'

'Whoa, hold on there!' I cried, trying unsuccessfully to regain the safe ground of masculine bonding. 'All I asked was why she wasn't around for your little pep talk. I didn't say anything about wanting to put any moves on her.'

Sam stood looking down at me. His smile had disappeared. I suddenly realized how dumb it was to think that I could ever find a niche for myself in something as dippy as what was going on here. I had to go, and the sooner the better, before anyone's feelings were hurt.

'Look, I'm sorry,' I told him, getting to my feet, 'I think maybe I'd better be moving on. It's been great to see you again, and this place is certainly interesting, but, you know, it's not really my thing.'

He looked at me in that set, level way he had when he felt challenged.

'You want to go?'

I nodded. He stared at me some more.

'When?'

'Any time tomorrow would be good.'

I had expected protests, but he merely nodded slowly, as though he regretted my decision but understood. Then he turned away.

'I'll see what we can do about that,' he said.

Sam didn't appear at dinner that evening, but Andrea did. She sat opposite me at the table, and kept looking pointedly in my direction. I didn't know how to respond. My main feeling was one of guilt for having shown an interest in her in the first place. If she was as desperate as Sam had suggested, this might loom a lot larger for her than it did for me. But the fact remained that I was leaving the next day, and that I would never see her again. I eventually decided that the only responsible course of action was to ignore her. I finished my meal as quickly as possible and then retired to my room, where I went to bed with a copy of Lewis and Clark's journal of their expedition to the coast in 1804. The account of their harrowing experiences put my little problems in perspective. It also put me to sleep.

I was awakened by the sound of voices. I couldn't distinguish what they were saying, but the tone was angry, a violent clash of wills and egos. Mark's smash-mouth delivery was recognizable enough, as were Sam's frosty responses, but their dialogue was punctuated at intervals by two other voices which I could not identify.

At first I tried to ignore the whole thing and go back to sleep, but a combination of curiosity and anxiety made this impossible. I knew that Mark was in a snit about my presence, and assumed that this must be the cause of the conflict. But in that case why didn't Sam just tell him I was leaving? If there was a problem with this, it was something I needed to know about. I was already uneasily aware that I could not get off the island without Sam's co-operation. The idea of being trapped there against my will, even for another day, seemed intolerable.

I got out of bed and crept to the door. I cautiously turned the handle, opened the door an inch or so and looked out, but the speakers were not in my field of view and I was afraid to draw attention by opening the door any further. Despite the flabby acoustics of the hall, I could hear much of what was being said, particularly when, as was often the case, it was actually being shouted. I was also able to put names to the other two men, Rick and Andy.

In the course of the next ten minutes, I gradually pieced together a few elements of the story. What escaped me was its significance, and above all any clue to why Mark was making such a big deal of it. What it seemed to come down to was that the guy called Russell, who was away, had failed to phone them. The whole thing sounded absurd to me, like Mom and Dad losing it because their twenty-year-old son hadn't called in to tell them what time he'd be home. There was also some talk about the one called Dale. I remembered Sam saying that he had left the group. It was now clear that his departure had created tensions, and that Mark was worried that Russell might go the same way.

'Anything could've happened,' he yelled at one point. 'We can't just sit around here with our thumbs up our butts. We got to find out!'

Sam's reply was too quiet for me to hear, but it evidently defused the situation somewhat.

'OK, it's a deal,' Mark said grudgingly. 'But if we don't hear tomorrow, we got to do something.'

Sam's response was again inaudible.

'Well, I do!' Mark snapped, his old charmarola self again. 'I'll run over to Friday, put in a call to one of the papers, radio station, something. If anything happened, they'll have heard. And they *better* have, or you're fresh out of excuses.'

Sam raised his voice for the first time.

'I have revealed the Secret to you, and raised you up unto eternal life! And what the fuck thanks do I get in return? You guys whining and bitching and scheming and sowing the seed of discord here in Beulah! Sure I was deceived by Dale. We *all* were. I just hope I haven't been deceived by you, Mark! For I am Los, prophet of the true God, and all those who seek to deceive me shall be exposed and cast out into Ulro, where the dead wail night and day!'

With this, Sam stomped off to his quarters on the other side of the hall, slamming the door behind him. Mark, Andy and Rick retired to Rick's room, next to mine, where they continued to talk until well into the night. I heard the drone of their voices through the wall, but it was impossible to make out what they were saying.

I lay awake for hours, trying and failing to make sense of all this.

Thirteen

By the time the uniforms reached the scene, there wasn't a lot that could be done. The black victim lay stretched out in a puddle of blood, his body contorted, scowling like a newborn baby. One of the white guys was dead too, with a hole in his chest you could have set a grapefruit in. The other had a stab wound in the side, and his left shoulder was almost blown apart, but he was still breathing. There was blood all over the sidewalk, soaking into the pages of an outspread copy of *The Watchtower* lying between the bodies.

'Poor guys,' murmured one of the patrolmen, who had recently accepted Jesus Christ as his personal saviour in the course of a three-day Pray-a-Thon on the Trinity Broadcasting Network. 'How come you let this happen to your people, Lord?'

Lamont Wingate was working another case when they paged him – a vagrant found beaten to death in a boxcar. A switchman had found the body that afternoon, but death had occurred at least twenty-four hours earlier. Lamont had contacted the Southern Railway office and learned that the train had come in the day before from Alabama, having stopped off at just about every town between there and Birmingham. The victim and his assailants could have boarded anywhere, separately or together.

Wingate imagined an argument during an interminable wait somewhere on the line, the heat pressing down like the covers when you crawled into your bed head-first as a child and then couldn't find the way out. They would have been wasted on Thunderbird or muscatel. One thing led to another, and then two or three of them ganged up on this guy, taking out all the frustrations of their miserable lives on him. Not only were there no suspects, there wasn't even a motive. This time, he was the one getting beat on, that was all. It could have been any one of them.

By the time Wingate got out to the Pittsburgh call, the medics had taken away the only victim they could do anything for, the medical examiner and the police photographer had been and gone, the corpses had been covered with plastic sheeting and the area sealed off with crime tape. A patrol car was parked so its headlights illuminated the scene, which was enlivened still further by the array of blue and white flashing lights on the roof. A policeman with crew-cut blond hair and acute blue eyes was trying to move on the rubberneckers who had descended on the scene, while brushing off the efforts of an elderly black drunk to interest him in some completely irrelevant calamity which had befallen him that day.

'Stand by!' the patrolman kept telling the guy. 'Stand by!'

Lamont Wingate peeled the plastic sheets off the bodies with a sense of mounting gloom. After fifteen years experience with the Homicide Task Force, he didn't harbour inflated hopes about the kind of cases he was going to get called out to, but after the battered vagrant he'd been hoping for something slightly more coherent, something that might fool you into thinking for a couple of minutes that the world made sense, even if the sense it made wasn't particularly good news.

But this was just another random act of violence, a mugging gone wrong or a racial confrontation that got out of hand. At first Lamont thought the white guys must have been looking for trouble, coming into the 'hood that time of night. Then he spotted the copy of *The Watchtower*, and the open suitcase with a stack of pamphlets on 'Eternal Life – An Offer You Can't Refuse' and similar subjects. That could explain it. Fundies from out of town, maybe even out of state, might not have realized what they were letting themselves in for by coming around here after dark.

But what about the small-bore revolver the dead white was clutching? Since when did Jehovah's Witnesses go around strapped? And if you were going to pack heat for protection, why not take something that would do the job, like the nine the black guy had dropped? The 9 mm hadn't been fired and no knife had been found, so there must have been at least one other person involved, maybe two.

Lamont bent down and went through the black youth's pockets. They yielded a packet of gum, a set of keys, some loose change, a small plastic bag containing a number of pills, a billfold with thirty-seven dollars and a driving licence in the name Vernon Kemp. The tabs were most likely moon rock, the cocktail of heroin and crack which was currently in favour with the wolf packs. If they'd beamed up before they went patrolling, that would account for a lot.

He walked over to the squad car, opened the door marked 'Buckle Up Atlanta' and ran the name Vernon Kemp past the computer. While he waited to hear the result, he patted down the white guy. This didn't take long. Except for a few loose bills and coins, maybe ten dollars in all, his pockets were completely empty. Lamont was still digesting that when HQ got back to him with details of Vernon Kemp's record: one conviction for assault, one for possession, plus eight arrests where charges were not brought. Six months skid-bid in all. Kemp was known to have links with a gang called the Jams, who controlled most of the drug trade on the west side of Capitol Avenue.

So far, despite a few anomalies like the God-botherer's pistol, it was pretty much the kind of thing that Wingate had expected. It was only when he looked through the contents of the suitcase that it started to get weird. He thought these would be as predictable as Vernon Kemp's background, but he was wrong. Underneath the upper layer of pamphlets and a Bible lay a box of ammunition, a Sony camcorder, a roll of duct tape and five sets of handcuffs.

This made it look more like a dirt-on-dirt hit, what cops called a twofer: two dead assholes for the price of one. Whatever these guys had been aiming to do with that stuff, they were not only ofay but very definitely *not* OK. And sure as hell not jamming for Jehovah, either.

Lamont's beeper went again, a drive-by at Central and Glenn, by the interstate exit. He told them he'd get over there ASAP and headed off to get a few statements to pad out the file. This being Pittsburgh, he didn't expect a whole lot of co-operation, and he wasn't disappointed. The only thing all the witnesses agreed on was that no Jehovah's Witnesses had come to their door that evening. Apart from that, the stories varied wildly. Some people even denied hearing shots, although the burner that punched that crater in the white guy's chest must have been a pound at the very least, and there was no way you weren't going to hear anything that size going off right outside the house. Others admitted hearing shots – estimates varied from one to a dozen – but with a single exception no one had seen anything except *Oprah*.

The exception was Donna Grifton, an elderly woman living alone at 322 Carson. It was she who had called 911 in the first place.

'I heard some kind of noise in the street,' she told Lamont. 'Like a car door slamming, something like that. I'd been expecting my niece to come and visit, thought maybe it was her. I was on my way over to see when I heard this other sound, real loud. I knew that weren't no car door. I heard guns before, and this was a gun all right.'

Lamont nodded.

'And what did you see?'

'Hardly nothing. Time I got across to the windowlight, it was over. The gun went off again, and then I hear'd some kind of hollering. Only thing I see'd was the three of them laying there up the street. That's when I called.'

Back at the scene, the garrulous drunk was still trying to tell his story to the beleaguered patrolman. Lamont Wingate felt the senseless shame he always did when a person of colour started acting up. He knew this was dumb, a kind of Uncle Tom reflex, but he went over anyway and told the bum to quit acting the fool or he'd 'bust him under statute 44471A'. There was no such statute, but Lamont had never known the threat of invoking it to fail. It was that 'A' that got to them, he reckoned.

But this particular citizen seemed unimpressed.

'I ain't acting no fool,' he protested civilly. 'I'm just trying to explain to this here *po*lice what happened here tonight.'

'The hell he was!' the patrolman retorted. 'What the sorry son of a bitch's been trying to do is tell me his entire life history since he got up this morning.'

'That is an arrant untruth,' the drunk replied in a hurt tone. 'I may have been a mite circumstantial, but you got to understand I got liquor goggles on. Yet I see life not darkly, through a glass, but whole and entire. Everything is connected, so where to begin?'

He turned to Lamont Wingate.

'You law?' he said.

Lamont nodded.

'I saw the whole thing,' the drunk said with an air of bravado.

'Name?' said Lamont, getting out his notebook.

'Ulysses Grant.'

'Right! And I'm Robert E. Lee.'

The drunk produced a laminated card from his pocket and handed it to Lamont. It was a library pass made out in the name of Ulysses Grant. Lamont inspected it briefly, then handed it back.

'Where do you live, Mr Grant?'

'Everywhere! In each creature and plant, and every human being that draws breath, as we all do, Mr Lee. But I stay in that house right there.'

He made a gesture taking in half the street. Lamont sighed.

'OK, what did you see? No, let me rephrase that. What do you have to tell me about what happened tonight? That might be of interest to a body who don't presently have the benefit of them goggles you mentioned, that is.'

Ulysses Grant frowned at him.

'Let me try and draw my mind up to these Lilliputian proportions. Damn, but it's difficult! Makes me feel all dizzy-headed. OK. Whitey one enters left, seen from my box up there on the rise. Moons along the street like he's subject to pull a car clout, something. Enter whitey two, stage right. Spies number one and comes over like he's seen a ghost, which I have on many occasions experienced myself, the spirits of the dead rising sometimes as thick as steam from a street grate, and not surprising when the soil beneath our feet is stained its fine rich tint with the blood of our ancestors, Mr Lee.'

Lamont Wingate tapped his notebook with the tip of his pen.

'I was on a cruise schedule, Mr Grant, I could stand here and listen to you all night. As it is, you don't cut to the chase, I'll have to carry you downtown, hand you over to someone with the leisure to do your fine rhetoric the justice it surely deserves.'

Ulysses Grant gave a glare which mingled apprehension and defiance.

'Downtown? I ain't been there in forty years. I don't need anything they got to offer, 'sides which I hear it's all been gussied up since these Yankee companies moved down here 'cos life is cheap. The War between the States might have broken the chains of slavery, Mr Lee, but it replaced them with the chains of wage slavery, which are a hell of a sight harder to … '

He broke off, catching the look in Lamont Wingate's eyes.

'The chase,' he said hurriedly. 'Whitey two blows up at whitey one. Then the brothers arrive.'

'How many?'

'Three.'

'Recognize any of them?'

Ulysses Grant smiled vastly.

'Them niggers all look the same to me,' he said.

Lamont Wingate nodded.

'Go on.'

'They go to clean out the white guys. Number one breaks bad, bucks Vernon there. Someone else takes the guy down, then the other. Exeunt right.'

'I believe the correct word is "exit",' Lamont observed with a malicious gleam.

'Then your belief is misplaced, Mr Lee, account of there was two of them. You exit. Y'all exeunt.'

Utterly defeated, Lamont Wingate packed up his notebook, returned to the patrol car and called in to find out why the guys from the morgue hadn't showed up yet. The dispatcher told him that one of the other detectives had gone to look into the drive-by, so Lamont went back to his car and drove off, munching on one of the light bread sandwiches his wife had packed and mentally composing his prelim on the Pittsburgh shooting.

On the face of it, it sounded like a no-brainer. Vernon Kemp and a couple of dudes he was down with see these two suits and go to hit on them. Kemp'd likely been aching to get a body for some time, keep any of the Jams from trashing his rep, prove he had the juice. That side of it he could see. The problem was the other guys. If the drunk was to be credited, they'd fired first, two on three, and staring down the barrel of some major ordnance. That didn't make no sense. And what the hell were they doing there in the first place, with a suitcase full of restraint equipment and a video camera, passing themselves off as a direct-sales team for the big kahuna?

'A pistol each, handcuffs, roll of tape, video camera,' he said out loud for the benefit of his father, who had died of a stroke two years earlier.

He hung a loose right on Georgia and drifted down to Capitol, past the construction site for the Olympic stadium. To the left, the IBM tower dominated the night sky, its lattice-work spire illuminated from inside like a Halloween pumpkin. Lamont thought about what the old drunk had said about the Northerners moving in. What broke the South wasn't the war, it was air-conditioning. Before that came along, the Yankees couldn't take the climate. Lamont smiled and shook his head, recalling one guy he heard of, moved down here from New England, who kept his AC going full blast in the winter so he could have a log fire. Go figure!

'Maybe a burglary?' his father whispered unexpectedly. 'Make like they're peddling religion to get the door open, then pull out the hardware and clean the place out.'

'What's to clean?' demanded Lamont. 'That area, even the cockroaches are on food stamps.'

He went north on Hill, past demolished lots lined with parked cars during the day and under the expressway opposite the grim Stalinist bulk of Grady Memorial Hospital. That's where they'd have taken the white survivor. He stood a better chance at

Grady than most anywhere else in the country. They saw so many gunshot wounds the army sent their surgeons there to gain field experience. Lamont hoped the guy would pull through, or at least hang in long enough to talk.

'A sex crime, maybe?' his father suggested tentatively. Even when he was alive, he'd never cared to discuss this subject. 'Like those perverts you read about in the paper. He threatens them with the gun, handcuffs and gags them, then videotapes the whole thing to watch later at home.'

'There were *two* of them, Pop. Sex offenders work alone, except it's gang rape or whatever, and then they don't bother with cuffs, all that shit.'

Rebuffed, his father fell silent. Lamont cruised on up to North Avenue, then swung right under a railroad bridge and into a humpbacked concrete sidestreet ending at the tracks. Looking at the Homicide Task Force headquarters, you would never have guessed that Atlanta had one of the highest murder rates in the country. A small one-storey brick block with a mean row of teensy windows, it might have been the workshop for the office stamp outlet next door.

Lamont went inside and called Grady. It took some time for them to track the guy down, since neither Lamont nor the hospital had a name for him. Presently tagged as 'Patient #4663981: Identity Unknown', the individual was said to be recovering from emergency surgery. His condition was described as stable but critical.

'So you didn't find any ID on him?' Lamont asked the voice on the phone, the fourth he'd been put through to. 'Driving licence, credit cards, nothing?'

'If we did, it'd be on the chit.'

This was getting weirder and weirder. It sounded like these guys had deliberately stripped their pockets before going out, just like a couple of professionals. Except no professional would go up against a trio of armed muggers with a twenty-two.

Lamont popped one of the little breath-freshening mints which were his only vice. He was up to two packs a day, maybe it was time to slow down. He pulled out the phone book.

Jehovah's Witnesses appeared under 'Business Listings'. There were about twenty numbers in all. Lamont called Central Congregation, the downtown branch. He got a recorded voice which explained that the office was closed right now and invited him to leave a message or dial another number if he wished to speak to a counsellor.

'This is Detective Wingate, Atlanta Police,' he recited after the tone. 'Couple of individuals have been sighted in Carson Street, off McDaniel, claiming to represent your Church. Could you let me know if you have anyone out working the houses in that part of town? We suspect they may be impostors.'

He left a number and asked them to call him back. This was just to cover his butt. He knew damn well the guys weren't Jehovah's Witnesses. What he didn't know, what he couldn't even begin to guess, was what in hell's name they were. The only person who knew for sure was 'stable but critical', which was the way doctors covered *their* butts. His father had been stable but critical for almost two weeks before he died. Another few days, they would have had to remortgage the house.

Lamont had spent the time at the bedside, reading his dad the mysteries he loved. Once he'd picked up the wrong one by mistake, read a chapter out of a whole different book. His father hadn't even noticed. That's when he realized for the first time that the man lying there beside him, still warm, still breathing, was no longer his father.

He pushed a sheet of paper into the machine and began typing up his notes on the vagrant in the boxcar. As for the other case, its condition was critical but stable. He might be able to track down Vernon Kemp's accomplices, maybe trace the weapon through a ballistics test on the spent ammunition, tie it in to some other shooting. Even if he didn't manage that, the result was merely a technical hitch which might be rectified at any time. The file would be left open, and when the perps fucked up in the future – which could only be a matter of time, seeing as they were so raw they'd run off without this seriously fly camcorder which was theirs for the taking – the loose ends would be tied up once and for all.

The white guys were another question. He might be able to figure out the back story on that one, or it might end up being one of those enigmas which infest police files like weevils in rice. There was one thing Lamont felt sure of. If he ever did find out, the truth would prove to be as disappointing as the solutions to those mysteries he had read aloud to his father.

*

Something stirred in his mind like dead leaves in a wind. Leaves of paper, torn pages, words.

My God, my God, why hast thou forsaken me?

He knew the words, the page, the book it had been ripped from, even the chapter and verse. Words ripped from a dying man. He knew the place too, the dull light and medicinal smells of the church hall where Bible Study was held. The rows of kids in their Sunday best, hating it in their different ways. He recalled the teacher trying to explain away that particular sentence, tying it back to some Old Testament reference and suggesting that Jesus was just reading from the script here, dutifully fulfilling all the prophecies about the Messiah. He'd never bought that, not for a moment. Of all the words in the New Testamant, those were the ones that rang most true. There was no rhetoric about them, no smart phrasing, just the despairing shriek of a man suffering an atrocious torture as a result of beliefs which, he has just realized, may be absolutely meaningless.

What if he *isn't* the Messiah? What if the whole thing was a delusion from day one, a scam of which he has been the principal victim? That's the terrifying possibility which Jesus had just glimpsed for the first time, the focused beam of darkness which shone down from the cracked heavens and made him cry out.

Russ recalled his parents once discussing someone's loss of faith in disapproving tones, as though the person had been caught red-dicked at some No-Tell Motel. He'd thought they said 'loss of face'. That's what it sounded like, something tacky and socially embarrassing, not as bad as going over to Rome, but in the same general league. No one ever mentioned that first loss of faith, recorded right there in Matthew twenty-seven, verse forty-six.

It was those memories which were the hardest thing to reconcile with the knowledge which had come to him now, stretched on his own cross. This was not an instant of doubt, a brief crisis which made the ultimate victory all the more glorious, but an enduring certainty as barren and intolerable as his pain. If God permitted him to suffer like this, it could only be because his suffering was meaningless. It didn't really exist. *He* didn't really exist.

Everything he had ever been was a sham, a mock-up like the flat exteriors they built for movies, hollow within. A cry broke through his clenched lips. How could he accept that? How could anyone? Those childhood memories brimming with feeling, with a depth and substance his life had long since lost, a sacred authenticity, how could they be anything other than real? What did the word mean, if not that?

He had no problem with the idea that he was a phoney now, that his life had become a sham and that the only reason his bluff had never been called was because other people were equally reluctant to play the truth game, having secrets of their own to hide. But he found it impossible to believe that he had always been tainted, from the very beginning. Yet how could it be otherwise? You didn't *become* a spectre. You either were or you weren't. If the adult stood convicted, the child was guilty too.

His cry had brought the night nurse over. She checked the schedule hanging from the footrail of the bed, headed *Patient #4663981: Identity Unknown*. The next dose of medication was not due for another two hours, but an optional top-up of analgesic had been provided for and the patient was evidently in considerable distress, struggling against the bonds designed to protect his wounds and muttering something incomprehensible. The nurse tore open a syringe packet, filled it from the ampoule and slipped it under the bare skin of the man's arm. Gradually the ravings diminished, fragmented, then ceased altogether.

*

The girl lay sprawled in the chair, naked under a pink cotton robe, legs splayed out. Her right hand stroked her exposed pubis, her left the channel changer. Even on cable, there wasn't much to see this time of the morning. She must have been all around the circuit fifty times already in search of something that would hold her interest. She hadn't found it yet, but anything was better than the idea of giving up and going to bed alone.

The sound of a car outside brought her to her feet. He'd said he would be taking the bus, but they'd stopped running hours ago. She pressed the mute button on the remote and went over to the window. Sure enough, a cab had drawn up outside the motel, its yellow roof bedazzled by the neon sign over the entrance. For a moment her heart lightened. Then a middle-aged couple emerged from the rear and lurched off towards one of the cabins at the far end of the court.

She wrapped the robe around her, shivering slightly despite the heat. She'd put it on for him, for when he got back. He'd given it to her the day before. Told her it was silk, which she didn't think it was, but it had a nice satiny feel and the colour looked good on her. And it was sweet of him to think of her like that when he was out buying a suit to wear to this job interview. She modelled it for him right away, with nothing on underneath, which was maybe kind of slutty. He'd sure liked it, though.

She lay down on the bed, rubbing herself and thinking about how he'd kissed her down there until she couldn't stand it any more, and her clumsy fumbling with his belt and buttons, and breaking out his cramped cock and pulling him on top of her. They'd done it for almost two hours, first one way, then another, until he saw the time and said he had to get ready for his appointment. He'd wanted her on top then, straddling him and bending low so he could squeeze and suck on her titties as he came.

She rolled over and sat up, looking at the clock radio by the bedside. It was now almost three. He'd been gone over eight hours, and for each of the last five of those she'd had to throw out the story she'd been using to explain why he wasn't back and dream up a new one. First she'd told herself the appointment had been delayed. Maybe there were a lot of applicants, although it seemed a kind of strange time to go for an interview.

But Dale had said it was for the night shift, and you had to see the people on duty then.

Her next version was that he'd got the job, and had gone out to a bar to celebrate. Or he hadn't got it, and was drowning his sorrows. After that, things started to get darker. The whole thing was a lie. There was no job. He'd gotten dressed up to go out on the town, maybe with another woman he had someplace. Or he was in trouble of some kind. The guy who'd phoned that morning had sounded like real bad news, hanging up in her face like that. Maybe Dale had been kiting cheques, or the skip-tracers or the repo men were after him. Maybe that was why he'd come all the way out here from Seattle.

Her darkest hour had been the last, when it occurred to her that he'd just dumped her, period. He'd got what he wanted and walked, probably leaving her to pick up the tab. That would be straight out of the guy manual, she told herself bitterly. Dale had seemed different, but then they always did at first. The fact that he seemed kind of weak, like he needed to be validated the whole time, just made it more likely he'd choose the coward's way out. Plus this scenario explained the one thing none of the others had, which is why he hadn't called her.

It was the only possible explanation, she thought miserably, getting up and returning to her chair. He knew she had no way of getting in touch with him. He hadn't told her where he was going, or even what kind of work it was. Said there was no point discussing it when he probably wouldn't even get the job. The only thing she knew was that it was somewhere down in the south end of the city. That was why he might be late getting back, he'd said, because it was a long bus ride.

She reached for the remote, unblocked the volume and started to surf through the channels, lingering a few moments on each. You kid yourself that you're tough, she thought, but really you're just a fool. You scoop this cutesie of a guy, put the moves on him and then act surprised when he gets bored of it and ditches you. She mashed the remote some more until she found a local station with a news roundup, and stuck with it to find out what the weather would be like that day. She'd need to get out

191

there and start looking for work before they caught up with the stolen credit card she'd been using till now. It was time to get real.

' … were killed this evening in a shooting incident on a cross-street of McDaniel in the Pittsburgh area of the city. Another man was taken to Grady Memorial Hospital with serious gun-shot and knife wounds. He is said to be in stable but critical condition. Police are searching for two other individuals who were involved in the attack, which is not believed to have been racially motivated. And now with today's weather, here's Howie!'

'Thanks, Gus. Well, this warm snap we've been experiencing over the last couple of days looks like it's going to be with us for at least … '

The girl pushed the mute button. She was no longer interested in the weather. McDaniel was the street where Dale had been going. She remembered him calling the transit company to check which number bus to catch.

She turned off the TV, walked over to where her clothes lay strewn across the floor and dug out the pack of cigarettes she'd bought last night while waiting for Dale to get back from meeting with that friend he hadn't wanted to introduce her to. Maybe he'd been bullshitting her about that too, she thought as she lit up. She really didn't know anything about him except his name.

She eyed the phone on the table next to her. But who could she call? The TV station? 'Hi, there! I'm a long-time viewer but a first-time caller.' That hospital? The police? All that'd do was stir up a lot of trouble for her, and maybe for Dale too. You're just tired, she thought. Tired and lonesome and dreaming awake. That would make a good title for a country song. She finished the cigarette with a smile on her lips. Everything would seem better in the morning. If Dale still hadn't shown up, she'd decide what to do then.

Fourteen

I lay awake for hours, trying and failing to make sense of what I had heard. It was past two o'clock when I finally realized that I was not going to be able to get to sleep. I turned on the light to read some more. As I searched for my book, which had fallen to the floor, I caught sight of the video cassette I had taken with me on my hasty exit from Sam's room that afternoon. I picked it up and read the label: *Russell (Rick): Seattle*. Russell was the guy that Mark had been giving Sam such a hard time about the evening before. Maybe the video might provide some clue to what was going on.

The hall was in darkness. The only sound was a soft persistent hushing of rain on the roof, punctuated by more percussive drips falling from the eaves. The fire had collapsed on itself, a dull mass of white ash, barely glowing. I switched on the television, turning the volume right down. The harsh glare of the screen seemed shockingly bright. I expected people to rush out of their rooms demanding to know what was going on, but all was quiet. I fed the video into the open maw of the VCR.

At first I thought I was watching some kind of amateur dramatic production – very amateur. The camera wobbled, the lighting was lousy, the sequencing crude and the acting a disaster. In fact the whole thing was *so* weak that I assumed it must be one of those 'experimental' efforts where bad production values are part of the 'artistic concept'. The action seemed to confirm this. It consisted entirely of a guy in his thirties breaking into a house and terrorizing people with a pistol. There was no attempt to contextualize what happened, still less establish character or motive.

The first person he encountered was a housewife in a nightgown and bathrobe. Holding the pistol to her head, he made her kneel down, then handcuffed her and stuck a patch of tape over her mouth. He then went into the bedroom next door, the hand-held camera bouncing along behind him like a dog. It approached a crib and panned in to show a baby asleep, then went back to the gunman. He seemed to be saying something to camera, protesting maybe. I didn't dare turn up the volume in case someone heard.

Eventually he nodded, as though in agreement. He left the bedroom and went down to the basement, the camera following. In one of the rooms downstairs, two boys, one of them Chinese, were playing a video game. The gunman made them lie down, one on the bed, the other on the floor. Then he handcuffed and gagged them as he had the woman.

It was at this point that I heard a noise. It seemed to have come from Sam's quarters. A crack of light showed under his door. I turned off the TV, extracted the video and stuffed it quickly inside my robe as the door opened, flooding the room with light.

'Phil?'

Sam stood in the open doorway, a dark silhouette.

'I couldn't sleep,' I explained. 'Thought I'd go raid the fridge.'

'The kitchen's that way,' he said, pointing to the other side of the room.

'Right,' I said. 'See you in the morning.'

He didn't reply. I walked across the hall towards the kitchen, the video cassette jammed up against my ribs. Behind me, the door to Sam's room closed. I altered course and headed back to my room.

I got back into bed and lay there, thinking over what I'd seen on the video. The idea that it was a crude attempt at drama no longer seemed credible. The only thing as lame as that was reality. Although I had no proof either way, I became increasingly convinced that I had been watching an actual break-in at an actual house. Judging by the label, it had taken place somewhere in the Seattle area. Russell had presumably been the gunman while Rick had done the filming.

Then it occurred to me that this might be the way the group financed themselves. They didn't go and work on the mainland, they broke into houses and stole whatever they could lay their hands on, then disappeared back to the island. But why bother making a video recording of the event? Unless this was Sam's way of keeping his followers in line. If anyone challenged his authority, he could threaten to send the video to the police.

Awash with these disturbing speculations, I eventually fell asleep. Because of my broken night, I slept late the next morning. Breakfast was over by the time I emerged, and the home-schooling session was in progress at the dining table. There was a different teacher today, a hard-looking blonde who seemed distinctly ill-at-ease in the role. The children looked sullen and bored, with none of the lively involvement they had displayed the day before. But when I went out to the kitchen, there was Andrea, washing dishes with one of the other women.

'Looks like I overslept,' I said lightly. 'I guess the coffee's all gone.'

Andrea immediately left the sink and went to the stove.

'I'll make you some,' she said without looking at me. 'Go to your room and I'll bring it to you.'

For some reason, I felt embarrassed by her eager solicitude.

'That's real nice of you, but don't … '

She gave me a glance which made me falter. I had no idea what it meant, but I felt its intensity like a blow.

'Well, if you're sure it's no problem … '

I hovered there for a moment, but she paid no further attention to me, busying herself with the percolator and a can of coffee.

'I'll be in my room, then,' I concluded awkwardly, and sidled out.

Shortly afterwards there was a knock at my door. Andrea stood there with a mug of coffee. She looked strained.

'I need to talk to you,' she said in a low voice.

'Come on in.'

She shook her head.

'Not here. Meet me by the water-tank.'

With that, she turned and walked quickly, almost running,

back to the kitchen. I closed the door and sipped my coffee thoughtfully. For a moment it crossed my mind that she might be acting under orders from Sam. But surely in that case she would have been more straightforward? What was all the secrecy about, and why was she so nervous?

I put on a jacket and went outside. The overnight rain had stopped, but the sky was overcast. A pair of seagulls skimmed overhead, crying plaintively. There was no one about except for two women hanging out laundry on a line. As I walked up the trail towards the water-tank, I tried to imagine what Andrea could possibly have to say to me. The only thing I could think of was that she'd heard that I was leaving and wanted me to take a message to someone, or to do some errand for her on the mainland. But in that case why hadn't she just told me when she brought me my coffee? Unless of course Sam had tabooed me after I made it clear that I wasn't buying into his little scam. 'Don't scare the horses,' he'd told me. Judging by the high-tech goodies I'd seen in his rooms, Sam had an awful lot at stake, and the last thing any con man wants is someone putting the suckers on their guard.

The water-tank stood all alone on a rocky elevation at the edge of the developed section of land, right above the well which yielded the island's limited supply of water. There was no plumbing, and all water had to be carried by hand. It would have been a relatively simple matter to run a pipe downhill to a communal tap near the hall, but evidently such a luxury took second place to Sam's need for the latest electronic toys.

It was another fifteen minutes before Andrea finally appeared, and when she did I was disappointed to see that there were two women with her. Since she'd made it clear that she didn't want to be seen talking to me, I took cover behind the shed which housed the electricity generator. Each of the women had a plastic bucket which they proceeded to fill from the tank, but it soon became apparent that this was only a pretext for the long, intense conversation that took place. Judging by the women's lowered voices and furtive manner, they too were anxious not to be seen talking, let alone overheard.

Eventually the discussion broke up and the women set off back together, carrying the heavy buckets of water. For a moment I thought that Andrea had forgotten about our appointment. But when they were about half-way back to the hall, she set down her bucket and said something to her companions, pointing back to the water-tank. The others also stopped, but Andrea shooed them away and started back. The other two continued on their way and soon disappeared below the ridge. I stepped out of hiding with the sheepish grin of someone caught playing a childish game, and walked up to Andrea.

'Hi there, honey!' I said in a parody pick-up voice. 'Want to take in a movie or something?'

A brief smile broke through the strain on her face. For a moment I caught a glimpse of another Andrea, a stranger yet the same, like a photograph from an earlier, half-forgotten period of one's life. There are said to be several hundred muscles involved in creating the human smile, but when everything's said and done, muscles are only pulleys, strings attached to flesh. How is it that such simple mechanics can create an effect which seems to give you the person entire, with all their complex chiaroscuro, their desires and potential, doubts and shortfalls?

'There's the new Nick Nolte and Susan Sarandon at the Bijou,' I continued, encouraged by her reaction. 'Then we could go grab a burger somewhere. What time do you have to be home?'

But her smile had already died.

'It's not safe here,' she said, glancing around quickly. 'Something's going on, I don't know what. Terri and Gloria say that Mark has gathered all the men together.'

'So what?'

Andrea shook her head impatiently.

'You know that rock-pool by the ocean, the one where ... '

She broke off, looking confused.

'Where you go swimming in the summer,' I prompted.

For some reason she blushed.

'Yes. Go there. I'll come as soon as I can get away.'

The key to everything which followed was right under my nose, if I'd been able to see it. But I could see nothing but the controlled panic in Andrea's pale brown eyes.

'I don't know if I can make it,' I said. 'I'm leaving today, maybe this morning.'

'You can't leave.'

I stared at her. Her eyes moved a fraction, fixing on a point just beyond my shoulder. I turned and saw Sam walking towards us. Andrea stepped past me without another word and picked up the bucket of water. As she passed Sam, he caught her arm and said something to her to which she replied quickly. Sam released her as I approached.

'Andrea and I were just having a little chat,' I told him. 'She says there might be some problem about me leaving today. Is that true?'

Sam glanced at Andrea, who had continued on her way down to the hall. Then he looked around at me.

'I just went into your room, Phil, and there was a video cassette on the chair by the bed. Do you know anything about that?'

'Oh, that,' I replied casually. 'Yeah, I found it in one of the drawers while I was putting my clothes away. I guess it must belong to Mark.'

I wondered if he'd noticed that the tape had not been rewound.

'Anyway, what's all this about me not being able to leave?' I asked.

Sam's eyes slowly defocused.

'We're having a little trouble with the boat,' he said. 'Can't seem to get the engine to start.'

'Any idea how long it's going to be out of action? I'm kind of anxious to get going.'

Sam nodded vaguely.

'It's hard to say. Rick's taking a look at it right now.'

Another thought seemed to strike him.

'You any good with guns, Phil?'

'Guns? What kind of guns?'

'Any kind. You ever fire one?'

'Hardly. I grew up in Europe, Sam. It's not really what you'd call a gun culture.'

He nodded in the same dreamy way, as though his real thoughts were elsewhere.

'Do you have guns here on the island?' I asked.

Sam gazed at me without speaking for some time. It seemed to cost him an effort to focus. I wondered if he was maybe slightly stoned.

'Sure,' he said at last.

'You do? Why?'

He smiled lazily.

'Because this isn't Europe, Phil. This is real life, and in real life a man has to be able to defend himself and stand up for his beliefs.'

He looked at me slightly aggressively.

'Right, Phil?'

I shrugged.

'I guess. Except I usually don't know what my beliefs are.'

Sam looked away at the dark border of woods which encircled the clearing.

'I used to be like that,' he said. 'Then one day I found out. I have a feeling that you're going to find out too. Maybe soon.'

I gestured impatiently.

'Well, it's going to have to be *real* soon. Another couple of hours and I'm out of here, boat or no boat.'

He took a step past me, then turned back.

'Oh, just one other thing. Don't believe everything Andrea tells you. She kind of overdid it with the dope back in the old days and her synapses are fried. She makes up stuff, doesn't even know she's doing it.'

'I'll bear it in mind.'

On my way back to the hall, I discovered that Andrea was not the only one who made things up. Sam had told me that Rick was 'taking a look' at the boat, but as I passed one of the pre-fab houses he and Mark emerged, along with a group of other men, all arguing loudly. I caught the names 'Andy' and 'Dale' before they saw me and fell silent. They stood staring at me in mute hostility as I walked past.

'Are we having fun yet?' I enquired sarcastically.

I'd given up trying to ingratiate myself with these jerks. I didn't even care whether Rick was working on the boat or not. Whatever happened, I was leaving that afternoon. If the boat wasn't fixed, I'd use Sam's cellular phone and call a water taxi from Friday Harbor. Screw the cost. All I wanted was out.

Back in the hall, the blonde was still sitting at the dining table with her three charges, but she had now given up all pretence of keeping order, still less teaching them anything. I wondered why Andrea had been replaced. Sam had given the impression that she was their regular teacher. The children were shouting and throwing things and teasing each other and generally carrying on the way children do. They paused for a moment when I entered, but immediately resumed their racket. Like everyone else, they had evidently realized that I was a person of no consequence in the life of the community.

Back in my room, it was immediately obvious that my belongings had been searched. No attempt had been made to disguise this fact. My clothes lay strewn all over the floor, my overnight bag had been emptied and the contents scattered across the bed. I did a quick check. Except for the video cassette, nothing seemed to be missing. In fact something new had appeared. A pair of jeans and a matching denim shirt in a child's size were draped over a wire hanger suspended from a hook behind the door. I repacked my bag and stashed it away in the corner. Then I took the child's clothing and walked out, leaving the door open. There were no locks or bolts on any of the doors, anyway. Presumably the Theosophists had thought such things beneath them.

'Any of you kids belong to this?' I asked, holding up the jeans and shirt.

They stared at me blankly. The blonde affected not to notice my presence.

'Pardon me, ma'am!'

Her cool eyes travelled a seemingly considerable distance to my face.

'Are you Melissa?' I said with a suave smile.

'Uh huh.'

My smile broadened.

'I'm Philip. Sam was talking about you. He told me about your gorgeous cat.'

A peevish look crossed her sharp features.

'I don't have a cat.'

I frowned exaggeratedly.

'Really? Gee. Well, maybe he used some other word. Do you happen to know anything about these clothes? I just found them hanging on my door, and they weren't there when I left. You've been sitting here the whole time, I figured maybe you saw who went into my room and put them there?'

Melissa gave a facial shrug.

'I didn't see anyone.'

I tossed the clothes on the table.

'Well, they sure as hell don't fit me. I guess I'll just leave them here, let the rightful owner claim them in the fullness of time.'

Outside, the cloud had thinned and perforated like a wet blanket worn thin in places. Rich blue sky peeked through, and the invisible sun chiselled the edges of the cloud masses into sculptural forms. I set off down the broad trail leading to the pier, watching out for the path which Sam had taken the day before. It was only then that it occurred to me how strange it was that Andrea had taken it for granted I would know where the meeting place she had named was, and above all how to reach it. But even now I failed to make the obvious inference.

I somehow managed to miss the path and found myself back at the pier. The boat was still there, securely moored. Wanting to check out Sam's story, I climbed aboard and had a look around. There was no sign of any mechanical work in progress. In a locker in the wheelhouse I found a chart which covered most of the local archipelago, known as the San Juan Islands.

I recalled that Sam had referred to the landmass across the strait as Orcas, and by working back from that I was able to identify where I was, a mere blip on the chart named Sleight Island. I also found the town of Friday Harbor on San Juan Island, the biggest in the group. I was dismayed to see how far away it was. As for the mainland, that was considerably farther.

In fact, the outlying islets of Vancouver Island across the Canadian border were a lot closer. If Sam and his buddies wanted to get away from it all, they'd picked the right place.

I returned to the pier and walked back up the trail, inspecting the undergrowth to my right for signs of the path. In the end I found it, a mere smudge leading off through soaring Douglas firs and yellowish cedars, interspersed here and there nearer the shoreline with madronas. Soon the ocean itself came in sight, heaving listlessly over the rocks. I walked to the brink of the bluff overlooking the cove. The tide was higher than it had been the day before, and the pool was almost entirely submerged.

There was no sign of Andrea. At the far end of the strait, a car ferry was passing on its way to or from somewhere. I was heartened by this evidence of life going on in a world that neither knew nor cared about Sam's half-baked, half-smart flimflam. Soon I would rejoin it, and all this would be a fading memory.

Over twenty minutes had gone by before I heard sounds on the hillside above and saw Andrea making her way down the path towards me. I'd had plenty of time to decide what approach to take with her. Sam had implied that Andrea was a brain-damaged fantasist, and while that wasn't necessarily true, there might well be something to it. If she had something definite to tell me, or some specific favour to ask, I was prepared to listen, but I wasn't going to stand for any more prevaricating or mystification.

She was wearing the same outfit she'd had on the evening I arrived, a baggy hand-knitted grey sweater and khaki slacks with a battered pair of brown work shoes. She had the kind of body which looked great in anything, but it was her face which stood out. With its regular features, good bones and flawless skin it must have looked almost tiresomely pretty when she was young, but age had rendered that banal bounty down to a lean, distinctive beauty with great character and just a hint of residual sweetness. Now, though, she mostly looked scared.

'Let's go down there,' she said, pointing to the rock ledge at sea level.

'Why?'

'Someone might see us.'

I looked around. We were surrounded by woods on one side and ocean on the other.

'That's bullshit. Anyway, what if they do?'

She looked down, shaking her head.

'You don't understand.'

'That's what Sam's always saying. I guess I'm just not up to the intellectual demands of living here. Fortunately I'll be back with my own kind soon. Now then, have you got something to tell me or what?'

She grabbed my hand and pulled me over to the jumble of rocks leading down from the bluff.

'Just come with me. Please!'

I decided to humour her. Below us, the sea swell slushed and slurped on the underside of the smooth basalt ledge. When we reached it, I turned to Andrea and smiled tightly.

'OK, lay it on me.'

She shrugged.

'I don't know where to begin.'

'Try the beginning.'

'It's … I mean, how do I know if I can trust you? Sam said that you were friends. You might tell him everything … '

I gestured impatiently.

'I won't. You have my word on that. Besides, we're not really friends. He's just someone I knew years ago, at college. Like I told you, I'm leaving soon and I won't be back. And the only regret I have about that is that I would like to have spent more time with you, Andrea.'

She pushed back her hair distractedly.

'Me? Why?'

I smiled at her.

'I thought women weren't supposed to ask that. Anyway, I don't know. I can only say that out of all the people here, you're the only one who seems completely real.'

She narrowed her eyes, as though suspecting some trick.

'You mean you think the others are spectres?'

I gave an expressive sigh.

'Please, Andrea! Don't give me that crap.'

'You don't believe in it?'

She seemed amazed.

'What's to believe?' I demanded. 'The gospel according to Billy Blake? You don't buy into that, do you?'

A seagull flew by, emitting sounds like a squeaky gate. Andrea swung around as though someone had touched her. She seemed to be getting more agitated by the moment.

'We all do,' she murmured. 'We have to.'

'But supposing you don't? Supposing you lose your faith, what happens then?'

She did not reply.

'Do you want to leave?' I suggested. 'Is that what this is all about, Andrea?'

Her head shook in a spasm.

'You don't understand!'

I turned and started to climb back up the rocks.

'Stop!'

It was a cry of desperation.

'You mustn't go yet! Please come back!'

She looked so helpless I found myself taking pity on her. Maybe she really was crazy, I thought. If so, she was in good company. I climbed back down.

'You're absolutely right!' I told her sharply. 'I don't understand a fucking thing. I don't understand why you asked me to meet you. I don't understand what you're so afraid of. I don't understand what you're doing here in the first place.'

She sidled past me, putting herself between me and the bluff.

'It's no use trying to cut off my escape,' I said. 'If you want me to stay and listen to you, you'd better start talking sense. Fish or cut bait, Andrea.'

She looked up above my head, as though seeking inspiration.

'You know about Lisa, right?' she said.

'Sam's wife, the one who drowned?'

'The one who drowned.'

She continued her circular movement, ending up back in her original position. I turned to face her.

'Lisa was a friend of mine. She invited me here when she bought the place. There were a bunch of us. Most of them left. I stayed.'

A movement caught my attention. Behind Andrea and slightly to one side, someone had appeared on the rocky outcrop high up at the other side of the cove.

'Someone's watching us,' I murmured.

I couldn't make sense of the perspective at first. The figure seemed to be farther away than the rock it was standing on. Then I realized that it was not an adult but a child, dressed in the clothes I had discovered in my room earlier, the denim shirt and jeans. The outfit now looked strangely familiar.

Andrea had turned to look.

'I don't see anyone,' she said with a puzzled frown.

I hardly heard. A terrible madness had gripped me, a senseless certainty I knew was impossible, but which I could not shake off.

'David!'

'There's no one there,' said Andrea.

The child stood rigidly still. His face was expressionless.

'David! It's me, your father!'

There was no reaction. I shoved my way past Andrea, sprinted across the cove and hurled myself at the rock face.

Fifteen

The day after the double slaying in Carson Street, Charlie Freeman came by Grady to check on the surviving white victim. It was a routine follow-up to a case which another detective had initiated, and in which he himself took no particular interest. Freeman was a good old boy of thirty-seven from a remote stretch of Wilkes County who had never pretended to take much serious interest in anything except fishing, hunting and his dog, Reb.

He parked his pick-up in a gimp slot right in front of the main door of Grady and walked on in. After lingering a little longer than was strictly necessary with the receptionist, a bottle blonde with buns of steel and alluring eyes, Freeman took the elevator up to the twelfth floor. The duty nurse on the ward he'd been directed to was one of those Germanic types, as broad as she was tall, and looked like she could plough the upper forty without the help of a mule any day. She told Freeman that the patient's condition had improved somewhat, but that he was still critical and could not be questioned.

'You get a name, anything?' asked Freeman.

'He hasn't opened his lips except to take a sip of water.'

Charlie Freeman looked around him vaguely.

'Stuff he had on him, where's that?'

'His personal belongings will have been bagged and taken to the depository.'

Freeman rode down with an extended black clan, all of them in tears except for one man who was fixating on something far beyond the modest dimensions of the elevator. Down in the basement, Freeman traversed a grid of aggressively lit corridors. On the far side of a pair of open double doors, a woman was mopping an empty operating theatre.

'Hey, that place's so clean you could do major surgery in there!' Freeman shouted, barking a succession of abrupt laughs.

The woman shrugged and said something in Spanish. Freeman continued on his way, scowling. Reason the country was going down the tubes, you couldn't share a joke no more. They either didn't get it or they disapproved. Pretty soon you'd have to run every gag past a committee of previously battered lesbians of colour or risk a lawsuit. Well, he didn't give a rat's ass. Live free or die.

The depository was presided over by a black guy tall enough to have been a basketball player maybe ten, twenty years ago. Charlie Freeman flashed his ID and asked for the belongings of Patient #4663981.

'You got a warrant?' the clerk asked.

'This here is a murder case and the guy is a suspect.'

'I can't release nothing without a warrant.'

It would take at least half a day to get a warrant, by which time Freeman would be off duty. Fine, it weren't no sweat off of *his* balls.

'I can let you look at it, you don't open the bag,' the clerk added, apparently intimidated by Freeman's silence.

He disappeared into a room lined with lockers. Freeman stood whistling tunelessly and staring at a photograph on the wall, some forest scene. Saturday, he'd go to Pete's, have supper, tie one on. They'd both get half a bottle of rye in the bag, then go jack-lighting Bambi's mother in the woods.

The clerk returned to the window with a large transparent plastic bag sealed with a sticker labelled 4663981. Freeman picked it up and inspected the contents: a Smith & Wesson revolver, a wad of twenty-dollar bills, some small change, a bus ticket and a flat metal key crudely stamped CENTRAL. He mauled the plastic, trying to turn the key over.

'You break that seal, you're in violation,' the clerk told him.

Freeman agitated the bag like a hound dog shaking a possum until the key flipped over. On the other side, the number 412 was engraved in the metal. He dropped the bag on the counter.

'Have a good one,' he said, turning away.

'You bet,' muttered the clerk.

Freeman walked up to the main floor, where he dished out another helping of intensive eye-contact to that sweet thing behind the desk. Now there was a body built for the long haul. He fired up a Camel and walked over to his truck. The bumper sticker read MY WIFE? SURE. MY DOG? MAYBE. MY GUN? NEVER.

Freeman unhooked the car phone and called in to tell HQ he was heading over to the Central Hotel, where it looked like the white perp had been staying. The Chief liked to keep tabs on everyone since it got out that three of the boys had been spending their afternoons playing pinochle in the back room of a midtown bar when they were supposedly trying to find the torso to which four recovered limbs and a head had originally belonged.

'We have a further development in that case,' the sergeant told him. 'Woman called in, wanted to know if either the guys involved was named Dale Watson. I tried to take her particulars but she hung up on me. Got the number off the tracer, though. She was calling from the A-1 Motel on Ponce. Probably nothing to it, she sounded kind of screwy. But it might be worth checking out.'

'I'll swing by there,' said Freeman, happy to have an excuse to stay out of the office. Anything beat riding a desk all day.

He shoved a Reba McEntire tape into the deck and cruised up Piedmont. One block before the corner of McGill, a Toyota four by four coming out of a sidestreet did a California stop, then swung right across the oncoming traffic into the turn lane, forcing Freeman to brake sharply and thereby miss the light. He leaned out the window and gave the elderly Chinese driver an emphatic number one, but she didn't notice that either, of course.

The Central Hotel was on Peachtree, a five-storey block of fancy brickwork with white bay windows overlooking the interstate. It would have been demolished years before, except for a political dispute over the future use of the land. Freeman got out of the truck and fieldstripped his cigarette, just like his daddy taught him to when they were out hunting. The lobby smelled of sweat and smoke and failure. A cadaverous bald man peered out over the desk top. Freeman shoved his ID in the guy's face.

'Detective Freeman, homicide. One of your guests ended up catching a bullet last night.'

A perfect, comic-book curve of a smile split the man's soft beardless face like a ripe fruit.

'Exit only!' he said softly. 'Ped Xing!'

Charlie Freeman peered at him.

'Yeah,' he said. 'So anyway, he's hovering between life and death like they say over at Grady and I'm here to find out who the hell he is plus any other details that might rise to the surface, you with me?'

The man's smile grew even wider.

'Wrong way!' he whispered.

'I see the register? Guy was in four twelve.'

The bald man stood up. His smile had completely vanished. He reached towards a bank of numbered pigeon-holes, with hooks for keys, drew a slip of thin cardboard from the opening marked 412 and laid it on the counter. It was only now that Freeman noticed that the man's right hand was a shrivelled knob, a vestigial thumb drooping at an angle.

He picked up the card. It had spaces marked 'Name', 'Address' and 'Rate'. Underneath was written ROOM MUST BE PAID FOR IN FULL BY 12 NOON – NO CREDIT CARDS – NO OUT-OF-STATE CHECKS. The occupant of Room 412 was registered as William Hayley of Grand Rapids, Michigan, no street address. He had checked in on the ninth and had paid the $55 in cash for three days running, the last time being the previous morning. Charlie Freeman pushed the card back. The man behind the desk was gazing at him with a look of utter despair.

'It's past noon,' said Freeman, 'and this guy didn't cough up his fifty bucks. I guess I'll go check out the room. You got a pass key, something?'

The man extended his deformed hand towards the registration card. Grasping the edge with his dwarf thumb, he flicked the card away to reveal a flat metal key. Freeman looked at it with a frown. He was certain the key hadn't been there before.

When he looked up, the clerk's uncanny smile was back in place, his whole face beaming with barely contained glee. He reached out suddenly and laid his stump on Freeman's arm.

'Pass with care!' he said with a stifled giggle.

Charlie Freeman nodded.

'Thanks, buddy. And listen, they ever get around to tearing this place down, give me a call. Maybe I can fix you up with a job as a street sign.'

The fourth floor of the hotel consisted of a single corridor running the length of the building. 412 was half-way along on the right. Charlie Freeman knocked perfunctorily, then unlocked the door and stood looking around. The air was hot and stale. Greasy light filtered in through the window. The bed was unmade, and there was a pile of clothes on the floor, a T-shirt, jeans, a pair of basketball shoes. On a shelf above the sink lay a toothbrush and a comb. There was a book beside the bed. Freeman picked it up and flipped through several pages. Poetry, it looked like.

In the corner of the room, half-hidden by the folds of the drape, was a wastebasket. Freeman poured the jumble of paper coils and twists out on to the table. Half the stuff was wrapping. Untwisting the rest, he finally found a till receipt for a suit, shirt, tie and shoes, dated two days previously. He bundled up the wrappings, clothes and book in a blue plastic tote bag he found in the closet. Down in the lobby, the guy at the desk was gazing up at the ceiling with a beatific smile.

'Seeing as Mr Hayley won't be coming back here for some considerable time, if ever, I'm taking his personal belongings for safekeeping,' Freeman told him. 'You need my John Hancock anywhere?'

The bald man transferred his grey eyes to Freeman's face. They were as blank as if he had never seen him before. Then he winked conspiratorially.

'Walk don't walk!' he breathed.

Freeman started to say something, then shook his head and walked out. An elderly black, his skin tough as an alligator hide, was standing on the sidewalk holding a sign that read GOD HATES GAY PRIDE.

'Seek ye the Lord,' he told Charlie Freeman in a voice devoid of all conviction.

Freeman unlocked his truck and slung the tote bag on the passenger seat.

'I already found Him,' he said. 'And I got bad news for you, gramps. He's a switch-hitter Hisself.'

Singing along in a penetrating baritone to Reba's 'The Greatest Man I Never Knew', he drove up Peachtree as far as the ornate fantasia of the Fox Theatre, then swung right on the avenue which had once divided north Atlanta from south, white from black. The sun showed pale in the sky, high behind a veil of haze. Must have been in the mid-nineties, easy.

The A-1 Motel was four blocks along, a fifties sprawl of two-storey rooms and cabins surrounding a large parking lot. Charlie Freeman pulled in and killed both the engine and Reba McEntire, who was instantly replaced by a barrage of thrash rock from a trio of baseball-capped dudes taking their ethnic briefcase for a stroll. Freeman picked a large manila envelope out of the file lying on the floor and heaved himself out of the truck.

'We're full,' called a male voice as he entered the reception area. The sound of sports commentary rumbled in the background.

'Sign says there's vacancies,' shouted Freeman.

'It's broke.'

Charlie Freeman looked around at the bulging walls, the fake ante-bellum furniture, the cases of plastic flowers, the green globs of goop circulating in a huge lava lamp. A man appeared in the open doorway behind the counter. He was wearing a Braves cap, a T-shirt and shorts. His face was pudgy and pugnacious, the skin riddled with broken veins.

'We're full,' he said, as if for the first time.

'You the manager?'

The man's glaucous grey eyes curled up the way slugs do when you salt them.

'This about the fire code? I told the guy already, we're going to upgrade same time we do the roof, right? Damn, all we're trying to do here is turn a buck and promote tourism.'

Charlie Freeman laid his ID on the counter and extracted two glossy six-by-eights from the manila envelope.

'I'd just like for you to take a gander at these pictures, tell me if you ever saw either of these individuals, then I'll let you get back to the game.'

The manager picked up the photographs.

'Damn, looks like they had a rough night,' he remarked lightly. 'I seen this one here. He in some sort of trouble?'

'He's dead,' said Freeman.

The manager's eyes widened.

'Dead? Damn.'

'When did he check in?'

The manager tapped at a computer keyboard.

'He was in one eighteen, right?' he murmured. 'Arrived the tenth.'

'Name?'

'John Flaxman.'

'Address?'

'Didn't give none. But I got some scoop on his girlfriend, if that's any use to you.'

Charlie Freeman tucked one of the photos back in the envelope and slipped the other into his jacket pocket.

'Can't hurt,' he said.

'She come by this morning, said her friend had left but she wanted to keep the room for a while and pay with a card. Gloria Glasser's the name, 2344 East 19th, Hopkinsville, Kentucky.'

He handed a smudgy carbon copy of the credit card imprint to Freeman, who studied it briefly.

'Thanks now,' he said, handing it back. 'Appreciate it.'

He walked along the line of cabins to 118 and rapped at the door. It opened almost immediately. The face which appeared was young, pale and drawn. Seventeen, maybe eighteen at the most.

'Gloria Glasser?' he said.

A momentary delay, a sudden obliquity of her gaze, confirmed Freeman's suspicions.

'Uh huh?'

'I'm from the police, ma'am. You called in about a Dale Watson?'

'You heard something?'

Her whole face was transformed.

'I come in?' said Freeman.

The room inside was a shade classier than the one at the Central Hotel, but a whole lot sadder. The other had just been a single guy's flop. Here something was missing, something which had been found and then lost again. The sense of that loss was as thick as the tobacco fumes in the air.

The girl closed the door and lit another cigarette.

'Want one?' she asked Freeman.

'Thank you kindly.'

She gave him a light from the tip of her own, just like they'd been best buddies for years. Cute little thing, thought Freeman, even if her name wasn't Gloria.

'So how can we help you?' he asked brightly.

'You said you had news,' the girl replied, her manner hardening up.

Freeman shook his head.

'You asked. I didn't say nothing.'

The girl's eyes narrowed.

'How do I know you're who you say? Show me your badge.'

Freeman did so.

'How about you?' he asked.

'Ain't no law that says I have to show you ID,' she retorted with a defiance as thin and hard as enamel.

'That so? But there *is* a law against using a credit card that ain't yours.'

'Who says it ain't mine?'

There was real apprehension in her voice now. Freeman gave her the eye.

'Honey, Gloria Glasser's held that card since 1988, it said on the print-out. You'd still've been in grade school then. Am I right?'

The girl bit her lip.

'It's my mom's. It's OK, she'll pay the bill.'

'And you are?'

'Cindy.'

'OK, Cindy. I've already got a pile of work right now, 'sides which it goes against my nature be ugly to a young lady. So you just answer my questions fully and frankly, I could overlook this little credit card matter. Deal?'

She glanced at him once or twice, then nodded.

'OK I sit down?' asked Freeman, doing so.

The girl perched on the edge of a chair covered in a heavy crimson acrylic weave.

'Now then,' Freeman said, 'why don't you tell me about this Dale Watson?'

Disjointedly, the girl related the whole story – how she'd met this guy on the bus, how she had nowhere to stay so she'd ended up coming here with him, how he was looking for work, how he'd gone out the night before and not come back.

'And then I heard on the news about this shooting, and it was where Dale said he was going, and I got thinking maybe something happened to him.'

'He tell you what kind of job this was he was applying for?'

The girl shook her head.

'And he said his name was Dale Watson?'

'Uh huh.'

'Only he signed the register as Flaxman. John Flaxman.'

She shrugged.

'Maybe he didn't want to use his real name.'

'And he was from St Louis, you say?'

'That's where the bus was coming from. But he'd been on the road a whiles, he said. Oh, and one time he mentioned Seattle.'

'*Seattle?*'

Like she'd said Seoul or Sydney.

'But I don't know if he was from there. He didn't let on too much about that kind of thing.'

Freeman eyed the girl in silence.

'You know what's happened to him?' she asked haltingly.

'I ain't even sure we're talking about the same person yet,' he said, taking out the photograph and passing it to her.

It was a head and shoulders shot, taken at the morgue. They'd done a pretty nice job. No injuries were visible, and the face appeared peaceful and indifferent.

'That's him,' the girl said with a lift in her voice that wrenched at Charlie Freeman's heart. 'Where is he? What happened? Is he bad off?'

*

Rosa Morrison was working on a lead article about racial integration in inner-city high schools when the call came through.

The piece was fascinating but an absolute bitch to sub: high-profile, extremely sensitive and site-specific. The two reporters who had researched and written it had done a good job, but the fine-tuning was down to her as assistant city editor. If she got the balance wrong, the various pressure groups involved would get on the case and the shit would hit the fan. On the other hand, if she watered it down into a feel-good McArticle, readers would complain that the paper was dodging the issues.

To make matters worse, this wasn't just a think piece. These were local schools. People whose kids went to them were bound to have their own opinions which they would feel outraged to find ignored or contradicted. Plus the whole thing had to be written as an inverted pyramid in case it got picked up by another paper and needed to be cut to fit around an ad for pantyhose or something.

So when the phone went with some gofer saying he had a guy on the line who wanted to check on a news item, Rosa's first impulse was to push the thing off on one of the other ACEs, only neither of them were at their desks. Bill was over by the water fountain flirting with Lesha Roberts, while Jodie was probably outside on the fire escape sneaking a cigarette. There were sometimes more people hanging out on that metal staircase than there were in the office. One of these days someone would drop a smouldering butt into one of the garbage Dumpsters below and start the biggest blaze since Sherman torched the city.

Rosa sighed and said to put the caller through.

'*Atlanta Journal-Constitution* city desk Rosa Morrison speaking how may I help you?' she recited all in one breath, highlighting a potentially inflammatory subordinate clause onscreen and blowing it away with the delete key.

'I wanted to check on a news story?'

The caller was male, youngish, with a Yankee accent. Midwest maybe, Rosa couldn't exactly place it.

'Uh huh,' she said non-committally.

'See, I live out of state. Arizona? There was like a report in the paper here about a shooting at a house on Carson Street. I have relatives there, like on the same street, and they haven't been answering the phone and I've been kinda worried, you know? I was wondering if you like had any more details.'

Rosa tapped a few keys, calling up a window with the library screen. She typed FIND 'SHOOTING'.

'What did you say the street was called?' she asked.

'Carson. 322's where my folks live.'

Rosa typed CARSON STREET and hit enter. Short high-pitched cries punctuated the fuzzy silence on the telephone line. They made her think of summer holidays at Palm Beach, all those years ago, before her father backed the wrong investment and pissed away the family fortune. She could still feel the hot squishy sand between her toes and see the vast indolence of the Atlantic stretching away before her like her own future.

The blue display flickered as the database responded. SHOOTING: 1047. CARSON STREET: 2. TOTAL: 0.

'We don't seem to have anything,' she told the caller. 'When did this happen?'

'Pretty recently. Last couple days.'

'I'm showing two mentions for Carson Street, but nothing involving a shooting.'

'Really? Well, I guess I … '

Jodie's head had appeared over the divider between their desks.

'Hold on a minute,' Rosa said, twisting the microphone of her headset aside.

'Was that something about a shooting on Carson Street?' Jodie asked.

'That's right.'

'I just subbed the story. Bottom of D2.'

Pecking away at the keyboard, Rosa killed the library window and got back into tomorrow's edition. There it was, a short news item tucked away in the local section.

'I've got it,' she told her caller, scanning the text. 'Correct, there was an incident last night in Carson Street. Not at a house, though. Two men killed, another in critical condition. One of the victims named as Vernon Kemp, fifteen, of 611 Garibaldi Street. The other two victims not yet identified. That's about it. We got it off the police blotter, didn't send a reporter out.'

There was silence on the other end.

'Hello?' said Rosa.

'The other two guys,' said the voice at last. 'You know anything about them?'

'Hold on a second.'

She leaned over to Jodie.

'Have you got the blotter report on this?'

Jodie hunted around amongst the papers on her desk, coming up with a stapled sheaf of fax pages which she passed to Rosa over the divider.

'Who is it?' she whispered.

Rosa shrugged.

'Some guy.'

She quickly found the police report of the incident, which Jodie had highlighted in fluorescent pink.

'OK, let's see. Blah, blah, blah. "The unidentified white victim was in his late twenties, five eleven, one hundred eighty pounds, light brown hair cut short, scar on left cheek." Looks like he was packing a .22 calibre revolver. The guy they took to Emergency was also white. Nothing more on him. "A suitcase recovered at the scene was found to contain some pairs of handcuffs, a roll of tape and a video camera." That's it. Hello? Hello?'

The phone had gone dead.

'Well, thanks a whole heap!' Rosa said savagely, cutting off the phone. 'Asshole!'

'He hang up on you?' Jodie murmured sympathetically.

Rosa dragged her school story back on to the screen. An African-American honours student was quoted as saying race was not an issue for her. Her best friends were Japanese and Jewish and they related on the basis of personality, not skin colour. That had to be balanced against a male student who supported segregated schools, claiming that students stuck to their own racial cliques and that talk of pride in diversity was just window-dressing designed to perpetuate white domination.

Rosa stared up at the suspended ceiling, inset with frosted glass panels diffusing a subdued, generalized light. There must have been forty people at work in the huge open-plan office, but the only sound was the hush of the air-conditioning and the occasional burr of a phone.

'How the hell did he know?' she said aloud.

'How's that, honey?' asked Jodie.

'If that story hasn't even run *here* yet, how did that guy know about it?'

'Maybe he lives around there.'

Rosa shook her head.

'He said he was phoning from out of state.'

She highlighted a paragraph and dragged it down the page, then froze again, staring sightlessly at the screen.

'Seagulls,' she murmured.

That was the sound she had heard in the background, the strident, mewing shrieks which had made her think of summer vacations at the beach.

'Do they have seagulls in Arizona?' she asked.

Jodie gave a raucous laugh which turned into an attack of smoker's cough.

'If they do, honey,' she said when the fit subsided, 'those birds sure as hell got off at the wrong exit!'

Rosa laughed, shrugged and returned to her work.

'I guess it's just one of those things,' she said.

Sixteen

I shoved my way past Andrea, sprinted across the cove and hurled myself at the rock face. It was almost sheer, with very few holds. After three vain attempts, bruised and bloodied, I gave up.

'What is it?' Andrea was shouting at me. 'What's the matter?'

I ran back to her and looked up at the rock ledge. There was no one there. I pushed past Andrea and climbed back up the way we had come down. The outcrop where David had been standing was about fifty feet away. Trees and thick undergrowth grew right down to the point where the rock surface fell away to the cove.

I forced my way through the prickly shrubs and around the trees, the branches whipping my face and tearing my clothes. At one point I lost my footing and almost slipped over the edge, but I managed to clamber back, driven on by the knowledge that my son was alive and somewhere close by. At last I reached the spot where I had seen him a few minutes earlier.

There was no sign that anyone had ever been there. Searching the undergrowth all around, I discovered a path leading off into the woods. I raced off along it. The path was obviously disused, but the vegetation had not yet reclaimed the central strip. I must have run for at least fifteen minutes, up and down hills, around zigzags and hairpin turns, on and on, always expecting to see the diminutive figure I sought just around the next bend or at the top of the next rise. When I could run no more, I trudged on for another ten minutes before finally collapsing, near tears, on a tree stump I had tripped over.

The path ran around the coast of the island, just above the shoreline. Because of its tortuous course, caused by the uneven terrain, it was a lot longer than the trail I had taken on my first day there, but I eventually discovered that the two were connected by the network of overgrown paths which I had been tempted to explore then. Convinced that David was somewhere on the island, I now beat my way up and down every single one of them. I didn't find David, but my persistence was not wasted. On the contrary, the knowledge I gained during those hours was eventually to save my life.

By the time I finally returned to the compound, Sam's Blake lecture was in full swing. Even at some distance from the hall, I could hear his urgent, bellowing delivery, every word in italics, every line a punchline, every stop an exclamation mark. It sounded even more brutal and peremptory than the harangue I had witnessed the day before. But I did not hesitate. Lecture or no lecture, I was going to have this out with Sam there and then. He had my kid and I was going to get him back.

I strode in through the open door of the hall, and stopped dead. The huge space was deserted. The voice I had been hearing came from the television, where an image of Sam strutting his stuff was playing to an empty room. The emanations of his screen image were printed all over the walls and ceiling, the sound boomed and echoed in every nook and cranny, but there was no one there.

I switched off the TV and opened the door leading to Sam's quarters.

'Sam!' I called. 'It's Phil. I need to talk to you.'

There was no reply. I went to the next room. Besides the pool table, there was an exercise machine, various weights and a set of wall-bars. The door to the bedroom was closed. I knocked. There was no answer. I opened the door and stepped inside.

'How are you doing, Phil?'

He lay sprawled on the bed in a white terry-cloth bathrobe, reading the Erdman edition of Blake's works. On one side of him was the Fender guitar, on the other a rifle. Then I spotted the cellular phone, on a chest of drawers by the window. I strode over and picked it up.

'I've seen David,' I told him. 'I'm going to call 911 and get the police out here.'

Sam turned back to his book. I switched on the phone and dialled. Nothing happened. I tried again.

'OK, what's the deal?' I asked Sam.

He set down the volume of poetry.

'There's a code number you have to enter to enable it. Prevents unauthorized use.'

'What is it?'

'Well, I don't actually give it out, Phil. The rates they charge for airtime, it would cost me an arm and a leg if … '

I threw the phone at him.

'Don't fuck with me, Sam!'

In one movement he rolled up off the bed and levelled the rifle at me. The muzzle looked enormous, like a tunnel. Neither of us spoke for what seemed like a very long time. Then Sam slowly lowered the rifle and heaved a sigh. I realized that he'd been holding his breath all along.

'Sit down, Phil,' he said. 'I think it's time we had a little talk.'

I edged backwards to a leather armchair. Sam perched on the end of the bed. The bedroom was at the back of the hall, and had a large picture window overlooking the strait. The setting sun had tinted the clouds with a delicate pink wash.

'I'm not going to give him up,' I said. 'You'll have to kill me first.'

'I thought he was dead,' Sam replied.

'You know about that?'

'I saw it in the papers. We get them once in a while. I figured you probably didn't want to talk about it.'

'He's *not* dead. I saw him just now, down by that pool you took me to yesterday. That's why you set up that meeting with Andrea, isn't it? That's how she knew I could find it.'

Sam looked at me expressionlessly.

'Did Andrea see anything?' he asked.

'She claimed she didn't, but she has to be lying.'

'Well, it wouldn't be the first time.'

He sighed.

'But I have to say, Phil, a lot of people, listening to you, would think you were just plain crazy. I imagine that's what the police would think.'

'I'm willing to take that chance,' I retorted.

He shook his head slowly.

'It's too risky, Phil. We aren't too popular with the locals. They'd love to have an excuse to give us a hard time. Plus I've got problems of my own, right now.'

'I'm not leaving without David,' I snapped.

Sam put down the rifle and walked over to the window.

'You're not leaving anyway,' he said.

He took a pair of binoculars from a hook and scanned the view outside.

'What do you mean by that?' I demanded.

'No one can leave right now. Mark and Rick have taken the boat over to Friday. They're worried about Pat and Russ, the guys who're gone. They haven't been in touch, and Mark thinks that something might have happened to them.'

'I don't care about that!' I shouted, standing up.

Sam whirled around.

'Well, you'd better start fucking caring!'

He glared at me.

'I had high hopes for you, Phil. I've been running this whole thing single-handed for years now. Do you have any idea of the strain I've been under? The only person I've been able to confide in is Mark, and he's got shit for brains. They all have. *You*'re the only person who ever really understood me, the only one I could talk to as an equal.'

He gripped my shoulders.

'Just say you're with me, Phil! That's all I ask, that leap of faith. Only you can make it, but once you do, everything else will come right!'

His eyes bored into mine. He was crazy, of course, but that didn't matter. As long as there was the slightest chance that David was still alive, I had to play along.

'All right,' I said. 'I'm with you.'

He stared at me, blinking. His eyes had filled with tears.

'Really?' he said in an almost inaudible voice. 'You really are?'

I nodded. He let go of me abruptly and moved away, rubbing his head.

'I can't believe this, Phil! It changes everything.'

He fell to his knees suddenly, hands clasped together, trembling with tension, head bowed in silent prayer. I felt a surge of nauseated terror. Whatever Sam was up to, this was no scam. He *believed*.

'OK, here's the deal,' he said, getting up. 'You saw the hall, right? No one there. It's the first time that's ever happened. Mark's turned them all against me.'

He measured me with his eyes for a moment. I tried to look sincere.

'What happened,' he went on, 'the last time some of our guys left the island, one of them didn't come back. That created problems, and now they've gotten worse. Andy, the guy who went along that time, told Mark what really happened. Mark told the others, and now they're all freezing me out.'

'What *did* happen?'

He shook his head impatiently.

'I can't explain all that right now. Just trust me, all right?'

He clapped his hands together and began striding up and down the room.

'What we need to do here, we need to buy ourselves some wriggle space. Unload Mark and get the others back in the zone, so if the news is bad and he tries anything, it won't gain traction. Get me?'

Thirty seconds before, Sam had been on his knees, now he was wheeling and dealing. I liked him better this way, but both seemed equally real to him.

'So the question is how we do that,' he continued, still pacing. 'Here's the deal. We get everyone together in the hall. I announce that Mark has rebelled and fallen from grace and that you've replaced him as Orc, my spiritual son. Then to clinch it, we have a big ceremony where you're reunited with *your* son.'

I felt my hands contract into fists, the nails digging painfully into my palms.

'So he's here?' I breathed.

Sam looked confused.

'Who?'

'David!'

He laughed.

'You think you were seeing things? Of course he's here!'

He shook his head.

'Man, the trouble we went to! First we had to follow you guys around for a month, work out what the deal was. Then Melissa and two of the guys had to move out there, get one of the kids here into that school, touch base with all the parents, buy a car, rent a place … It cost us a fucking fortune! But that time I talked to you in the bar, I knew that was the only way. You needed to be broken before you could heal. I still remembered the way it used to be back at that house, the two of us studying Blake together and rapping about everything under the sun. Those times were precious to me, Phil, but you'd retreated into this prison of work and family. That sickened me! And I swore then and there that I'd free you, whatever the cost.'

I fought to control my anger. That wouldn't save David.

'So where is he?' I asked.

Sam waved vaguely.

'You'll see him soon enough. It'll look better if you don't meet until we do it in front of the others. It'll come across as more genuine, know what I mean?'

This was too much to take. The rifle was still lying on the bed where he'd left it. I grabbed it and pointed it at Sam.

'*Where is he?*'

His eyes seemed to glaze over.

'I thought you were with me,' he murmured.

'I want my son! Now!'

Sam stood staring down at the floor. His expression had become infinitely weary.

'Then go find him,' he said.

I stabbed the rifle at him.

'Tell me where he is, you asshole!'

Sam sighed deeply.

'Guy was killed, I was in Vietnam.' he said. 'Best buddy of mine. Had a Purple Heart he got leading a patrol to rescue a downed aircrew deep in Cong territory. Know how he went out? Another guy went out on the toot one night, came back to barracks and started fooling around with his MK-16, making like it was a guitar, dig? And it went off and this guy gets one through the spine. Since then I never keep loaded weapons around.'

We looked at each other. He took a step towards me, reaching for the rifle. I pulled the trigger. There was a dull click. Sam took the gun from my unresisting hands. He opened a drawer in the chest and took out a metal pack which he clipped to the underside of the rifle. Then he turned to me, holding the weapon loosely.

His eyes did not leave mine. The barrel of the rifle moved languidly up and to one side, crossing over my body, until it was pointing at the wall. There was a shattering noise, a burst of explosions, maybe four or five. The air convulsed briefly and a sleet of splinters fell all over the room. I looked at the wall behind me. The bullets had passed straight through the solid tree trunks, gouging out a huge crater.

I turned back to Sam. The gun was now pointing directly at me.

'What do you think would happen if I pulled the trigger now?' Sam mused quietly.

I gazed back at him, my heart racing. The organ itself suddenly felt absurdly vulnerable, lodged right there at the front of the chest in its cage of fragile bone.

'That's what you should be asking yourself, Phil,' Sam continued. 'The answer to that question is the answer to all questions. Think about it.'

I nodded, as though we were having a normal conversation.

'OK, I will,' I said.

Leaving that room was one of the most difficult things I had ever done. Sam held the gun on me the whole time, and I had no way of knowing whether he would use it or not. It felt as though I was learning to walk all over again after a stroke. Every movement had to be planned and willed and then painstakingly executed.

Dusk was drawing in, filling the empty reaches of the hall with darkness. The fire had gone out and the air was cold and damp. I walked across to my room, the floorboards squeaking underfoot. My brain was awash with a mixture of fantasies with a factual solidity and facts which I would have dismissed a few hours earlier as fantastic. Which was harder to believe, that David was alive or that Sam had engineered his kidnapping? That my son and I might soon be reunited, or that we were both in the hands of a God-intoxicated maniac and his wayward gang of followers?

At first I was inclined to dismiss the whole thing as a cruel trick. After all, the kidnap victim had been selected at random. Each child chose their own coloured thread, and only one led out of the room. Then there was the question of David's clothing, drenched in his own blood. I'd only seen the child on the rock for a brief moment. Maybe Sam had just dressed up one of the kids to look like David. His picture had been in all the papers.

But I soon realized that these factors did not really create a problem. The kidnappers could easily have had another bag of threads which were all the colour of the fatal trail, and simply substituted this for the other when David came to make his choice. If it had been obvious that he'd been targeted, I might have suspected Sam earlier. As for the blood, they could have drawn off some of David's and used it to soak the clothing. Sam had told me that Melissa used to be a junkie. She would be good with needles.

I switched on the light and looked around my room. My overnight bag was where I had left it, all packed and ready for my abortive departure. On top of it lay a piece of paper neatly folded in two. I picked it up and opened it. On the inside was a rough plan of the compound, showing the hall and the shacks all around. Most of this had been done in blue ballpoint, but one of the houses, the furthest downhill, had been drawn in red. There was no message and no signature.

I lay down on the bed and closed my eyes. Just a few hundred yards away, on the island across the strait, normal people were getting on with their normal lives. There were telephones and TVs, cars and ferries, police and mail carriers, schools and libraries, stores and bars. Just a few hundred yards, but it might have been another continent, even another century.

I picked up the paper and looked at it again. Maybe there *was* a message after all. I put on a coat and went outside, taking the map with me. So far I hadn't explored the cluster of buildings to the east of the hall. This area had a slightly raffish, run-down, shanty-town air. The cabins had all been made from scratch, using a mixture of roughly trimmed tree trunks and a few planks and boards which looked like they'd been recycled from earlier constructions. The roofs were mostly corrugated metal, but a few consisted of a simple sheet of canvas thrown over a timber frame. One even had a turf roof, where wild plants had seeded themselves, put down roots and sprouted happily.

The house marked in red on the chart stood slightly apart from the others beside a huge first-growth cedar which had been left standing at the fringes of the clearing, where the zone of stubbly scrub began. The house was in fact partly supported by the tree, to which it was lashed by two rusty metal cables. It was a ramshackle structure made of boards and beams, some of which, judging by their smoothness, had been scavenged from the beach. The roof was hard to make out in the fading light, but seemed to consist of mottled camouflage canvas which might have started life as a piece of army equipment. A dim light was visible inside. Then something touched my back, and I whirled around.

It was Andrea. Without a word, she led the way along the side of the shack and opened a badly hung door made out of what looked like a cut-down ping-pong table. We went inside, stooping under the low door frame. The furniture consisted of the bed, an old outdoor table and a green metal chest which might well originally have served as packing for the canvas which sagged from its rudimentary supports overhead. An oil lamp was burning on the table. Andrea blew out the flame. She sat on the bed. I remained standing.

'I've been waiting behind that tree for over an hour,' she said. 'I didn't know who might come. I didn't dare leave a message in case one of the others read it. I just hoped you'd understand.'

'How do I know this isn't another set-up?' I demanded.

She sighed.

'You'll just have to believe me.'

'Why should I? You lured me down to the pool so that Sam could stage that little dramatic tableau. There's no use denying it! Sam has admitted the whole thing.'

She stood up, facing me. I couldn't make out the expression on her face in the gloom, but she sounded angry.

'Has it ever occurred to you that I might not be a free agent? Has it ever entered your head for a second that you might not be the only person in Sam's power? Do you have any idea of the risk I took in leaving that map in your room?'

I shook my head.

'Well, let me tell you what happened to one of the other women,' she said in a hard tone. 'She went along on a shopping trip with Lenny and Rick, and tried to sneak off. Said she had to go to the bathroom, then climbed out the window. They found her trying to hitchhike out of town and brought her back here. Sam had her stripped and tied to the wall-bars in his room. They left her hanging there by her arms for three days, taking turns raping her. When they finally cut her down she couldn't move her arms for a month. She's still in pain, even now, but they won't let her see a doctor.'

I sat down on the metal chest and buried my head in my hands.

'But this is crazy!' I exclaimed. 'He can't keep all these people locked up here against their will!'

'Yes, he can. Anyway, most of them want to be here. They believe everything Sam tells them.'

'What, this shit about Blake? Studying his poems like they were the Bible or something?'

'That's what they believe they are. They believe that William Blake was divinely inspired, and that his work is the word of God. They believe that Sam is the prophet Los, the second coming of Jesus. They believe that the world will come to an end soon and that they will be the only ones to survive. I thought you knew all this! I thought you believed in it too. Why else would anyone come here? That's why I was so afraid this morning. I thought Sam was testing me, using you as a spy to find out if I could be trusted.'

She shivered. There was no heating in the cabin, but I didn't think it was just a matter of the temperature. I went over and sat beside her, taking her hands in mine. Her thin, bony fingers were as cold as a corpse's.

'What about you, Andrea?' I asked. 'What are *you* doing here? Why didn't you leave after Lisa drowned?'

'Because I saw it happen.'

'So?'

She was silent a moment.

'What did Sam tell you about it?'

'That Lisa tried to swim across to that other island and didn't make it.'

'Did he say *why*?'

I shrugged.

'He said she was a good swimmer, only this time she over-reached herself.'

Andrea stood up and moved away into the shadows.

'Lisa *was* a good swimmer. A champion. We were at UW together, and she was on the Huskies team. But she was also far too smart to try and swim across to Orcas. The water around here is icy and the currents are fierce.'

'So why did she do it?'

She emerged from the darkness and stood in front of me.

'She didn't. Sam did.'

'Did what?'

'Drowned her.'

I stared up at her.

'She and I were swimming down at that pool,' Andrea went on. 'After a while the boat appeared. Sam was at the wheel. He called to Lisa. She swam out and climbed aboard. Sam took the boat out into the middle of the strait and threw her overboard.'

I was silent.

'That's why he'll never let me leave,' Andrea went on. 'He

made me write a letter home saying that I was going to Nicaragua. One of the guys who was going to Texas mailed it from there. When they didn't hear any more, my parents eventually came looking for me here. Mark took me up into the woods while Sam talked to them. I don't know what he said, but he can be very persuasive when he wants to be. They haven't been back.'

I stood up.

'But what about the others?' I said agitatedly. 'You can't just make all these people disappear without someone getting suspicious!'

'Sure you can, if you pick them right. There are a million homeless kids in this country. It's no problem to find someone with no roots, no hope, no paper trail. A couple of the guys go out recruiting every so often. They befriend these kids, give them some money and a big line about Sam having all the answers. If they decide the guy's no good, they let him go. All he knows is that some religious nut tried to get him to sign up. If they decide to take him, then he has to write a letter the same way I did. Sam always quotes that line from the Bible about leaving your parents and brethren and wife and children for the kingdom of God's sake. Most of these people weren't getting much return from those things anyway, so giving them up in exchange for board, lodging and the secret of eternal life is not a big deal for them.'

'Did he try and convert you too?' I asked.

She shrugged.

'I have to pretend to go along with it, but they don't really care what the women think. It's basically a guy thing. The women aren't initiated into the Secret. They just have to turn up for the lectures, take care of the scutwork, and spread their legs whenever Sam asks them to.'

I couldn't believe what I was hearing, and I didn't particularly want to. If what Andrea had told me was true, then the situation was far more dangerous than I had ever imagined.

'OK, you've told me your story. Now hear mine. My child was kidnapped and apparently murdered. As a result, my wife killed herself. Sam now tells me that he master-minded the whole thing because, quote, I needed to be broken before I could heal, unquote. Maybe that's true, maybe it isn't. I only saw that boy for a moment, and from a distance. It might have been some other child, dressed up to look like David. Sam could have got all the other details from the newspaper stories at the time. I don't know what to believe. I feel like I'm going crazy.'

Andrea gave a deep sigh.

'I'll tell you what I know. Melissa left the island for a while, a couple of months back, I guess. I lose track of time. When she got back, she had a child with her. We were told he was her son, and that one of Melissa's sisters had been looking after him all this while. No one thought anything of it.'

'Did you meet this boy?'

'Of course. He came to my classes.'

'How did he seem?'

She shrugged.

'Normal enough. He used to have coughing attacks, that was the only thing. Sometimes he seemed to find it hard to breathe. But after a couple of weeks here that stopped. Plus he used to ask when he'd see his mother and father again. Melissa told us that he'd been with her sister so long he thought she and her boyfriend were his parents.'

'And where is he now? With this bitch Melissa?'

'I don't know. The day you arrived, he disappeared. When I asked why he hadn't come to class, Sam warned me not to talk about it.'

'Well, I'm going to find out!'

I tried to push past her, but she blocked me with her body.

'No,' she said decisively. 'I will.'

We stood there in the darkness, holding each other.

'They won't tell you anything,' Andrea went on. 'They might talk to me.'

She released me.

'You'd better go,' she said. 'And be careful. If you're seen leaving here, we'll both be in serious trouble.'

'Do you have any children, Andrea?' I asked.

'I missed out on that.'

Her tone was flat, almost flippant.

'You must still be young enough,' I said.

'That's not what I meant. I haven't set foot off this island for what seems like a lifetime, and the breeding stock here doesn't impress me. Now go. Tomorrow morning I'll tell you what I've been able to find out.'

She accompanied me to the door. Outside, the darkness was now complete. I found Andrea's hand, squeezed it one last time and slipped away towards the fringes of the clearing.

Back in my room, I began to have doubts about the wisdom of trusting her. For all I knew, Andrea might be reporting back to Sam even now. Or perhaps he had set up this meeting too, to gain time, or work on my emotions in a different way. But this, I knew, was what Sam wanted, what he stood for. He revelled in obscurities and ignorance, in dysfunctionality and doubt. If I allowed them to overwhelm me, he had already won. I had to have faith, not in his hallucinogenic theology but in my own experience, and in the irreducible reality of another human being. Losing on those terms would be less destructive than winning on Sam's.

My thoughts turned to David. Was he warm enough? Had he been properly cared for? Would he recognize me again? How could I ever explain to him what had happened, and break the news of his mother's death? Above all, I wished I could *do* something. I felt so helpless. Everyone on the island, except maybe Andrea, was my enemy. There was nothing to be gained by single-handed heroics. I turned off the light and tried to sleep.

I awoke shortly after dawn to find a figure standing beside my bed.

Seventeen

Kristine Kjarstad was in tears when Steve Warren brought in the fax. Oh fuck, he thought, wondering if it was too late to 'eclipse himself', as his mother used to say. She had a load of oddball expressions like that. People thought everything had been easy for Steve, that he'd been born with a plastic spoon in his mouth. Nothing could have been further from the truth.

His mother was a war bride with whom his father had spent a pleasant few days during the liberation of Paris and then returned after the armistice to discover, as he put it, that 'there were *two* Battles of the Bulge, and we lost the second one'. The result was Steve's oldest brother, George, with an optional 's', who was born a few weeks after their marriage. Three months later, the newly-weds arrived back in Dick Warren's home town of Aberdeen, a logging community on the Washington coast.

The first month they were there, it rained non-stop for twenty-three days. Shortly afterwards, Françoise ('Frankie') Warren had the first of her spaz attacks. These took a variety of forms, all of them frighteningly unpredictable, from appearing at a wedding in what looked like a strapless nightgown and no bra, to serving dinner guests a boiled pig's head with the snout and ears still on.

Steve's siblings had dealt with this by copping out and acting weird themselves. Georges, who now insisted not only on this spelling but also the pronunciation that went with it, was a mainstay of the Blue Moon Tavern in the U District, where he gave recitations of his poetry. Annie lived in a cabin on Vashon Island, communing with the womanspirit of Puget Sound and 'invoking her intercession for our sins against the environment'.

Only Steve had possessed the grit and guts to transcend his unconventional upbringing and seize the lacklustre prizes which life has to offer those who do OK: a tract home in Bellevue he'd still be paying off when he was a hundred and ten, a car he could never find in a crowded parking lot because it looked just like all the others, a wife who could walk into a strange mall and locate the Hallmark store in seconds. Some men are born to mediocrity, some have it thrust upon them. Steve Warren was one of the very few who achieve it by their own unaided efforts. Despite the almost overwhelming handicap posed by his home environment, he could look back on his life and tell himself proudly, 'I did it *their* way.'

As a result, he felt he had the right to demand the same high standards of others, and Kristine Kjarstad had never let him down before. She could be a little snippy at times, yes, but he'd never seen her in tears.

'You all right?' he said, trying for the New Man image, concerned but not wimpy, like one of those sporty house-husbands you saw jogging around Green Lake with the baby.

'All right?' she snapped, pretending to blow her nose so that she could dab the tears away. 'Sure, I'm just fine. I just got through phoning the prosecutor in the Selleck case to tell him we can't proceed after all.'

Steve Warren dimly recalled the case she was talking about, some fourteen-year-old who'd been raped while walking home from her aunt's house. The victim had named a local kid who denied the charges, claiming that he had been drinking with friends at the time. The friends had corroborated his alibi, but Kristine Kjarstad had been sure they would back off once the forensic results came through.

'You mean the tests showed it wasn't him?' Steve asked in a solicitous tone.

'The tests never got done!' Kristine exclaimed. 'They've got a backlog of hundreds of cases down at the labs. Nothing gets processed until a trial date is set. Meanwhile the swab we took from the victim's vagina gets stored in a fridge down in the basement, right? A couple of months ago there's a power failure, and pretty soon you've got a couple of dozen samples of assorted bodily fluids turning green, growing legs and heading back to the farm. Result, the suspect's alibi will stand. We know he raped a fourteen-year-old, and he knows we know. And he's going to get away with it, and there's not a fucking thing that anyone can do. All right? Sure, I'm just *fine*. No problem.'

She passed a hand through her wavy brown hair and gave a long sigh.

'So what's new with you?'

Steve Warren held up the fax.

'This just came through from SPD. I took a look at it and … '

He broke off. The whole idea suddenly seemed flaky, maybe even slightly wacko. What if he told Kristine, and she looked at him and said, 'Are you feeling all right?' Steve took several deep breaths, trying to control this *crise de nerd*, as his mother used to say. It was so hard to be normal all the time!

'Yes?' said Kristine Kjarstad pointedly.

'Well, I just, see, OK, like, the thing is … '

'Are you feeling all right?'

Steve Warren dropped the fax on her desk.

'Just read it,' he said, and walked out.

Kristine skimmed through the fax, wondering what had produced this rare glimpse of spontaneity in a droid like Steve Warren. The fax was a standard request for a criminal record search, commonly known as a D and B after the credit check agency, Dun and Bradstreet. This one had originated in Atlanta, Georgia, and was made out in the name of Dale Watson, a.k.a. John Flaxman. It had been sent to the Seattle Police Department, and they had routinely copied it to the King County force, whose territory surrounds the city on three sides.

Neither of the names meant anything to Kristine, but she dutifully went down to the basement and ran through the files to see if there were any rap sheets lying around from before her time. There weren't, but on her way back she finally spotted the detail which had provoked her partner's personality attack. It was in the section dealing with the crime itself. Kristine had skipped this first time around, having discovered that it was a street incident of no interest, the kind of thing she imagined happening all the time in places like Atlanta.

Now, trapped in an elevator which stopped at every floor, she read it through out of sheer boredom. Two sentences leapt out at her: 'Subject was armed with a .22 Smith & Wesson revolver, as was his accomplice. They were also carrying a case with religious literature, a video camera, several sets of handcuffs and a roll of tape.'

The covering note from SPD was signed Don Krylo. Thirty seconds after she got back to her desk, Kristine had him on the phone. Krylo, a harassed-sounding sergeant in Central Homicide, was delighted when Kristine offered to deal direct with the original source of inquiry.

'You got a contact name?' she asked.

'I'll need to look it up. Let me call you back.'

'I'll hold.'

If she let Krylo go, she'd probably never hear another thing. While she waited, Kristine tried to get a firm grip on herself. She'd only just succeeded in putting the Renton case behind her. The last thing she needed was to open up that can of worms again to no purpose.

'Here we go,' said Don Krylo. 'Guy's name is Wingate. Lamont Wingate, Homicide Task Force, Atlanta City Police.'

'Great.'

'You think you got something on this guy?'

'I don't know. I need to check it out a little. It's tough for us here in the county. You know how it is, Don. We make a mistake, everyone starts cracking jokes about hayseed sheriff departments.'

Krylo, who had probably made more than a few himself, indignantly denied the possibility.

'It's just this is the second CRS we've received in this name,' he said. 'Both out-of-state, too. I thought maybe you might know why this guy's such a celebrity.'

Kristine Kjarstad felt her heart racing. She took a deep breath.

'This is the second one?'

'That's what it says here. There's a reference number to the other request, but I don't have it right … '

'Could you look it up?'

Her tone was eager, almost peremptory.

'I guess. Might take a little time. You wouldn't believe the mess we've … '

'I'll call you back in fifteen minutes, Don. That give you long enough? This is kind of urgent.'

'It is?'

Don Krylo sounded as though he suspected that something was maybe getting away from him here. Kristine tittered girlishly.

'No, I just mean I'm going out to lunch, right? And I'd like to get this wrapped up first. You know how it is,' she finished lamely.

'No kidding,' Krylo replied in the tone of a man who knew only too well how it was. 'Catch you in fifteen.'

Kristine put down the phone with a shaky hand. Fifteen minutes to fill. A thought had occurred to her while she was talking to Don Krylo, but for a moment she couldn't track it down. Then she remembered that she'd been meaning to call Paul Merlowitz. Her lie about going out to lunch had jogged her memory.

The original idea had been to pass on the information about the Wallis house. Paul was the perfect networker for a deal like this, with a ton of contacts all over the country. If anyone could find a short-term tenant with a kid Thomas's age, it was him. The problem was that Paul had this thing for her, and if she phoned him he would think she was coming on to him and she'd have to deal with the consequences of that.

In fact it was more than just a thing: he'd practically proposed to her. A lawyer's proposal, phrased in such a way that if she turned him down, as she had, he could make it look like he'd never made a firm offer in the first place. Nevertheless, they both knew what had happened. She'd expected him to drop her after that. God knows he wasn't short of other possibilities.

It wasn't that she didn't like Paul, in a way. But there were problems. For one thing, she didn't want to end up as some hotshot lawyer's trophy wife. For another, she didn't feel physically attracted to him, or not enough to make the difference. And then there was his work. They had met in court, a case in which she had appeared as a prosecution witness of a man charged with the murder of his business partner plus his wife, child and mother-in-law who were all in the house when it burned down.

As Merlowitz had privately admitted to her after the acquittal, there was no question that his client was 'guilty as fuck'. But he got him off by stacking the jury, working the ethnic angle – the accused was Korean – and plugging away at inconsistencies in the prosecution case and irregularities in the police investigation. None of these had the slightest bearing on the basic facts of the case, but they were enough to persuade at least one member of the carefully chosen jury that the accused's guilt had not been proven beyond all reasonable doubt.

Kristine had never tried to tackle Merlowitz about the morality of what he was doing. She knew exactly what line he would take: every citizen has the right to the best defence money could buy, better let ten guilty men go free than convict one innocent one, etc, etc. She acknowledged the force of these arguments, just as she acknowledged the need for a nuclear defence capability, but that didn't mean that she wanted to marry a B-52 pilot. Nor could she imagine letting into her life a man who earned obscene amounts of money dreaming up ways to free someone he himself admitted was guilty of a callous, premeditated murder.

Nevertheless, expediency won out in the end. Kristine had her principles, but she knew there was also a grey area where she could be bought. Whether or not she managed to come up with a vacation playmate for Thomas, she would certainly get a fabulous lunch. And if Paul Merlowitz didn't come up to her exacting standards, there wasn't anyone else around at the moment who did. She lifted the receiver and dialled.

After all her agonizing, Merlowitz wasn't taking calls. Instead, she got to speak with a secretary who ran through a whole repertoire of moves from the elaborate tai chi of commercial intercourse, concluding with the statement that Mr Merlowitz was 'in conference'. Kristine left a message, and immediately regretted it. Now she would be waiting, if only subconsciously, for the phone to ring. Merlowitz had her on a string. She should have hung up and called again at her leisure, instead of handing him that power.

Only ten minutes had gone by, but she called the Seattle Police back anyway. Not only was Don Krylo there, he had the information she'd requested.

'I was kind of doubtful for a while,' he told her. 'We're going on line here and everything's ass over tits, whole boxloads of stuff I could put my hand on a week ago've just like, you know, disappeared. Watch it be one of those, I told myself, either that or someone's circular filed the damn thing. Anyway, looks like you lucked out. The previous CRS on this guy originated in – you got a pen? – Evanston, Illinois. Detective Eileen McCann's the name right here on the docket.'

'Right. And thanks for coming up with this so quickly. I sure appreciate it.'

'Hey, that's what we're here for! Your tax dollars at work.'

'Have a great one, Don.'

'You too.'

Kristine Kjarstad lay back in her chair and closed her eyes. Her breath came irregularly, in spasms. It was almost like being in labour again. She called the switchboard and got the numbers of the Atlanta and Evanston City Police, and then a kind of paralysis descended on her. Every time she dialled, she found herself setting the receiver down the moment the ringing tone began. This was the moment of truth. The whole edifice she had constructed in her mind was either about to be revealed as a delusion, or not. It was hard to say which prospect she found more disturbing.

Finally she just steeled herself and dialled the Evanston number. She discovered that Eileen McCann did in fact exist – for some reason even this had seemed doubtful – but that she was 'away from her desk'.

'My name is Kristine Kjarstad. I'm with King County Police, in Washington State. It's about a suspect named Dale Watson. Could you please have her call me?'

Once again, Kristine found herself in the classic female position of waiting helplessly for the phone to ring. She was just about to call Atlanta when it did.

'Kristine? Paul Merlowitz.'

'Oh! Oh, hi. Hi Paul.'

'You called.'

'Right. I did, yeah.'

'So how you been?'

'Good. You?'

'Good.'

'Good. The thing is, you caught me at kind of a bad moment, I'm expecting a call, but I was wondering, maybe could we get together some time? The thing is … It's kind of difficult to explain on the … There's this house … '

'Thursday any good for you?'

'Thursday? That's … '

'Or I could do Tuesday next week. We're talking lunch, right?'

'That sounds … '

'The Painted Table, Thursday, noon, OK?'

'OK.'

'Great to hear you, Kristine.'

The line went dead. But the moment she put the phone down, it started to ring again.

'Hello?'

'Am I speaking with Officer Carstad?'

It was a woman with shoulder-pads built into her voice and a crisp, pedantic delivery.

'That's right.'

'This is Detective Eileen McCann, Evanston City Police. I understand you have information concerning our inquiry with regard to an individual named Dale Watson.'

'I may have.'

There was a pointed silence at the other end.

'And when will you be sure?'

Kristine Kjarstad took a deep breath. This was clearly going to be one of *those* calls.

'I'd like to know a little more about the present status of the case,' she replied.

The Evanston detective sniffed audibly.

'The basic information is on the inquiry we sent. It is not the policy of this department to give out progress reports regarding on-going investigations over the telephone.'

'Wait a moment!' Kristine snapped. 'I don't work for some tabloid TV show. Can't you cut me a little slack here?'

'I repeat, it is not department policy to … '

Kristine cracked.

'OK, if you won't talk, listen! The reason I'm calling is because I've received notice that a Dale Watson is currently being sought by another law enforcement agency in connection with a case which has certain resemblances to one on our files. Let me just run the outline past you. If it means nothing, go ahead and hang up. All right?'

'I'm listening.'

'Our case involves an apparently motiveless quadruple homicide. The attack took place in broad daylight at the family home. The victims were restrained with handcuffs, gagged with lengths of duct tape and shot at point-blank range in the back of the head. The weapon was a .22 handgun, probably a revolver, loaded with Stinger cartridges.'

She had spoken fast, the words gusted along on a tidal current of adrenalin and anger. Now she'd done, and sat tight, grasping the receiver tightly, probing the long silence the other end.

'You are describing a crime which you currently have under investigation?' the Evanston detective enquired at last.

'Correct. And I know of at least one more.'

Another silence.

'Then I consider it expedient that we should meet up as soon as possible,' Eileen McCann pronounced at last.

Success went to Kristine's head.

'Thursday any good for you?' she demanded. 'Or I could do Tuesday next week. We're talking lunch, right?'

'That's logistically problematic,' was the unruffled reply.

'OK,' said Kristine, getting a grip on herself. 'Fax me through details of your case, and if it looks like we're on to something here I'll get out there to see you within forty-eight hours. How's that sound?'

'Let's diarize.'

Whatever Eileen McCann lacked in charm, she made up for in efficiency. Twenty minutes later, Kristine had the entire dossier of the Maple Street shootings on her desk. She was still poring over it when Steve Warren appeared. He handed her a waxed cup filled with a creamy foam.

'Thought maybe you could use this,' he mumbled. 'Double tall's how you like it, right?'

Kristine barely looked up.

'Steve, you're a fucking genius!'

Warren flinched. He didn't deserve this! OK, so he'd screwed up earlier, but he'd tried to make it up to her, running over to the espresso stand and getting her a latte. There was no call for mockery.

'This thing has hair all over it!' Kristine exclaimed almost hysterically. 'And if it hadn't been for you, it would have passed us right by. No one else would have bothered to read those details about the MO that tie in with the Renton case.'

Steve Warren shrugged awkwardly.

'Hell, I'm just an average Joe … '

Kristine shook her head decisively.

'No, you're not, Steve. You're one of a kind.'

He looked at her as though she'd slapped his face, then turned without a word and walked out. Kristine shook her head and returned to her reading. She kind of liked Steve, but there was no getting away from the fact that the guy was a total fruit-cake.

It took her another thirty minutes to get a clear fix on the Evanston case. As soon as she had, she called Atlanta. At first it seemed that she was in for another round of the old crapola with some dickette who'd flunked out of charm school, but the woman who answered the phone turned out to be merely a call catcher. Detective Wingate, she informed Kristine, wouldn't be on duty for another three hours.

Kristine glanced at the clock. The idea of waiting seemed intolerable.

'Can you give me his home number?' she begged.

The steel magnolia replied that she was not authorized to give out such details, and offered instead to connect her to Wingate's colleague, one Charlie Freeman. There was silence, then another ringing tone.

'Homicide,' said a male voice.

'Detective Freeman?'

'Yeah.'

'My name is Kristine Kjarstad, I'm a homicide detective working out of King County Headquarters in Seattle. You want to call me back, check my credentials?'

'That's OK, ma'am, I know a cop when I hear one. Besides, this way it's your nickel. What can we do for y'all?'

Freeman's voice was deep, slow and sexy. Kristine found him easy to talk to. It remained to be seen whether the opposite was true.

'I've just seen a CRS from your Detective Wingate regarding an individual named Dale Watson. I was wondering if you could tell me a little more about that case.'

She braced herself for another bout of stonewalling, but Charlie Freeman apparently took a more relaxed view of his work than Eileen McCann.

'Sure. Not a whole lot to say, though. Two white guys go for a stroll in a black neighbourhood, for some reason we don't get. They meet up with three of the brothers and someone pulls a gun. One guy on either side gets dead and the white survivor is in IC. Half an inch to the left and he's history too, the doc says.'

'And he's Dale Watson?'

'No, Watson's the one who got whacked. He was shacked up with a teenage runaway. We got the name from her, plus the idea he was maybe from Seattle, which is how come we faxed you guys. You got anything on him?'

'Not under that name. But we've got a case on the books which looks similar.'

Charlie Freeman sounded sceptical.

'You sure about this, ma'am? I have to say the incident here looks like one of those classic street things.'

'This guy in the hospital, have you got a name?'

'Booked himself in as John Flaxman at the hotel, but that don't mean jackshit. He's out of danger now, but he still won't say a word about what they were doing that evening. Just lies there staring up at the ceiling.'

'Does he have any links to Seattle?'

'Not that we know of. I searched his hotel room, but he didn't have no ID, no tickets, no nothing. These guys were stripped. All I found was a pile of clothes and some athletic shoes, could have been bought anywhere.'

'Athletic shoes?'

'That was his own stuff. They dressed up as holy rollers that night, see? Bought themselves the outfits right here in town.'

Kristine stared at the wall. It seemed to be moving, bulging in the centre like a sail.

'What kind of athletic shoes were they?' she asked.

'Well, I don't rightly recall, ma'am. Some kind basketball shoe. But this is a doozy whichever way you look at it. Take the hardware they went in with. You go looking for trouble in a neighbourhood like that, you gotta pack enough gun. Now sure, a two-two can be a work of art, I got a couple at home, but out there on the streets you're up against Uzis, Cobrays, you name it. The toddlers pack magnums in their diapers, even our guys are outgunned half the … '

'If we could just get back to the shoes for a moment … '

Freeman sighed.

'What can I tell you? They were standard basketball shoes, the kind all the kids wear.'

'What brand?'

Her tone was almost rudely abrupt. Charlie Freeman sounded taken aback.

'I don't recollect, ma'am. What's with the shoes, anyhow? They were black, far as I recall. Yeah, and there was some kind of logo, a little red outline. Some guy doing a slamdunk.'

'Was the brand Nike?'

'How's that?' asked Freeman.

'N, I, K, E.'

'Is that how you say it? I always thought it rhymed with "Mike". Let me just look up my report here. Yeah, that's right.

Nike Air Jordan. You sure it's spoke like that? Sounds kind of weird.'

Kristine Kjarstad let out a long, slow breath.

'That's because it's a Greek name, Mr Freeman. Nike was the goddess of victory.'

'Well, hey, learn something new every day. Nike, huh? So who was she? Some kind of feminist?'

'Just a woman who hated to lose. You're talking to another. One more thing. Were there traces of paint on the soles of the shoes?'

This time there was a lengthy silence.

'Now you come to mention it,' Freeman replied in a different tone, 'I think there *was* something on them. I figured it was bubblegum or some ... '

'Because it was pink, right?' Kristine interrupted.

Another long silence.

'Now how in hell did you know that?' asked Charlie Freeman quietly.

'I'll tell you when I get there.'

'You're coming down south?'

'Correct. I'll call you back once I have my reservation. I'll want you to set up an interview with this guy in the hospital. Make it as long as possible. I plan to go to work on him, and I don't want the doctors getting in the way. This is our one chance to crack this case. It may be the last we ever get.'

'But I told you already, he refuses to say a goddamn ... '

'I think he'll talk to me, Mr Freeman. I'm pretty sure I can get him to talk to me.'

Eighteen

I awoke shortly after dawn to find a figure standing beside my bed. My dreams had been unusually vivid and elaborate, and for a moment I thought the intruder was another illusion, an escapee from that nocturnal melodrama. Then it moved, and I saw that it was female, and naked.

The covers were stripped back and I felt flesh touch mine at many points, chill on the surface but brimming with internal warmth. A face was buried in my neck and hands roved over my body. Firm breasts were crushed against my chest, the nipples knotted with cold. My cock, already thick with early morning tumescence, stirred and hardened as wiry pubic hair brushed against the bud.

I was still in that ambiguous state between sleep and waking, where the normal rules and standards do not apply. The woman was shivering, so I hugged her. It must be Andrea, I thought drowsily, come to bring me comfort and news of my son. Then the woman turned and raised herself slightly, looking down at me. The light was dim, seeping in through the cracks in the exterior walls and under the door, but it was enough to reveal my mistake. This was not Andrea. It took another few minutes, by which time we were almost coupled, before I realized who it was.

My erection immediately began to sag. I pulled away, giving myself space, studying the plain, feral face with its high cheekbones and stubby nose. My companion was none other than Ellie, the plump nymphet whose enthusiastic compliance Sam had so brutally vaunted the day before.

'Fuck me,' she whispered imploringly. 'Please fuck me.'

It should have been a perfect wet-dream scenario. Maybe it

was its very perfection which gave it away, that and the fact that her desperation was evidently not erotic. Certainly she played her part well. She sucked on my lips and her knee pushed in between my legs, and as my traitorous cock stiffened up she grasped it and squeezed so hard I gasped. In any other situation I would have been only too happy to go along and ask questions afterwards, but I knew I couldn't afford that luxury.

'What are you doing here?' I croaked.

'Just fuck me!'

She sounded impatient to get it over. The next thing I knew she was on top of me, her breasts in my face, trying to cram my flaccid cock inside her. We tussled like that for a while, but she was dry, and her clumsy and increasingly frantic attempts to force penetration removed any remaining traces of desire on my part. My prick had collapsed to a little bundle of slack flesh, as though trying to make itself invisible. I rolled her off me and pushed myself up on one elbow, looking down at her.

'You've got to fuck me!' she cried with a mixture of petulance and fear. 'You've got to!'

'You don't even want to.'

'Just do it!'

She heaved herself up with surprising energy and started wrestling with me again. I pushed her off.

'Cut it out, Ellie!'

'What's the matter?' she cried in what sounded like real distress. 'What am I doing wrong?'

I stroked her hair.

'It's not you,' I said. 'It's the whole thing that's wrong. I haven't even spoken a word to you, and here you are climbing into my bed and trying to rape me. What the hell's going on?'

She fixed me with a determined stare. Just as she had been trying too hard to be sexy, now she was trying too hard to be adult.

'Sam sent me. I'm supposed to bring you to see him. But first we've got to fuck.'

I ran my eyes over the chunky, pubescent body which wore its womanhood like a badly fitting prom dress.

'Why?' I asked.

'I don't know! You've just got to do it! If you don't, he'll say it was my fault and he'll beat me up.'

I looked her in the eyes. There was no doubt that she meant exactly what she said.

'Has he beaten you before?' I asked.

But she was already regretting her candour.

'Listen, you going to fuck me or what?'

I got out of bed.

'Consider it done.'

'But we *haven't* done it!'

I started to get dressed.

'So? Who's to know? Is he going to give you a swab test or something?'

I tossed over a light cotton bathrobe I found lying on the floor, which she must have discarded before I awoke.

'Listen, Ellie, I'll tell him you fucked me all ends up. I'll swear you were the best piece of ass I ever had in my life and you made me come ten times in a row. And if he lays a finger on you, you come straight here, OK?'

She pulled on her robe with a sniff of disdain.

'I don't need nobody to look after me,' she said in a tough lit-tle voice. 'I can take care of myself *just fine.*'

Even though she had been acting under orders, I got the dis-tinct impression that Ellie felt resentful that her advances had been spurned. I followed her out into the open spaces of the hall, barely illuminated by the early-morning light. There was no one around. Ellie marched resolutely across the boards to Sam's door and knocked four times, a little rhythmic figure that sound-ed like a code.

'Who is it?' said a voice inside.

'Me,' Ellie replied.

'Phil there?'

'Yeah.'

'Anyone else?'

'No.'

There was a loud thump. The door opened a crack and Sam's ferrety features appeared. He inspected us for a moment with a beady eye, then threw the door open. The automatic rifle in his hands was pointing right at us.

'Come on in,' he snapped. 'Close the door after you. Ellie, put the bar on.'

The girl picked up a length of wood from the floor and slipped it into the metal brackets bolted to each side of the door frame. Only then did Sam lower his weapon.

'Hi, Phil,' he said tonelessly. 'Did Ellie show you a good time?'

'She sure did! Best wake-up call I ever had.'

Sam smiled coldly. He nodded at Ellie.

'Get in the bedroom.'

She obeyed without a word. Sam laid the rifle down on the sofa and waved me to a chair.

'We've got a problem,' he said.

'I kind of figured we might.'

He sat facing me on the sofa.

'We're going to have to move along a lot faster than I was planning. It's too bad. It's way better to let the whole thing grow on you gradually, until you're not just ready for the truth but *hungry* for it!'

A look of power took possession of his face for a moment, then faded.

'In my dreams, it was all so different! You were ready, open, desperate! And then we'd have done the whole thing right, with a big hit of acid. The stuff you can get these days is twice as powerful as anything we ever had! It completely rewires your brain, lets you see the truth that's been staring you in the face all along. But there's no time, and anyway I need you straight.'

He leapt to his feet.

'Remember I told you Mark'd gone to Friday to find out what happened to Russ and Pat? Well, it turns out the news wasn't good. They called late last night. They'll be back soon, Phil, and they won't be bringing flowers.'

I stood up.

'Look, Sam, I wish you all the best in whatever doctrinal disputes you may be having with your followers, but you've got to understand that none of this has a fucking thing to do with me.

Just tell me where my kid is, give me the phone and let me call a boat. I'll be out of here in an hour, and you guys can hash out your exegesis of Blake's later epics to your hearts' content.'

He stabbed me with his eyes.

'I gave you Ellie,' he said quietly. 'She's my woman, Phil. No one else around here has had her. I mean, I'm trying to bond here!'

I didn't say anything. Sam shrugged.

'You want the phone? It's next door.'

I walked through to the middle room and looked around at the exercise equipment, the pool table, the wall-bars where Andrea said that one of the women had been tortured. Then I saw the twisted mess of plastic on the floor, and the bullet holes in the boards themselves.

'I guess I kind of lost it when Mark called.'

I turned around. Sam was standing in the doorway, the gun in his hands.

'He said a lot of bad stuff about me,' he went on. 'A load of insulting bullshit. After a while I'd had enough, so I picked up this baby and … '

He pointed the rifle at the remains of the cellular phone and mouthed a soft explosion.

'Well, that was really smart!' I said. 'Now if they do come back and try and make trouble, there's no way you can call for help.'

'We don't need help, Phil.'

He went over to the far wall and opened the doors to what I had assumed was a cue rack. Inside were about twenty weapons like the one he was carrying.

'We got the firepower and we got the manpower,' he said. 'I spent the whole night working on the other guys. They're all on deck. That just leaves you, Phil. Come on, let's get to work.'

He strode back into the other room. I followed, stopping in the doorway.

'First I want to see my son,' I told him.

Sam stretched out on the sofa and yawned massively.

'No problem. I'll send for him. Sit down.'

I took a seat on the chair facing Sam. He leaned forward intensely.

'Have you ever heard of the Secret of the Templars?' he asked.

My heart sank. I don't know what I was expecting, but it was certainly something more original than this. One of the guys I worked with at the community college was a conspiracy buff who used to press books on me about supposed secret societies dedicated to concealing the fact that Jesus had survived his execution, married Mary Magdalene and founded a dynasty which had controlled the destiny of the world ever since. He also believed in flying saucers and the prophecies of Nostradamus, and was an avid chess player and computer nerd.

'The Templars,' Sam continued without waiting for an answer, 'were the richest and most powerful bunch of motherfuckers in the medieval world, yet they were ruthlessly wiped out to the last man in this like show trial, right? The charges against them didn't make any sense, but they were tortured into making confessions and then burned. So what was the deal? Lots of people believe that the official charges were just a cover for something too terrible to be mentioned. The truth is that the Templars were the guardians of a secret which they had learned from the Cabbalists, who were these Jewish mystics ... '

'Sam,' I said, holding up my hand. 'Excuse me, but could we skip the history lesson?'

He wasn't used to being spoken to like that. For a moment he looked at me in a way I had never seen before, and which scared me. Then he shrugged.

'Maybe you're right. I've never done it this way before. It's kind of hard to know where to start.'

He looked down at the floor for a moment.

'OK, let's try something more recent. You remember that night at the Commercial Hotel? You remember that baby we were talking about, the one got cooked by its junkie mother? Have you seen what's been happening in Africa? Sometimes they just cut the kids' arms and legs off with machetes and let them bleed to death. Sometimes they ... '

'I don't need a catalogue of horrors, Sam. Sure, bad stuff happens. So what?'

He seemed to make a deliberate effort to fix me with his eyes.

'So what about God?' he breathed.

I sighed.

'That's not a problem for me, Sam. I don't believe in God.'

Sam smiled unpleasantly.

'So what *do* you believe in? A universe controlled by the laws of the jungle, where species come and go and the individual counts for nothing, and in the end the whole schbang collapses into a black hole? Is that the kind of world you want to live in?'

'I don't have a choice. But if I did, I'd rather live there than in a world ruled by an omnipotent Deity who lets all these horrors happen.'

Sam leapt to his feet and slapped his hands together.

'You've put your finger on it, Phil! How can He permit such things to happen? That's the whole point.'

'What about David?' I said.

Sam waved impatiently.

'Let's look at it the other way. Supposing God did use His power to prevent evil, what would happen?'

'We'd all be a hell of a sight better off.'

'Materially, sure! But what about spiritually? If the innocent never suffered and the guilty never prospered, faith would be meaningless. We would be *forced* to acknowledge God's existence. It'd be like trying to deny the law of gravity.'

I nodded.

'So you're saying that baby got boiled alive as exhibit A in an on-going theological demonstration?'

Sam smiled.

'God is both just and loving, Phil. He's not into playing sadistic games. Never for a single moment does he permit one of his creatures to suffer.'

I stood up.

'What about when you beat up Ellie?' I demanded. 'Are you saying her pain doesn't really exist? That she's just pretending to be hurt because she knows it turns you on?'

Sam searched me with his eyes.

'Ellie!'

The far door opened and Ellie walked towards us in her cotton robe.

'What?'

'Did you tell Phil here anything about our bedroom secrets?'

The look of betrayal she shot me was answer enough. Sam grabbed the rifle and jabbed the barrel into her stomach with a swift bayonet-like thrust. Ellie grunted and fell to the floor.

'Stop it!' I shouted.

Sam turned the rifle on me. He smiled lazily …

'I didn't do that to punish her, Phil. I did it to enlighten you.'

Ellie lay at his feet, clutching her abdomen.

'Initiation usually takes us over a year,' Sam went on. 'Sometimes longer. We don't have that kind of time, so I'm having to come up with some new methods.'

He pointed to the injured girl.

'Tell me what she's feeling, Phil.'

The rifle was still pointing at me.

'Is she in pain?' Sam asked.

'Of course.'

'How do you know?'

I fought to remain calm, to play this appalling game by the rules Sam had imposed.

'Because I know that if you get hit like that, it hurts.'

'That's not what I asked, Phil. Sure, you've taken hits and they hurt. *But how do you know this one hurt her?*'

I stared at him blankly.

'You don't!' he exclaimed. 'You can't! There's simply no way we can ever know what another person is feeling, or whether they're feeling anything at all!'

'"Hath not a Jew eyes?"' I murmured. '"If you prick us, do we not bleed?"'

Sam stepped over Ellie's prone form, gesturing rhetorically with his free hand.

'Yeah, I remember that class. The professor, what was his name? That old guy in the tweed jacket. Remember how he set fire to his pocket one time, putting his pipe back when it was still lit?'

There was a low moan from the floor behind him. Sam turned and prodded Ellie with his boot.

'Get the kid,' he said. 'Bring him back here.'

The girl got to her feet, bent over, still holding her stomach. Sam waved towards the bedroom.

'Come on, Phil.'

I followed. Sam evidently had a point to make, and since he was holding both my son and the gun it seemed best to let him make it. He threw the rifle down on the bed, picked up the binoculars and scanned the scene outside.

'Where were we?' he asked without looking round.

'You were saying that we can never be sure another person really feels pain,' I replied. 'But by the same token, we can never be sure they don't.'

'*Wrong!*' Sam retorted, whirling round. 'That's the whole basis of the Secret! All the top theologians and philosophers have wrestled with this whole question for thousands of years, but they've never come up with the solution! That's because you can't get there using mere rational thought. God has fixed it that way, because if the truth ever got out, His plan for the world would be destroyed. But He reveals the Secret to a few people in every age so that it won't be lost for ever. It's kind of like a covenant.'

I found myself nodding thoughtfully, as though we were discussing steelhead fishing techniques.

'And you're one of those people?' I prompted.

Sam nodded.

'It all happened that night I dropped that shit on the way back from the bar. Right there in that crummy house in Minneapolis, with you guys snoring your heads off all around. Divine revelation can happen anywhere, I guess. Kind of like Jesus being born in a stable. But it wasn't till I got back from the war that I really saw the significance of the whole thing. Even then I found it hard. I thought I was alone, you see. I thought I was the only person who had ever been granted this terrible vision of the truth. It seemed like a curse which I had to bear on behalf of all mankind.'

He sighed heavily.

'That was before I realized there was a tradition of the Secret stretching back to the beginning of recorded history. It has taken many different forms, but the one which inspired me to start this thing here was the Templars. They had this inner group of twelve Professed Knights who had all been initiated into the Secret. The great task I've been entrusted with is to recreate that holy community. I always wanted you to be part of it, Phil, from the very beginning. And now you will.'

He looked out of the window again.

'Let's go back to the baby that got scalded to death,' he said. 'How could God permit such a thing? That's the question, right? OK, here's the answer. He didn't.'

I frowned.

'You mean it never happened?'

Sam leaned forward and fixed me with his intense stare.

'*There was never any baby in the first place,*' he whispered.

We confronted each other in silence. Sam kept staring at me fixedly, as though trying to will me into acquiescence.

'So what was there?' I asked.

'There was something that looked like a baby and sounded like a baby,' he went on in the same hushed undertone. 'Only it wasn't.'

He relaxed now, pulling back and breaking eye-contact, as though the critical moment had passed.

'Think of it as a doll,' he said in his normal voice. 'The most advanced doll in the world, a million times more realistic than anything you can buy in the shops. It mimics a baby perfectly, but inside it's empty. It has no thoughts, no feelings, no capacity for joy or suffering. In a word, no soul.'

I tried to look as if all this made perfect sense, but that there were one or two details I hadn't quite got straightened out.

'But if we have no way of knowing whether other people have feelings or not, then it's impossible to distinguish the imitation baby from a real one. So the distinction is meaningless.'

Sam sighed and shook his head.

'You're still thinking logically, Phil! It's not just that baby we're talking about here. It's also the baby's junkie mother and the abused wife in the apartment next door and the kid knocked down by a hit-and-run in the street outside and the guy dying of cancer in the hospital across town and the family of ten crushed in an earthquake who called for help for five days before dying. It's every single victim of evil and injustice and catastrophe in the whole world ever since the beginning of time!'

I wondered if Ellie had brought David yet. Perhaps he was even now just a few yards away from me. But Sam had the gun, and I was increasingly convinced that he might be capable of using it. I had to keep him in play, at least for now. On the other hand, I knew he wouldn't buy it if I just pretended to go along with everything he said. He had to believe he had convinced me intellectually.

'OK, let's see if I've got this,' I said. 'Bad stuff appears to happen, but it may not really, because we have no way of knowing whether the people it happens to are real.'

Sam shook his head vigorously.

'We *do* know. That's the whole point!'

'But how? You just got through saying there was no way of telling the difference!'

He made an impatient gesture.

'Listen! If God is love, He won't let anything bad happen to someone real.'

I shrugged.

'So?'

'So if it *does* happen to them, it means they can't be real!'

He stamped his foot on the floor in delight.

'Get it? It's so simple, so elegant, as only the truth can be!'

His expression suddenly became deadly serious.

'That's why the Secret can only be revealed to a few chosen individuals. You understand what it means? It means you can do what the fuck you want! You can beat people, shoot them, burn them, torture them, anything at all! Because if God allows you to do it, the victim was never really there in the first place. He was what Blake calls a spectre. An emanation, a mere shadow. "Why wilt thou give to her a body whose life is but a

256

shade?", *Jerusalem*, chapter twelve, verse one.'

He broke off, listening. Then he moved back to the window and reached for the binoculars.

'Course, this is just the bare theory I'm giving you here,' he said. 'To become a full initiate, you have to prove your faith in practice. And I have the feeling you might get the chance real soon.'

'How do you mean?' I asked.

He adjusted the focus of the binoculars.

'Jesus!'

'What is it?'

He handed me the binoculars without a word. I raised them to my eyes. Over the tops of the trees, a wide swathe of the ocean inlet was visible, a choppy sullen grey. Then I spotted the boat bouncing through the waves towards the island. It was painted blue with some kind of white marking on the side, and was smaller and trimmer than the one on which I had arrived. The man at the wheel seemed to be wearing some kind of a uniform. As the boat slowed and turned, making for the pier, I was able to distinguish the marks on the hull, large white letters reading POLICE.

Nineteen

The day after she had spoken to Charlie Freeman, Kristine Kjarstad caught the red-eye to Chicago, arriving at five a.m. Considering the hour, O'Hare was a hive of activity. It had a buzzy, big-city feel in striking contrast to the quiet, deserted spaces of Sea-Tac the night before. Kristine could remember nothing in between except one glimpse of some town on the prairie, lines and clusters of lights like molten plasma showing through cracks in the black surface crust.

She went into a café staffed by two male Hispanics sporting huge gilt rings, and ordered a bran muffin and a mug of coffee which would have put the place out of business in a week back in latte-land. Dawn was just breaking, patches of dark blue sky appearing against the lowering clouds. Living in a city defined by hills and water, Kristine had been amazed by the scale and regularity of Chicago as they overflew the vast grid of streets which seemed to stretch away for ever, with highways and rail-road lines overlaid on it like cross-hatching.

Here at the airport, it paraded its character in a different way, in the sheer variety of the people around, and in the way they presented themselves. Two paunchy men wearing tractor caps and baggy leisure outfits sat opposite two scrawny women in thick-rimmed glasses, stud earrings and floppy pantsuits. Next to them, a group of businessmen in Italian suits were trying unsuccessfully to ignore a woman making a full-frontal fashion statement in a slinky, skin-tight sheath. There was a hip black dude too cool to look at anyone, a slutty woman of about thirty with heavy make-up and come-on hair, a crop-haired guy with tattoos on his arms and macho-military clothing, women in two-piece suits with a full complement of matching accessories.

It all made Kristine feel dowdy and provincial. Seattle was a pleasant place to live, but it was not a sexy city. No one dressed to impress, there was little eye-contact and street life was like her mother's cooking: bland, wholesome and homogeneous. She was so used to being invisible that it was a shock to find all these people eyeing her, sizing her up, weighing and measuring her. A sense of anxiety came over her, a panicky suspicion that this whole trip was based on a delusion which would instantly collapse under the weight of scrutiny it would be exposed to out here in the real world.

Rather than go through another humiliating interview with Dick Rice, she had taken a couple of days off, parked Thomas with his father and bought the ticket herself. If she came up with the goods, she would bill the department. If not, she was stuck with the tab. But it wasn't the money that worried her so much as the prospect of being revealed as an unsophisticated, self-important hick, like some small-town genius who keeps bugging the Patent Office with plans for inventions you can buy for twenty-nine cents at any drugstore.

Outside the terminal, she picked up a cab to Evanston. The vehicle was an old Dodge with spongy shocks, a high-pitched whine from the transmission and a tendency to pull to the right when they braked. The back seat was covered in a crocheted afghan, like a sofa in a blue-collar living room. The driver was a Pakistani who had been in the country for two months. He was courteous and voluble, but seemed to have only the vaguest grasp of the local geography.

'Evenstone, Evenstone, Evenstone,' he chanted softly. 'Nice town, nice streets, nice people, but is not a good place to go from here. In the city, no problem. I am seeing signs, 'Evenstone', even though I do not myself go there at this time. But from here is very difficult, I think.'

Kristine finally went back inside and bought a street map from which she gave the driver directions. The route turned out to be very straightforward, north a ways on Highway 294 and then east along a street called Dempster running dead straight for eight miles to the shores of Lake Michigan.

The cab let her off in the wedge of shops and offices a few blocks wide which constituted the miniature city's downtown area. She tipped over-generously, got a receipt, and then spent about five minutes going over various possible routes back to Chicago. The driver listened with a look of increasing desperation, like a man who suspects that he may never see his family again. Eventually Kristine gave him the map as well, and the Dodge lurched off, leaving a smudge of black exhaust smoke on the still air.

Her appointment with Eileen McCann wasn't until eight o'clock, and since nothing in Evanston was open yet, she decided to wander around and pick up the feel of the place. The broad, tree-lined streets leading to the lake were lined with brick apartment buildings fixed up like fake castles, with leaded windows, crenellated roofs and turrets with arrow slits, and huge mansions in Tudor or New England style, each standing on a lot big enough to accommodate six houses like her own.

She spent a while walking along the lake, then wandered back under a low iron railroad bridge into a neighbourhood of slightly less grandiose properties a few blocks inland. This area may have been on the wrong side of the tracks, but it wasn't exactly skid row. The houses were spacious and well-proportioned, the yards deep and well-tended with mature trees, the streets broad and quiet. It was only when she saw the sign reading MAPLE that she realized she had stumbled on the site of the crime which had brought her there.

The house itself was four blocks farther south. She spotted it at once by the FOR SALE sign. The name of the realtor had been changed from Bonnie Kowalski to Evan Krebb. It was a lugubrious half-timbered affair with a ground floor in brick, a fancy arch over the front door, and steeply angled roofs rising to gothic peaks. After all the unwelcome publicity the property had received, moving this home was going to be a real test of Mr Krebb's salesmanship.

Kristine walked on, shaking her head slowly. Of the many questions to which she wanted answers from the wounded gunman in Atlanta, none obsessed her more than the choice of target. Between the Sullivans' home in Renton and this Victorian pile lay a socio-economic gulf as wide as the distance between the two towns themselves. What conceivable criterion could bridge such a gap?

There were plenty of other mysteries, of course. The Dale Watson who had been involved in the Evanston case was dead, but another one had appeared in Atlanta. Was this just a coincidence, or was there a generic 'Dale Watson' of whom these two were simply examples? Above all, what was the purpose behind such senseless killings? With any luck, Kristine thought as she strolled back to the centre of town, she would have the answers to all these questions by that evening. Her connecting flight left at one-thirty, getting into Atlanta three hours later. By five, or shortly after, she would be at the surviving gunman's bedside.

Despite what Charlie Freeman had said, she didn't think it would be too hard to make him co-operate. The detail of the Nike Air Jordan basketball shoes clinched it. She felt sure that the man in intensive care in Grady Memorial Hospital was one of the two who had taken part in the Kansas City shooting, where he had stepped in the pink paint hurled in a last act of desperation by Winston Jones, the handyman. And he had also been at the house in Renton, where Jamie had seen the shoes from his hiding place. But their owner didn't know anything about this. He thought he was safely anonymous, supposedly the innocent victim of an unprovoked street attack. Best of all, he had no idea that Jamie Sullivan had survived.

Kristine had already put together her game-plan. She wouldn't ask questions, she would make statements. She'd start by describing the Renton and Kansas City killings in great detail. Then she'd confront him with a copy of her interviews with Jamie, carefully edited to exclude the fact that the boy hadn't actually seen the killers. Finally, at the psychologically precise moment, she would drop in the detail of the Nike Air Jordans. That would be enough to make him talk, she calculated, particularly in his weakened condition. The case against him was airtight, and in a death-penalty state. The shock of discovering that his crimes were known, documented and witnessed, added to the prospect of enduring weeks of agony in the hospital only to end up dangling from the end of a rope, would surely be enough to break even the strongest and most stubborn spirit.

At exactly eight o'clock, Kristine Kjarstad presented herself at the front desk of the police station and asked for Eileen McCann. While she waited, she surveyed her reflection in a glass door across the room. With the image she had formed of Eileen McCann in mind, she had given some thought to her own. Finally she had settled for a grey cotton-blend suit, sober but expensive, with a stiff backbone of polyester to help resist the rigours of an overnight in cattle class. Add her executive-style briefcase, and she figured she was a match for anyone.

It turned out she needn't have bothered with any of these elaborate preparations. In person, Eileen McCann was a sad frump, overweight and out of shape, a chain-smoking fashion victim for whom every day was a bad-hair day. She greeted Kristine coolly and invited her into a small, immaculately neat office. The walls were bare, the papers and books neatly stacked, the furniture modern and functional. Even the cigarette butts in the ashtray were aligned as precisely as they had been in the pack.

'Do you have an interesting life, Ms Carstad?' McCann asked when they were seated. 'Professionally, I mean.'

Kristine shrugged.

'King County is pretty big. It stretches from the ocean all the way up to the mountains, and surrounds Seattle on three sides. So we get our share of action.'

McCann crushed out her cigarette and laid it beside the others in the ashtray.

'I envy you. Crimewise, Evanston is strictly bush league. The most interesting case I've had until this thing was an alleged date rape involving two students from the Garrett Evangelical Theological Seminary. And the only interesting thing about that was trying to figure out which of the parties involved was lying most about what. So yesterday, instead of trying to break through to a new level in the video game which my partner thoughtfully downloaded into our computer, we worked the phones and the fax and contacted four hundred law enforcement agencies and state prosecutor's offices across the country. Correction, three hundred ninety-two.'

Kristine looked suitably impressed.

'That must have taken hours.'

'Jeff went home at five, but then he has a home to go to. I stayed till eleven. I made a few more calls out west, where they were still at work, then collated the data we'd come up with. I didn't even notice the time, to tell you the truth. I was too damn excited.'

'You found something?'

Eileen McCann wrinkled her unlovely nose.

'I would hardly have brought the matter to your attention otherwise, Detective Carstad.'

'Call me Kristine.'

The other woman appeared to consider this offer carefully.

'OK. And you can call me Iles.'

'Iles?'

'That was my father's name for me. My mother always referred to me as Miss Eileen. "Well, Miss Eileen, straight As again, huh? Looks like you must have brains, at least. Let's hope so, child, because that face sure as hell won't pay your freight." She was typical lace-curtain Irish, hypocritical with outsiders, ruthless with her family.'

She passed Kristine a sheaf of neatly typed pages.

'OK, here's my homework from last night. As you'll see, our makeshift poll elicited six matches to add to the two we already know about.'

'Make that three. After I called you, I found out about what looks like another one, in Atlanta.'

Eileen McCann lit another cigarette.

'I'd like to hear about that later, Kristine. As I was saying, we came up with six cases which fit the broad parameters you outlined on the phone. In reverse chronological order, they are St Louis, Los Angeles, Oklahoma, Columbus, Salt Lake City and Houston.'

Kristine scanned the first sheet, which provided brief details of location and timing for each crime. The earliest was four years ago. The rest had occurred at irregular intervals since then, anywhere from a few weeks to several months.

'You sure got a quick response out of the LEAs involved,' she said, partly to cover her embarrassment at not having done the same thing herself weeks before.

'They mostly didn't even have to consult their files,' McCann replied crisply. 'The kind of thing we're talking about here is so unusual it tends to stick in the minds of the investigators however long ago it was. Most of them were able to tell me what I wanted to know then and there, over the phone.'

She consulted a copy of the document she had given Kristine.

'As you can see, Houston is chronologically the first of the presumed series. The victims were three males in their twenties and a prostitute they had brought back from a bar. The men were living in a trailer. They had a dog loose in the yard. A lump of raw steak was wedged in the chainlink. When the dog came to investigate, it was shot with a .22 calibre automatic silenced with the nipple from a baby bottle which was found discarded at the scene. One of the guys comes to the door and is shot between the eyes. One of the others tries to grab a rifle on the wall, doesn't make it. The other and the hooker are both shot in the head at close range.'

Kristine had been following the typed report.

'They used regular CSA ammo, no handcuffs or gags, and an automatic, not a revolver. Apart from that, the MO fits.'

'You'd expect some variation. They'd refine the details as they gained more experience. For instance, realizing that the benefit of being able to suppress the noise from an automatic was outweighed by the disadvantages of leaving behind identifiable ejected cartridges or wasting time hunting around for them. On the other hand, the similarities may just be superficial. The Houston PD wrote it off as some kind of low-life feud. The victims all had records going way back. Maybe they'd made one too many enemies.'

Eileen McCann tapped the ash from her cigarette.

'But take a look at the next one. Salt Lake City, a widow living alone with her cat. No criminal connections there, and no hint of a motive. The victim had almost eight hundred bucks in a vase sitting in plain view right there on the mantel, but it was untouched. Plus there's a second victim who just happened to be there at the time, a neighbour's kid who came by for piano lessons. He heard the shot and ran, but they caught up with him at the back door, which was locked, and took him down too. Which is maybe why they've started using the restraints and the gags by the time we get to Columbus, Ohio. That way they can go through the house and secure all the victims before they start shooting.'

Kristine turned the page. Her heart was pounding with a mixture of excitement and apprehension. If this *was* a series, it was one of the biggest things in years. The investigation would make or break her career, and not just her career. 'It's theirs to screw up,' Dick Rice had told her. Now it was hers.

'What happened in Columbus?' she murmured.

'A doctor and her teenage son are having dinner when someone comes to the door. A neighbour sees two men on the stoop but pays no attention. She remembers the time, though, because *Jeopardy* is just beginning. When the woman's husband gets home shortly afterwards, he finds his wife and child shot dead. A patrol car a few blocks away is there within seconds. Not more than ten minutes have elapsed since the shootings, but the killers have disappeared.'

Kristine nodded absently, following the script in front of her.

'And then Oklahoma,' she remarked, just to make it look like she was on the case.

'Right. Two gay guys. It looks like one of the killers posed as a delivery man that time. The cops found the pizza still in the box on the porch. Bought as a take-out, paid cash, no record. Guy comes to the door, sees the box, relaxes. "There must be some mistake, buddy." "Isn't this 3468 Roanoke?" "Sure, but we didn't order a pizza." Blam, blam. Los Angeles, an illegal immigrant and three friends playing cards one evening. Nothing new there. St Louis's kind of instructive, though. This is a classy high-rise with a security guard, closed-circuit TV, the works.

Our guys turn up in overalls and say they've got a sofa which Mr Miller in 308 ordered from the store. Mr Miller isn't home, as they've no doubt ascertained by phoning a few minutes before. The guys show the guard the sofa they've got right there blocking up the lobby. "We just need to stick it inside the door of the guy's apartment," they say. "It'll take two minutes." So the guard lets them into 308, where they pull guns and cuff and gag him. But – get this – *they don't kill him.*'

Kristine Kjarstad looked up with a puzzled expression. She'd lost track of her place in the text, overwhelmed by the other woman's dominant personality.

'So who did they kill?'

Eileen McCann stubbed out her cigarette and added it to the growing pile.

'Some newly-weds who'd just moved in. They used the guard's master key to get in. But that's not significant. The point is, why didn't they shoot the guard too? The guy was with them for almost ten minutes. He was able to give the police a full description. If these guys are so ruthless they kill kids and babies, why do they spare a witness who could send them both to the gas chamber? They make a big point of not leaving any evidence behind, no prints, no spent cartridges, no traces of any kind, yet they have this guy at their mercy and let him live! Why?'

Kristine Kjarstad shrugged. She felt good again, in charge. By this evening I'll have the answer to that, she thought.

'Beats me,' she said.

Eileen McCann nodded.

'Are you religious, Kristine?'

'What's that got to do with it?'

She felt the ground give way beneath her again. Eileen McCann smiled for the first time.

'It's just that I don't want to offend anyone's sensibilities,' she said. 'It seems to be so easy to do these days. I myself am a Catholic of the cafeteria variety, and last year I received from an ancient aunt a perfectly hideous calendar featuring photographs of the present pope which I put up on the wall in here, largely to get it out of the house. A co-worker who recently converted to Islam objected to this, and the Chief made me take it down. His secretary had taken him to court about a Matisse print he had bought to brighten up his office, on the grounds that the semi-nude subject was, quote, demeaning to her as a woman and a blatant act of sexual harassment in the workplace which made her feel raped by proxy, unquote. So you have to tread delicately.'

'I'm kind of a go-along, get-along Episcopalian,' Kristine replied.

Eileen McCann nodded.

'That's sufficient for my purposes.'

'Which are?'

'To remind you, and myself, that the human brain favours connections over disjunctions. In other words, we are programmed to privilege data which appear to generate patterns over data which call patterns into question. Hence the eternal temptation of God, and the corresponding necessity of an organized theology by means of which these temptations can be safely controlled.'

Kristine sat looking at her in amazement. How little we know about anyone, she thought, and how much we presume.

'Descending from the theological to the criminal,' McCann continued, 'we are faced here with a situation in which the temptation to make connections is almost overwhelming. These killings seem to exemplify all the things we fear most about the society we live in. Random violence, the killer at the door, your name on some unknown agenda. We need to construct a theory to connect and contain these events. What worries me is that in satisfying that urge, we may find ourselves ignoring the facts which tend to contradict any such thesis.'

'Such as?' Kristine demanded.

'Such as the absence of any conceivable motive. People don't just travel all over the country committing acts of violence without some reason. If it's a terrorist group, how come they aren't publicizing their activities? And who are they targeting? In your case they killed a baby, in Kansas a cripple, here a realtor and a lawyer. What's the connecting thread? It doesn't exist. There's no discernible victim typology, by age, gender, ethnicity, profession, religion or social level.'

Kristine Kjarstad nodded.

'I see what you're saying here, Iles. But I still think there *is* a pattern.'

'Because of this Atlanta case? Tell me about it.'

Kristine hesitated.

'It doesn't sound like much. Two whites and three blacks in a fire-fight. One on either side was killed, the other white is in the hospital.'

'I don't see the connection.'

'There may not be any. But the white guys were armed with .22 Smiths loaded with this Stinger ammo, and they were carrying a case with handcuffs and a roll of duct tape. I figure they were on their way to hit a house when they ran into a different kind of trouble. Anyway, I'm going down there to speak to the survivor.'

Eileen McCann raised her eyebrows.

'You're going to Atlanta?'

She sounded disapproving. Kristine felt a need to justify herself.

'I know it's a long shot, but this could be one of the biggest things in years, Iles. We'd be national celebrities!'

She immediately regretted this last remark. I've been spending too much time with Steve Warren, she thought.

'*You* might, Kristine,' Eileen McCann replied pointedly, 'but it would take more than a mere homicidal conspiracy to get this mug on coast-to-coast television. Anyway, I think you're allowing your dreams of stardom to run away with you. Our presumptive killers don't have a monopoly on Smith & Wesson handguns or fragmenting bullets. Nor is there any reason to suppose that they are the only ones to have realized that handcuffs are the best way to … '

'There's something else,' Kristine interrupted. 'The guy who was killed was going under the name Dale Watson.'

Eileen McCann waved her hand impatiently.

'Dale Watson's dead. That's one thing we know for sure. His father went to the morgue and ID'd the body.'

'So the guy in Atlanta is using the name as an alias. But why *that* name?'

They stared at each other.

'Maybe he read about it in the papers,' McCann suggested. 'A kind of copycat thing.'

'Maybe. But that's kind of weird too. Like you said, these people seem to go to enormous lengths to avoid leaving any clues. So you'd think they'd be smart enough not to use a name which is already known to the police in connection with a similar crime.'

Eileen McCann looked at her for a long time.

'What time is your flight?' she asked.

'I have to check in by one.'

McCann glanced at her watch.

'I'll give you a ride. We can pick up a bite to eat on the way.'

Much to Kristine's surprise, Eileen McCann turned out to be something of a foodie. The 'bite to eat' consisted of eight helpings of delicious dim sum at a restaurant in a predominantly Jewish neighbourhood called Lincolnwood. Eileen was relaxed, witty and informative about her work, colleagues and the socio-cultural microclimates of the northern Chicago suburbs. By the time they reached the airport, they were talking like friends.

Instead of dropping Kristine at the kerb, Eileen parked in the short-term facility and accompanied her inside, then abruptly dashed off to use the bathroom without saying goodbye. Kristine headed for the gate, where the plane was boarding. She found her seat and settled back with a copy of *Vanity Fair* she had bought at Sea-Tac the night before.

The plane had levelled off at cruise altitude when she looked up to see Eileen McCann walking down the aisle towards her.

'What are you doing here?' she demanded.

'God, I hate flying!' the other woman exclaimed. 'Two hours without a smoke.'

She smiled and shrugged.

'Here's the deal. You get the TV coverage, and they can stick me on NPR and local radio. Even my mother conceded that my voice wasn't so bad. Or as she tactfully put it, "If you could date by phone, the guys'd be all over you like an old coat."'

She settled into an empty seat across the aisle, pulled out a battered paperback and didn't utter a single word for the rest of the flight. Kristine dozed.

The descent into Atlanta was bumpy, the landing hard. It was pouring with rain, sheets of it falling from a sky the colour of mud. They exited the plane, passing through an intermediate zone of clammy air before the air-conditioning took over. It was like walking through a hot shower. Among the crowd at the gate was a tubby black man with glasses and a moustache holding a piece of cardboard with Kristine's name written on it in pink marker.

'Were you sent to pick me up?' she asked him.

'You Miss Kjarstad?'

He pronounced it perfectly.

'That's right.'

'I figured you far taller, more intense,' the man went on with a broad smile. 'The Nike type. Charlie told me about that. He was very impressed, you knowing Greek and all.'

She recognized the voice now. He had called her the day before to make final arrangements for her visit.

'You're Lamont Wingate, right?'

The man stuck out his hand.

'Pleased to meet you.'

Kristine turned to introduce her companion.

'This is Detective Eileen McCann of the Evanston City Police. She also has an interest in this case.'

Lamont Wingate shook Eileen's hand too.

'It's my pleasure to welcome you to Georgia, ladies.'

'But I thought we arranged to meet at the hospital,' Kristine said. 'There was no need to come all the way out here to the airport.'

Lamont Wingate suddenly looked serious.

'Yeah, well, there's been a change of plan, you see. I've been trying to reach you all day. If I'd known you were in Evanston, I'd have called there. The thing is, I'm afraid you've made a wasted trip.'

Kristine felt her stomach contract painfully.

'What do you mean?'

'That guy you came to talk to? He's dead.'

'No!'

It was a shriek. Eileen McCann put her hand on Kristine's arm.

'You mean he had a relapse?' she demanded.

Lamont Wingate shook his head.

'Did it hisself. Called the night nurse as she passed on her way back from tending to another patient and asked her for a drink. She went off to get it, he lifted a hypodermic needle off her cart. Time they found him, it was too late. "Exsanguinated", they called it at the hospital. Found an artery and stuck the needle right in there. Blood pressure does the rest. The mattress was soaked right through.'

He shook his head sadly.

'I sure am sorry you ladies had to come all this way for nothing.'

Twenty

As the boat slowed and turned, making for the pier, I was able to distinguish the marks on the hull, large white letters reading POLICE. I almost broke out laughing.

'Well, Sam, looks like the cops have decided to pay you a visit anyway!'

I set down the binoculars and turned to relish my moment of triumph. Then I saw the rifle lying on the bed, and remembered the doctrine which Sam had taught his followers, the Secret which gave them the power of life and death over everyone else. I suddenly had visions of a violent clash with the law followed by a long siege with an uncertain ending. The essential elements were all in place: a tightly knit group of people in the grip of mass psychosis who believed themselves to be chosen and protected by God, and who had access to an arsenal of automatic weapons.

Sam had been staring at me all this while, biting his thumb compulsively. Maybe he sensed what I was thinking, because at the same moment I dived at the bed and grabbed the rifle, he hurled himself at me and almost knocked it out of my hands. But I managed to hang on, twisted around and freed myself enough to smash the butt down on his head. He let go and sank to the floor with a moan.

I backed away, pointing the gun at him.

'OK, Sam, you want to test your little theory? Go right ahead! Let's see if God miraculously stops the bullet in mid-air before it has a chance to blow your fucking brains all over the wall! Or maybe it'll just bounce off you. What do you think?'

I was hysterical with rage and loathing. I wanted to riddle him with bullets, blow him away, demonstrate once and for all the reality of my existence by annihilating his.

'I guess I was wrong,' Sam murmured, sitting up. His head was bleeding, I noted with pleasure.

'I guess you were! Hey, looks like I cut your scalp open when I hit you back there. Tell me, is your pain real? You see, I have no way of knowing. Maybe you're one of those spectres you were talking about, just a piece of scenery in the great cosmic farce!'

'First Dale, then Russ and Pat, Mark and Rick. And now you, Phil. I was wrong about all of you. I've been wrong all along. Maybe there *is* no one else. Maybe I *am* alone.'

Bursts of gunfire resounded in the distance, one-two-three, one-two, one-two-three-four. Sam crawled to his feet.

'Hold it!' I told him.

He didn't pay any attention. Throwing a quick glance out of the window, he ran from the room.

'Stop or I'll shoot!'

But I didn't. Despite my fantasies of blasting him away, when the moment came I couldn't pull the trigger. Then I remembered the rack of guns next door, and ran after him. But Sam rushed straight on through and out into the hall. His footsteps hammered briefly over the wooden boards and then fell silent.

I had no idea what he intended to do, but my priority was to contact the police. I was so intent on this that I didn't notice the diminutive figure in the doorway of the last room until we collided. The child went sprawling. I barked an apology, and then time stopped as I realized that he was *my* child, my son, David.

He recovered before I did.

'Hi, Dad,' he said.

He seemed more shy than surprised to see me.

'What's that?' he asked, pointing at the gun I was carrying.

I whispered his name, my eyes filling with tears. I could see at once it scared him. Here he'd been for so long, trying to pretend that everything was all right when he knew it wasn't, and now the person he'd always counted on to make it right was falling to pieces in front of him.

'Hi, guy,' I said casually, drying my eyes and giving him a hug. 'How've you been?'

'OK. Is Mom here?'

I should have expected this, but it threw me. I could only shake my head.

'Where is she?'

It was only then that I noticed Ellie, stretched out on the sofa with an air of petulant abandon.

'She's not here,' I said to David. 'Look, we've got to … '

The sound of gunfire filled the air again, a long burst followed by several single shots.

'Fuck's going on?' grumbled Ellie, gathering her robe around her.

I took David's hand and led him outside. It sounded as if the situation down at the waterfront was deteriorating rapidly. If the police had come under fire, they couldn't be expected to care too much about any given individual's exact role in the island community. The last thing we needed was to get caught up in a fire-fight between Sam's latter-day Templars and a SWAT team who saw everyone on the island as a potential cop-killer.

The scene outside was one of frantic confusion. Everyone there had heard the shots, and they were milling about in the yard in front of the hall, waiting for someone to tell them what to do. Maybe I could have swung them behind me if I'd had the right speech ready, told them that Sam was the false Messiah and that I had come to bring them the truth. They might have believed me, or at least enough of them to influence the outcome.

As it was, I just said, 'The police are here. Sam's gone to talk to them.'

They stared at me with a kind of mute horror, as though they had just been addressed by a domestic animal. I was a non-person for them, I remembered, a mere mock-up of a human being. The sounds I made were of no more significance than the cries of the gulls overhead. Gripping David's hand, I started to push my way through them. At first the crowd melted away as we approached. Then I saw the lean blonde standing in our way.

'Hi, 'Lissa,' said David.

'Leave the boy,' she told me.

She sounded mean and determined. The crowd started to close in around us.

'You're going to have to take him,' I said, raising the gun. 'And it won't be so easy this time.'

I turned so that I had the wall at my back. I don't know how the confrontation would have ended, but at that moment Sam appeared, sprinting at top speed up the trail, arms and legs pumping, face white and strained.

'The apocalypse is at hand!' he shouted. 'The dark powers are massing in the vales of Ulro!'

This wasn't addressed to anyone in particular. Sam was in rhetorical mode, singing arias to the crowd teeming in his mind. Then he saw me and David and Melissa and the others, and switched registers. This was part of his power, I realized, the ability to move at a moment's notice from front to back stage, to be at once the star tenor and the theatre manager.

'There are three of them,' he gasped. 'Mark, Rick and Lenny. They're disguised as cops. They shot Andy and they're coming here. We've got to be ready to deal with them.'

He looked at me, then turned to the crowd with a sad smile.

'I thought this man was my friend. I offered him the secret of life. I even brought his child back from the dead. Yet he rejected me.'

He lowered his head, displaying the clotted blood.

'Like the first Christ, I have been scourged. Like Him, I have been betrayed. But where He had only one Judas, I have a legion of traitors and spies at work amongst my disciples. But now the hour of reckoning is at hand! Now is the time for the true believers among you to stand up and be counted!'

He looked around them all with a sweeping gesture.

'Do any of you guys want out? If so, get moving! Because we don't want anyone here who doesn't belong here, *right*?'

There were scattered cries of 'Right!' No one made any move to leave.

'OK,' said Sam quietly. 'Everybody get inside the hall. Break out the guns and assume your positions, but don't fire till I give the command.'

The crowd started to disperse. The only one to linger was the scrawny blonde.

'The kid should stay,' she said.

Sam glanced at her. He shook his head.

'We don't want them here, Melissa. They're dead. They always were, and soon they will be.'

This threat was clear enough. Sam's people were arming themselves, and David and I would be legitimate targets. I picked him up and ran as fast as I could up one of the alleys between the cabins, getting into cover.

'Where're we going?' asked David. 'Why don't we stay with 'Lissa?'

He sounded scared. I was too shocked to say anything. In the coming showdown between Mark and Sam, we would be legitimate targets for both sides. Neither would hesitate to shoot us down. They might disagree about Sam's leadership, but both accepted the truth of the 'Secret' he had been peddling. And stripped of its theological pretensions, this was simply a licence to kill. Our only hope was to get as far away from the hall as possible. I made it as far as the last of the outbuildings before pausing to rest. In front of us stretched the zone of rough-cut scrub we had to cross to reach the relative safety of the woods.

'I want to go back,' said David.

'Don't you want to see this neat place I found the other day?'

'What kind of place?' he asked doubtfully.

'It's really cool. Kind of like a cave.'

'Is Mom there?'

I picked him up again and trudged on through the underbrush and around the stumps of the culled trees. When we were about half-way, there was a burst of gunfire from the hall. I crouched down, holding David tightly. Several more bursts of firing followed. They didn't seem to be aimed at us, but I decided to keep down.

There were sounds on the hillside just above us. I threw myself down, hugging the ground, one hand over David's mouth. A black-clad gunman had broken cover from the trees about twenty feet to our left. Even in his uniform and cap, I had no difficulty in recognizing Mark's huge frame and menorah-like beard. We must have been visible from where he was standing, but fortunately his attention was fully occupied elsewhere. A further burst of gunfire from the hall was silenced by a single shot, deafeningly loud, from Mark's weapon. The next moment he plunged past us down the hillside. By the time I risked taking another look. he had reached one of the new buildings and taken cover behind the end wall.

There were further bursts of gunfire from the far side of the hall, and down towards the pier. It looked as though the attackers were executing a prearranged plan, two of them using the coastal path to circle around the hall while the third made a frontal approach. I knew that Mark and Rick had both served in the army, which might give them a slight advantage, but they were heavily outnumbered, and if they attempted to storm the hall they would be cut down. The most likely outcome seemed to be a stalemate, with the attackers unable to enter the hall and the defenders unable to leave. It occurred to me that Sam might come to regret having destroyed his phone link with the outside world.

'This is a *stupid* game,' David whispered.

I couldn't have agreed more, even though I knew, as he mercifully didn't, that it was a game of life and death. The stakes were about to be made very clear. I had just noticed that there was a third person marooned in no-man's-land. That first burst of gunfire from the hall had not been directed at us or at the attackers, but at Andrea. Now she was working her way up the hillside towards us, bending low and taking cover every so often. I got up and waved to her.

'Over here!'

She saw me and stopped. A spray of bullets seethed through the vegetation all around, followed by an answering shot from Mark's assault rifle. Andrea fell sideways, collapsing into the undergrowth. Without thinking, I jumped up and ran downhill towards the place where Andrea had disappeared. I saw her lying on the ground and threw myself at her like a football player going for the line.

She was alive. In pain, but alive. She had been hit just below the left elbow. By the way the arm was hanging, it looked like the bone was broken. There was a lot of blood.

'Dad?' said a panicky voice behind me. 'Where you go, Dad?'

I turned, horrified. David was wandering around in the open with a look of terror on his face.

'Get down!' I called.

His face collapsed and he started to cry.

'Can you move?' I asked Andrea.

She shook her head.

'Go back to your son. You were doing fine until I butted in.'

'So were you, until I started yelling and waving. I'll go get David, then we'll fix you up.'

I crawled back to find David. He was terrified by now, though more by my sudden disappearance than by what was happening all around us, and I had a hard time getting him calmed down. We slowly made our way over to where Andrea was lying, going on our hands and knees. I foraged around until I found a reasonably straight length of fallen wood, which I lashed to Andrea's forearm using strips of material torn from my undershirt. I did the work, while she gave me directions through clenched teeth. She had taken a first-aid course at some point and knew a lot more about it than I did. David looked on with interest.

'What are you doing here anyway?' I asked Andrea. 'Did Sam throw you out?'

She shook her head.

'I walked. He sent Terri and me to get water. I saw you running up the hill, and … Ow! That's too tight.'

I loosened the binding.

'It's like I've been under a spell all this time,' she went on. 'Somehow you set me free again. It wasn't anything you did, just you being here. I guess it could have been anyone. Ow!'

'Sorry.'

'I don't understand what I've been doing all these years. It's like I turned into someone else.'

'Someone and anyone,' I said. 'We'll make a great team.'

She touched my face with the back of her hand.

'It doesn't make any difference, anyway,' she said.

'What doesn't?'

She glanced at David, who was watching and listening attentively, and fell silent.

When Andrea's arm had been bound to her breast, we moved off. She obviously couldn't crawl, so I got up on one knee, ready to provide covering fire if necessary, while she ran the remaining distance to the edge of the woods. There were only a few sporadic shots, none of them directed our way. It sounded as though the two warring parties had settled down for the long haul, and were trying to conserve ammunition.

Once Andrea had reached the cover of the trees, David and I set off, crawling the whole way. The ground was hard and hostile, full of sharp shoots, jagged branches, bumpy roots and thorny plants, and we had to move on our hands and knees, keeping as low as possible. We were soon covered with cuts and abrasions, but David was a good sport about it. The sight of Andrea's bloodstained clothing seemed to have impressed him more than anything I could have said.

Once we reached the cover of the trees, the ground became softer, a spongy mass of dead pine needles and velvety moss. We crawled another few yards, and then at last it was safe to stand up. After that, it was downhill through the trees until we found the path running along the coast. The sun had broken out from behind the clouds, flooding the scene with a soft, warm light. The water glinted and bristled, the outlined islands receded like flat cut-outs in a theatre set. The contrast between that tranquil beauty and what was unfolding just over the hill was almost more disturbing than anything else.

The sight of the ocean gave me an idea. I told David that I had to go and get something, and that he was to stay there with Andrea. He agreed with surprising ease. Andrea herself was harder to convince, but I was adamant. It was our best chance, I told her, and we couldn't pass it up.

I left them there and set off back along the path. It took me about five minutes to reach the bay where the pier was, and as long again to reconnoitre the area. Once I was sure that it was safe to break cover, I made my way down to the trail. Then I saw the body stretched out on its back, arms outflung, a huge red stain on the shirt. It was Andy.

This was the first evidence of violent death I had seen, and it changed everything. I had somehow convinced myself that Sam's talk was just that, the ramblings of a bar-room philosopher whose portentous pronouncements get more and more extreme as closing time approaches. But this was real.

I looked down to the pier, searching for the boat which had brought Mark and the others to the island. It was nowhere to be seen. Then I noticed that the whole pier was tilting to one side, and saw the taut mooring ropes leading down into the water. Once on the pier itself, the submerged launch was clearly visible. Either Andy had managed to sink it before he was killed, or Mark had deliberately scuppered it to prevent anyone escaping. Whichever, my plan was in shreds.

When I got back, Andrea was telling David a story. He was calm again, and even seemed mildly annoyed to have the story interrupted. I took Andrea aside and told her about the boat.

'But it's OK,' I went on. 'All we have to do is lie low somewhere until the police arrive.'

Andrea looked at me with surprise.

'The police?'

'Someone's bound to hear all this shooting and call the cops.'

She shook her head.

'The islands around here are all uninhabited, except for Orcas, and hardly anyone lives on this side. Anyway, no one's going to think twice about hearing shots. We used to have gun practice every morning until you got here. People figure this is some kind of survivalist group. They think we're crazy, but Sam pays his taxes and the guns were all bought legally. No one's going to come after him.'

She looked over her shoulder. David was busy stomping on a line of ants making their way across the path.

'But someone's going to come after *us*,' she continued. 'That's what I meant when I said it made no difference.'

'What do you mean?'

'Just listen. The shooting's almost stopped. Mark's made his point. Pretty soon now he and Sam will start talking. They'll work out some deal together.'

'But Andy's dead!' I exclaimed. 'I saw him lying back there by the pier.'

She nodded in a cool, detached way I found terrifying, a peephole into a psychological abyss.

'Andy was the cause of the whole thing,' she said. 'Melissa told me the story last night, while I was trying to find out about David. She and one of the guys called Dale were an item for a while, so she was the first to hear. We were all told that Dale had killed himself. But Mark and Rick went to work on Andy the other evening and he confessed that he shot Dale. Sam made him lie to the others. That's what Mark couldn't stand, the idea that Sam was deceiving him. But now Andy's dead, they'll be able to patch things up.'

I shook my head.

'There's still a corpse down there by the pier. They can't talk their way out of that.'

'They'll bury him in the woods somewhere. No one will ever know.'

'I know!'

Andrea looked at me.

'They'll just have to make that grave in the woods a little larger,' she said.

'What you guys talking about?' demanded David.

He had grown bored with destroying ants and drifted back towards us, resentful about being left out.

'Look, a boat's bound to come by sooner or later,' I told Andrea. 'Maybe even a plane. When it does, I'll fire a few shots at it. *That'll* get the cops out here fast enough.'

'It could be days before anybody comes by. This place is very remote.'

I smiled.

'That's no problem. I know a place we can hide up for a week and no one'll find us.'

She sighed. Then, getting up on tiptoes, she kissed my cheek.

'They don't need to find us. The only water on the island is down by the hall.'

'I can sneak down there during the night and get some.'

'And get shot? They may be crazy, Philip, but they're not stupid.'

'Where's this place you're going to show me?' demanded David peevishly.

'We're going there right now,' I said, taking his hand.

I looked at Andrea.

'How's your arm?'

'It hurts like hell. But I don't care. I'm so glad to be here. I'm so glad you're here.'

I wanted to kiss her, but David's presence inhibited me.

'It'll be all right,' I whispered in her ear. 'Everything's going to be all right.'

We walked on along the path, David and I hand in hand, Andrea following close behind. The weather had turned warm and summery, bathing the woods in a benign light which seemed full of the promise of things to come, of growth and change and new life.

Eventually we reached one of the side paths which I had explored the day before. It was overgrown and steep in places, and Andrea especially made slow and painful progress. About half-way up, erosion had caused a gully to open up, almost obliterating the path. Some trees had collapsed into this cleft, coming to rest at an angle over a boulder in a way that formed a natural shelter. Inside, we would be invisible from anyone on the path, but with a good view out over the strait which separated us from the distant islands to the south.

Before we climbed down, Andrea got us foraging for food. Lisa and her friends had apparently been into living off the land and food-for-free, and Andrea still had all the old skills. Before long we had a collection of berries, leaves and nuts which looked extremely unappetizing, but which gave us something to chew on. Then I climbed down to the uppermost tree, and helped the others to scramble down the chute of dry mud. The shelter was home to a family of seagulls the size of ducks, who squawked and flapped their wings proprietorially as we invaded their domain, but once we got rid of them we were left in peace.

The trees had retained enough of their root system to keep their leaves alive, and it was very beautiful under the canopy of foliage, the light filtering down and the sun warming every surface. Andrea resumed the story she had been telling, but before long David fell asleep. Andrea and I stayed awake a while longer. I asked her about her life, her family, her background and beliefs. She answered haltingly at first, then with increasing confidence, like someone speaking a language they hadn't used for a long time.

The light slowly began to fade, tucking shadows in around us like a comforter. Our conversation became more and more desultory, and in the end we must have fallen asleep too. I remember waking once, and automatically reaching for the body I found beside me, without even knowing who it was. I may have mentioned Rachael's name. If so, Andrea pretended not to notice. We huddled together and fell back into the soothing solitude of our respective dreams.

It was dark outside when we were awakened by a loud roaring noise, and a lurid glare which made our shadows revolve like a carousel.

Twenty-one

Joe Quinlan was driving a truckload of hay back to the barn when his pager sounded. The low beams of early evening light which showed up every detail of the meadows to his right had turned the woods on the other side to a jagged sheet of black. Quinlan swung into the Cooks' drive, backed out facing the way he'd come and jammed the pedal to the metal, swooping around the curves and over the belly-wrenching undulations of the two-lane blacktop which meandered the length of the island.

The grass in the fields was burnt to a deep ochre, the driest Quinlan could remember for years. Lying in the rain shadow of the Olympic mountains, the San Juans had a microclimate totally unlike the prevailing conditions along the rest of the coast. Tourists, off-island immigrants and elderly convalescents loved this 'banana belt' effect, but for the islanders themselves it was a mixed blessing. After a month in which the sun had blazed down almost every day, water supplies were now dangerously low. The whole county was like a primed barbecue waiting for a flame.

It took him twelve minutes to reach the outskirts of Friday Harbor, and another five to get through the convoy of cars, trucks and RVs which had just disembarked from the ferry. When he finally pulled up outside the Fire House, the doors were closed and both engines still inside. In the office, he found Jim McTafferty and Ed Boyle sipping coffee. McTafferty was wearing jeans and a Hawaiian shirt, Boyle a pair of combat pants and a T-shirt inscribed 'Accordions Don't Play *Lady of Spain* – People Do'.

'What's the idea?' he demanded.

McTafferty looked up with a pesky smile.

'Hi, Joe. We got a reported blaze at the old camp on Sleight. Thought we might take the boat over, have ourselves a look at the situation.'

Joe Quinlan stared at him incredulously.

'You drug me all the way down here for that? Sleight's private, you know that. Those hippies don't pay taxes. Fuck 'em if they've got a fire. Let it burn itself out.'

'What day's it today, Joe?' asked Ed Boyle.

Quinlan frowned.

'Hell's that got to do with it?'

Boyle looked at McTafferty.

'He don't get it,' he said sadly.

Jim McTafferty shook his head.

'I guess he don't.'

'OK, Joe,' said Boyle, 'you better run along now. Wouldn't want you to be late for charm school.'

Joe Quinlan felt a sinking sensation in his gut. He'd forgotten all about the function that evening. At seven o'clock, they were all supposed to assemble at the high school to attend a 'Communication Skills and Stress Management Seminar'. Some salesman had gotten to the Chief and convinced him that the 'emergency response capability' of San Juan County would be 'enhanced' if all personnel participated in an 'interactional growth experience providing a neutral space in which to ventilate feelings and promote team cohesion through the development of problem-solving strategies and coping mechanisms'.

'This facilitator they brought in from the mainland sounds like she really knows her stuff,' McTafferty said. 'That seven-page questionnaire they sent around sure made me realize my communication skills need to be upgraded. I couldn't understand a fucking word.'

'I hear they're going to have role-playing too,' Ed Boyle chimed in. 'I sure hate not to get a chance to express my true feelings. I remember going to those Lamaze classes when Jean was pregnant. That was so much fun. I really miss all that touchy-feely stuff.'

He wiggled his fingers in the air.

'Hell, yes,' said McTafferty. 'We'll be thinking of you, Joe.'

'Let us know how it goes,' added Boyle.

Joe Quinlan looked at them.

'The Chief said it was mandatory.'

'Mandatory *this*!' said Boyle, stabbing a finger in the direction of his crotch.

'Thing is,' McTafferty explained, 'we've had this report of a fire on Sleight, like I said, and in my capacity as deputy I consider it incumbent on me to investigate personally and if need be inform the state authorities pertaining to the risk of environmental damage.'

'Way to communicate,' murmured Ed Boyle.

'I'm taking Ed here along 'cause it's getting dark and he knows the waters around here better than anyone, and I was also hoping to draw on your considerable experience, Joe, to assist me in any decision I might feel called upon to make. Plus I know you just love watching things burn. But it would mean missing out on this seminar, and I can see you don't want to do that.'

Joe Quinlan broke into a broad smile.

'Hell, Jim, since you put it like that … '

They drove the two blocks to the waterfront in one of the motor pool trucks which the Fire Department shared with other county officials, then strolled down the wooden walkway past the sheriff's spanking new speedboat to a battered red vessel marked FIRE – RESCUE. It was almost thirty years old and could make eight knots, flat out.

'So who reported this?' Quinlan asked as they chugged out of the harbour into the San Juan channel.

Ed Boyle gave the wheel a wrench to starboard.

'You know Bert Rigby over at Eastsound on Orcas?'

McTafferty laughed.

'He and Kathy Monroe still a number, or did she wear him all out? Now there's one spunky babe. She's been through half the men on Orcas since she got her divorce squared away.'

'Probably looking for a meal ticket,' said Quinlan. 'Knowing Gregg Monroe, she'll never see dime one.'

'Perry Fletcher told me Bert's already got a couple by-blow kids somewheres on the mainland. Someone should buy him a pack of Trojans.'

Ed Boyle pushed the throttle up to full revs.

'Anyway, Bert was up on the Turtleback with his gun and spotted smoke on Sleight,' Boyle continued. 'Called in when he got back home. "Thought you should know," he says. "But to be honest, them hippies burn themselves out, it'll be the best news since we won the Pig War."'

Quinlan smiled sardonically. Off-islanders were never more than tolerated by the locals, although most of them were pleasant enough folks: boat-butts, retired military personnel, convalescent oldsters, a reclusive millionaire or two. The only real pains were the tree-huggers, granolas in Birkenstocks who'd moved out there from the cities to have a meaningful relationship with nature. They were constantly banging on about stuff the islanders had been doing since Christ was a corporal, like burning off the stubble and dumping their sewage in the ocean. Joe couldn't see it made a damn bit of difference, the tonnage of raw shit the Canadians pumped into their side of the straits every day.

But at least the eco-nuts lived in regular houses, paid their taxes, sent their kids to school and supported local businesses. A few of them even had jobs. The people out on Sleight were different. Always had been. There was something about that island seemed to attract weirdos. When the first-growth was logged, back in the last century, one of the crew had gone crazy and killed two others with an axe while they slept. Then some kind of religious cranks had set up there, Quinlan could never remember the name, Theo and Sophy came into it. They were there for years, and when that brand of voodoo finally went out of style a bunch of goddamn hippies moved in. It was enough to make you believe the story someone had told him, that the Indians used to avoid the island because it was inhabited by bad spirits.

The boat shoved its ungainly way through the water shimmering in the last faint rays of the vanished sun. Ed Boyle consulted his watch.

'Well, the seminar should be underway by now. Wonder if they're in the hot tub yet.'

At last they cleared the cluster of islets at the southwestern tip of Orcas, and Sleight Island finally came into view, a dark mass hunkered down on the shifting waters. There was no sign of any fire.

'Shee-it!' breathed McTafferty.

'Looks like we might have to start something ourselves,' said Ed Boyle.

Joe Quinlan sighed.

'I knew I shouldn't have let you boys talk me into this. It looks like we ditched out on purpose, the Chief'll go ballistic.'

'Bert wouldn't kid us about something like this,' said Boyle. 'Maybe she just burned herself out.'

He switched on the searchlight mounted on the cabin roof, illuminating the coastline and the wooden pier.

'No sign of their boat,' McTafferty remarked.

Ed Boyle throttled back to bring the launch alongside, while Quinlan and McTafferty went out on deck to get the mooring ropes ready. Then there was a jarring crunch, and the launch stopped dead, hurling Quinlan painfully against a winch.

'What the fuck?'

McTafferty got up from the deck, rubbing his thigh. He looked overboard.

'Something down there.'

They backed off and angled the searchlight down into the water. All three men gathered at the bow.

'Jesus!' said Quinlan.

In the depths alongside the pier lay a submerged boat. Taut mooring ropes secured it to the pier, which was leaning over at an angle under the weight. On the blue hull of the wreck, white lettering spelt the word POLICE.

'Where the hell's that from?' asked McTafferty.

Ed Boyle brought the launch in on the other side of the pier, and they all went ashore. The bulk of the island rose massive and black behind them. There was no sound, no light, no trace of human presence.

'Guess we should go see what's cooking,' said McTafferty.

'Guess so,' said Boyle.

Neither man moved.

'You guys get on the radio,' said Joe Quinlan. 'Find out if the cops have been here. I'll go check it out.'

McTafferty walked a ways along the pier with him.

'If you're not back here in ten minutes, Joe, we'll … '

He broke off, catching sight of the body. It was lying on its back in the dirt at the landward end of the pier, the arms and legs stretched wide.

'Christ almighty.'

'Give us some light here!' Quinlan yelled to Boyle.

The searchlight moved jerkily up and across. Quinlan approached the body, processing information as he drew nearer. A man. In his thirties. Blond hair. Beard. Work boots. Jeans. Blue flannel shirt with a large red stain. No pulse. Skin cold. Been dead some time.

He glanced up instinctively at the screen of trees all around, the tips barely etched in against the night sky.

'Kill the light!' he shouted.

The searchlight went out, leaving him blind for a moment. He groped his way back to McTafferty.

'Well, we don't have to worry about skipping that seminar,' he said.

'Is he … ?'

'Yeah. Get the sheriff out here.'

*

Darrell Griffiths was a massive man with flinty eyes, a bushy moustache, an impressive gut and a permanently morose expression. He had owned the islands' only drugstore for years, but when his oldest daughter graduated from pharmacy school at the university he turned it over to her and ran for sheriff. Since then, Darrell had supervised whatever law enforcement the county needed – not a whole heck of a lot, to be honest – as well as raising the four younger children his wife had dumped on him when she ran off to Spokane with some guy from the mainland. It had been the talk of the town for months, but

Darrell had never said one solitary word about the whole business, and he wasn't the kind of guy you could ask.

The fire launch was lying at anchor about half a mile off of Sleight. It was the first time they'd had the hook down as long as anyone could remember, but the damn thing worked perfectly, showed the maintenance programme must be OK. The sheriff's boat came alongside, and Griffiths and his two deputies went aboard the launch to confer with the firemen. After a brief conference, the two vessels continued to the pier, where they tied up side by side.

The six men walked down the pier and surrounded the body.

'Anyone recognize him?' asked Griffiths.

Pete Green, one of the deputies, spat mellifluously into the undergrowth.

'One of the guys that lives out here,' he said. 'Time I came over last year he met me right here, we talked. Not that bad a guy … '

' … *for a hippy*,' the others all concluded silently.

Griffiths recalled the occasion. The police had been called by a group of rich yuppies from Boston who were spending a couple of weeks in the islands, cruising around in a fancy yacht they'd chartered. They'd dropped anchor off Sleight and gone ashore in a dinghy to have a picnic. Next thing they know, these guys are standing around them with guns, telling them the island's private property and they got sixty seconds to get their butts off of it. The hippies were within their rights, of course, and the sheriff didn't have a whole hell of a lot of sympathy for Easterners anyway, but he'd sent Pete over to have a word with them, suggest maybe next time they could tone down the attitude some.

Joe Quinlan knelt down and inspected the massive entry wound in the chest.

'Looks like a high-velocity rifle,' he announced to no one in particular.

Quinlan had been in the war, and was the only one of them to have much experience of gunshot wounds. Lorne Fowler, the other deputy, voiced the question which was on all their minds.

'Think whoever done it is still up there some place?'

The sheriff sniffed loudly.

'Bring me the bull-horn, Pete.'

Pete Green brought the megaphone from the boat. Griffiths switched it on.

'This is the sheriff speaking. If any of you are armed, lay down your weapons and come out with your hands on your heads. I've got five men with me and we're coming in now.'

He drew his revolver and started up the trail. The others followed. The dusk was gathering rapidly now. The woods on either side were already in darkness. The six men walked quietly, at an even pace, without speaking. A startled bird flew off into the woods with a rapid squawking. Something scuttled away in the shrubbery. The moon had risen, a perfect white crescent cut as though with a razor out of the black board of the sky.

As they turned the final bend of the trail and came in view of the clearing, they all stopped. The camphouse, the only building of any size on the island, had completely disappeared. In its place lay a heap of charred timber and ashes from which a flaccid plume of smoke rose into the evening air. Some of the undergrowth on the far side of the clearing was smouldering quietly, but a more serious conflagration had been avoided, thanks to the absence of wind. There was no one in sight, and no sound other than a creaking and settling from the burnt-out timbers.

'Jesus,' said Griffiths quietly.

He led the way across the open ground between the trail and the ruins of the hall. The silvery veil of moonlight made everything look unreal. Then they all heard the noise, and stopped again. It seemed to be coming from the piled ashes and debris, a kind of moaning sound. It had a human edge, like the wail of a baby you can't ignore. The men looked at each other, none of them wanting to be the first to admit what they were all thinking.

At first they were almost relieved when the other noise cut loose, loud and insistent, mechanical, masculine. Its clamour chopped up the silence into orderly segments, and proved its reality by chipping timber off the trees with vicious slashes. By the time they realized what it was and had thrown themselves to the ground, it was over. They lay panting, retrospectively terrified.

For a long while, no one spoke. They all knew that if the gunman had aimed a little lower, they would now be dead. They also knew that unless he had aimed high on purpose, they would soon be dead anyway. The guy had some kind of rapid-fire weapon, a machine-gun or assault rifle. Returning fire would only draw attention to their position, and in any case they had no idea where the shots had come from.

'Pete?' said Griffiths eventually.

'Yeah?'

'You have your radio?'

'Nope.'

'Lorne?'

'Didn't think we'd need it.'

There was another silence.

'OK, I'm going to try and make it back to the boat,' Griffiths said. 'You guys cover me.'

He crawled backwards through the scrub and rocks, high enough to make progress difficult but too low to give a man any serious cover. Hearing a sound behind him, he whirled over on his back, revolver pointed.

'It's me,' said Joe Quinlan.

'Jesus, almost blew you away!'

'Two of us should go. That way one of us might make it.'

'I don't believe this,' muttered the sheriff.

'It don't need you to believe it,' Quinlan replied.

They had almost reached the woods when Griffiths stumbled on something. Another body, a guy in his forties this time, short but solidly built. He had a blond moustache and a ponytail and that was about all you could tell, because the whole back of his head wasn't there.

'Ah, fuck it,' said Quinlan.

He stood up.

'Get down!' yelled Griffiths.

Joe Quinlan kept on walking. The sheriff wasn't his boss. When he reached the trees, he started to run, dodging and weaving, feeling a thrill he hadn't experienced for years, not since he was a boy playing war games up at English Camp with the Whitney kids and Lorne Fowler. It was fun! He tore through the woods, emerging on the trail about twenty yards from the pier. Only then did it occur to him that this wasn't a game.

He backed into the trees again and worked his way down beside the path. He could see the pier now, the two boats riding at their moorings and the dead man. If this had been a trap, these were the jaws. He stayed there for a full five minutes by his watch. There had been no further firing back in the clearing. Then he stepped out on to the trail and strolled down to the pier. There was no point in hurrying. If there *was* anyone up there in the trees, they'd get him anyway.

He climbed over the police boat into the fire launch moored alongside. Sheriff had some kind of smart radio he wouldn't know how to operate. Quinlan switched on the set and sent out an 'Officer Down' call, adding that they'd found two bodies and were under fire. No one had actually been hit, but he wanted armed back-up, and he wanted it now. If these guys were going to play hardball, let them play the pros.

*

Thirty minutes later, Sleight Island was thick with cops. State troopers, a SWAT team from Seattle, units from Skagit County and Bellingham, even a squad of MPs from the Navy Flyers base at Oak Harbor. A helicopter hovered overhead, pouring a cone of brilliant light down on to the clearing.

In the meantime, Pete and Lorne, the two deputies, had split up and circled around the remains of the hall to see what they could find. Joe Quinlan was about to offer to join them when he realized that would be uncool. He'd already upstaged the cops by volunteering to go to the boat and call HQ. He hadn't even been thinking, but they had. He was in Vietnam, they thought. He figures he's the hot-shit jungle warrior and we're just a couple of farmer's boys.

Actually, nothing had been further from Quinlan's mind. He hadn't been trying to make anyone look bad, he'd just done what felt good. But he could see it from their point of view, and sat tight while they loped off through the bush with their .38s drawn, wagging their tails around like they were playing flag football. Quinlan prayed to God some guy out there wouldn't blow their well-meaning asses over Orcas before they even figured out what they were doing wrong.

Ten minutes later, Pete Green was back, white-faced as a kid whose Halloween has turned bad on him.

'Another guy dead up there!' he exclaimed, pointing to the hillside. 'Stripped down to his underwear. Jesus, made me sick to look at him!'

The five men crouched down, scanning the darkness for signs of movement, alert to every rustle in the surrounding undergrowth, trying to shut out the sporadic unnerving moans which emerged from the burnt-out structure of the hall.

'I better go take a look,' said Darrell Griffiths.

Pete Green went with him. Joe Quinlan kind of tagged along. They found the corpse right behind one of the outbuildings. He was a big guy, over six feet tall, with a long beard divided into miniature pigtails looped together with some kind of silver threads. A ring in one nostril dangled suggestively over the bloody ruin of his skull, which had been dismantled with a brute force that even Quinlan found sickening. Mostly because it reminded him of other times, other deaths.

'Looks like someone shot him from behind,' Griffiths remarked, as though this wasn't obvious.

'From about a foot away,' Quinlan added.

Then they heard the siren of the first back-up team to arrive, and returned to the others. Lorne Fowler was back. He'd found a body too, on the far side of the clearing. This one had been shot in the chest, just like the guy down by the pier.

An hour later, with overwhelming force on their side and all the equipment and back-up they needed, they still hadn't found the shooter. The cleared area around the burnt-out hall had been searched meticulously, as well as all the smaller buildings which had survived the blaze. They had located the source of the unnerving moans, a girl in her teens with a broken leg and severe burns lying in the dirt to one side of the charred hall. She was airlifted to the hospital in Bellingham by Medevac helicopter along with another woman and a man, both of them suffering from third-degree burns.

Other than that, the search yielded only corpses. Some had been hauled from the wreckage of the hall, burned beyond recognition. Others were scattered outside the doorway, apparently shot down as they had tried to flee.

None of the survivors was in a condition to fire a gun, and no weapons were found anywhere near them. The conclusion was obvious. The person who had loosed off those shots after Griffiths's warning had slipped away into the woods and was still at large. It was impossible to search the whole island until daybreak, but the sheriff wasn't worried about the delay. Members of the SWAT team had secured the perimeter of the clearing, preventing any further threat to the safety of the law enforcement personnel on the ground, and there was no place the guy could go. Let him shiver alone in the dark. They'd pick him up the next day at their leisure.

There might well be more bodies in the burnt wreckage of the hall, but that too could wait. Helicopters cost money, and the taxpayers of the county were going to get a stiff enough bill for the night's operation as it was. Griffiths had the site sealed off with tape, and arranged for the loan of a set of mounted floodlights and a generator from the state. The Coast Guard agreed to provide a vessel with sleeping accommodation and communications facilities. Everyone was pulling together, the way they always did when things got tough. Griffiths was just beginning to think he might get to bed that night after all when one of the SWAT personnel called in to report intruders.

'Is he armed?' asked Griffiths.

'One of them is.'

'How many are there?'

'Two. No, wait … '

Joe Quinlan stood beside the sheriff, staring starkly up at the helicopter spraying light like some deadly defoliant.

'Use your discretion,' Griffiths told the SWAT man curtly.

Quinlan was peering towards the edge of the clearing, beyond the water tank on its metal trestle, his eyes narrowed. The helicopter blades whopped monotonously overhead. Then he started to run.

'Hold your fire!' shouted Griffiths into the radio. 'One of our guys is ... '

He broke off. What the fuck *was* Quinlan doing? Sprinting up the trail as if his life depended on it, towards the figures who had emerged from the woods. He reached them, turned and walked with them down the trail.

'Joe's with them,' Griffiths told the men scattered around the clearing. 'Hold your fire.'

The policemen waited, looking towards the three figures moving towards them. No, four. A child had detached itself from the grasp of one of the adults and was walking between them, holding their hands. Joe Quinlan walked to the right of the group, a little apart. They came steadily forward down the trail into the scorching circle of light, staring at the semicircle of armed men, who stared back.

Twenty-two

It was dark outside when we were awakened by a loud roaring noise, and a lurid glare which made our shadows revolve like a carousel. A moment later it had gone, leaving us in the dark.

I got the automatic rifle I'd taken from Sam and crawled outside. I could hear a strong rhythmic pulsing, but nothing was visible from where I was standing. It took me several minutes to clamber back up the chute of fallen earth to the path, and from there to the top of the largest rock-mass I could find.

At the eastern end of the island, a blinding glare shone down from the sky, an inverted wedge of brilliant light against which the tips of the trees between stood out stark and black. This also seemed to be the source of the noise. It was much louder here, a throbbing mechanical racket which came and went at intervals, ebbing and flowing.

'What's happening?'

A figure had appeared in the darkness below. I recognized Andrea's voice.

'It's a helicopter! It must be the police. Get David!'

It seemed to take for ever to get them both up the slope to the path. I had been astonished at how well David had coped with the extraordinary events of the day, but I knew that there would be a payback. Unfortunately he chose this moment to throw a major fit, screaming his head off and trying to wrestle himself away from both Andrea and me. Since her arm was still out of action, and the terrain had been difficult to negotiate even in broad daylight, the timing could hardly have been worse.

I was terrified that the helicopter might swirl off into the night at any minute, its reconnaissance mission completed. Presumably someone must have been alarmed by the sound of gunfire and called the police, but I had no way of knowing what the situation was by now. Maybe Sam and Mark had patched things up, as Andrea had predicted they would, and would put on a united front to get rid of the cops. A few people smiling and waving might convince the helicopter crew that it had been a false alarm. If they flew off, we would be stranded there at the mercy of whoever had gained the upper hand.

So it was with increasing desperation that I hauled David and then Andrea up to the path, picked the boy up and started to run as fast as I could up the steep hillside. Everything looked different in the dark, but the knowledge I had gained of the island stood me in good stead and I was able to find the trail meandering through the woods to the clearing. I put David down. It was totally dark here, all light soaked up by the tall trees to either side. We tripped continually over roots and outcrops of rock. I fell heavily once, gashing my forehead on the branch of a tree and almost putting my eye out. I didn't even feel the pain. Nothing seemed to matter except reaching the clearing before the helicopter abandoned us to our fate.

It was only when I at last emerged from the woods into the felled area above the compound that I realized that my panic had been unnecessary. As well as the helicopter hovering fifty feet above, there was a substantial force of uniformed men on the ground. The clearing looked bigger than I remembered it, more open and raw. It took me a moment to figure out why. The hall had completely disappeared. In its place lay a heap of ash and smouldering timbers.

'We're safe!' I told Andrea, and kissed her impulsively.

'Dad?' said David. 'Who's that funny-looking man?'

I turned to look, and my elation vanished. A man in a blue uniform was crouched in firing position about twenty feet away, a large gun trained on us. For a moment I thought it was Mark. Then the man spoke into a walkie-talkie, and I realized that it was some kind of police sharp-shooter.

'Throw down the gun!' someone shouted.

It was a man running up the trail towards us. It occurred to me for the first time that my sudden appearance, covered in blood and holding an automatic rifle, might be misconstrued. I tossed the rifle aside and picked up David. The running man reached us. He wasn't in a uniform and I had never seen him before.

'Stay close to me,' he said. 'They won't fire as long as we're together.'

I decided that he was crazy but friendly. We marched down the trail, David in my arms, Andrea at my side. As we approached the cleared space where the hall had been, a stout man wearing a khaki uniform and a Nelson Eddy hat advanced. He raised a bull-horn.

'Put your hands on your heads!'

I looked at Andrea and smiled. It was all so ridiculous. But we did what he said, as one humours a child.

'Move away from the woman and the kid,' said the fat guy in khaki.

I realized that he was talking to me. I started to explain who we were and what we were doing. Then I noticed that every officer present had a gun that was aimed in my direction. Everyone seemed very tense.

'Just do what he says!' shouted the man who had run up the trail to meet us.

I obediently took several paces sideways.

'Lie down on the ground,' continued the man with the megaphone. *'Real easy now. No sudden movements. Just keep calm and nobody's going to get hurt.'*

Again I obeyed, sensing as I did so that I had already surrendered some considerable part of my constitutional rights. My arms were dragged behind my back and handcuffed securely together.

'Better Miranda him,' said a voice above me. 'This one's going to be huge. Watch some slick lawyer try and make a career by springing the son of a bitch on a technicality.'

Strong hands hauled me to my feet and patted every inch of my body while I was told I was under arrest and my rights were recited. I was not really paying attention, but I remember that the charges included assaulting a police officer. For the first time it occurred to me that this was not just a silly mistake which would all be cleared up in a few moments.

'This is ridiculous!' I said. 'We're innocent victims. They would have killed us if they could.'

The character in the hat cut me off.

'You can do all the talking you want back at the courthouse, son. No need to rush things. We're operating on island time here.'

He turned to another man, also in a khaki uniform.

'Take him across, Lorne. Pete, you go along too. Keep him cuffed the whole time, and don't take your eyes off of him.'

Other policemen surrounded Andrea and David as I was led away. I protested loudly that David was my son and begged them not to separate us, but no one paid any attention. It was as though I hadn't spoken, as though I weren't there. The man called Lorne gripped my arm and pushed me along. I noticed that there were dead bodies everywhere. I recognized Melissa, the blonde woman who had kidnapped David. Her face and hands were badly burned and she had a terrible gaping wound in her back. As I surveyed the other corpses, strewn across the ground all around the burnt-out shell of the hall, the full scale of what had occurred became apparent to me, and the gravity of my presumed involvement in it.

The two policemen steered me down the trail to the pier, holding me in a tight, impersonal grip. They kept up a bantering dialogue about the number of reporters and television people who would shortly descend on the islands, but neither spoke to me. I felt that I had been reduced to the status of an object to be moved from place to place, some large piece of furniture which no one wanted.

'Shit, it'll be worse than a long weekend in August,' said the one called Lorne. 'They'll be crawling all over Friday. Show your ass on the street, someone'll shove a microphone up it.'

'And the ferries? Forget it. Still, I guess it's a two-way street. I was supposed to visit my sister tomorrow, over in La Conner, but now … '

'Looks like you got lucky, Pete. You might get over there with the car OK, but westbound? No fucking way.'

The scene at the landing was transformed out of all recognition. There were boats everywhere, some by the pier, others anchored offshore, maybe ten in all. Most had their engines running and their searchlights on, illuminating the scene in a weird pattern of intersecting beams. Two men in overalls and another wearing shorts and a Hawaiian shirt were bending over Andy's body. The civilian nodded to the two deputies.

'What the hell happened here?' he asked in a shocked tone.

The one called Pete gestured up the trail.

'You think this is bad, wait'll you see what's waiting for you up there. This thing's a regular massacre.'

'Guess I can forget about that cookout, then.'

'You get through here, Dick, you won't want to eat charbroiled meat for a long, long time, I promise you that.'

We walked down the pier and boarded a launch marked SHERIFF. My handcuffs were fastened with another set to a guardrail support. The launch was lying between the pier and a red fire boat, and it took a few minutes to re-rig the mooring lines and back the launch out. Then we did a high-speed turn and scudded off over the dark waters.

Despite my humiliating and painful position, I felt an enormous sense of relief just to be off that island at long last. Whatever happened from here on in, the worst was over. It looked as though Mark and his two allies had torched the hall, maybe using gasoline from the generator shed. If one of them had approached the south end of the hall, where there were no windows, he would have had all the time he wanted to start a serious blaze. And since there was no source of water inside the hall, once the timbers caught there would be no way to put the fire out. If the people inside stayed put, they would be overcome by the smoke and flames. If they tried to leave, they would be shot down. Mark, Rick and Lenny would have had no compunction about this. Every killing validated their contention that they alone were fully human, empowered to mete out life and death.

We rounded a headland and turned into a sheltered bay with the lights of a town at the far end. As we drew closer, I saw that it was a sizeable pleasure port, with a large marina and a loading dock where a car ferry was tied up. The police launch cut up the channel to the landward end of the marina. One of the two deputies unfastened the handcuffs securing me to the rail. We disembarked, walked up a gangplank to the street and drove off in a police car.

After my enforced exile, I greedily took in every detail of the scene. There was a main street back of the harbour and a few smaller ones off of those. We went about three blocks, pulling up in a parking lot before the courthouse annexe, a long one-storey building from the fifties with an overhanging flat roof. There were lots of pretty trees, shrubs and flowers planted in front. The sheriff shared the office space with the county's Building and Planning Department, as well as the Public Health and Community Services.

Inside the front door was a cardboard box with a slit and a handwritten sign reading COMMENTS AND SUGGESTIONS, a large plastic recycling bin, and a set of grey metal lockers marked WEAPON DEPOSIT BOX. In my heightened and febrile state, they seemed to symbolize the essential trinity of American life: democracy, idealism, violence. We entered a warren of cramped offices where I was formally placed under arrest. My name and other details were recorded and my fingerprints taken. I was allowed one phone call, which I used to contact my parents. It was the middle of the night on the East Coast, but they were very sympathetic. My father told me that he couldn't fly out immediately because my mother was too sick to be left alone, but that he would get in touch with people he knew in Boston and hire the best defence lawyer in the Northwest. They both said they loved me and that everything would be all right. I wanted to tell them about David, but it didn't seem the right moment.

The deputy called Lorne had meanwhile broken out a first aid kit which he used to clean and dress the cut on my forehead. Then I was taken to a holding cell at the end of the block, a small bare space with a bunk bed and a window of opaque glass bricks. My handcuffs were finally removed and I was locked in. I paced up and down, thinking about David and Andrea. I wanted so much to see both again. Although it sounds absurd, I had come to think of us as a family. The intensity of the experiences we had been through together seemed to constitute a lived history at least as substantial as the one I had shared with Rachael. But time dragged by and no one appeared. Eventually I lay down on the bed and fell asleep.

I was awakened by the arrival of two different policemen. One pushed a breakfast tray into the room while the other covered his partner from the doorway with a revolver. Then they backed out of the cell and relocked the door. I got out of bed and retrieved the tray. I was starving, and it was a good breakfast, biscuits and gravy and scrambled egg with a big mug of fresh coffee. After that, nothing happened for several hours. Then the door was unlocked again and the sheriff stepped inside, accompanied by the deputy named Pete.

'How're you doin'?' the sheriff asked.

I shrugged.

'Best breakfast I've had in a long time.'

The sheriff nodded.

'Molly'll never be the cook her mom was, but she does an OK job. We have to send out. Don't have cooking facilities here. These cells are hardly ever used, except some drunk needs to dry out overnight.'

I'd had enough of this bantering.

'Where's my son?' I demanded.

The sheriff leaned up against the wall.

'The boy and his mother are staying with Lorne and his wife. They've got plenty of room now the kids have gone. We got a doctor to attend to the woman's injury. They're both OK.'

I was about to point out that Andrea was not David's mother, then decided to keep this to myself.

'I want to see him!' I said. 'You have no right to do this. We've just been reunited and now you've separated us again!'

The sheriff held up his hand.

'You're way ahead of me here. I don't know a thing about you except your name. Assuming it is your name.'

I strode towards him, waving my hands dramatically.

'Call the FBI! David was kidnapped. They'll tell you … '

'Hold it right there!'

The deputy had drawn his revolver and was pointing it at me. I stopped. There was a moment's silence.

'OK,' said the sheriff. 'How about we all go into my office, where a man can rest his butt, and you tell me the whole story from the beginning?'

My handcuffs were replaced and I was taken out of the cell and down the hall to a small cubicle with a desk decorated with framed family photographs. The sheriff sat opposite me, while Pete perched on a filing cabinet and operated the tape recorder. I told them everything, from the very beginning: how Sam and I had met at college, how I'd run into Vince by accident, how David had been kidnapped and Rachael had killed herself, how I'd sunk into depression and then decided to hit the road. I spoke openly and naturally, making no attempt to hide anything. I wanted them to realize that I had nothing to hide.

I must have talked for almost an hour. Sheriff Griffiths, as the sign on the desk proclaimed him to be, made no attempt to cross-question or interrupt. I finished by describing meeting Rick in Anacortes and the drive to the house.

'I don't know where it is exactly, but it shouldn't be too hard to find. It's situated on a headland, down a dirt road. There are some outbuildings and a pier just like the one on the island.'

'What kind of a car were you driving?' asked Griffiths.

'A big old Chevy,' I replied promptly. 'It has Minnesota plates, 469 AUK. It's kind of an aquamarine colour. There's an antenna and whitewall tires.'

The sheriff glanced at the deputy.

'OK,' he said. 'Now tell us what happened when you got to the island.'

I was about to answer, but something about the look the two policemen had exchanged made me think better of it. Filling in the background was one thing. My experiences on the island would form the basis of any case against me, and it might be a mistake to discuss that without legal representation. I could easily end up saying something which looked damaging. It didn't

304

help that most of the other witnesses were dead.

'I asked my father to get me a lawyer,' I told Griffiths. 'I'd prefer not to say any more until he gets here.'

The sheriff nodded lazily.

'Guy phoned already,' he said. 'Name of Merlowitz. Supposed to be here this afternoon. He's chartering a floatplane from Seattle. Sounds like he must come expensive.'

He got to his feet with a sigh.

'I sure hope so, son. Because you're going to need the best there is.'

'But I haven't done anything!' I protested angrily. 'My only crime was to be in the wrong place!'

The sheriff smiled very slightly.

'Not just you.'

'What do you mean?'

'That Chevy you just described to me? We found it OK. Only we didn't find it at Fidalgo, like you said. It turned up on a dock in Bellingham, right next to the marina where that blue motorboat was stolen yesterday. The one that was faked up to look like a police launch.'

Back in my cell, I tried to come to terms with this latest development. It didn't take long. I'd left the key to the Chevy with Lenny when I arrived. Mark and the others must have realized that the painted VW van was too conspicuous for their purposes and taken my car instead. It made no difference. Since I'd never left the island, I couldn't be implicated in anything that might have happened in Bellingham.

The lawyer recommended by my father's friends in Boston arrived shortly after three o'clock. He was in his mid-thirties, thin and balding, with a heavy five o'clock shadow and shrewd eyes. He wore a crumpled linen jacket, a white T-shirt with a silkscreened Gary Larson cartoon involving rats and lawyers, black jeans and Banfi loafers. He introduced himself as Paul Merlowitz, shook my hand and looked me in the eye.

'OK, first off, did you do it?'

'Of course not!'

Merlowitz continued to stare at me for a full ten seconds.

'If you didn't do it, you didn't do it,' he said in a studiously neutral tone. 'Only it's going to make it tougher.'

I was staggered. Here was the guy I'd been counting on to champion my innocence, presumably at vast expense, and he was making it pretty clear that even he wasn't convinced of it.

'Tougher? How come?'

Merlowitz looked around my cell like a realtor sizing up the selling points of a property.

'Because if this comes to court we're going to have to plead you not guilty, which means showing reasonable doubt. If we pled you guilty, we could go straight to mitigating circumstances, of which there look to be plenty. You haven't any priors, and none of the police were hit. It was dark, you were confused. They'd probably let you cop a plea. Worse case, I could get you a short sentence in some tennis prison. Not guilty is a way tougher route to go.'

'Gee, I'm sorry, Mr Merlowitz,' I retorted sarcastically. 'What can I tell you? Next time I'll make sure and pull that trigger.'

The lawyer smiled faintly.

'I'm just telling you what the deal is.'

Ten minutes later, we were all back in the sheriff's office. It was an extremely tight squeeze, as Merlowitz commented caustically. Griffiths nodded.

'We've been asking for new facilities for near ten years now, but there just isn't enough crime in the islands. Maybe if this case attracts enough attention we'll finally swing it.'

He looked at me.

'OK, son, we've had the back story. Now let's hear what happened after you got here.'

I'd had plenty of time to organize the narrative in my mind, and I told it concisely and fluently. I gave my first impressions of the island and of the community living there, and how these had gradually changed. I mentioned the daily study sessions, and my discovery that the group believed that William Blake's poetry was the Third Testament and Sam the second coming of Jesus Christ.

I talked about my attraction to Andrea, her account of Lisa's

306

death, and my son's dramatically staged appearance on the rock. I went over the split between Mark and Sam and his attempts to win me over. Finally, I described the arrival of the fake police boat and the shoot-out which followed, and how Andrea and David and I had eluded the others and taken refuge in the woods.

The sheriff nodded.

'Well, that's all very interesting. But what really concerns us here is what happened when we got to the island. And in that respect we've got a real problem believing what you say.'

'How come?'

Griffiths lay back in his chair, sighed and looked up at the ceiling.

'It's like this. We still haven't figured out exactly how many people were living there, and we haven't accounted for all the ones who died yet. We've got a forensic team out there now, but it's going to take a while. They've got to sift through every pound of ash and work out what's cinder and what's human bone, then add up all the bones and see how many complete cadavers we've got. We're talking weeks, maybe months.

'In the meantime, here's what we've got. When Lorne and Pete here and I reached the island, I made an announcement over the bull-horn telling everyone to drop their weapons. Then we started up the trail with the three guys from the fire department. When we reach the clearing where the camphouse used to be, someone opens fire with an automatic weapon. We hit the dirt and call for reinforcements. Soon as they get there, we secure the area and search the place. We find a girl with a broken leg and a woman and a man, both of them badly burned. The man has since died. None of them had an automatic weapon anywhere near them, or were in any shape to use it if they had.'

The sheriff stirred the papers on his desk with one hand, as though embarrassed.

'Soon as it got light, we searched the island from one end to the other. We used a helicopter, a K-9 team from Bellingham and a couple of boats to check the shoreline. We didn't find anyone.'

'I fail to see the relevance of all this,' Merlowitz interrupted.

Sheriff Griffiths held up his hand.

'I was just coming to that, Mr Merlowitz. You see, Sleight's only a small island, and there's nowhere to hide. So we can be sure that there's no one still there we don't know about. We can also be sure that no one left the island last night. I never heard of anyone swimming across those straits, least of all in the dark. Even if they had, they'd have been seen on Orcas. Everyone knows everyone around here, and any stranger's going to get noticed. And the only boat on the island besides our own launches was riddled with holes and six feet under water.'

He looked at my lawyer, then at me.

'So at the time we came under fire, the only people on the island who weren't dead or critically injured were you and the woman and child you claim were with you. And you had an automatic rifle.'

'I took it from Sam's room so as to be able to defend me and my son. But I never fired it.'

Sheriff Griffiths raised a massive eyebrow.

'A bunch of bullets are gone from the clip.'

I suddenly remembered Sam blasting away at his bedroom wall. I was about to explain this to the sheriff when Paul Merlowitz told me not to answer any more questions. He looked distinctly uncomfortable.

'We recovered some of the bullets that were fired at us,' the sheriff continued unperturbed. 'Luckily the aim was high, kind of like you'd expect from someone without too much experience in using that particular kind of gun. A couple of the shells ended up embedded in the tree trunks. The ammo's the same as what's left in the weapon you discarded.'

'That doesn't amount to conclusive proof,' Paul Merlowitz retorted. 'My client has stated that there were a large number of such weapons on the premises. They probably bought the ammunition in bulk.'

The sheriff nodded.

'That's possible. But there are also other possibilities.'

'Name one!' I snapped. 'Just give me one good reason why I should have been involved in any of this!'

Sheriff Griffiths looked at me calmly.

'Well, let's say this woman Andrea found out about your boy being kidnapped and felt bad about it. Let's say she called you up in Minnesota and told you where he was. I could certainly understand if you decided to take revenge on the people who had seized your son and caused your wife's death. That would explain why you three were the only ones to survive unscathed, plus a bunch of other things which don't make a whole lot of sense right now.'

'That's unsupported hypothesis!' said Merlowitz dismissively. 'Your case against my client amounts to nothing more than a bunch of circumstantial details, none of which prove that he was anywhere near the scene when the shooting occurred, still less that he was responsible for it.'

'I was just outlining our thinking as of this time, Mr Merlowitz,' the sheriff replied mildly. 'Our investigation is continuing.'

I was taken back to my cell and locked up.

Twenty-three

Long, low rolls of surf broke ceaselessly on the shore, collapsing into shallow sheets of water sweeping up the level beach, then draining away again, leaving the sand smooth and glistening. The sun stood high in a flawless blue sky, but a strong breeze kept the air cool.

The beach stretched away for miles in either direction, apparently as endless as the Pacific itself. The few people in sight – adults sunning themselves, children playing in the sand, an older couple walking their dog – made the landscape appear still emptier and more vast.

A woman basking in the sun looked up and called to a boy paddling at the edge of the waves.

'Thomas! Don't go in any further!'

'It's OK, Mom.'

'Just keep nearer in, OK?'

Testosterone, thought Kristine Kjarstad. He knows there are dangerous currents and that the water is icy, but he sees those facts as a challenge, not a threat, something to test himself against. And it will get worse as he gets older, until in the end I'll lose all control. A father could still impose his authority, even once the child grew bigger and stronger than him, simply by drawing on years and years of conditioning. But all a mother had to offer was love and indulgence, and one day that might not be enough.

Such moods came on her very rarely, and were more frightening as a result. Most of the time, Kristine felt vaguely ashamed of being such an irredeemable optimist, convinced against all the evidence that things were basically OK and that the exceptions she encountered in her everyday work somehow conspired, in some way she had chosen not to examine at all closely, to prove that rule. But her abortive trip to Chicago and Atlanta seemed to have broken her spirit. Everything seemed bleak and hopeless, even her ability to do her job. I've been faking it all these years, she thought, and they just found out.

'They' meant her Chief, Dick Rice, who'd summoned her on her return. The worst thing was that he'd been pleasant, too pleasant, the way you are with people you think don't quite get it and never will.

'You had the makings of a nice little case there,' he'd commented. 'Too bad the perps can't talk, but at least they got what was coming to them. We ought to be grateful to those gangsters, they saved us all a ton of time and money. Now, Kristine, what I want you to do is forget the whole thing and get on with your job. I realize that everyday crime here in King County may not have the same glamour as a nationwide murder hunt, but the work is there and somebody's got to do it.'

Kristine had tried to take the Chief's advice, but it hadn't helped. She just didn't seem able to accept the fact that she had come so close to cracking such a huge and obscure conspiracy, and had failed. As Dick Rice had said, the perpetrators were dead, along with an unknown number of their victims. No one would ever know exactly how many people they had killed, let alone why. In one sense it was over, but in another and more important one it would never be over, not for her. She felt that she had been presented with the great chance of her life, and that she'd blown it. Nothing would ever change that.

This realization had triggered a severe attack of depression, in the course of which she not only lost all interest in her work but also came down with a bad cold. It was only when the physical symptoms appeared that Kristine did what she should have done right away, and applied for two weeks of the leave she had coming. Since the weather was good, she had decided to get away not just from work but from the city itself, away to this remote beach on the Olympic peninsula, the very edge of the continent.

They were only staying a few days, but already the change

had done her some good. Thomas, too. He was in mourning for Brent Wallis, who had finally left for Europe with his parents. For a while Thomas had been inconsolable, but in this different environment he finally seemed to have accepted the loss of his friend.

Looking up to check on him, Kristine was relieved to see that he had teamed up with an older boy. The two were busy whipping a beached log with lengths of the tough, snake-like seaweed with which the tideline was littered. The boy's parents, a hearty couple with a red Jeep 4x4, had gone off jogging along the beach. If only a family like that would take the Wallis house for the summer, Kristine thought wistfully. But the chances were almost nil, although she'd mentioned it to Paul Merlowitz at the lunch they'd had when she got back from the east. That had been one of the few good things that had happened to her since then.

She'd forgotten just how funny Paul could be, and how closely connected laughing and loving were in her mind. No sooner had she sat down than he'd launched into a story about some guy he knew, a state prosecutor who'd been questioning a child witness in court during a sexual abuse case. The point had been to establish whether the kid knew the meaning of the terms involved, and the prosecutor had led her gently through a verbal multiple-choice exam.

'Is this a penis?' he'd asked, pointing to his ear.

'No,' the girl had replied.

Pointing to his nose, 'Is this?'

'No.'

Paul Merlowitz had broken off to order a bottle of Oregon pinot noir.

'Then he points to his head, says, "Is this a penis?" And the kid nods and goes, "Yes." Result, he not only lost the case, he's now known around the DA's office as Dickhead.'

While she was still laughing, Merlowitz suddenly demanded, 'OK, what did the guy do wrong?'

Feeling put on the spot, Kristine shrugged. Merlowitz smiled and answered his own question.

312

'He broke the oldest rule there is in this business. Never ask a witness a question if you're not sure what answer he's going to give.'

'Maybe we should worry a little less about the rules and a little more about justice,' Kristine replied, nettled by his condescending tone. 'If the jury system means anything at all, it means ordinary people working out the truth for themselves.'

Paul Merlowitz closed his eyes.

'Kristine, Talmudic scholars teach that every verse in the Torah has forty-nine different interpretations, each equally valid. Truth isn't some commodity you buy at Fred Meyer. We're talking about an exercise in damage limitation. The best we can hope to do is to recognize and control our ignorance.'

And to make a damn good living off of it, thought Kristine as the wine and the first course arrived. But she didn't say anything, and the lunch had passed agreeably. When she mentioned the Wallis house, Paul – punctilious as ever – had promised to see what he could do. As she watched him noting down the details with his Mont Blanc pen, Kristine had felt a stab of pain at the contrast between his organized, methodical efficiency and her own sketchily improvised existence. Paul Merlowitz would never have wasted his time agonizing over something he couldn't control the way she had with the Dale Watson fiasco. If he had a failure, as even he must occasionally, he would forget it and move on.

Trying to shake these gloomy thoughts, she rooted around in her beach bag for something to read. She had brought a novel along, but wasn't making much progress with it. Eventually she found a copy of the local paper they had given her at the motel, or 'Inn' as the place called itself. Besides the expense, another good reason for not staying longer was the management's attempts to give the place what they imagined to be an upscale feel. Every item on the menu came 'complimented' with something or 'served on a bed' of something else. If she hadn't had to look after Thomas, Kristine would have taken her chances at a bar in the hard-bitten logging community a few miles down the road.

The best thing about the newspaper was that it had no time for such ingratiating gentility and mock cosmopolitanism. The tone was that of the reader board she'd seen at a café in Hoquiam on the drive over: WE DON'T SERVE ESPRESSO. The lead stories concerned a crisis in the logging industry, the on-going political fight about the threat to the habitat of the spotted owl, and a controversial proposal to upgrade the coast road by building a short cut through an Indian reservation. Buried on an inside page were short items off the wire about the situation in Bosnia and the likely consequences of the US intervention in Haiti.

On page six, in a border around a huge ad for a local furniture store, she found a follow-up piece about the shoot-out among that religious cult on the San Juans. Kristine had been following this vaguely – it had been big news for a few days – but she found it hard to get interested. It sounded like one of those Waco-style things, or that guy in Guyana who got all his followers to kill themselves. You knew these people were out there, but it didn't seem to have much to do with real life. She felt sorry for the children who'd been dragged into it, but apart from that it was like the drug cartels or the Mafia. Let them kill each other off as much as they wanted. It just saved the taxpayers money.

Kristine raised her eyes from the paper. Someone else had said that to her recently. Of course, it was Dick Rice, talking about the shoot-out in Atlanta. Well, it was cynical, no doubt, not the kind of thing you could admit to in public, but none the less true. Ideally criminals should be brought to trial and sentenced according to the law, but in practice the police were overextended, the jails bursting and the streets unsafe. Despite Paul Merlowitz's Talmudic wisdom, anything which helped even the score was welcome as far as she was concerned.

She returned to the story. Two women who had escaped from the blazing building were said to be co-operating with the authorities. The police didn't seem to be giving much away at this stage, beyond saying that the killings had been the result of a power struggle for control of the cult. One other survivor, a man, had initially been detained but then released pending further enquiries. Forensic work was continuing, but was hampered by the fact that none of the victims had as yet been identified. It wasn't even clear how many people had been living on the island in the first place, let alone who they were.

Kristine Kjarstad folded the paper up and stuffed it back into her beach bag. It was time to forget all about stuff like this and just veg out. She should make it a rule not to read the paper or watch the news, maybe not even answer the phone once they got home. The good weather was supposed to hold up through the next week. She would just lounge around the yard, maybe do a little gardening, bask in the sun and try to forget all about the violence that her work brought her into daily contact with. She needed to put things in perspective, to get centred again. And when her vacation time was up, she would go back healed and strong, ready to tackle the cases that came her way one by one, not obsessing about any of them, no longer feeling that it was her business to solve the problems of the world singlehanded.

She checked her watch and called Thomas, who turned, eyeing her warily.

'*Vær så god!*' she called, using her mother's Norwegian expression for calling people to table.

'Whaaaat?'

'It's time for lunch, darling.'

'Aw, Mom!'

'Aren't you hungry?'

'But we're just killing these guys!'

'All right, five minutes.'

Shrieking their delight, Thomas and his new friend got to work with the seaweed whips again. Their delirium reminded Kristine of her confrontation with Eric when she picked up Thomas on her return from Atlanta. Her ex-husband had objected to two aspects of his son's life. The first was an 'apparently uncontrolled amount of time spent playing video games', in excess of the norms laid down in a parents' guide to the subject he had bought and insisted on her reading too. The second concerned Thomas's current 'obsession' with toy guns.

Eric had brought up all the usual arguments on this subject, from the need to teach children not to see violence as the solution to their problems, to the undesirability of reinforcing gender stereotypes. In theory, Kristine agreed with all this. The trouble was that her mother had bought the gun in question for Thomas's birthday after taking him to Toys 'R' Us and hashing out at some length exactly what he wanted. It was an air-driven model which fired a brightly coloured foam dart, and he and Brent had had endless fun chasing each other around the back yard with it.

It was all very well for Eric to remind her that the Parenting Plan in their divorce decree included a stipulation that toys would be chosen by both parents in consultation. He didn't have to deal with the day-to-day business of looking after Thomas, and for that matter didn't want to. What he wanted, and what he thought he'd found, was a way to extend his control over areas of Kristine's life which he was no longer able to influence directly but could continue to manipulate through their son.

She got to her feet, shook the sand out of her towel and put it in her bag.

'Thomas!'

Seeing her poised for departure, he contorted his face into a pathetic mask. Kristine almost gave in, then decided that it was time for her to demonstrate some control too. Taking her son by the hand, she led him over to the red Jeep. The other child's parents had come back from their run and were now relaxing over a power snack of carrot juice and tofu. For a moment Kristine found herself sympathizing with the author of that yuppie-bashing reader board in Hoquiam, but she would gladly have kissed up to the biggest nerd in the world if Thomas got on with his kids.

In fact the couple turned out to be perfectly pleasant, for Californians. Kristine quickly firmed up an arrangement which would leave her two hours of blissful solitude that afternoon. As she led Thomas up the flights of wooden steps from the beach to the lodge on the cliffs behind, she felt her familiar old Pollyanna self re-emerging. It had been a good idea to leave Seattle, but she was always glad to get back. She would just laze around the house and let the rest of the world look after itself. Maybe Eric's lingering influence had been partly responsible for her crisis. She should take a tip from Paul Merlowitz, and stop worrying about things she couldn't control.

*

About the time that Kristine Kjarstad and her son left the beach to have lunch, a man walked into the office of a motel on Aurora Avenue North in Seattle. This was very different from the one at Ocean Shores. Aurora had once been a bustling thoroughfare, part of Highway 99 linking British Columbia and Mexico. Now all the through traffic used the interstate, and Aurora was a run-down strip of discarded dreams and broken promises. The motels which had survived were mostly on the brink of Chapter Eleven, while some of the sleazier ones functioned as business locations for the prostitutes who worked the avenue.

The one the man had chosen was on a long narrow lot between a gun shop and an auto-wrecking yard. A massive neon display on a stand sunk in a brick planter read Tuk-Inn Motor Lodge. The office was a fake log cabin with access lanes on either side leading to the rooms. It smelt of mould and cheap air freshener. There were dirty lace curtains over the windows, sad plants in pots, wallpaper with a photograph of mountain scenery repeated over and over, and a plastic sign in mock embroidery stitch which said IF YOU WANT A PLACE IN THE SUN, YOU HAVE TO PUT UP WITH A FEW BLISTERS.

As the man approached the desk, an electronic bleep sounded in the back room. He dropped the black tubular bag he had carried six blocks from the stop where the Greyhound bus had set him down. A woman in lurex hot pants and a tight-fitting sweater drifted in through the open doorway. Her nails were elaborately painted, her feet bare.

'How are you today?' she said.

'You got a room?' the man asked. 'Yeah, I guess you got a room.'

The woman made a show of consulting a large ring-binder with handwritten entries.

'How long you staying?'

The man shrugged.

'Maybe a few days.'

'Forty bucks gets you a suite with a kitchenette.'

'Whatever.'

He handed over two crisp twenty-dollar bills. The woman examined them carefully, then glanced at the man and flashed a smile, as though apologizing for her caution.

'First time out for these babies, looks like.'

She caught the look in the man's eyes and her smile vanished.

'Third on the left-hand side,' she said in a hard voice, plucking a key from one of the hooks on the wall. 'Check-out is at ten. You want to keep the room, it's another forty.'

The man picked up his bag and walked down the driveway to the sunken parking lot. The cabins were built of brick patched with sheets of metal. The matt beige paint was flaking off like diseased skin to reveal a drab green. He unlocked the door corresponding to his key number and went in. There was a bed, a table, a sofa, a television, a toilet and shower. The one small window had the same lace curtains as the reception area. It did not open. The air was stuffy, with a sickly scent of mildew. The man set down his heavy bag, locked the door and lay on the bed, staring up at the scabrous rows of ceiling tiles.

How long would he be staying? As long as it took. He was in no hurry. From now on, everything must be perfect. One call, to establish the address, then the visit. He had no idea where it would be. He didn't even know which state he'd have to go to. It would most likely be some place back east, but it could be anywhere, even right here in this town. There was simply no way of knowing.

In the old days, every detail had been worked out weeks and even months in advance. The system had seemed so flawless. The prophet Los selected those worthy of initiation. He gave them a life and demanded a life in return. That was only just. After that, everything was controlled by the rigorous lottery of chance. The target city was located in the state where the novice had been born. That was where he had entered the false life, the state of Generation, and that was where he must return to perform the ritual which freed him from his native state. Mark had been born in Texas, so his initiation had taken place in Houston. Lenny was from a small town in Missouri, so he'd gone to St Louis to become his eternal self, Palambron. Russell was from somewhere around here, so he'd come to the Seattle area to celebrate his passage into the state of Eden.

And now they were all dead. It was a bitter blow, when so much loving care and attention had gone into their rebirthing. First the novice's personal number was calculated. You took an ordinary pocket calculator, the kind you can buy at any drugstore, powered by a solar cell – by Sol, which is another name for Los. You keyed in the month, day and year of the subject's birthday, then pressed the square root key to obtain the magic string of numbers which expressed the root of his existence, the secret DNA code of his eternal self.

It was so beautifully simple! Say the person was born on September 11, 1958. You tapped in 0, 9, 1, 1, 5, 8, then hit √. That gave you the sequence 30192383. The novice and the initiate who would accompany him then took the boat across to Friday Harbor, where there was a public library. They went to the reference section and consulted the White Pages phone book for the city in question. They looked up the page corresponding to the first three digits of the personal number and took a photocopy of it which they brought back to the island.

Now began the arduous task of determining the exact address. Each page of the phone book contained approximately 440 entries, arranged in four columns. The calculation involved running through all the permutations of the remaining digits of the novice's personal number. In the case of the man born on September 11, 1958, this meant finding the ninth entry from the beginning, then the 92nd from that, then the 923rd, the 9,238th, the 92,383rd, the 2,383rd, the 383rd and the 83rd. The third entry after that one was the target address.

It wasn't necessary to count the entries by hand, of course, although some people preferred to do so. One of the men with a mathematical flair had come up with a formula for calculating the correct result once the number of entries in each column had been counted, and this was always used as a check. So there was never the slightest question in the novice's mind that the house to which he would go had been selected in accordance with the divine will, expressed through the agency men call chance. As a result, he was freed of all doubt and empowered to perform the ritual, knowing that the victims were mere spectres created by a loving God to permit the illusion of evil in a world where only good existed.

The man rolled up off the bed, covering his face with his hands and gasping as though struggling for breath. When he finally removed his hands, both they and his face were wet with tears. It was such a joyful, liberating truth, and they had laboured so long and hard to demonstrate themselves worthy of possessing it! Yet it had come to nothing. They were all dead, and that could mean only one thing: they had never been alive in the first place.

Chance might appear to be a mere lottery, but he knew that it possessed a rigorous logic, and one that must be obeyed. Whatever it cost him, he had to submit to God's will. If his friends and allies were dead, it was because they had been spectres from the beginning, every one. It wasn't just a question of this or that person not working out, a Dale Watson here, a Russell Crosby there. The wholesale nature of the holocaust which had occurred demonstrated that once and for all.

He alone had survived. That proved his reality, but also his solitude. From now on, he would have to shoulder the terrible burden of the Secret all by himself. The mystics of the cabbala had taught that as long as there was one enlightened man left alive, God would spare the world for his sake. It was an awesome responsibility to hold the destiny of all Creation in your hands, but he had no choice.

There would be no more mistakes, no more false disciples. From now on, he would trust nobody but himself. He would live quietly and alone, invisible to every eye but God's. But first he had a debt to pay, a sacrificial offering to mark his acceptance of the great task which had been entrusted to him. He had pledged his faith in blood, and now that pledge must be renewed. Only thus could he be cleansed, and all the errors and confusion of the past erased.

He opened the black bag and lifted out the handcuffs and the roll of tape he'd bought in Everett, then the Cobray automatic pistol. He wouldn't use that, though. Some time in the next few days he'd swing by the gun shop next door and pick up a .22 revolver and some Stinger ammunition. A couple of boxes should be enough. Whatever else might have gone wrong, there was nothing wrong with the method itself. It was tried and tested, and he would stick to it.

He weighed the Cobray in his hand, thinking over his next move. It would be best to let things settle down for a couple of days before doing anything. This was a perfect place to hole up. All they wanted was money, and he had plenty of that. It hadn't always been that way. Back in the early days, each initiation had to be funded by the novice going off and taking some lousy job for a couple of months. But that had all changed with Rick's arrival. His was the only case where the victims had been selected personally instead of in the regular way. But Los made the rules, and he could break them. As he'd said at the time, the test of faith was even greater when the individuals concerned were your own father and mother.

There had been a stunned silence when the news was announced. You could see them all wondering if they'd have been able to do it themselves. It had been hard enough for some of them to agree never to see their parents again, never mind having to hold a gun to their heads and expose their sham existence for what it was, a mess of meat and bone and tissue. But Rick had *wanted* to do it. He hated them both, especially his mother, who had never lifted a finger to stop the abuse he had suffered as a child. He figured his father didn't know any better, but she should have stepped in and done something. Well, she hadn't, and now he would.

Whatever Rick's feelings were, the financial rewards for the group had been substantial. The sale of the family house, plus the life insurance and various investments, had netted almost a quarter of a million dollars. The other son, Matt, would have got a share of that, but Rick had scores to settle with him too. A telephone call had been enough to send Matt, who had a plumbing business, out in response to a non-existent emergency around about the time the cops arrived at the parents' luxurious suburban house, alerted by a neighbour who had seen flames. They found the father and mother dead, their chests blasted away by a shotgun. The weapon was not recovered. The fire had been caused by a pan of oil which the mother had apparently been heating on the stove when she was attacked. There was no sign of forced entry, and neither the sophisticated alarm system nor the family's German shepherd dog had responded to the intruder.

Since Rick was supposedly in Mexico – he'd crossed the border a week before, then paid a coyote to smuggle him back with a group of illegal immigrants – it was only a matter of time before the police began to suspect the other brother. No one was surprised when Matt was found in his truck up in the mountains, his head blown away by a blast from the shotgun he was holding, and which had also been used to kill his parents. Rick had set up the meeting, stressing the need for secrecy, on the pretext of working out a fake alibi if Matt was arrested.

As a result, the estate had come to Rick, and through him to the rest of them. The money had been deposited in a bank in Bellingham and was accessible via the Accel and Interlink systems at any one of millions of cash machines all over the country. He could afford to wait weeks, even months, until it was perfectly clear that the police suspected nothing.

The thought made him reach into the bag again. He took out a pair of pants and jacket in a dark, heavy material. They needed to be cleaned and pressed, but it might well be a nice touch to wear them when the time came. But first he had to find out where the house was and figure out the bus schedules. It might take days to get there, but that didn't matter. He didn't care how long or uncomfortable the journey was, just as long as he arrived safely.

And he would! He knew it, suddenly, with a surge of confidence and courage that made him want to leap in the air and holler exultantly. He would arrive and the others would depart, revealed for the shams they were. And the survival of the Secret would be ensured for ever, sealed in their blood.

Twenty-four

It was a Sunday morning, ten days after I was released. I had gone to run some errands at the local stores and now I was walking home, relishing the warm sunshine and the cool breeze and the stunning views of snow-capped mountains above the wooded ridges and valleys of the North Seattle skyline.

We had been in the house a week, and were still settling in. It had been made a condition of my release that I should remain in the state, available to the San Juan County investigators. At the same time, both Andrea and I wanted to get away – and to get David away – from the islands themselves which, beautiful as they were, held such horrific memories for us. When my lawyer mentioned a house in Seattle which was available for a few months at a reasonable rent, we jumped at the idea.

When I was finally given my conditional freedom, I had no expectations about anything or anyone from my former life. All that had been wiped clean. After being charged with crimes I had experienced only as a victim, nothing seemed impossible, or even unlikely. Normality had become a meaningless concept. I wouldn't have been surprised to find that David had vanished again, and that everyone was conspiring to convince me that he had died back in Minnesota months before. As for Andrea, I no longer had any firm belief that she had ever existed in the first place. She was just one among many phantom figures I seemed to have encountered in the course of my hallucinatory experiences on the island.

So I was even more amazed than pleased to find her waiting for me when I emerged from my cell. Thanks to a benign sexism on the part of Sheriff Griffiths, Andrea had never been regarded as a suspect, and once he had taken a full statement from her she had been free to go. But she had stayed. That made all the difference. We both had to make plans, and it seemed the most natural thing in the world to make them together. After what we had just lived through, any arrangement was bound to seem provisional. Why not take the path of least resistance, rent this house which my lawyer had found and see how things turned out?

It had been Andrea's testimony which had finally convinced the sheriff of my innocence. We had each been questioned separately and in great detail about the events of that fatal day, and our answers matched to a degree which ultimately made it impossible to believe that we were making it all up. One of the two survivors from the hall was Ellie, and she had been able to corroborate my story about the events leading up to the final horror. Finally, the police had talked to David. His story, told with the idiosyncratic clarity of a child's vision, corresponded fully to Andrea's and mine. That clinched it.

The investigators were now working on the theory that one of the dead gunmen had still been alive when the sheriff and his men approached the compound. Thinking they were enemies, he had opened fire, and had then died in the long interval before the helicopter arrived to illuminate the scene. All in all, I got the impression that the cops were asking me to stick around not because they had any further intention of charging me, but to try to lend an air of credibility to the fact that they'd arrested me in the first place.

That was fine with me. I had no wish to go home, and for that matter no home to go to. The events I had lived through had cut me off for ever from my past, and called into question everything I had ever imagined in the way of a future. I was left with the present, and for the present I was content to settle into this pleasant house, knowing that whatever happened we would have to move out in a couple of months, but not oppressed by that knowledge. I no longer had any interest in long-term plans. I was content to live one day at a time, as long as I could live it with Andrea and David.

Through all this, David had of course been my major preoccupation. My feeling that his previous acceptance of the situation had been too good to be true had been confirmed. It seemed somehow to be linked with his being on the island. The moment we left, everything changed. He became withdrawn and intensely clinging. I couldn't even go to the bathroom without finding him outside the door in tears when I came out. There was also the question of Rachael's death, which I had ducked before. Now I told him the truth, although without mentioning that she had died by her own hand. He at first refused to believe that he would never see her again, then became preoccupied with the physical details of her present whereabouts. In fact Rachael had been cremated, but I spared David that knowledge too, particularly after what he had seen on the island. I said she was buried underground, and he wanted to know how deep and where and whether she had enough food and a phone. I explained that that was just her body, and that his mom was not really there. I added, with a twinge of hypocrisy, that some people believed that she was in heaven. David immediately decided this was right, and that she could see him and hear everything he said. I decided to go along with this and let him work out the truth for himself at a later date.

One very important factor in David's stability was completely fortuitous. The woman who owned the house in back of ours happened to have a boy about the same age, and the two made friends one day over the fence. This was the more surprising because David had never been very outgoing, even in the old days back in St Paul. But although it would be absurd to suggest that the ordeal he had been through was what we would once have called 'a growth experience', there was no question in my mind that he had changed, becoming more independent and less tentative with other children. The only thing he absolutely insisted on was my continual physical presence. I'd only been able to sneak out to the store because he was plugged into some TV show he'd become hooked on.

The main problem with David's understandable dependency on me was that I wanted to be with Andrea – alone with Andrea. Her problems of readjustment were not as serious as David's, but they were just as real. After living in seclusion for so many years on the island, she had lost many of the skills that we all take for granted. Going almost anywhere was a torment to her. Travelling in a bus or car made her sick, the sight of strange faces made her panic. She couldn't deal with answering the telephone or going shopping. Like a prisoner released after many years, she found herself unable to cope with the demands of organizing a life in which she was constantly called upon to make decisions.

All of this would simply have been irritating if I hadn't been in love with her, but I was. Whenever we were apart, even for an hour or two, I felt unreal, drained of substance, like one of those spectres whose meaning Sam had so totally perverted. What Blake meant, as far as I can recall, is that every one of us has a male and a female component, and that we can only achieve full humanity when the two are commingled. Split from that whole, the male component becomes a 'spectre', a reasoning machine spinning abstract theories and arbitrary rules and then enforcing them ruthlessly. The female component similarly degenerates into an 'emanation', jealous, moody, nagging, envious.

Something like that had happened to me. Without Andrea, I felt reduced to a pale parody of myself. I wanted to be with her all the time, to care for her in this difficult transitional phase she was going through, to help her find her feet in the outside world. I never discussed these feelings with her, or asked her what she felt for me. It would have been forced and intrusive. Once we had both settled down there would be time enough to talk, and to decide what we were going to do next. For now, it was enough that we had these few months together, without conditions or promises.

I walked home unhurriedly, enjoying the mild summer day. Our house was in a pleasant neighbourhood called Wallingford, with just enough yuppie input to have excellent bread and coffee and microbrews and similar amenities readily available, while retaining a solid core of long-time residents from the days when it had been an unpretentious blue-collar community, blighted by fumes from the gas works down by Lake Union. The paper bag I was carrying – I had rapidly learned that in Seattle the question 'Paper or plastic?' means 'Responsible tenant of Condominium Earth or unrepentant Eco-Nazi?' – contained a crusty French loaf, a bottle of good olive oil, tomatoes, basil, pasta and a selection of local goat's and sheep's cheese, together with a couple of bottles of Hogue Cellars' fumé blanc. Life seemed good.

As I turned the corner into our street, I saw something that brought me crashing down. At the other end of the block, coming towards me, was a policeman. He passed the house next door where the students lived, then turned up our steps and disappeared behind the fence.

For a moment I was tempted to go hole up at the trendy café where the local house-husbands went to sip herb tea and write in their diaries. It wasn't that I was seriously concerned about being arrested again, although there was always the possibility of some unexpected development in the investigation. But even the prospect of having to answer another set of questions designed to trap me into some inconsistency seemed too grim to contemplate. I just wanted to be left alone.

But I knew this was dumb. If the police wanted to question me, there was nothing I could do. Better to get it over with now. I carried on down the hill, clutching my sad sack of goodies. Our gate was open. I walked up the steps to the porch. The lace curtains of the living room window were drawn. I opened the front door and called, 'Hi, I'm home.' There was no answer.

Setting the groceries down on the table in the hall, I walked through into the living room. It seemed to be empty, but I could hear a strange noise, like someone humming tunelessly. Although it was such a lovely day, the blind over the window looking on to the garden was lowered. A black bag I'd never seen before lay on the pine table. I rounded the section of wall forming a kind of proscenium arch into the dining area, and stopped. Andrea was on her knees in the corner of the room, looking up at me imploringly. Her wrists and ankles were handcuffed together and a patch of tape covered her mouth. She was trying desperately to speak, but all that emerged was the inarticulate humming I had heard. Then something cold and hard touched the nape of my neck.

'Hi, Phil. I'm home too.'

I felt my skin prickle. I couldn't see who was standing behind me, but I knew the voice. I also knew that the person it belonged to was dead.

'Put your hands behind your back.'

I couldn't move, couldn't speak, couldn't think. What was happening was impossible.

'Do it, or I'll blow your brains out right now!'

Mechanically, I obeyed. I felt a handcuff bite into one wrist, then the other. Then a vicious kick at the back of my knees sent me crashing to the floor.

'Kneel!' said the voice.

By pushing with my shoulder against the sofa, I managed to get to my knees. My ankles were locked together with another double click. There was a tearing sound, and then a hand was clamped to my face, pressing a sticky surface hard over my lips, gluing them together. A figure moved into the space between me and Andrea. I looked up, and the impossibility was confirmed. The man in a black uniform standing over us with a gun in his hand was Sam.

'Big surprise, huh?' he sneered. 'Ripley's Believe It or Not. And you didn't, did you, Phil? I laid it all out for you. I shared the Secret with you, and you still didn't believe. Mark and Rick and the rest, they didn't believe either. They demanded proof. Well, they got their proof, just like you're going to.'

He burst into a savage laugh.

'They accused me of making mistakes! And I *did* make a mistake. The mistake I made was thinking that they were worthy of sharing the Secret. I didn't want to be alone, you see. I didn't want to have to bear this great burden alone.'

He nodded gravely.

'Like the first Christ, I wanted the cup to pass from me. I told myself that there were other people out there as real as me, and that I could recognize them. Well, I've been punished for my weakness, justly punished. I accept the bitter truth now. I am alone, and always will be. What happened on the island proved that. They were all destroyed, but I survived. Plus you two, and the kid.'

He broke off, as though a confusing thought had just struck him. Then he reached forward and ripped the tape off my mouth.

'Where is he?'

I could hear the faint sound of the TV down in the basement.

'At a friend's,' I said.

Sam nodded reflectively.

'In that case he gets to live. That's the way it works. That's how God protects his chosen ones. You thought maybe he suspended the laws of physics for us, so a bullet fired into our brains wouldn't penetrate the skull? I told you, Phil, things are set up like this to make faith both possible and necessary. If some people got a special deal, it would be obvious that God was protecting them. But it doesn't work like that. This gun would kill me just like it's going to kill you two. The reason it doesn't is because it's never fired!'

He laughed again.

'I'm living proof of that! There I was, trapped in the hall with all the others, surrounded by three crack shots who gunned down anyone who came out. The hall is torched and burns to the ground, and pretty soon afterwards the whole island is crawling with cops. Yet I walk out of there without a scratch on me, as easy as checking out of a hotel! You want miracles? There's a miracle!'

'So how did you do it?' I asked.

The longer I kept Sam talking, the more chance there was someone might come to the door and scare him off. Or maybe he'd crack up and go over the edge. The way he was acting, it looked like he was high on something. If I could spin things out, it just might turn on him. It was a chance at least, the only one we had.

'How did I do it?' he echoed. 'I had faith, Phil, the faith that moves mountains. I knew I couldn't be harmed. I knew God wouldn't let that happen. But I also knew that I couldn't just sit there and expect Him to stop the world and let me get off. God helps those who help themselves!'

He had started pacing up and down the dining area, swivelling around every four paces. His face was pale and strained with a manic energy.

'Those fuckers had us pinned down, right? Mark on one side, Lenny on the other, Rick out front. Lenny was the one I went for. I knew he was only going along with the others out of weakness. Lenny was too scared to stand up to Mark, but I knew he couldn't stand up to me either. I opened the window in my room and called to him, told him I wanted to talk. Then I climbed out and walked over to him.'

Sam looked at me with contempt.

'You couldn't have done that, Phil, for all your fancy talk. Walk up to a guy who's crouching down twenty feet away holding a Cobray automatic on you, just staring him down! I knew he wouldn't fire, you see. I knew God wouldn't let him. I kept on talking to him the whole time, telling him how this was all a terrible mistake, urging him to come over to our side. In the end he lowered the gun. He knew he couldn't use it. I walked right up to him, and when I was close enough I pulled out this little baby and shot him in the face.'

He paused, listening. I too had heard something, a faint click, then a scuffling sound. I knew it must be David. The programme he'd been watching was over and he was now coming upstairs. I glanced at Sam, and realized that he'd read my expression perfectly. He ran through to the kitchen and I heard the door to the basement open. I turned my head towards Andrea, but I couldn't bear the look of helpless anguish in her eyes. There was nothing either of us could do for David now.

It seemed an eternity before Sam returned. When he did, he was alone.

'How come the TV's on?' he demanded.

I shot another glance at Andrea. Had David managed to hide somewhere? Perhaps God really was protecting him. I hoped someone was.

'He always leaves it on,' I said. 'He thinks those are real people in there, and if you switch it off they die.'

Sam's eyes bored into mine. He had seen the look on my face earlier, and was still suspicious, but his desire to maintain an aura of omnipotence made it difficult for him to show any uncertainty or doubt.

'But how on earth did you get off the island?' I asked, to get him back on track. 'The police searched the whole place with dogs.'

Sam smiled, secure and superior again.

'How did I get off?'

He burst into raucous laughter.

'The police escorted me ashore, Phil!'

By now it was obvious that he was out of his skull on something or other. His whole mood had changed in a few seconds, and he seemed to have forgotten the question of David's whereabouts.

'I let Rick and Mark torch the hall and pick off the suckers inside as they tried to escape,' he continued in a rapid burst. 'It was a regular turkey shoot. I could have taken them any time, but it suited me just fine that there wouldn't be any survivors. They were so busy covering the hall they didn't see me creeping up behind them. They had no reason to watch their backs. They thought everyone was inside getting barbecued. I took them out one at a time at close range. They never even knew what hit them.'

He patted the black jacket he was wearing.

'Mark had this phoney police uniform he'd put together to get past Andy, some kind of security guard outfit. I stripped it off him and changed into it. When the real cops showed up I fired a burst over their heads with the Cobray to make sure they called in reinforcements. After that I sat tight in the woods and watched the whole thing. I saw you guys come in, and I saw the reception you got. That beat everything, Phil, watching you get led away in cuffs!'

He started pacing up and down again, seemingly trying to relieve the surges of nervous energy which threatened to overwhelm him.

'Once they figured they'd caught the guy who shot at them,

they all relaxed. I just moseyed on down to the pier and waited around till I saw a boat leaving. Some guys from the Coast Guard, it was. "Hey, fellas, any way I could catch a ride with you? Our boat's gone back to the mainland and I'm kind of stranded here." They were real nice about it, ran me over to Friday Harbor and I got the last ferry out.'

He stopped in front of us.

'Now all I have to do is take care of you two, and I can head off into my new life.'

'How did you find us?' I blurted out, desperate to distract him a little longer. I could face the idea of dying, but not now, not so soon.

'I called your father. Told him I'd heard you'd had some kind of beef with the cops and I wanted to get in touch at this difficult time. He gave me the address right there, over the phone.'

I dimly recalled my father telling me that a friend of mine had called a few days earlier. I hadn't paid any attention at the time. I certainly hadn't thought of Sam. As far as I was knew he was dead.

'This won't hurt,' Sam went on in the same rapid patter. 'I watched all the videos we made those other times, to get the new guys used to the idea. You can tell they didn't feel a thing. Spectres don't have feelings. That's the whole point.'

He stepped towards us, hefting the revolver. Since it didn't matter what I said any more, I wanted my last words to be the truth.

'We aren't the spectres, Sam. You are.'

He grinned tightly.

'We could argue all day about that, Phil. But there's an easier way to prove you wrong.'

I knew that any resistance was hopeless, but just to wait passively to be killed seemed inhuman. As Sam moved towards Andrea, I hurled myself against his legs. He stumbled and fell. The gun went off with a sharp crack. For a moment we both lay sprawled on the floor. Then he wrenched himself free, whirled around and smashed the barrel of the revolver into my face.

'You stupid bastard!' he screamed. 'Do you think you can

change the will of God? You're nothing, less than nothing!'

He got up and grabbed me by the hair, hauling me back to my knees. The pain was excruciating. I felt blood flowing from my cheek and nose. Sam went over to Andrea and stood behind her. He pressed the gun against her head. I gave her one last glance, to assure her that I loved her, that she wasn't dying alone.

But she wasn't looking at me. Her face was turned to the far end of the room and her eyes were stretched open in amazement. I turned, and at that moment the window looking on to the porch imploded in a shower of glass. Fragments flew everywhere, tinkling off the walls and furniture, cracking like sheets of ice on the floor. When the fallout ceased there was another person in the room, a figure of savage splendour, half-naked and covered in blood from head to toe.

*

Kristine Kjarstad was stretched out on a canvas lounger in her front yard wearing a black-and-white one-piece swimsuit. The book she had been reading lay face-down on the patio beside the remains of a glass of iced tea. Her eyes were closed, her face relaxed, stunned by the hot sun.

The yard was enclosed by a tall wooden fence, built as high as the code allowed, which made the space feel like an annexe of the house, another room. A border of native shrubs in varying shades of green surrounded the brick patio: wax myrtles, ferns, viburnums and the ground-hugging evergreens which Kristine had planted because they were drought resistant. It seemed like a bad joke that a city where it rained as much as in Seattle should be subject to periodic water shortages, but a mild winter with little snow-melt to fill the reservoirs had resulted in yet another watering ban.

This was the last day of Kristine's vacation, and she was making the most of it. Thomas was spending the weekend with his father, leaving her to luxuriate in peace, quiet and idleness. She had slept in, ate a boiled egg, ploughed through several pounds of newsprint, then smeared herself with sun block and gone outside. She knew that tanning was now regarded as seriously incorrect, but it was a pleasure she refused to give up. It was almost as good as sex, she thought, and better than some sex she could remember. She stretched out luxuriantly and gave herself up to a gentle, pervasive sense of well-being.

When the gate clicked open, she thought for a moment that it was the paperboy or the mailman. Then she remembered it was Sunday, and the paper had already come. She straightened up slightly, raising one hand as a screen against the sun. The front gate was still closed, but the one at the side of the house was open. A child was standing just inside it, at the very edge of the patio, as though afraid to advance any further.

Kristine blinked rapidly, trying to focus her sun-drenched eyes.

'Hi there!' she said.

A moment later she recognized the boy as Thomas's new friend, the one who'd just moved into the Wallis house.

'Thomas isn't home right now,' she said lazily.

But the boy wasn't listening. He was talking, blurting something out in one long continuous sentence punctuated only by frequent gasps for breath. He must have run over from his house through the back yard, Kristine thought. She rolled up off the lounger, replacing a strap which she had slid down. She still couldn't figure out what he was saying, but he seemed to be in distress. He backed away as Kristine approached, still gabbling, seemingly on the verge of tears.

'What is it, David?' she asked gently. 'What's the matter?'

Now the tears came, making the boy's speedy patter even more incomprehensible. Karen crouched down, making herself look smaller and unthreatening.

'Is something wrong? Where are your mom and dad?'

She'd only spoken to them once, apart from phone calls to arrange for the children to get together. The father was one of Paul Merlowitz's clients – Paul hadn't disclosed anything about the case, of course – and had been an English professor. They seemed a pleasant enough couple, although they'd managed to deflect her questions about where they were from and what they were doing in Seattle. Kristine hadn't insisted. If she had been one of the framers of the Constitution, she would have added 'privacy' to 'life, liberty and the pursuit of happiness'.

After listening to the boy's staccato delivery for another few minutes, she finally began to tune in to what he was saying. It was like doing a jigsaw puzzle, picking out a few phrases here and there, then trying to fit them together. The picture which emerged seemed harmless enough at first. A man had come to the house. He was a friend, or at least someone known to the family. Then David added a few more pieces to the puzzle, and the pattern abruptly became more sinister. The man had hurt his dad. He had started shouting angrily. David had been watching TV. He had got scared and run away. He was afraid the man had come to take him away again.

Kristine didn't particularly want to butt in on some domestic dispute, but the boy's terror seemed real enough. Then he added one final, decisive detail.

'He's got a gun.'

Kristine Kjarstad ran up the steps to the porch.

'Stay here!' she told David. 'Don't leave this yard!'

She raced upstairs to her bedroom and opened the blue chest, painted with elaborate red and yellow designs in traditional Norwegian style, where she kept her issue revolver. It took her a few seconds to load the weapon – she'd seen the results of too many accidents to keep a loaded gun in the house with kids – then rushed downstairs again and out into the sunshine.

The boy was nowhere to be seen. As she hurried along the side of the house, it occurred to her that she might well be making a complete fool of herself. The whole thing could well be some fantasy the boy had dreamed up. Men with guns coming to a private house in broad daylight? Things like that didn't happen in Wallingford.

She ran across the mangy lawn pitted with weeds and past the unpruned apple tree whose crop had already started to fall and rot. Next door, Mr Shadegg was tending the immaculate beds of vegetables and herbs which his wife pressed on Kristine continually. He looked up at the figure in the bathing suit running by, revolver in hand.

'Call 911!' Kristine shouted at him. 'The Wallis house!'

Mr Shadegg just stood gaping. Kristine opened the gate in the picket fence and ran on across the Wallis's yard to the back steps with their ancient stencilled notice NO PEDDLERS. It made her think again about the wisdom of what she was doing. If David had made the whole thing up, the story might end up in the papers. People would be coming up to her at Food Giant for months with an ironic glint in their eye.

She went around the side of the house and up the front steps to the porch. The lace curtains were pulled across the window and all she could see was a vague silhouetted figure at the rear of the room. She was about to ring the bell when she heard the sound of a gunshot inside. A man shouted something in a tone of fury. There was a cry of pain.

She tried the door. It was locked. Someone could be injured, even dying. There could be more shooting at any minute. Closing her eyes and saying a swift prayer, Kristine took a step back and hurled herself at the window. It shattered under the impact and she fell into the room, stumbling over some piece of furniture. She quickly recovered her balance and straightened up, grasping the revolver two-handed. Thin seams of blood seeped from her exposed skin, but she didn't notice the pain, riveted by the scene at the other end of the room. The couple who lived here were kneeling on the floor. They were both handcuffed, and a patch of silvery tape covered the woman's mouth. A man in some kind of uniform was holding a pistol to her head.

'Police!' Kristine shouted. 'Drop it!'

The gunman smiled.

'You shoot, so do I,' he said in a quiet voice. 'You might miss. I won't.'

'There's no way you can escape!' Kristine rapped out. 'I called 91⒈ already. There'll be a squad car here any second. You haven't killed anyone yet. Don't make it worse for yourself.'

The gunman's smiled broadened. He seemed to be enjoying himself.

'Great tits!' he said. 'I bet you have a cute ass, too. Even the blood's kind of a turn-on, tell you the truth.'

Kristine ignored the taunts. She knew she had to take the initiative in the next few seconds or the situation would get out of control. But what was the situation? The set-up looked like one of the cases she had been working on before her leave. Was this a copycat, some jealous lover who had read about the Renton case in the papers and decided to borrow the MO?

'Looks like we have a stand-off here,' the gunman said, staring at her intently. 'I'll tell you what we'll do. We'll let God decide.'

'God?' echoed Kristine faintly.

'Isn't that best? After all, we're only human. We could make a mistake. But God doesn't make mistakes.'

His tone changed abruptly, from ruminative meditation to rapped-out instructions.

'We both raise our guns so they're pointing at the ceiling then break out the cylinder, cover one of the shells and let the rest fall to the floor, engage the cylinder again and spin it. Then we lower our guns at the same time and fire. If nothing happens we try again. Sooner or later one of us will get lucky. God will decide which.'

'No fucking way!' Kristine snarled.

The gunman's smile vanished. He jammed the pistol against the woman's skull so hard she winced with pain.

'Five seconds. Four. Three. Two … '

The bound man kneeling on the floor spoke for the first time, a howl of despair.

'For God's sake!'

'OK, I'll do it,' Kristine shouted.

She had no choice. Even if she fired now, the gunman would have time to blast the woman's head apart. This way, he would at least be forced to remove the pistol from his victim's head. Once he did that the odds would be even, and there was a possibility that Kristine might get a shot at him. But she would only have one chance. She wished she had spent more time on the range.

'I know what you're thinking,' the man said. 'You're thinking you can maybe get the drop on me while we're unloading the guns. Well, think again.'

Keeping the pistol rammed up against the kneeling woman's head, he reached into the black bag lying on the dining table and produced a snub-nosed lump of black metal. Kristine recognized it as a Cobray M-11/9 semi-automatic submachine pistol, long the weapon of choice among drug gangs and other connoisseurs of violence. 'Semi-automatic' described the way the weapon came set up, in order to evade the provisions of the 1934 National Firearms Act, but converting it to full auto was simply a matter of sending off for a kit to form the lower receiver frame. After that, the thing was capable of delivering a full clip of thirty-two 9-mm pistol bullets in a couple of seconds.

The man laid the Cobray down on the table.

'This is going to stay right here,' he told Kristine. 'If you try anything funny, or your buddies come to the door, this house is going to be full of corpses in no time at all.'

Kristine stared right into his eyes. The stinging pain of her lacerations was beginning to tell.

'That's not fair,' she said. 'You could blow me away while I'm unloading.'

The man smiled and shook his head.

'You don't get it, do you? No one seems to get it! I'm not going to try any tricks. I don't need to. I already know what's going to happen. As long as you play straight, I won't touch the automatic.'

In one smooth gesture he whisked the pistol away from the woman's head and pointed it at Kristine. Her finger tightened instinctively on the trigger, then relaxed. I'm outclassed here, she thought. I could never have done that so quickly. The gunman seemed to have endless reserves of confidence and capability.

'Let's go!' he said.

Locking eyes with her, he began to raise his pistol in a slow, smooth arc. Kristine found herself doing the same. She had the tunnel vision of the shooter, focused only on what is happening up front, rigid, inflexible, locked into combat.

'Now we're going to break out the cylinder,' the man said, as though talking to a child.

The two clicks were practically simultaneous.

'Cover one of the shells and let the rest fall to the ground.'

If he tries anything, I can dive behind the chair and take him from there, Kristine thought. But it seemed a faint, weak memory from a previous existence, with no force or relevance to what was happening. She blocked one hole in the cylinder with her thumb and let the other bullets fall to the floor. In the background, she could hear a television blatting away.

'Put it together again and spin the cylinder three times,' the man said.

Kristine obeyed. The man nodded. She had done well, he was pleased with her.

'OK,' he said, 'here's where we play.'

She tightened her hold on the wooden grip of the revolver and started to lower it in time with his, the two guns describing twin parabolas through the still air. Someone was weeping somewhere. It was the kneeling man. She felt irritated with him for disturbing them at this important time.

'I want to play too,' said a voice from the kitchen.

Something flew through the air, striking the gunman in the face. He whirled around to face this new threat. The moment his eyes left Kristine's, the spell was broken. She pulled the trigger, but the gun just clicked emptily. She was vaguely aware of a shape in the doorway to the right, small and indistinct. The gunman was turning back now, taking aim. Click. Click. Click. Kristine pumped the trigger desperately, all her force in that one finger, aiming for the centre of mass in the upper chest area, and then felt rather than heard the gun come to life in her hands, and saw the gunman reel back clutching himself, his mouth open in amazement.

He sagged towards the table, reaching for the Cobray. Kristine rushed him, but there was a sofa blocking her path and she was only half-way there when the automatic went off. Lumps of hot metal flew through the air, striking her in the face and body, and for a moment she thought how easy and painless it was to die. Then she realized that they were the ejected shell casings. The bullets themselves were ripping into the walls and ceiling, having passed through the body of the collapsing gunman.

The clattering stopped as his finger released the trigger. Kristine started trembling all over. She looked at the bound couple, then at the boy standing in the doorway to the kitchen. He was holding the dart-gun which her mother had given Thomas. The foam projectile lay on the floor beside the dead gunman.

David looked at his father, then surveyed the scene of carnage with an expression of awe.

'Coo-ul!' he said.